EVERYTHING

Full Murderhobo Book Three

DAKOTA KROUT

MOUNTAINDALE
PRESS

ACKNOWLEDGMENTS

To my Patreons who are supporting me directly, thank you all so much! Especially to Lilly Hawk and Mike Rylander.

And to my family, always.

PROLOGUE

As the first hints of daylight began to transform the false dawn into a beautiful morning, Zed the Bard admired the sky as it was painted by the forces of creation.

"What a beautiful day to achieve everything I have always wished for." His murmured musings were short-lived, abruptly interrupted by the commander of the forces of the Hollow Kingdom opening the door. "Bartholomew! My dear Commander of the Inquisition, I'm shocked and surprised... that you took my request seriously. Are you here to stay a while and listen?"

"You told me what I needed to do in order to learn of the fate of the Queen." The Commander spoke heavily, a drawn expression on his face hinting that there was more at play than he wished to divulge.

Zed eyed the man up and down, studying every detail of the opponent that had chased him across territories, kingdoms; abyss, the entire *continent*... for years. "You look tired. I must ask, did you bring the gold?"

"The... gold?" The Commander seemed nearly afraid to ask the question. To voice confusion in the presence of the

Mindbender was tantamount to opening himself willingly to coercion or trickery, no matter how well he had trained to resist.

"Why, yes, of course! Surely you didn't forget that I had named only two requirements for you today?" Zed may have been gently teasing the man, but he was firm on his stipulations. "I told you that, if you wanted to come and listen, you needed to simply walk through the door... then pay the tab for the entire room!"

A cheer burst from the assembled townsfolk, who seemed far too relaxed for Bartholomew's tastes. To him, it merely signified that the Mindbender had them completely enthralled. Every last one would need to be eliminated before they could become problems upon leaving the building. He closed his eyes, overcome for a moment by the fact that this exact scenario had played out dozens, if not *hundreds* of times while he was hunting this monster of an Ascender. Something about the presence of the Bard forced his inner monologue to surface, and he whispered, "So many dead at your hand..."

"Very *few* at my hand, in fact." At this provocation, Zed's calmly serene expression shifted to a stony glare. "Is it so wrong for me to walk from town to town and tell them the truth? Is there a single word that you can identify where what I have said has been false? If knowing the truth is a crime worthy of death, then... hmm. I suppose we have proof that you believe it is. In that case, there is no further reason for us to throw insults at each other. I know the truth, *you* know the truth, and soon, the entire world will as well."

"What have you done, Mindbender?" Bartholomew's eyes went wide as Zed held up a hand, cocking his head to the side and listening.

A wide smile, one completely devoid of mirth, spread across the face of the Ascended Bard. "Sneaky, *sneaky*. A moment, if you'll indulge me. How *interesting* that you would go this far... using yourself as a sacrificial pawn in an effort to bring my guard down? Adorable! If only I hadn't already known that you would do something like this, perhaps I would have been caught by the trap. Alas, it's been a while since I've had to use this, but I suppose it is fitting, both for my narrative today and as perfect punctuation for the tale I have promised you all."

He snapped his fingers for dramatic effect, allowing a burst of mana to spread from his hands, from his lungs, and out of his mouth as he spoke the words, "*Echoes of Reality: Peace Lily.*"

The mana coalesced into a shimmering image that hovered above the crowd of people packed into the building shoulder-to-shoulder. As it came together, it formed a beautiful plant with the most intricate array of leaves that Bartholomew had ever had the misfortune to lay his eyes upon. He immediately knew what it was. What he didn't know was how a Bard could use *Druidic Abilities*. "No… *no!*"

"Surely you must feel some relief?" the Bard chided the opposing Ascender. "Are you *truly* so ready to throw your life away for a cause you know is wrong?"

Before either of them could say another word, a high-pitched ringing momentarily filled the air as an artillery spell impacted the side of the structure with enough force and compressed power to reduce the people, the tavern, and a dozen paces of ground in a twenty-foot diameter into motes of dust. Bartholomew stamped his foot, hard enough to hurt himself, yet somehow he didn't. "You did it…? You actually replicated the powers of the Archdruid! I thought it was hearsay, but you truly have found a way around the restrictions… this is heresy."

"Ah, finally! Not only do I get to claim sedition, treason, and abuse of power; *finally,* I get to add heresy to the list of random crimes of which I'm accused." Zed shook his head then watched placidly out the window as the crackling orb of power rolled along the ground outside, completely unable to damage anything. At some point, he knew that it would move beyond the edges of his ability to keep it contained, and it would detonate as originally intended. "With that well out of the way, I guess we can move on with our story."

Turning to the crowd—which had remained in rapt attention ever since the troops of the Hollow Kingdom had begun to arrive—Zed lifted his hands and cheerfully called out, "I know that we have usually started in the evening, but today, my tale nears its end. My power will allow us to remain here all day, then all night, coming to a dramatic conclusion at the break of dawn upon the morrow! This last installment of my tale is significantly longer than my previous ramblings, and I hope you'll forgive an old man for starting a little early today."

He glanced up fondly at the Peace Lily, knowing that it would ensure that not one of his listeners would become hungry, tired, or thirsty. "Let us discuss what happened after the establishment of the Scarrocco Nature Preserve. Reclaiming the land that had been lost to the desert, combined with rescuing and enhancing the Ley Line, allowed the Hollow Kingdom to blossom even beyond its former glory. The Nature Preserve turned the kingdom into a potential superpower, and as we all know... a threat to the major powers surrounding our once-weak kingdom."

Zed took a deep breath, calming and centering himself before continuing. "This story is tough for me to relive... but I will do all I can to be honest. When the Dynasty of Dogs provoked the Hollow Kingdom, The Four were forced from their seclusion. No matter what the propaganda tells you, the end results of the war were *not* the fault of The Four. What we are living through today, as the baseline human grows in power —and as the Ascenders begin to weaken—was the direct result of King Vir coming to power, and then breaking the trust of the people sworn to the crown."

Inquisition Commander Bartholomew winced at the bold declaration, glad that he had waited until that moment to acti-vate the communication stone that would relay the words spoken here to the Inquisition, and from there, to the armies of the kingdom. By the order of the king, everyone was to observe what happened to those who committed treason.

"As I'm sure you can all remember, just shy of five years after the establishment of the Nature Preserve, an *abrupt* death occurred in the Royal family, and a drastic shift took place in the direction of the leadership."

The Bard waved his hands once more, and reality faded away, replaced with his memories. "When it all began, The Four were only just beginning to recognize the limits imposed on them…"

CHAPTER ONE

Luke the Murderhobo slouched in a chair crafted of vines and living wood, staring sullenly at the lush, verdant paradise he found himself in. Every once in a while, a tree branch would slightly extend toward him, offering fruit, nuts, or vegetables— strangely enough. The oddly solicitous vegetation was not why he was in a funk. Luke didn't mind the ready access to food, and the view was enjoyable... even if the unnatural motion of the encompassing flora screamed at his senses that it must be destroyed for invading his space.

No, the reasons for his displeasure were far simpler than his idyllic haven might suggest. Five years had passed in this world since he'd had a true challenge. With the death of the Corrupted Nature Dragon, along with the exquisite growth that he had been able to find for himself and Cookie, he had imagined that the next several years would be filled with opportunities for advancement and combat.

Instead, he had spent nearly half a decade scouring the edges of the expanding forest, searching for any annoyance-relieving open Scar that he could step into without his Sigil setting his nerves on fire and forcing him to step away. Each time he had found something that *he* had deemed useful, Luke had been forced to close it, due to the sheer threat level of the contents of the portal. To his ever-mounting irritation, every time he had found something boring and not worth pursuing, his Skills wouldn't allow him to close it, identifying it as useful to the kingdom that controlled him.

Frankly, there had been another annoyance he had been forced to deal with. When their party had first defeated the Corrupted Nature Dragon, Taylor had sent a report to the kingdom. With her mind unchained from its original level, no longer forced to its innately inflexible, duty-bound, or practically childish temperament, the Mage had allowed herself to keep the details sparse. Specifically, she had not destroyed team morale once again by divulging each of the rewards they had earned, thereby offering them to the kingdom on a silver platter.

However, because the report had been so bare of details, The Four had been punished with a 'reduced ability' to enter their alternate worlds and gain power easily. In Luke's case, he had gone from being able to enter Murder World once per thirty days to once per *sixty*. Directly *halving* the amount of time that he was able to enter that world had infuriated him beyond belief. Luke had spent the greater part of his time searching for any form of combat challenge—any way to hone himself or maintain his battle sense at his desired level—but once he had reached the maximum range of the Scarrocco Desert and visited each training opportunity, he found himself completely idle.

It was then that he decided on a new plan, and the five years had moved as a blink to him, in an almost literal way. His Skills forced a certain amount of growth—actual growth, in one of the cases—but the enforced idleness had been on the verge of causing a mental collapse. Before he stooped to destroying plants, attacking boulders that were slightly too different in shade, or screaming at clouds, Andre the Druid had come up with a far simpler solution. Between his ventures into Murder

World, Luke had a tendency to spend a few minutes in the Descender portal they had found upon their original entry to the desert.

A few minutes was all it took for *weeks* to pass in their world. He quickly adopted the habit of popping in for a few minutes, stepping out, and absorbing all the changes that had been enacted by the Druid during their time apart. It was strange enough that he often wondered if he was somehow under an illusion effect created by Zed, having his perceptions subtly altered in order to keep him calm. It turned out that the reality was far stranger than any fever dreams that the Mindbender could place in his skull.

Andre had spent the entire time that they had been... exiled? Protected? Hidden? Imprisoned? No matter how Luke looked at it, it was simply more time away from the rest of humanity, let alone the accoutrements and benefits that he had *earned*. The Murderhobo shook his head and tried to remember what he had been thinking about... luckily, simply looking around allowed for an easy transition back into reminiscing. The Druid had spent the entirety of the last five years *working*. Planning, growing, crossbreeding and pollinating plants and animals; all for the express purpose of maximizing the benefits this land now provided.

Since the Ley Line and the Earthen Node had increased in potency, and the Druid had access to literal miles of ideal fertilizer, Andre had single-handedly generated explosive growth. Five years in, he had expanded the boundaries of his idealized paradise to hundreds of miles, with only a thin strip of desert still remaining between the Nature Preserve and the grasslands that surrounded it. His efforts had not gone unnoticed, and The Four had caught hundreds of spies and scouts searching their land. Still, without concerted effort, it was going to be impossible for an enemy—or even a presumptive ally—to locate them in the Druid's territory.

Andre was connected to the land and to every plant and animal within it. There was no way for anyone to sneak in without The Four having knowledge of the intruder's presence prior to their arrival. If the Ascended exiles didn't want to be seen, they'd never be found. That, more than anything, kept Luke from destroying the far-too-solicitous trees that were always offering him treats. "Abyssal strange is what that is. *I* wouldn't offer someone my arm, hoping they'd take a bite out of it. These plants just aren't *right*."

The Murderhobo had recently exited the Descender portal and was awaiting the delivery that Zed had promised him. Once upon a time, Luke had commissioned enchanted gear from the kingdom's best armor and weapon smiths with instructions to send it wherever he might be. In general, his orders had been fulfilled, and delivery had been attempted many times, yet he had only obtained a *fraction* of the items he had specifically requested. In all fairness, it wasn't entirely the fault of the craftsmen he had paid in advance. No, it was the fact that every wagon shipment was laden with spies, magical orders, or some other contingent sent to remove or withhold autonomy from The Four.

It had become such a consistent occurrence that they had taken to sending a clone of Zed to approach the wagons, and if it detected even a hint of an ambush or Royal decree, the clone would self-destruct, fading away into oblivion before the orders could be magically passed along. The Bard had made many enemies this way, since he would typically laugh in the faces of whoever had arrived, be it mercenary or Inquisitor, before fading into nothingness. Of the very few wagons that did arrive without passengers, most of the vehicles contained Spells, tracking devices, or other methodologies designed to corral the bounty hunters that The Four had become.

Every last one was dismantled by the combined efforts of the Bard and the Druid. Vines couldn't read royal decrees or writs, and Luke swore the coiling lengths rustled in satisfaction as they snaked out to pull the equipment into the underbrush. Tracking Spells or other various magical effects were dispelled by Taylor, and usually the enchantments imbued into the commissioned gear were hearty enough not to be impacted. Overall, it was a time-and-resource-intensive proposition to acquire those goods, and frankly... it most often wasn't worth doing.

Luke looked at the results of their successful raids on wagon deliveries which had been meant for him in the first place, huffing out a deep, disgruntled sigh at the fact that this was the best that their highest-quality Enchanters could create. "Look at this. Fifteen spears, with only minor variations between them for each individual spell effect. All of them 'on touch'; not a single one is able to cast magic at range. I didn't pay a Tier-one Enchanter; I paid for the masters of the craft to be the ones working on this. If nothing else, these should be capable of ranged use and have multiple effects. Not this... inadequate *garbage.*"

"I think you might still be thinking too highly of the 'Masters' of the craft," Zed informed him with a dramatic shake of his head. "You must remember that this is the Hollow Kingdom, not the Starfall Imperium nor the Dynasty of Dogs. Frankly, the fact that we even *have* Enchanters is already fairly shocking, if for no other factor than the sheer power required to be able to travel to those worlds. If I remember correctly, the Hollow Kingdom has one of the weakest connections to all the various planes, making any interplanar connection difficult for a potential Ascender."

"Are you meaning to tell me that physical location—where we are standing on this planet—impacts our ability to step into neighboring worlds?" Luke rolled his eyes at the absurdity. "Something tells me that it has more to do with mana density than with where we are *standing* at any given time."

"Yeah, most likely." Zed chortled darkly. "But when Andre finishes his little project here, something tells me that isn't going to be an issue anymore. I'm really looking forward to seeing what happens at that point. I will have new stories to tell people for *decades.*"

Taylor glided over as Luke lifted another spear with a small grunt of displeasure. She waited patiently, watching as his mana reached out from his body, engulfing the entire weapon, only to utterly obliterate it in the next moment. The Mage waited, and sure enough, a ghostly blue version of that exact weapon appeared in his hands. With a slightly manic grin, the Murder-hobo tested out his ability to use it, causing the air to whine and snap as he thrust and slashed. "It's always interesting to watch you do that, since it isn't supposed to be possible. Forget about consuming a weapon and still being able to use it; destroying the enchantment pathways should make it so that even if you could replicate the weapon, it would be a simple, powerless, mundane tool."

"Hello, Taylor!" Zed waved cheerfully at her. "Anything interesting to report today?"

"You'd be happy to know that I haven't looked at the 'instruction manual' they sent along with us since they reduced our capacity to visit our worlds," Taylor reminded him dryly. "No point in giving up even more of our freedom, right?"

"I really like the new you. Have I said that? I feel like I say that a little too often these days. I hope you don't take offense to it." Zed rambled, his hands beginning to subconsciously mimic the rapid tumble of thoughts spilling from his lips. "Kind of like if you had been in combat and had all your hair burned off, and I explained to you each day how nice it looked that your hair had grown out a little bit. I think we should-"

"Zed," Luke muttered with quiet annoyance, "you've already tested out all your ability to earn Potentia from us. You should know that rambling to us all the time isn't going to help you increase it. It's only going to boost the odds of you accidentally getting stabbed by a spear and shoved into a tree trunk."

"You know what? That might be better than just hanging around these trees all the time." Zed shifted focus instantly. "Then I would actually have some purpose in this forest. Suck up some water, get some nutrients, stretch out in the sun... maybe I'll see if Andre is open to having a Bardic Dryad."

"Not funny, Zed." Taylor softly murmured as she shot him a

warning glance. "You know how he feels about that, now that he's had time to consider what he had to do to create them."

"Yes, yes, we all know that he feels bad that he made trees that ate people and grew through their bodies. Even so, how many people have come into this paradise seeking eternal life as a tree? How many people have *wanted* that? He always tells *them* yes!" Zed's complaints didn't have any heat to them, because frankly… the idea of becoming a tree and therefore being unable to leave and seek out new population centers went against *everything* he truly wanted in life. "Fine. Well, if Andre is going to be a giant spoilsport, what do you guys think of my idea of joining Luke the next time he is able to pop off to his world?"

"*Pop* is the right choice of words there, Zed," Taylor reminded him firmly. "Even with our empowered Mana Channels, I still believe that none of us would be able to survive there for any length of time."

"It's been half a decade! Let me *try!*" This time, Zed's request was in earnest as he pleaded both with the Murderhobo and the Mage. "My body has been able to accept mana at a far higher volume; my cells are practically *saturated* with it! I think I could make it. Abyss, I can stand in the center of the outflow when he opens his portal and only feel refreshed and invigorated. I haven't spontaneously combusted even a *single* time!"

"Zed, you know that we'll just die-" Taylor started to argue, only to have Luke cut her off.

"Fine." The Murderhobo locked eyes with Zed. "You want to take the risk? At least you're doing something to grow. Even if it kills you—and it probably will. Almost certainly. I'm practically positive that you'll die in the first few minutes. But, like I was saying, if it does, I'll only have respect for you. I'll remember you fondly for being willing to suffer to get stronger. At least until I start thinking about something else."

A long, tense silence stretched, broken by the Bard jumping in the air and whooping for joy. "You hear that? I'm going to Murder World!"

CHAPTER TWO

Zed, Andre, Taylor, and Luke stood together in person for the first time in nearly three months. They had grown comfortable with each other and were aware of each other's presence in a way that eliminated the necessity for constant interaction. Luke, especially, was not one for extravagant or idle chatting for the sake of being social.

The Bard looked around, his unfettered joy showing on his face at all times. "This is nice. Isn't this nice? How are you all doing? I know that we've all-"

"I'm sorry to interrupt, but I think this is a bad idea, and I don't want to lose a friend over his desire to subject himself to a Mana Baptism that will cause his body to shatter and melt away like an icicle," Taylor burst out, cutting off Zed's flow of words and glaring at Luke the entire time.

"Well," Luke paused for an uncomfortably long duration, then shrugged. "If you don't like it, force us not to do it."

"Stop throwing that in my face," Taylor hissed at the smirking trio of men. "We have all determined that our minds were not our own and *agreed* to let the past stay in the past. We have all grown and changed. Yes, this *is* your decision, but I'm not going to let you do it… without at least reminding you how much you mean to us and that losing you would devastate our team."

"*Aww.* Taylor, I had no idea you cared so much!" Zed attempted to pull her in for a hug when a small arc of lightning forced him to leap away from her with a yelp. "Well, that was rude. Still, I'm going. Thank you for your concern, but we both know the kingdom never gave you instructions on keeping me safe or alive. Frankly, I'm surprised they didn't give you direct orders to off me at the first opportunity."

Taylor winced visibly, and Zed's mouth dropped open. His finger shot out to point at her accusingly. "They *did*! I *knew* it!"

"No, they didn't. I flinched at the fact that you have such low trust in the people in power." Taylor waved him down with a long sigh. "But… you're correct. If you can get in there, I can't stop you. Something tells me you *won't* be able to; your Sigil knows it is almost certain death for you. I think you're going to take a single step and lose control of your legs."

"Oh right, I forgot about that. Abyss. Still, I'm going to do what I can to make it happen." Zed's expression had shifted through a half dozen emotions during the conversation, but it finally settled on confidence and grim determination. "Luke, whenever you're ready, I am as well."

"To be clear, you want to go into Murder World no matter what happens, right?" Luke's eyes seemed to be boring a hole directly into Zed's skull, so the Bard simply gulped and nodded. "Great."

Wham.

Without any further warning or notice, Luke's fist lashed out and sent a cascading reverberation through the air as he dumped mana into the space in front of him. His other fist followed, echoing the sound and enhancing it as the world seemed to bend and warp. Faster and faster his fists went flying, impacting nothing… as well as reality itself. With a final strike, the world gave way, tearing open a portal between the two dimensions. As far as the eye could see, only blue landscapes and minor variations of the same monochrome hue could be found.

The Murderhobo was heaving for breath, not from exhaustion or any form of feeling tired, but from the sheer mental fortitude it took for him not to dive in and let the portal close behind him. "If you want to come, you'd better move *now*."

Zed sprang toward the opening as rapidly as he could, only for his legs and body to collapse like a puppet with its strings cut. He slammed his fists on the ground in a tantrum. "No! It won't let me! I *want*—**uup*!*"

Luke scooped up the caterwauling Bard in passing and chucked him into the portal just ahead of himself. He followed through the Scar and let it close behind him, cutting off the shocked expressions on the faces of the other half of their team. "Congratulations. You made it. Try not to die."

"Yeah. About that. Any recommendations?" Zed was sweating and chuckled nervously as he glanced around. "Honestly... I didn't expect to make it this far. I have no plan from this point forward."

"I told you your plan. Try not to die." Luke set off, paying the Bard no further attention. "Don't breathe too hard; don't drink any of the water. It'll make you explode. Same with the pearls. I don't recommend trying any of the food from this place, either. It's delicious, but again... it will make you explode."

"You know, I have my proof of concept now. I'm able to walk around and am not on fire or actively dying, so I should be able to come back another time, right? My Sigil will just let me walk in?" Zed's rambling wasn't drawing any response from the Murderhobo, so he tried a new tactic. "Any chance that you could let me out of here? You know, now that I have my proof-"

"I can't open the way out from here," Luke informed the Bard without a backward glance. "After Zone fifteen, things changed a little bit. Now I get an exit portal every five Zones, but an entrance portal every three. We're going to need to make it to the end of Zone twenty or backtrack to fifteen for you to get out."

"The end of Zone twenty? Wait, haven't you been telling us that you've been stuck in Zone nineteen for something like... four years?" Zed hurried to catch up, eventually resorting to a flying tackle to grab onto Luke's shoulders as the Fitness-focused Ascender accelerated to a sprint.

"Yes."

"Would you care to expand on that answer at all?" Zed was doing his best impression of a cape, clinging to Luke's neck and shoulders for dear life as the man sprinted ahead at speeds an avalanche couldn't hope to rival.

"It is a very long distance, and I have a very specific amount of time before I'm forced to turn around." The last detail was practically growled; the maximum amount of time that Luke could spend in his world was thirty days of subjective time. That translated into approximately two days in the outside world, which made it nearly impossible to cross the vast distances required while maintaining effective combat readiness.

Zed decided against nodding or performing any other movement that might impact his stability on his ride. Still, he had long since mastered the art of being able to continue a conversation, no matter the circumstances. "You say it's a long distance to Zone twenty; what does that look like? I feel like you've explained this before but, frankly, I never thought it would be pertinent to me."

"System notifications have a measuring function," Luke begrudgingly offered after a few minutes of silence. "The size of each chunk of land increased by half all the way until I got to Zone sixteen. After that, it only increased by one tenth. Probably a limitation on physical land, as there is no shortage of mana."

"Mmkayy..." Zed tried to draw out more information but remembered exactly who he was talking with. "Could you give me an exact measurement for how long until we reach... what, Zone nineteen? We are in eighteen right now, yes?"

"You're not getting any of my world's direct information. That is fine. We should be reaching Zone nineteen in the next few hours," Luke told the Bard in a crystal-clear voice.

Zed blinked a few times as he realized that he was hearing the Murderhobo speak through a smile, and it was impacting the tones of his normally flat and slightly angry voice. "Are you… is this you being *happy*? Also, I don't know how fast you're moving right now, but a few hours seems like a long time, since you're… I want to say running a mile every minute or so? Maybe a little bit farther?"

"I have Cookie, I'm in my world, and I'm going to get stronger. Why would I not be happy?" Luke nodded solemnly, nearly dislodging his uninvited jockey. "If the distance calculations are correct, Zone one was ten miles long and half a mile wide. By Zone five, that was fifty miles in length and two miles wide. At Zone fifteen-"

"Hold on; wait, wait, wait." The Bard had a spectacular mind, and he tried to formulate the statistical increase of Luke's claims. "That means at Zone fifteen, we were looking at… you don't mean to tell me that we have to run nearly one thousand, four hundred miles before we reach the edge of the next area?"

"Zone," Luke corrected him blandly. "Yes. This *Zone* is one thousand, three hundred sixty-three miles long, one hundred and one miles wide. Zone nineteen is a little bit longer, but Zone twenty is the real problem."

"If you don't mind me asking, where are all of the monsters?" Zed had heard so many horror stories about this place, though they were delivered in a nonchalant and slightly annoyed tone. He had remained tense from the moment he knew he would be able to survive the air until right now.

"I cleared them perfectly on previous runs. The ones that respawn while I'm out of this world are trying to gather together to launch sneak attacks on me once they get strong enough again. There were only fifty thousand of them… or so. Nothing like Zone twenty," Luke elaborated only out of great consideration for his guest.

"Well, now I'm properly concerned about our destination. Seeing as you brought it up a couple of times, and even called it an issue for you, what's going on?" Zed was starting to be drawn into the excitement that his friend was exuding despite himself; he felt a wide smile growing across his own face as his body literally *thrummed* with power. His Mana Channels were Pristine, allowing for a cycle of power to flow through him and into his cells, which he had previously considered to be utterly saturated.

"Most of the issue is the fact that I need to return to the base world in a timely manner." Luke let out a long, uncharacteristic sigh of annoyance. "I haven't been able to figure out the trick to the next Zone yet. I'm hoping that, this time, I can get into the Zone to understand what the issue is."

"You don't even know what the problem is? Wait, you haven't been *into* the next Zone yet? I'm confused."

"Just wait until we get there, and you'll see the problem for yourself," Luke explained with a grunt that signaled the end of the conversation. No matter how the Bard wheedled him from that point forward, he simply kept his mouth shut and kept running.

CHAPTER THREE

"I have officially seen the issue for myself, and I think we should vacate the premises immediately." Zed cautiously released Luke's neck when the man didn't stop running, tucking and rolling immediately to his feet and springing into a run that ensured he would be diverted away from Luke's path. "Whew, good thing I'm a Bard. Any Bard worth their salt can *tum~ble*."

The Murderhobo didn't take any time to concern himself with his friend's wellbeing. The edge of Zone twenty lay directly ahead, over a thousand miles long and just over one hundred miles wide... with monsters standing shoulder to shoulder, literally filling the entire boundary as far as his enhanced eyes could perceive.

He knew from experience that this wouldn't inhibit their combat effectiveness even a fraction. In fact, these creatures not only had ranged attacks in addition to melee attacks, but they would also use cooperative tactics to work together in their attempts to take him down. Even so, the Murderhobo was always afforded at least a single full power strike against them before they would open fire. As he sped closer and closer, their weapons and the clicking machinery they had instead of eyes tracked him until he was right on the edge of the Zone.

"*Bum Rush!*" Hurtling at his absolute full speed, he twisted and hopped on one foot, swinging Cookie around with all the force that he could muster. The Dragonbone Greatmace hit the leading creature, and the world was instantly filled with death and weaponry. "*Shockwave Cleave!*"

A heartbeat after his attack landed was when things went sideways. The monsters were strange amalgamations of ivory, metal, and cloth, as though they had been assembled in some form of deranged laboratory or factory. They parodied a near-humanoid form, although the bases of their torsos split into four legs for stability, while four arms brandished what looked like oversized needles. The vivified mannequins used the metallic spikes like javelins, either shooting them out in a straight line from where they stood, or expertly wielding the makeshift lances to thrust and parry whatever he could bring to bear against them.

Luke didn't yet have a name for the creatures. He didn't understand what they were, or what their purpose was. Still, as an enemy, he respected them. They were unchangingly silent, attempting to deal with his intrusion ruthlessly and efficiently. Even so, he was frustrated beyond belief as they died in droves from his initial attack. As the Shockwave hit, dealing absolute death to hundreds of the creatures in a conical pattern, he watched with his own eyes as they were reduced to mere scraps of cloth and twisted metal. Skill Pearls fell like rain, igniting his greed and his ire alike.

His anger had a simple explanation. There was no way to scoop the Pearls up and either shove them down his gullet or into Cookie for combination and enhancement. By the time he was blasted backward from the rebound of his own blow, the only proof that his attack had been successful was the layer of remains and Skill Pearls that new monsters were standing atop. All the space his slain enemies had occupied was already completely refilled with exact replicas of the fallen.

The resulting burst of Potentia was already far less than what he had been able to gain from these creatures when he had first met them.

Damage dealt: 35,090 blunt. (6,923 weapons in range, average maximum damage 50 per weapon.)

Potentia gained: 2,800.

Damage taken: 428 damage from rebound.

Current health: 502/930.

Only the fact that Cookie appeared to be utterly unbreakable saved the weapon from shattering as Luke's Source-cerer's Armory activated, boosting his total damage dealt by ten percent of the maximum weapon damage of all weapons in range. The resulting detonation had sent him flying backward, bouncing off the ground for nearly a tenth of a mile before skidding to a stop. Luke lay face down, taking deep breaths for a few minutes before he was able to regain his footing. The endless enemies in the next Zone were well and truly agitated, and a trail of metal projectiles followed his path near perfectly for over half of the distance he had been knocked back before they started to lose accuracy and petered off.

He could only growl and shake his head in frustration as he heaved himself to his feet and started advancing once again, only to pause in confusion when a non-hostile stepped in his way.

"Luke… what just happened?" Zed was shaking like a leaf on a newly created Dryad. "I was nowhere *near* all of that, and I still nearly died. What *were* those needle things? Is this what you've had to deal with the whole time you were trapped here? Just a continuous attack, nearly die, repeat? I know that's what you told us, but… I didn't really understand it. Not until now."

The Murderhobo huffed and shook his head irritably. "No, it has not always been this bad. Not for a long time. I'm not sure what's going on, or if there is a particular trick to clearing this Zone, but all I can do is keep attacking until I break through. In the face of overwhelming power, trickery just doesn't matter."

"Yeah, sure, but *feces*, man! I watched your arms turn to

shredded meat!" Zed stared uneasily as the final wounds on Luke's arms closed, though the skin certainly didn't look healthy. "How did you not die from that attack? Every single part of what just happened should have killed you."

"Giga reached Tier one, level six the last time I was here," Luke offered in lieu of proper explanation. With every word, ambient mana started to compress into his body and create shockwaves intense enough to be felt by everything in this and the next Zone. However, since it was a low-Tier Skill, the process would be over in practically no time flat. "Abyss; speaking of, it looks like I'm getting an upgrade as we speak. Two Skills at the same time? Nice."

He sat down to read over the messages, simultaneously refreshing his knowledge of his Characteristics and Skills. Once he'd brought himself up to speed, he decided to stare at his hands until the Skill increase was complete.

Automatic allocation of Etheric Xenograft Potentia has allowed Skill: Bum Flash to begin breaching Tier three!

Skill increase complete! Bum Flash -> Bum Thunder.

Effect 1: At the cost of 10 mana, once per minute, you can empower your forward charge, allowing you to cross the distance in one second that you can normally sprint in five seconds.

Bonus 1, at range: At the cost of $10n$ mana, you're able to instantly traverse $1+n$ meters of space (maximized at 10 meters) while rushing toward an opponent, where $n =$ Skill level. There is no longer a cooldown restriction on this Skill.

NEW! Effect 2: No longer is your instant travel a quiet and non-disruptive Skill! Now, all items between yourself and your destination will take 50% of your weapon damage as concussive damage. This will generate a small shockwave which might further disrupt anyone unlucky enough to exist in your path.

Giga has reached level seven!

Cal Scan
Level: 13
Current Etheric Xenograft Potentia: 2,799/61,000 to level 14!

Body: 35.85

- *Fitness: 46.7*
- *Resistance: 25*

Mind: 22.3

- *Talent: 19.7*
- *Capacity: 24.9*

Presence: 21.5

- *Willpower: 27*
- *Charisma: 11*

Senses: 29.85

- *Physical reaction: 37*
- *Mental energy: 22.7*

Maximum health: 1020 (Giga)
Maximum mana: 378
Mana regen: ~~*6.57 per second*~~ *Overridden: 100 per second.*

<u>Skills: Tier: Level</u>

Source-cerer's Armory: 9: 9
You Need to Stop: 4: 9
Bum Thunder: 3: 0
Hobo Holler: 3: 0
Pristine Balance: 4: 7
Rift Hunter: 7: 9
Feather's Fall: 4: 2
Shockwave Cleave: 4: 0
Giga: 1: 7

Happy with the changes and delighted to once more have access to the entirety of his Skills, Luke allowed a ghost of a smile to cross his face as he stood up fluidly. "I *knew* that was the Skill I needed to do this right. That whole swarm of enemies is a giant defensive line."

"What...? You're awake again?" Zed's astonishment removed the smile entirely from the Murderhobo's face.

"What're you talking about?" Luke glared at the Bard in confusion. "I was never asleep."

The Bard frowned at the man before him with great concern. "Are you being serious right now? All of a sudden, all the mana in the area was being drawn toward you, enough that I was actually able to hang out pretty comfortably—thanks for that, by the way—but then you just sat there for *hours* as you... I don't know any other way to say this... I think you grew a little bit?"

"Yeah, that makes sense; Giga hit level seven."

"You know that means pretty much nothing to me, right? Do you have a Skill that makes you larger? That doesn't... none of this makes sense." Zed was clearly full of frustration, but Luke could only shrug and continue forward. "You don't have any food, let alone any of the other nutrients that would be required for a change like that! You're a walking paradox."

Luke was about to refocus his mental efforts onto the situation at hand, but he decided to throw the Bard a bone. "I can *tell* you everything; I can't make you *understand* everything. If you want to learn something, you need to ask what you actually want to know. Be specific."

The Bard tried to respond, but Luke merely waved him off and walked away. "I don't have time to give you an introduction to this entire world. I have things to kill."

It was time for a tried-and-true method. The fact that each of the monsters—of which he still didn't know the name—were capable of a ranged attack meant that using Feather's Fall to attempt to glide over them was tantamount to intentional self-harm. He would have tried it regardless, but unfortunately, his

Sigil wouldn't allow him to even attempt the action. Finally, Luke had access to his preferred method once again; a way to simply careen through the enemy.

Running downhill, he slowly increased his speed until he was barreling toward the creature-choked boundary at a full-on sprint. Without activating any other Abilities, moving as quickly as possible with no other burdens allowed him to cross the distance in only a handful of seconds. Just before he reached the front line of the quadrupedal monsters that were waiting for him to make the first move yet again, the Murderhobo activated Bum Thunder.

The Skill allowed him to cross ten meters in a single instant, at any angle or direction that he desired. The new upgrade allowed for the ability to send his enemies flying away from him thanks to the blast of noise coming from directly behind him, and Luke was counting on that benefit to clear a path for him to follow back out after he got the Zone information.

What he had *not* been counting on was the Skill absolutely failing to allow him through the front line. The Murderhobo merely slammed face-first into an enemy and was sent tumbling backward as the Skill failed to live up to its promises. Unfortunately, the impact laid him practically prone on the ground for a quarter second. Though he launched himself to his feet and leapt backward, Luke was unable to dodge the first handful of ivory needles, and they penetrated his flesh.

He only felt the three in his left arm. The first started by slicing through the armor that sprang up over his shoulder, then bounced off just below his elbow and stopped directly over the skin of his palm. A few **pinged** off Cookie's impenetrable surface, and he mentally thanked her for helping him avoid taking additional damage.

Damage taken: 11 penetration damage!

Since these rudimentary weapons could inflict enough damage to make it through his armor, he performed a tactical retreat to mull over his next move. First, Luke decided that looking over his combat logs would help him determine exactly what had just happened.

Bum Thunder activated! Attempting to knock aside enemies. Error! Density of target location indicates that target is terrain. Skill is unable to compress terrain. Deactivating Skill!

Damage taken from void-tipped ossified iron needle. Armor attempting to mitigate damage! Property 'void-tipped' adds 80% armor penetration. Resolving... Metal Gauntlet (Stone Ape) completely blocks damage. Resolving... Simple Metal Pauldron fails integrity check. Approximately 20% of damage has penetrated.

That made sense, though it was frustrating beyond belief. "If I could only get some armor that could withstand those needles, I could wade right in and attack until I can make my way deep enough into the Zone."

This realization did two things for him. The first was to make Luke utterly frustrated and ready to take out his anger on these creatures. The second was to light a fire under his rear to hunt down better armor until nothing could damage him as he rained blows down on the bodies of his enemies. He ambled back to his Bard friend, not sure what to do or say, so he merely turned around and stared at the agitated monsters until they finally settled nearly a score of minutes later.

In an eyeblink, he engaged them once more, this time with Cookie leading the way. Once again, the Murderhobo hit the front line with everything he had, sending out a Shockwave Cleave that tore through hundreds of the monsters before spreading out to damage *thousands*. The returned damage dealt nearly half of his Total Health in retribution as he was sent flying uphill. He rolled to a stop at Zed's feet, looking up to see the gleeful Bard grinning down at him—hanging off the earth like a bat from Luke's perspective.

"I've got to know, is this what you do all day long when you're alone here? I mean, you come here, kill a whole bunch of creatures, recover, and do it all over again?" Zed didn't bother offering Luke a hand to stand up; between the weight of the massive human and his weapon that likewise weighed hundreds of kilograms, there was no point in trying to help. "I have to say, this sheds a whole lot of light on your attitude in combat. You don't bother to avoid attacks because, when you're here, you just heal up by taking a sip of... 'water'. You don't need to bother learning a combat art, as most things die with a single hit. Frankly, this entire experience has been incredibly enlightening for me."

"Be useful or stay out of the way. Distraction means death."

"Incorrect; in fact, distraction means 'a thing that prevents someone from giving full attention to something else'." Zed started whistling to himself, going silent as he realized that the Murderhobo wasn't going to listen to him anytime soon. "You know, I wonder if there *is* something that I could do to be helpful here? Hey, Luke! Wanna hear a song or something?"

Moments later, a bruised and bloody man impacted the ground and tumbled toward him, seeming to have a knack for coming to a stop at Zed's feet. This time, he not only bore the damage he had done to himself, but several needles were protruding from the weak points of his armor. "Right. Forgot. Gotta give them a chance to calm down."

"I know just the song!"

"I'm not going to bring you back the next time I come here."

"*Lu~uke*! Don't be like that!" Zed demanded playfully. "I have just the thing."

The Bard cleared his throat, pulled out a lute, and closed his eyes. "Hush, little Berserker, don't you roar; rage and fury, let them be no more. Close your eyes and take a deep breath; let the calmness ease your mind from death-"

"Stop."

"There's only two more verses!"

CHAPTER FOUR

Weeks later, from their perspective, Luke and Zed stepped out of the portal and back into the lush green forest Andre had created. The Murderhobo exhaled a deep sigh of disappointment as he peered around the mana-lacking environment.

To be fair, compared to everywhere else on the planet he had been so far, this oasis was more mana-dense by a substantial margin. Most of that was passively influenced by his mere presence, since opening his portals within the boundaries of the Preserve allowed a fresh influx of raw mana to be dumped into the immediate environment.

In truth, it was thanks to the efforts of the Druid that mana was captured, diverted to fertilize the earth, and generated a fresh harvest of power. Life generated mana, and when mana was in balance with the world around it, the entire planet would slowly increase in potency over time.

This was one of only *two* ways for a planet to naturally Ascend, but theirs had been greatly stunted by the efforts of the Corrupted Archdruid that had set a dragon to feast off the Ley Lines and Earthen Node. The resulting loss of power had caused the planet to slowly start forming new lines, but they were stunted things that had never cycled power throughout the world as they should. By repairing and furthermore increasing the potency of the local damaged Earthen Node, they likely regained hundreds of years that had been thought to be lost.

That was the *upside* to the influx of raw energy that he leaked into this area; just as whales breaching the surface before diving deep into the ocean would carry fresh air to the depths. Luke studied the grass he was standing on, watching as hundreds of fresh shoots withered and died in a slowly expanding ring. He shook his head and grumbled with soft annoyance, "Right there is the downside."

Unfortunately, the truth of the matter was that neither the weak nor the unlucky could survive the Mana Baptism that increased magical potency brought. Increasing the density too rapidly would merely destroy everything; from plants dying, to rocks exploding, to civilizations falling.

He was shaken from his thoughts as the Bard's voice rang through the area. "Taylor! Andre! I have so many stories for you. First off, look! I survived!"

"I'm glad." Andre came over and threw an arm around the Bard's shoulders. "I admit, I was worried for you, my friend. That stunt was reckless, not to mention dangerous in the extreme. Furthermore, even if you didn't die from the mana exposure, how are you alive right now? I didn't see a pack of food or drink."

Zed lifted his shirt to display his pronounced ribs, his sunken gut, and involuntary trembling. "Correct! I'm wildly malnour-ished and literally starved nearly to death. Thanks for noticing! I was able to survive with only drinking a few mouthfuls of water a day, and luckily, I had a couple waterskins on me."

"For the love of apples, Zed!" Andre growled as he waved his hands at the land around them. Fruit and vegetables started rolling toward them, dropping from their trees or vines to tumble end over end as the grass collected and transported the small orbs until they began arriving at their feet. "Eat something."

"Honestly, I feel great." The Bard punctuated that assertion by picking up a cucumber and biting it directly in the center. It split into two jagged chunks, and he alternated between hands, chomping on the succulent veggie as soon as his mouth was empty. "Something about the sheer amount of power in that world sustained me pretty well. Not great, clearly, but pretty good. But that's not the exciting thing!"

Andre watched nervously as the Bard picked up a banana and ate it, peel and all. "You are clearly near death."

"Yes, yes, we've been over that!" Zed's eyes were shining, and he wasn't about to be stopped. "The sheer *enlightenment*! Andre, you don't understand; we have these incredible Mana Channels, and we have never been given the opportunity to use them! Put that big, beautiful mind of yours to work. When we have higher-capacity Mana Channels, what does that mean for us? Think on that for a second; imma eat that rabbit."

The Bard lunged for the small animal, missing terribly as the beast contemptuously avoided him and hopped away. Andre watched the interplay with a heap of concern and a hint of mirth in his eyes. "Well, if conventional wisdom is to be believed... having greater Mana Channels will allow for a higher capacity of understanding on... *everything*."

"Exactly!" Zed's voice was muffled, as his face was pressed against the dirt and grass from his failed attack on the bunny. Still, his hand was in the air, one finger pointing up. He rolled over, and that finger pointed directly at the Druid's face. "It is literally *enlightenment*! Having the capability for greater things, for understanding things at a higher level, being able to learn things more easily. All of this can be traced to our Mana Channels. Sure, it might not directly give us new Masteries or 'Abilities' in your case, but it allows us to explore them more fully... so long as we have the *required mana* to run through those Mana Channels!"

"This all makes sense, but I don't see how it is overly useful? We still need Potentia in order to increase the level of the Abilities." The Druid crouched down and hoisted the Bard to his feet, handing him an apple. "Would you like a pair?"

"Sure?" Zed answered, frowning as another apple was handed to him. "Huh? Oh! Haa, you took advantage of a homophone. You are clever; I like that. No! Focus, Zed! Endless mana is useful for you because you'll be able to test your capabilities constantly, endlessly. Do you know what my mana regeneration was in there? *Fifty*. Fifty mana per second. I was able to play with almost all of my Masteries, and I gained a far deeper understanding of all of them. You would obviously benefit from that, as would Taylor, but I directly need to master my Masteries in order to gain new Masteries to master!"

"I see a nap in your future," Andre chuckled softly, inspecting the disgruntled Murderhobo as he gently led his friend towards a bed of soft moss that he'd started to grow for this special occasion. "How was your play time, Luke?"

"Deeply unsatisfying. I was unable to overcome the blockade that has been placed in my path." Luke ruminated on this failure in silence as he watched the Archdruid settle the Bard onto the cushioned greenery. "Hitting harder has not been helping, and I'm unable to hit *faster*."

"I made you hit a little bit faster," Zed sleepily called over. "That song of vigor gave you a three percent increase to your attack speed at the start. It's not *my* fault that Cookie weighs the same as a small house, or that the fastest attack you can make with it is almost as fast as the slowest attack you can make with it."

"*Her*," Luke corrected his friend warningly. "Not 'it.'"

Taylor strode into the glade that had resulted from the unfortunate forest fire effect of Luke's re-entry into their world. Looking at the Mage's face, Luke could see the obvious signs of her mental age catching up. The shift had been fast, only occurring over the past five years, and he hoped that the effects were permanent.

In conversation, this growth manifested as calmness in the face of the mess caused by their return. Instead of launching into recriminations or stirring up issues, as she would have before the updating of her mental state, Taylor merely made sure that everyone was healthy and leaned against a tree to patiently wait and see if she was needed.

Zed was already snoring as Luke struggled to maintain the fragile human connections that he had been able to build up. "How. Are. Things."

"Things are going very well. We only have a few dozen more miles to complete before the desert is fully eradicated, and the Ley Line is reintegrated with the magical framework of the Hollow Kingdom. A couple of months, at most? I'm *hoping* it will be weeks." Andre paused as his friend nodded woodenly, the Murderhobo's eye twitching and nostrils flaring. "Thank you for asking. Is there anything I can do for you?"

"I need better armor." The sound of Luke's teeth grinding against each other didn't exactly shatter the silence, but it certainly added an unnerving auditory effect. "If I can boost the armor values of my legs and shoulders, I will be able to send a constant deluge of kill notifications to my Sigil. It looks like about one hundred points of armor is necessary to outright ignore the void-tipped needles."

Andre nodded sagely as the explanation washed over him. "I have no idea how to translate armor into numbers, so I can't guarantee that we will be able to determine how to make that possible. Still, I'm on the lookout for any caravans coming this way with the gear you have commissioned. Nothing has made it through in the last couple of months. Also, are there any further details you can provide about the problem you're having? What is a void-tipped needle, for example?"

"Ask the Bard," Luke scoffed as he glanced at the snoozing man. "Uhhm. Uh…"

"You can be done with the conversation; thank you for trying this hard." Andre nodded understandingly at the instantly relieved Berserker.

"Yeah. Good." Luke felt a wave of exhaustion roll over him.

Too much social interaction was not good for his mental health. "Right, I'm off. See you in five weeks."

Taylor stepped in his path, holding her hand up in a clear request for him to wait. "Are you sure that you want to do that again, Luke? I don't know anyone else that willingly and intentionally enters a Descender portal over and over again. We don't even know what the long-term effects are going to be."

"Are you going to tell me not to go?" Luke waited patiently, not a hint of concern on his face.

"You're going to do whatever you want to do and can do. So long as those two things overlap, I'm not going to try to stop you." Taylor eased closer, taking a deep breath before reaching out and putting her hand on his arm. When they had first started this journey together, that same motion would have allowed her to touch his shoulder, showcasing just how much he had literally grown over the years. "I just worry about you. I worry about all of you, all of us. The raids have grown more frequent, and the traps have become more sophisticated. If anyone has noticed you going into that portal… well, each time you go, there is a greater chance that they will catch you. I know that you know it."

Luke could only shrug. "It's either wait out the time in only a few minutes or go crazy trying to do it out here. You know as well as I do that the order you were given to make me wait sixty days between each delve into Murder World was intended to make me a beacon of destruction for them to follow."

That put a small, if sad, smile on her face. "On the plus side, it was worded poorly. Otherwise, your time in that Descender portal would result in forcing you to still need to wait sixty days."

"Then we would be found immediately!" Zed shouted, drawing the group's attention in collective bewilderment. As far as they could tell, he was still asleep.

"Yeah, *that's* not at all weird," Andre muttered as he took a couple small, careful steps away from the sleeping Mindbender. When he glanced back, Luke was already gone. That didn't stop him from knowing exactly where their brusque companion was: this was *his* forest, after all. "Okay, bye, I guess!"

The Murderhobo was sprinting through the dense foliage, charging directly *through* trees if they were small enough that he figured his Druid friend could replace them with a wave of his hand. He had no concerns about his wake of destruction being followed; the forest behind him was being repaired as quickly as he moved through it. Sound that would normally travel in such a quiet environment was instead absorbed by leaves that shifted to impede the movement of the air vibrations. By the time he got up to speed, he was moving so fast that standard humans would never be able to track him, and with the help of the encompassing forest, it was unlikely that any but the most impressive scout would be able to detect signs of his passing.

The portal he was aiming for was outside of the forest, but not by much. He exploded through the final curtain of greenery, mulching leaves and wood in his frenzied charge. Someone shouted, and he narrowed his eyes. Before he could be restrained by any instructions, demands, or a writ that would force him to march his unhappy feet back to the control of the kingdom, he uttered the words 'Bum Thunder' and appeared directly in front of the portal, the thunderous clapping of his passing echoing and drowning any sounds that had been aimed his way.

He launched himself into the bright orange portal, keeping his eyes closed as he waited for the next few minutes. To him, this world was abstract: a place of bizarre colors, muted sensations, and such low mana density that the world looked like it had been created by a child with watered-down ink. Finishing his countdown, he jumped backward, directly out of the portal.

Weeks had passed, exactly as he had expected. Yet time was not the only change that his absence had accelerated. Now, the desert was gone, as far as his eyes could see. Riotous foliage and underbrush blanketed the landscape, stately trees soared into the sky, and countless small animals rustled in the underbrush. Just like that, he instinctively knew that an ambush was *not* waiting for him. There was no way Andre would allow an incursion into his forest, and that awareness allowed him to take his time wandering back to the group.

"Looks like you were right again, Cookie. Having good friends does matter. Good call."

CHAPTER FIVE

- ANDRE -

The Druid stood in the center of his terraformed paradise, ankle deep in mud rich with fertilizers and nutrients necessary for the final push. He sucked in a deep breath, letting it out slowly as he expanded his awareness of the area to his maximum capability. As an Archdruid of the Third circle, he was able to feel not only the sensations of the plants, but also the animals and the topsoil of the planet.

Layer by layer, he intently inspected all of his work, feeling each discrete sensation vividly. As far as his powers and knowledge extended, he sensed that everything was... perfect. Still in his semi-trance state, he murmured notes to himself for future usage. "A few more uses of Brute Migration to even out the predator-prey cycle, likely only a few more gallons of blood to nourish the last stretch of flora, and it will be done."

At that thought, he couldn't hold back the suffocating dryness that instantly parched his throat, or the simultaneous release of a single tear from his right eye. "They said it would take more than a century to fix this, but to accomplish such a thing in only five years? What other Druid will be able to make the same claim that I do, that I have completed *two* great acts of service for the world?"

So close to achieving the goal he had been sprinting toward his entire life, he was unwilling to pause for rest. Tendrils of his power, along with vegetative tendrils of mycelium and roots, spread outward into the dead perimeter that still completely encircled the hundreds of miles of regenerated paradise. Three-quarters of a mile, half... less than a quarter. He wiped away the annoying trickle of blood streaming from his left nostril, using it to further amplify his powers, and fully trusting in his forest to heal the damage that he was dealing to his body.

"Andre!" Taylor's melodic voice pushed its way into his ears, and his eyes snapped open. Her face was mere inches from his, her hands outstretched to grab and shake him. "Are you snapping out of it? Are you okay?"

For a long moment, he didn't answer. Instead, he simply studied her face. He had known her since they were children, and yet he continually found what he saw to be utterly fascinating: the small lines of worry that were slowly being carved into a permanent look of concern, the beautiful hair that cascaded down into silken waves that Luke had voiced envy of more than once upon returning bald from his world.

Her skin was flawless, and though they lived within a botanical extension of his nervous system, she was somehow able to maintain perfect hygiene without ever leaving his *presence* to bathe or swim. Even now, years into their enforced exile, there were so many details that he didn't understand about her or have the courage to ask.

As her concern threatened to shift to alarm, he found his voice. "I'm fine, it's just... I'm so *close*. Another day, maybe two, and I will be able to reconnect the Scarrocco Paradise to the Hollow Kingdom. The land is humming with anticipation, the dead land is nearly all eradicated, and my quest is *finally* almost complete."

"Andre... I fully understand what it means to be motivated

to reach that success." Taylor locked eyes with him as he tried to avoid her gaze. "Let me ask you something, and please be as honest as you can. If you were to do nothing else, if you were to relinquish active cultivation right now, today... would the land still finish healing?"

"Well... I mean, nowhere near as fast as I can make it happen. Really, it will only take me another day, day and a half at the most-" The Druid's deflection was met with silence and pursed lips. He sighed, and his body practically crumpled in as he allowed himself to feel the bone-deep exhaustion that had been building. "Fine. You win this one; I will take a break. But as soon as I'm-!"

"Of course. As soon as you're in the right state of mind— rested both physically and mentally—you'll return the kingdom to its former glory," Taylor lightly teased him, fully aware that her friend literally cared more about a large hole filled with decomposing feces and plant matter than he did about the political benefits of the rehabilitation of a dead zone impacting the health of the kingdom's citizens. In fact, both Taylor and Andre were fairly certain that, upon completion of the work, they would be caught up in a political feces storm, and not the kind that could be used to grow anything pleasant. "How is your blood? Have you been making sure to eat well, and drink plenty of water and get the nutrition that you need?"

"Humph," he grumped at her, his true age shining through with the absolutely verbose reply. "Just because I use my own blood to augment my Abilities to their maximum effect does not mean that I'm a fool. I'm ensuring that I heal myself properly and restrict the bloodletting to the absolute minimum."

She stared at him silently, a small smile playing about her lips as her gaze drilled into him. After an uncomfortably long silence, he began fidgeting, then rolled his eyes and let out an exasperated sigh. "Fine! Eating some red meat and leafy greens certainly wouldn't be harmful to me, but if you want meat, you'll have to hunt it yourself. I'm not going to betray the trust of my creatures by hunting them when they cannot escape."

"You really *were* out of it." She smirked at him archly, sweeping her hand back to gesture at a small table already loaded down with food. Now that it had been pointed out, Andre could easily detect the succulent smell of savory roast game, as well as a steaming vegetable medley that had been spiced with saffron. His mouth instantly watered, and he nodded his appreciation at his counterpart.

"Thank you, once again." His words were heavy, as were his thoughts. When this commission was complete, none of them knew what would happen next. Currently, they were under orders to remain in the Scarrocco Desert, but when that had been fully converted, what would happen? Would they be forced to stay within this area, or would the order become meaningless, allowing them to roam under their own discretion until they were eventually found by the King's men?

The Druid knew which he hoped for. His plans were simple and fully aligned with his class. All he really wanted was to travel throughout the kingdom and begin binding the land to his power. It wouldn't only benefit him, but also the people of the kingdom, not to mention the land itself. He was jostled from his optimistic reverie as Taylor poked him in the back, jabbing the exact same spot that she had consistently targeted in an attempt to bruise him once upon a time... closing in on a century ago, by his own subjective time. "Gah! Don't *do* that; you know I hate it!"

"It's nice to see that I can still command your attention." Taylor coyly sauntered toward the table, pulling out a chair, twirling it around, and plopping herself down like a soldier returning from the front lines of the battle. "We should make a plan."

"I have a plan."

"*We* need a plan. Us. The Four," Taylor countered instantly. "You're likely planning on going off to lose yourself in some other form of self-sacrifice, which is so like you that your Spell set got tailored to your mental state. However, I don't want to lose what we all have. We have companionship, a history together, and a high-functioning team."

"I have Abilities, not Spells," Andre absent-mindedly deflected, trying to read between the lines and predict what she was getting at. "I don't see any situation where the four of us can stay together and maintain not only our freedom, but also expand our powers further."

The Mage dramatically plucked a piece of fruit coated with cinnamon off the table, popping it into her mouth and chewing slowly and blatantly. "Yum, yum! Look how easy it is to do multiple things at once."

Andre rolled his eyes, but he begrudgingly started to eat as Taylor laid out her thoughts. "I have to admit, I think Zed was onto something. The way he was describing our Mana Channels? The fact that he, *Zed*, of all people, was able to survive visiting Murder World? I think we have been missing out on an opportunity that would be beneficial to all of us."

"He came back literally starving to death, clearly has not slept in days if not weeks, and was ranting like a lunatic about 'fantastic opportunities for mass murder,'" Andre stated incredulously. "If you think that sounds like a good idea, or a team building exercise... well, I've got to tell you, it doesn't to me."

"Sure, he came back sounding a little more like Luke than I wanted to hear, but that guy was Zed's only companion for a month. Beyond that, you know what *does* sound like a good idea? Fifty mana regeneration per second. When was the last time that you managed to increase the Tier of even one of your Abilities?" Taylor's eyes were *glistening* as she spoke hungrily.

"Both of us have uses for endless practice, and you know it. Think of the sheer number of things that you could practice, even with a mere thirty days in which to do so. If you had unlimited mana, what *couldn't* you do? On top of that, if you were there, we wouldn't be facing any food or starvation issues. All we would need to bring is enough water... wait, you could handle that as well by growing juicy fruits. We could survive on juice, correct?"

"Yes, we potentially could, *if* the fruit doesn't absorb the mana from his plane of existence and convert into artifacts of immense power that either explode when we bite into them or cause us to explode." Andre shook his head in wonder as he studied Taylor with new eyes. "You really have changed over the last few years. The old you would never have suggested putting ourselves at risk, let alone taking a gamble that could backfire in terrible ways. You know what? ...I don't hate it."

They ate for a while in silence, a small smile dancing across both of their faces. Each of them felt that they had suddenly gained something and were trying not to mess it up by pushing too hard one way or another. Andre felt a sudden energy signature in his mind just as he attempted to resume the conversation, wincing as one of his trees was reduced to toothpicks. "Luke is out of the portal, and one of the trees waved at him too excitedly."

"He mulched it?"

"Yes." The Druid took a calming breath, intentionally connected to his forest, and guided that tree to regrow from a distance. He and Taylor had moved their camp from the last site that Luke had visited, so he opted to open a path through the forest that would guide the mana-saturated fighter in the most direct way possible. "I have no idea why he is so adamant about smashing trees or rocks every few feet. Seriously, he just went out of his way—*Luke*! Ugh. There goes an entire acre of flowers. He seriously hasn't figured out that those are magical plants? Or does he just hate the fact that they're magical?"

"What was special about those ones?" Taylor asked with a chuckle, resting her chin in one hand.

"They're an upgraded version of the Mountain Willow Wind flower; these ones don't just chime in the wind, but I planted them in a specific order so that they are constantly singing a song. It is supposed to be *soothing*!" Andre pulled irritably at his beard, which he had been letting grow out for the last few years. "Zed helped me compose the tune. Now we're going to have to start all over, because they needed to be individually transplanted after we figured out what note they would sing, and how often."

Taylor nodded sympathetically, continuing to enjoy her meal as she listened to his half-muttered rantings. "I'm very happy that you have taken time to make your work uniquely beautiful, and especially that you have a hobby instead of just constantly working to achieve the most efficient results possible. If you don't mind me asking, what song did the flowers sing?"

"It was the tune to a lullaby that Zed had made up. He didn't tell me the words yet; said he was still writing them." Andre's disgruntled explanation was met by a deep laugh as Zed approached the table, and the two dining friends frowned at him in consternation as he fell to the ground, choking on his own hysteria.

After an impressively lengthy duration, he started flapping his hands above his still-prone body. "I think I know why he went out of his way to kill those flowers! Every time he was getting on my nerves, I sang that lullaby to him. He once got so annoyed that he picked me up and threw me at a group of monsters."

Andre snorted; it was extremely easy to picture Zed tumbling through the air. The Bard had the capability to either truly integrate himself with any group he encountered or annoy the ever-living daylights out of them. "Only *you* could turn a lullaby into a Murderhobo's blind-rage activation sequence."

"I know! Am I not *awesome*?"

CHAPTER SIX

After a short rest, a good meal, and gathering his friends around him, Andre was certainly in a better place mentally. Each of the others were looking on with excitement, interest, or absolute apathy, depending on their own temperaments. "Thank you all for being here; I'm sure you know exactly how much this means to me."

"Make with the magic, plant boy! I want to see what happens!" Zed held a notebook and plant-based ink that had been supplied by the Druid, and he was furiously writing even while he heckled.

"As you know," Andre continued without acknowledging the Bard, "we aren't certain what this is going to do to our future, nor to the kingdom, but we do know that it is necessary for the world. There's a good chance that reconnecting this section of land to the world at large will cause mana storms, spontaneous rifts, or any number of other strange effects."

"Hold up." Luke looked interested for the first time. "You mean to tell me that just by growing some plants, you might open a bunch of Scars that need... *inspecting*?"

"That's what I'm trying to tell you: *everything* is possible."

Andre couldn't keep the nervousness out of his voice, but fear of the unknown was not something they slowed down for. "Here I go."

Drawing on the power granted to him by his connection to their sanctuary, Andre pricked his fingers with small thorns, drawing a thin stream of blood up from each digit of his outstretched left hand. The blood was captured by his outpouring mana and shunted into three thin circles that raised up into the air to focus the channeling of his will. As the circles were completed, they allowed him to bind to plants, animals, and the world, in that order.

Seeds that had been packed into the layer of fungus and plant matter burst into bloom. Grass speared through the earth in a rippling carpet, flowers opened their petals, and small trees began to sprout. His eyes firmly closed; Andre instead sensed his power working through the bindings. The second circle allowed him to guide insects, worms, arachnids, and all sorts of other humble organisms that were necessary for balancing the ecosystem. The Druid pushed them to expand their territories and briefly increase their reproductive rates, ensuring that the plants would have the caretakers they needed.

As the flora and fauna collaborated to cover the last remaining sliver of desert, Andre turned his focus to the final, most difficult portion. Connecting with the planet itself, he poured mana into the network of crisscrossing Ley Lines that balanced the energy of the world. He smoothed out the endcap portions, growing the healthy lines to connect to the world outside, lastly connecting the lines from the Nature Preserve to the surrounding countryside.

As the connection stabilized, an undulation of mana squirmed out from the forest, causing the ground to shudder, plants to tremble, and animals to cower. Over the next few minutes, the thick power in the air that had collected over the course of their exile was sucked away, further empowering the Ley Lines and moving along with the will of the world to balance other regions that had suffered from the artificial mana drought.

Each of The Four reacted differently to the abrupt drop in potency, but all of them could feel the strain clearly. In its wake came the realization that they had been feeling it the entire time they had lived in other areas of the kingdom. Taylor was the first to voice it, even though Luke appeared to be suffering the most. "That feels... disgusting. How could I even describe it? I don't know... transporting from the flatlands to the peak of a mountain in an instant, and expecting the air to stay just as dense? Is it *actually* harder to breathe, or does it just feel that way?"

"This place is becoming less real by the second," Luke asserted sadly, inspecting each of his friends with a surly stare, clearly trying to determine if they were actually caricatures—as he had suspected all along. It seemed they passed the test, because he diverted his intense gaze after a few disquieting, incisive seconds.

Zed had frozen under that stare, paralyzed by the relentless bloodlust that had seemed to chill his very soul.

Andre didn't particularly care for the byplay, as he was busy reveling in his success. He knew for certain that he had succeeded, as the only quest he had ever gained from the Hollow Kingdom's Archmage was showing... as complete.

Quest complete: Return life to the Scarrocco Desert! You've completed a legendary task appointed to you by the Hollow Kingdom. Return to the Capital, triumphant, to claim your reward!

"Oof. Yeah, no," Andre muttered softly to himself as he reread the message his Sigil had provided. Frankly, he had not expected to earn too much from the kingdom for this quest, but he was still hoping to receive a reward from the world itself. He didn't have to wait long, and he was not disappointed.

Nearly five minutes had passed since the aggressive draining of power from their haven had concluded. Just then, at the very edge of his senses, he felt it. Andre's eyes shot open as he realized that the land that he was bound to was, for the very first time, expanding *on its own.*

An outside entity that is bound to you is altering your Abilities.

Ability mutated! Bind by Blood (Tier 6, Level 7) → *Bloodflood Binding (Tier 7, Level 2).*

Bloodflood Binding (T7): 0/300 to level 3!

Effect 1: By using your blood when creating a Druidic binding circle, you can gain additional benefits from the bond.

Bonus 1, at range: Circle can be created within line of sight.

Effect 2: Bond is 30+n% more likely to succeed in any circle your blood is added into, where 'n' = cumulative levels after Tier 2! (T3 level 0 and beyond counts toward the percentage.)

Bonus 2, Multitarget: Increases resource gain among bound presence from $r*5^{-6}$ to $r*5^{-5}$ of offered resources, where r = offered resources!

Effect 3: Offered resources now include any Etheric Xenograft Potentia generated by bound beings within touch distance.

Bonus 3, AoE: 'Touch' distance is now considered anywhere within the circular binding. Any future Abilities generated that require 'touch' can be activated by any plants you're connected and in communion with.

Effect 4 NEW!: Areas in the world that are bound to you will expand on their own if there is a surplus of blood or mana in the area. Having both requirements filled will double the speed of expansion. This expansion occurs at a rate of 1 meter per 5 units of blood, or 1 meter per 50 units of surplus mana.

Although it was the only Ability increase he saw, something within himself also changed. Turning his attention inward, he focused on that change and realized that he had become some-what sturdier both physically and mentally. He could not exactly quantify how, but when he opened his eyes, he found Luke staring at him in wonderment. The huge man stepped closer, then reached out and poked Andre in the chest. "You just became more *real.* How did you do that?"

The Druid was lost for words, until he remembered what that meant to the Murderhobo. "Are you telling me that my Potentia has become more stable?"

"Call it whatever you want to call it, but you look like you'll fall apart less easily now." Luke nodded solemnly. "Whatever you just did, I want to do it, too."

Taking his time to think of a proper answer, Andre identified exactly what had changed within him. "I think my inner Potentia has condensed. If I recall correctly, you once told the royal guards that they looked like fluffy fakes? My hypothesis based on this latest increase is that I'm better primed to gain power, Abilities, and who knows what else. Would you say this is fairly accurate?"

"You words too much. How *I* do what *you* did?" Luke remarked slowly, as though Andre was the one having a difficult time understanding *him*, rather than the other way around.

"I think I've got this one, if you don't mind." Zed pulled out a lute, strumming it gently as he stared into Luke's eyes. "The Druid went out and performed a mighty work. The Earth itself rewards him! To do what he does, be who he is. If you can't do that, quiet down and do your job. Comparing yourself to others… is the true thief of joy!"

The other three stared at the Bard as he played his janky song, but somehow it penetrated their minds and cleared up any lingering confusion. Taylor shivered as she pondered the tune, both in revulsion at the actual lyrics, as well as the fact that he had blatantly used some form of Bardic Mastery on them. "It always makes me feel icky when you do that, even if it somehow clarified things in my head. It doesn't change the fact that we don't know what happened, and yet… I kind of care less?"

"It's a work in progress." Zed carefully backed away from Luke, who appeared to be debating whether or not to slap the Bard across the grove. Luke didn't enjoy having his head messed with, and it took a lot of effort and power to make such a thing happen. "Also, I didn't *intentionally* use a Mastery on you; I was just singing you a song."

"Hmmph." Luke grunted as he turned his attention back to the Druid. "Now what?"

"Now?" Andre read over his newly upgraded Ability, and a wide smile stretched across his face. "I don't suppose you have any liquid mana you would be willing to donate to a good 'cause'? You know, be-*cause* it'd help me out?"

"Mooch." Luke didn't fight against the request. After five years of living together, it was a fairly common occurrence among the group, as each of them had been donating their usefulness in various ways to help each other. Andre was glad the big man didn't begrudge him the boost, even if he would never use the fact that he had kept them fed, hidden, and sheltered for the last five years against them.

Accepting the oversized waterskin Luke offered a few moments later, Andre merely opened the top and set it down. Zed and Taylor simultaneously sucked in a harsh breath, staring at the apparent waste of mana that would be worth a medium-sized fortune in the outside world. Only Luke was paying attention to Andre's face as the Druid's smile stretched wider and wider into a maniacal caricature.

"I earned a new Ability; when there is surplus blood or mana in an area I control, it increases my 'bound' boundaries by a flat rate over time. With just this small container of mana leaking out, I've already acquired over one hundred meters of new land and counting."

He blinked as he felt something new. Small tremors that indicated something, or in this case, *someone,* walking. The number of steps increased rapidly, and his wide smile slowly started to collapse. "There are people approaching. They're…"

Only a pained grimace remained on his face, all of his previous joy completely eradicated. "They are everywhere. We are completely surrounded."

"Surrounded?" Zed scoffed at the despondent Druid. "So, drop us into the ground, and we'll hike along to a new part of the forest. How far away are they?"

"I'm not talking about us personally; I'm talking about the Scarrocco Nature Preserve. The entire area is surrounded, and if I'm judging the input accurately, an entire division of the army has been deployed to slowly close in toward the center of the forest," Andre informed them with a hint of dread.

"When you say that we're surrounded… you mean the several hundred miles of forest that used to be a desert is encircled by tens of thousands of people?" Zed lazily waved around the clearing. "They will never find us, if you don't *want* them to find us."

"Actually, based on the fact that a ton of Spells are going off in the process of expanding my range of territory even farther, I think that they *will* find us, unless we do something fairly drastic." Andre's mouth was set in a grim line, his brows drawn down in concentration and slowly mounting fury. "If my guess is correct, those are a mix of 'Detect Human' and various other scouting Spells."

"Sounds like the kingdom isn't very happy with us." Taylor took a deep breath and nodded firmly. Her companions tensed in anticipation, then relaxed as she assuaged their worries over where her true loyalties lay. "Our job in the desert is done. Let's find a way to get the *abyss* out of here."

CHAPTER SEVEN

"I'm not sure if anyone else has noticed this yet; is it just me...
or is there a giant pillar of light going from the ground to the
sky from the spot where Andre finished his quest?" Zed pointed
straight up, and they collectively groaned. The only reason the
rest of them hadn't noticed the glowing column was that they
were standing within its circumference and had been focused on
their own concerns. "Is that because he finished a legendary-
difficulty quest?"

Without a word, Luke turned on his heel and dashed away,
leaving the others to scramble after him as they abandoned the
beacon that would swiftly bring the kingdom's forces down on
them.

Andre snarled at himself. If they were caught because of his
actions, he would feel terrible. Using his ability to connect with
the world around him, he shaped the earth in front of them to
constantly be a downhill slope, speeding up their progress
immensely as trees and shrubs shuffled out of their way.

Often, it still was not fast enough for the Murderhobo,
forcing the Druid to take a moment to revitalize pulped foliage
as they ran. "Luke, stop smashing things. It's splitting my focus!"

"Where are we even going, if we're totally surrounded?" Taylor called over, and Andre had to admit that was a very good question. Part of his mind was still connected to the forest, allowing him to track the rapid movement of the encircling troops, especially the Ascenders at the front of the pack who were sprinting toward the beacon.

"If we maintain this course, we are going to run into kingdom forces in under three minutes. We need to get to one of our safe houses." His words were firm, and he called after Luke to divert to fallback point 'tree eight'. "After we secure the location, we can jump into another world and travel across the kingdom before leaving. I think—and correct me if I'm wrong —it's fairly certain that we are no longer stuck here?"

"Only way to know for sure is to try it out," Taylor agreed with a nervous smile and a shrug in an attempt to inject cuteness into the serious situation. "But I hope so!"

"I don't get lit on fire when I go into people's worlds anymore!" Zed enthused, clearly comfortable with their spontaneous plan. "Which is my way of saying that your plan sounds great, since I'm not in danger of immediately dying anymore. Last thing, why didn't we have this plan in place *before* we completed your quest?"

No one had an answer, but it seemed that the tree branches got out of Zed's way a little less frequently after that comment. After dodging through a particularly dense thicket, the small party dove into the compact base that had been formed within the hollow of an oak tree's roots, then expanded with druidic magic. Andre closed the exit behind them with a simple stomp of his foot and looked around at the others hopefully. "Who's making the portal?"

"Can't," Luke informed him with a grunt.

"Don't feel bad about it. The fact that you can perform at *all* at your advanced age is already a huge success." Zed held out a single thumbs up with a lopsided grin. Luke had gotten plenty of practice in ignoring the Bard, and he continued to perfect that state without even twitching an eyebrow.

Taylor shook her head, folding her hands into her sleeves to hide her nervous fidgeting. "I won't be fast enough to get us out of here in time; can you do it?"

The Druid nodded, stifling his frustration while pulling his LivingWood staff out of the earth where it tended to travel along near him. With a flourish, he pumped mana into it and drew out a circle. The portal began forming just as Andre sensed a wash of mana that seemed to cling to him and pull in a specific direction. "King Alexander's saggy staff, I think they just got a lock on me!"

"It hit all of us; keep going," Taylor advised him, her words carefully chosen to avoid sounding demanding or nervous. She was simply encouraging, which was exactly what he needed at that moment.

The Druid focused more intently on his task, and the portal flared into existence. He held it open as Zed stepped through, followed by Taylor, but as Luke attempted to pass through, his Sigil flared brightly and sent him stumbling back and away, faltering at the abrupt loss of strength in his legs and core. Andre wrapped him with vines and tried to throw him in, but the Sigil audibly *chimed*. With an irritated grunt, the Murder-hobo exploded from the bindings and threw himself to the ground. Andre met his friend's eyes, and Luke merely nodded at the open escape.

"Looks like I'm not going with you," the scarred warrior stated heavily. "Get out of here while you can. I'll hold them off for as long as possible."

Andre shook his head mulishly. "We are a team, and I'm not going to leave you here."

"Get out of here. Go put down roots somewhere. You had a taste of freedom. Solid appetizer. Now get a whole meal out of it." Luke didn't wait for an answer, hopping to his feet and lightly slapping the Druid—sending him flying at breakneck speed through his portal.

The Scar in the world's membrane closed with a *snap* as Andre smashed headfirst into the stone wall that stood on the other side of the portal. His head twisted to the side, skull attempting to cave in from the impact. Frankly, there was a good chance that he would have died if he hadn't been tossed into his personal grove, where the Peace Lily was in full bloom and preventing death. "*Ow-ah!* Luke, you absolute lunatic…!"

"What happened? Where's Luke?" Taylor searched the grove anxiously as she grabbed Andre and helped him up. It was clear the huge man hadn't joined them in their attempt to escape. "You *left* him?"

"I did nothing!" Andre indignantly declared, "His Sigil refused him entry to my portal, and he nearly killed me by fighting to stay on that side because of it."

The trio sank into doleful silence as they stared at the empty space the portal had occupied, mulling over their strategy without Luke. Zed drummed his fingers on his chin, calculating aloud. "The time dilation on this world is about eight times greater than the kingdom's time, correct? That buys us some time before he's in real trouble. We need to make a plan."

"Time shift is only six times greater. I think we should cut our losses and run for it," Andre stated without a moment of hesitation. "That's what he wanted us to do. I say we figure out where the connection points to our world are, and bolt to a safe location. Once we're out of range, I can make it exponentially harder for us to be found."

"Look how well that worked last time!" Taylor raged as she punched the wall hard enough to split her skin, only for her hand to take no damage whatsoever. "At least when we're here, we have the defenses you have put in place—food, safety thanks to your flower—and we're able to help nurture your World Seed."

"I *still* think you should grow it into a dragon," Zed muttered almost too quietly to be heard. Seeing as he was not offering any useful advice, let alone participating in the conversation in general, the other two decided to focus on each other.

"The difference is that I would be dropping us in the *kingdom*, not a smallish area that can be easily surrounded and searched." Andre argued with the Mage, "If we are hiding in the kingdom proper, any search Spells that are looking for humans are not going to be effective in finding us. If we get out there, we are *free*."

"So long as we never read a document, get found by the guaranteed *hundreds* of bounty hunters that will be looking for us, or run into any kingdom official that would be able to order us around," Zed chimed in unnecessarily, and far too cheerily. "I don't know about you guys, but when I see a notice posted, my first inclination is to read it. That's going to be how they get me, guaranteed. That, or I'll lure an army to a tavern and make them listen while I ramble at them for free Potentia."

"This isn't helpful. Like Taylor said, we bought some time." Andre tried to calm himself down, only to find that he was seething with a raging sea of emotions. Disgust with himself for leaving his friend behind, annoyance that they'd been forced to flee directly after his moment of triumph, and finally, bone-deep weariness from constantly working to finish healing the desert over the last five years. For him, it had taken closer to nine years, thanks to the constant need to return to his world and experiment without impacting the forest. Nearly a decade of backbreaking work, only to be capped with impending capture.

It was an insult of the highest measure.

He stalked away from the clearing without another word, the walls of roots and stones shifting out of his way as he traipsed through the wilderness that he had made intimately and intrinsically *his*. With a sigh that carried equal relief and exhaustion, he meandered into the main cavern and found Arthur, his Dire Bear companion. Leaning into the side of the great Beast that was chuffing in greeting and happiness, the Druid internally mused how wonderful it was that this magnificent creature was able to dwell within a domain that disallowed degradation. Arthur hadn't aged a day since he had made this cavern his home, needing neither sustenance nor sleep.

The perfect guardian of his secrets, his successes, and all too frequently... his failures. Stroking the coarse, wiry fur, Andre closed his eyes and heaved a great sigh. "Yet another loss after a glorious win, my friend. This time, I'm not the one paying the price for my failure to properly plan, and it is already eating at me. What do I do?"

Warbling a low growl, the bear showed his teeth. Andre shook his head, a slight smile curving his lips despite his agony. "No, unfortunately I cannot eat this issue. If any of these people get close to me—it's humans that we are attempting to escape from, by the way—they will conscript me into service once more. My vacation of an exile is at an end, and I will be forced into constant mobility…"

Arthur swung his head to the side, looking pointedly at the massive cavern filled with plant life and bioluminescent moss. Truly, this was a fairytale slice of Elysium, and the bear's meaning was clear. Even so, the Druid shook his head in the negative, sorrow weighing down his face and limbs. "Until I'm able to achieve level twenty, I will not be able to remain here permanently. Even then, I will be attempting to Ascend to a higher world, and this will merely become my base world at best. You do know you're coming with me, right?"

Huff. The Dire Bear snorted agreeably, rolling his massive shoulders and settling in on the floor. Even though the Beast was laying down, his shoulder was at eye level for the extremely tall Druid.

Andre couldn't have been more pleased. His bear was his ideal companion and guardian, happy to listen to him and without muddying the waters with morals or ethics. Have an enemy? Eat them. Have a problem? Hibernate for a while; maybe it will go away. Andre sighed as he started to relax. "If only mankind didn't need to complicate their lives to such a degree."

As he leaned comfortably against his warm, dozing companion, he considered his life for the last near decade and decided to take a look at his Sigil in order to review his quantified growth.

Cal Scan
Level: 12
Current Etheric Xenograft Potentia: 17,843 / 37,700 to level 13!
Body: 13.15

- _Fitness: 10.4_
- _Resistance: 15.9_

Mind: 39

- _Talent: 28_
- _Capacity: 50_

Presence: 14.8

- _Willpower: 20.5_
- _Charisma: 9.1_

Senses: 10.25

- _Physical reaction: 12.3_
- _Mental energy: 8.2_

Maximum health: 209
Maximum mana: 662
Mana regen: 9.3 per second.

Ability: Tier: Level

Bloodflood Binding: 7: 2
Hemoflora: 4: 9
Earthblood Terraformation: 4: 9
Brute Migration: 8: 5
Call Of Nature: 9: 0

It had been interesting to observe how his Potentia had

continuously increased, albeit slowly over the years, thanks to having bound himself to such a rich, and highly mutable area. Hardly any of his growth had come from defeating other creatures; it had all resulted from his work, along with the donations of the flora and fauna of his bound areas. Still, it had been enough to achieve the great milestone of level twelve, as well as allowing him to increase his Abilities beyond their previous limits.

Not spectacular increases, in most cases, as he felt that he had neither truly mastered nor understood each of those imparted Abilities to their fullest extent. Regardless, he had made great strides with his Druidic Circle Magic especially, and he noticed that many of his characteristics had greatly increased. Even though he personally had only been able to allocate twenty total points—thanks to his increase in levels—being around Luke, Taylor, and Zed had been fantastic for training his Willpower and Charisma.

Something about them made it extremely difficult to simply give in when pressed on an issue. His constant resistance to domination, intentional or otherwise, had pushed the growth of his Willpower to new heights. Of course, the ability to train in an area with extremely saturated mana density was also a major factor in his growth. It had likewise given him a particularly keen insight into how Luke had become such a monster of a man.

That line of thinking brought him full circle, of course, and he sagged in place as he remembered his failure to rescue his friend.

Wub.

He sat up with a frown, straining his ears for several heartbeats. The sound that had just intruded on his private reminiscence increasingly annoyed him as he attempted to place it. "What in this *world* makes that sound?"

Wub. Wub.

His eyes widened in fear as he realized that he did, indeed, recognize it. He had been right to be confused. There was nothing *in this world* that made that sound.

Not unless the Murderhobo was coming.

"Andre!" Taylor's distressed tone pierced through the foliage a fraction before she burst into his cavern, eyes wild. "Luke is smashing his way in through your closed portal!"

"That's impossible! He was unable to enter... no! Someone has control of him." Andre's blood froze in his veins at the realization, and the ramifications were bone-chillingly clear. By the horror in her eyes, they were clear for Taylor as well. "They are sending him after us... to bring us home. Scatter! Run for it!"

CHAPTER EIGHT

- LUKE -

At the sight of the portal *snapping* shut right in front of him, it was all Luke could do to not fly into a rage and start smashing things. Squinting his eyes, he tried to make a plan. Thinking that hard made his head hurt, so he decided against it and fell back on 'smashing things'.

Andre hadn't left him an exit, so there was no real alternative. He ran over to the walls and dirt he knew were the weakest, spinning around and slamming Cookie into the earth at an upward angle. At least a half ton of dirt, stone, and splinters went flying at a velocity that almost touched the speed of sound. Not quite, but the blow was loud enough to alert anyone who had been unaware of his presence to his exact location. With that knowledge, he took a deep breath and followed the raining debris by activating Bum Thunder. With nothing in his way, he instantly shot about eight meters above the ground, an echoing *boom* canceling out any shouts of surprise or bellowed orders.

He wasn't overly worried about being captured; he only needed to make sure that he didn't look directly at anything anyone was holding or let himself hear what they had to say. To make sure that happened, he let go of Cookie for an instant and clapped his hands over his ears, bursting his eardrums and effectively eliminating half of the threat. Blood trickled out of his ear canals, and he chuckled to himself.

"Just like old times! Those banshees in Zone seventeen were a pain in the rear until I figured out this trick. Afterward, they were just a pain in the ear."

Luke could sense that people were closing in on him, since the standard movement of the forest was not enough to mask the trembling of underbrush, the swaying of trees, or the half-dozen people that were sprinting toward him. He kicked off a towering oak with a laugh, leaving deep foot-shaped indentations in the wood, and launched himself through the air with all the force his forty-six-point-seven points in Fitness could manage. Between that and Giga increasing his overall physical output to seven thousand, two-hundred and thirty-eight kilos of force, he blasted into the air at a slight angle like a ballista bolt targeting a peasant militia while noblemen cackled.

At the peak of his parabolic arc, he activated Feather's Fall and hummed gently to himself as he drifted through the forest at a breathtaking pace. He couldn't hear the sounds he was making, but as much as he hated to admit it, Zed's song had really stuck in his head. "In battle you're fierce, a force to behold. It's time to let your muscles unfold. Feel the peace of the night around you. Let your spirit rest and renew."

The second verse of the annoying lullaby that the Bard had slipped into his brain was far less soothing to the hordes of people shouting for his attention. Particularly when his eyes were closed, someone had jumped directly in his way as he was saying 'feel the peace of the night'. Just as the line left his lips, Cookie sliced directly through the Ascender who had gotten in his way. Luke didn't even notice, thanks to the passive effect of Feather's Fall, which converted his momentum into penetrating damage.

"Huh." Luke wiped his face as he continued soaring

through the air, planning his next launch point as Cookie dragged him down faster than he wanted to drop. "Must be raining tonight."

He kept his eyes closed as often as possible, as Zed's warning about written documents was fresh in his mind. As he slowly plowed into the ground, Luke rolled and scanned his surroundings for a bare fraction of a moment to get his bearings, then shot forward, hoping he wouldn't run into a tree that he couldn't plow through. To make doubly sure, he used Sourcecerer's Armory to materialize a long spear in front of him. His reasoning was simple: if the spear could pass through whatever lay in front of him, so could he.

A small frown grew on his face, as he recalled that he had been unable to absorb the void-tipped needles that had been shot at him by the as-of-yet unnamed monsters of Zone twenty. Even though they were considered a weapon when they were being held by the creatures, they were not considered as such by his Skill when they were separated. The silver lining was that—since his Skill *did* consider them weapons—when he was able to walk into that Zone, he would hopefully be able to consider the entirety of the felled creature as a weapon instead.

The Murderhobo wasn't certain if being able to summon one of the towering monsters was going to let him summon something to fight beside him, or if it was going to turn into a stationary, useless weapon. Either way, it would be an exciting addition to his repertoire. If it worked.

Unbeknownst to him, his smiling, blood-coated face was striking terror in the hearts of those pursuing him. After the first utter failure, no one had been foolish enough to get directly in Luke's path, and for some reason, he was able to ignore their shouted orders, even though they *knew* they were in audible range of the Murderhobo. Their only remaining hope was to take him down before he breached containment, as they had been warned that he would be nearly impossible to capture if he escaped.

The inevitable happened, unfortunately for Luke. He was in

a forest, in one of the densest areas, which meant several extremely broad and durable trees. He ran into one, feeling the resistance thanks to the spear, and he was forced to open his eyes for a brief moment to scout a new path. In that instant, one of the Ascender tracking teams came up with a brilliant idea: they cast a taunting spell on the large parchment they were holding, forcing him to focus on it.

It certainly held the Murderhobo's attention long enough for him to read the words, but the order on it didn't come into effect fast enough to stop him from lashing out and destroying the offending item—and the person holding it. "Whoops."

In a flash, Luke was surrounded by dozens, then scores, then hundreds of soldiers. As they arrived, he remained unable to move, having read the order of the king. "I should have *known* that reading was going to be my greatest enemy. Books are printed on paper; paper comes from trees. Unnatural trees that can tell me what to do. Ugh."

No matter how highly ranked the people around him were, he was not compelled to comply with their shouted orders, instead remaining frozen in his current position as the written order had commanded. Eventually, one of the Ascenders spotted the blood trickling from his ears and connected the dots. After they pulled over a Healer, Luke's ears were repaired in a matter of moments. Then a high-ranking government official ordered the Murderhobo to sit down, and the mountainous man plopped to the ground like a puppet with cut strings. Everyone in the area, except the Murderhobo himself, breathed a sigh of relief.

"Finally, things are going how I expect them to go." The ranking Ascender stepped closer to Luke, scornfully looking him up and down. "I didn't know what to expect from you, but deafening yourself and running with your eyes closed until you faceplanted into a tree was *not* it. Where are your companions? I order you to tell me."

"They skipped out on this world," Luke informed the Ascender shortly, glaring stonily at his captor.

"Abyss!" The man slapped his side as he brought a hand up against his forehead. "Which one opened the path out? Was it Taylor, the prospective Archmage? Or was it the Druid? I order you to answer all my questions."

"The Druid."

"*Abyss!*" Now the man threw his hands in rage, shouting at no one and everyone. "If it was the Mage, at least we could have gone after her! We only have one Druid, and he was just released back to his country after they recalled him for mandatory service! Spread the word; we need to find someone who can go after them. Does anyone know a roaming Druid, a different mercenary company who could open the way? Anyone? *Someone*, please? Does *anyone* have *any* idea how we could go after them? Give me answers, people!"

"Yes." Luke was forced to begrudgingly answer, though he kept his voice as quiet as possible, since the Ascender was not addressing him directly. Even so, the man's incredibly heightened senses caught the muted reply, and he whipped his head around to stare at Luke.

"What did you say?"

"I said 'yes'," Luke responded in a deadpan tone. "Before that, I said 'The Druid'. Before that, I said 'They skipped'-"

The man irritably waved his hand to cut Luke off. "What do you mean, 'yes'? Do you have an idea of how to go after them?"

"Yes."

"What is it?"

"A thought or suggestion of a possible course of action," Luke explained carefully, earning a look of confusion in return.

"Why did you just say that?" the Ascender quizzed him cautiously. "Answer."

"You asked me what 'an idea' was."

Releasing a long **hiss** of air through clenched teeth, the Ascender attempted to control his temper. "You think you can get away with malicious compliance? You're going to take *everything* literally?"

"Yes. No."

"Explain those answers!"

Luke shook his head. "I can't take everything, literally. I cannot hold that much weight."

"I order you to explain how we can pursue the others on your team if they have escaped into a world that no one else has a way to enter," The Ascender ordered with a smile that promised violence later.

Luke attempted to keep his mouth shut, and the imprint of his Sigil became brighter and brighter as it attempted to force him to follow the command of the ranking Ascender. Finally, his mouth moved seemingly of its own accord. "I can open the way."

"Can you, now?" the man murmured in a considering tone, not sure how such a feat would be possible. Even so, Luke had been ordered to answer his questions, so Luke at least *believed* he could do so. "Then I order you to open the way and retrieve the other members of your team as rapidly as can be done... safely! As rapidly as can be done *safely*!"

That last part had been hastily added as Luke leapt to his feet and sprinted through the ranks of soldiers. He let out a gentle snort of derision as he glanced down at the nearest squad of men in front of him, some of whom had large, wet stains traveling down their pant legs. "It seems I made an impression."

CHAPTER NINE

It took Luke slightly longer than he'd wanted to find his bearings, as he had run through the forest with his eyes closed. Yet, without Andre present to repair the damage that he had left, it was fairly obvious which direction he needed to go. "Follow the path of destroyed forest. Can do."

Without delay, he made his way toward the location of tree eight, deliberately spending as much time as possible picking out the *safest* route. Would it be *safe* to go through those saplings? Who knew for sure? Perhaps he would get poked in the eye. Was that bush poisonous? Probably. Better make sure to not step on anything that appeared even mildly unsafe.

The other Ascenders watched incredulously as the enormous Murderhobo picked his way through the forest, tiptoeing so delicately as not to disturb even a leaf if at all possible. Half an hour into his journey, he had barely made it ten feet from the point where he had received his orders. The ranking Ascender was practically pulling his own hair out, stomping over to shout at Luke. "Why are you doing this? I told you to go open the portal!"

"Just trying to be safe," Luke informed him with an absolutely serious face. "Who knows what kind of dastardly trickery that Druid could have put in place. Lots of dangerous natural *stuff* out here."

While his tone seemed sincere, the way he eyed the people around him left no room for imagination. The man in charge took a deep breath, then addressed him in a pleasant tone. "Hello, Luke. You get to know me as 'Sir', as the idea of giving you my name so that you can find me in the future seems like a terrible idea. Most people that know me think of me as someone that is very pleasant to work with, as well as driven to succeed. I have less than a decade of service remaining before I get to Ascend, and I would like to complete those years on good terms with the people that are in charge of my Sigil. How about you help me out?"

"I can send you on permanent retirement, if that is what you're asking." Luke hoisted Cookie into the air, hoping that the man in front of him would give any indication at all towards a 'yes'.

"I was tasked with bringing you and your team back to speak with the king. He has gifts for you, as well as a new assign-ment." Sir's incentives seemed to have no impact on the over-sized Berserker, so he tried a different tactic. "Do you know that people have been singing your praises ever since you came back from your first mission rolling a house-sized ball of gold to the castle? Now, you've clearly had some role to play in fixing the desert that was expanding and threatening to engulf our entire kingdom. As word of that spreads, *all* of you will be heroes to the kingdom."

"*Nn-neat.*" Luke held the word in his mouth until it carried two syllables, as he could not be certain that using only one syllable would be 'safe'. He swore that he could hear Cookie chuckling at his antics, and he was glad that she approved. "Back to my offer… I'm not hearing a 'no'."

"You want to do this the hard way? Fine. Harming neither myself nor any of my troops, go and retrieve the remainder of your team as quickly as possible without dealing permanent damage to them." A strained hush hung in the air between the command leaving his mouth and Luke acting upon it. In that time, Luke's Sigil glowed with increasing intensity, eventually releasing an audible *chime* that continued until the Murder-hobo finally started moving forward.

He activated Bum Thunder, launching forward and sending out a small shock wave behind him. It wouldn't be his fault if those troops were injured from it, he was certain. Smashing through trees, crushing bushes, only a small detour to punch a specific noisy flower, and he was back at the fallback point where his team had made their escape. Pulling back his fist, he eyed the faint distortion in the air that he was almost certain only he could see. "Ready or not, here I come."

His fist launched forward as he activated 'Rift Hunter', lamenting over the fact that he didn't currently have enough stored Potentia to start Tiering up that Skill, effectively locking it away until it would be too late to open the portal. His knuckles tapped against the spatial membrane that kept this world separated from the next dimension over, sinking in slightly as power rushed through him.

The membrane rebounded, attempting to remain closed. A deep thrumming radiated out from the point of impact, rapidly punctuating the impact of punch after punch.

Wub.

Wub. Wub.

As his fifth strike landed, the portal had absorbed enough energy and damage to stabilize and pull itself open. Without a moment of hesitation, Luke stepped through the Scar and snorted out an annoyed exhalation. "Feces. I had been hoping that wouldn't work. Andre, Taylor, Zed! Run away; don't let me know where you are! Then again... if you think you can't escape, you're probably correct, and you should stay within the influence of the Peace Lily, so I don't accidentally hurt you."

He bellowed the warning at the top of his lungs while simultaneously running through the honeycomb of tunnels that greeted him upon exiting the portal. Luke let out a swift smile as he realized that the layout had changed. "I like that you're thinking ahead, Andre. Sorry to say it's not going to matter."

Because he knew the rules and restrictions of this world, specifically the grove that Andre lived in, Luke couldn't allow himself to *walk* the meandering halls that most likely connected back onto themselves. Instead, he tossed Cookie up and down in his hands, forced to use both of them since her absorption of the Corrupted Nature Dragon's leftover carcass. Howling to warn them of his imminent approach, he shot forward, slamming Cookie into the stone wall blocking his path, as he knew it blockaded the most direct route towards the center of the grove.

Chips of stone pelted him, bouncing off of his mana-materialized armor. Anything that would have been able to deal damage, such as a boulder that dropped onto his head, simply fell to the side thanks to the fact that this place made it impossible for health to degrade. Another strike revealed open air on the other side, the blow having tunneled through a dozen meters of solid rock in an instant. The second sent shards everywhere. Yet, when he swung again, Cookie was stopped dead in her arc as she walloped a tree root that had sprung out of the stone.

"Do more of that, Andre! Surround yourself with roots so that I cannot tear you away from here!" Luke bellowed desperately, hoping that it would be enough. He was literally unable to stay still, and rushed to blast through ahead of Andres' ability to grow things. Speed, or a lack thereof, was the major downfall of the Druid's power set. Without access to endless mana such as Luke could provide, he was limited by the plants already in place, as well as what he could accomplish with his own internal reserves. By his own admission, the redhead only had command over a small slice of paradise and was otherwise surrounded on all sides by barren wasteland.

Luke knew that he could move faster than Andre could defend himself, and he *had* to take advantage of that. Another strike, slightly to the side, sent the slowly extending root system flying into the air, accompanied by the shattered stone. For only a few moments, the path forward was clear, and the Murder-hobo dashed forward to take advantage of that fact.

In the next moment, he was forced back by a barrage of flames that sprang out of nowhere; clearly Taylor had not heard his instructions to run away. He was disappointed but unsurprised. Even if they would have run, he knew it would only have taken him longer to catch up to them.

It certainly didn't mean that they would escape.

Walking through the flames dealt no damage to him, exactly as he had expected. He growled at the fact that the Sigil interfaced with his thoughts and memories, else he would have happily tricked it into thinking that he was in danger from the normally harmful fire bolts. Unfortunately for everyone involved, a simple activation of Bum Thunder brought him in range of the Mage, and her eyes widened fractionally as his hand darted forward. She dodged his grasp smoothly and attempted to vanish from view. It was close, so close that he *tried* to allow it to succeed, but instead of heeding his senses, his hand shot out and closed around what appeared to be empty air. Without looking, he knew that he had wrapped his hand around her neck.

Luke picked her up and carried her over to a bare section of the stone floor, which he smashed with Cookie to make a roughly human-sized hole. Tucking her into the space with a regretful grimace, he rolled a boulder over the opening so that she couldn't escape from the makeshift prison cell. A small *scuff* echoing down a side hallway was all he needed to launch himself in that direction, and a moment later, he had captured Zed as well. He closely inspected the scrawny man, nodding in solemn consideration. "I don't know if you ever knew that I could always tell the difference between your clones and your real body; sorry you have to find out this way."

He threw the clone to the side, then swung his hammer around and blasted away the opposing wall, revealing a terrified Bard that should have died simply from taking the massive Greatmace to his chest. A few moments later, the Bard was deposited adjacent to the Mage in a small cell designed just for him. "Last and certainly most annoying, I need to go find Andre."

As far as Luke could determine, it was unlikely that his friend would leave the others to their own fate, seeing as how the man had nearly lost his mind upon being forced to leave Luke behind. It *certainly* wouldn't happen twice more. Therefore, the Druid's most probable location would be at the center of his domain, where his power was the greatest. That wasn't too difficult to pinpoint, as the Murderhobo had visited before. Running down the hallways, it quickly became apparent that he was traversing the enormous underground cavern teeming with mutated and interesting plant life.

However, Luke was only interested in the animal life he faced, namely the Druid and the massive bear that had interposed itself between the two humans. "Andre. I'm fairly certain that vines are pretty much unbreakable here, right? If you can manage to loop them around my feet and arms, you can keep me contained until we figure out a way to break the control they have over me."

The Druid nodded, fully understanding that Luke was not in control of his own actions at present. Even so, both of them had a certain gleam in their eye. There had always been one question that they had been unable to answer: which of them would win in a fight? Luke was all direct aggression and physical power, while Andre could command the entire planet around him to fight on his behalf. The thought of such a clash nearly made Luke salivate. "If I fought a planet, who would win? I bet I could turn it into a moon, at minimum. Maybe not fast, but I could do it."

Crinkle.

In the absolute stillness of their tense stalemate, the sound of a plant bud breaking through the surface and dislodging a few grains of sand and pebbles was enough to alert the Murderhobo to his impending predicament. As much as he wanted to stay still and accept being bound, his orders wouldn't allow him to do so. "Bum Thunder!"

An instant later, he hovered above the massive Dire Bear, Cookie pulled over his head, angled so far back that the flat of his feet were pressed against her top. As he descended, he pushed up with his feet and swung down with his arms, generating a massive overhead two-handed strike that blasted into the floor like a meteorite.

Andre hadn't stayed still and accepted the blow, which would have been foolish even if it wouldn't have dealt damage to him. Even the possibility of getting knocked off-balance and captured was enough to ensure that he took the fight seriously. His LivingWood staff jumped out of the ground and into his hands, a vine already strung along its length to convert it into a longbow. Arrow after arrow was grown and fired at the Murderhobo, who danced around the projectiles easily, expertly avoiding the embedded seeds and spores that would begin growing on him if he was impacted.

Arthur the bear joined combat, swinging a paw the size of a dinner table at the massive human, only to be directly caught by Luke as he dropped Cookie. The Murderhobo used both hands as he twisted and flung the bear over his shoulder, lifting it completely into the air and slamming it into the ground. Another swift motion brought his weapon into his hands once more, and he swung down and up in a parody of an uppercut, striking the bear's jaw and sending the beast flailing through the air.

Even before it could hit the ground and begin tumbling, Luke had moved once more to be above the Druid. In an expert swing, his weapon struck out, but Andre lifted his staff and caught the blow, the wood supported by two vines that had shot out and wrapped around it. The weapons stopped dead, even as a resounding *boom* shook the room and sent any remnants of dust flying away from the epicenter of their battle. Just before Luke could rebalance himself in the air, the reinforcing vines released the staff and snaked around his torso and one leg.

Unable to contain himself, the Murderhobo shouted in glee, "Yes! You did it!"

The vines reeled him in, Andre making a point to keep him suspended in the air and give him no ability to push off a wall or other surface. Anytime he tried to generate movement, such as swinging back and forth, the lines would go slack on one side and taut on the other. Since he couldn't damage them, they were the perfect capture device.

"Release him at once!" an authoritative voice shouted into the cavern, turning the Murderhobo's jubilation into instant grim resignation. Luke dropped out of the sky, hitting the ground and launching himself at the Druid. "Nobody move!"

Instantly, both of the members of The Four were held fast and merely regarded each other with expressions full of resignation. 'Sir' had followed Luke into the portal and took their distractions as an opportunity to succeed in his own mission. "You will both follow my commands. We are going to return to the capital of the Hollow Kingdom immediately. Wait... what is *that*?"

His eyes widened as he took in the fact that two artifacts of incredible power were sitting right next to each other. One was a flower, and one resembled an egg but radiated such immense Potentia that it had to be worth an *unfathomable* amount of gold. "If you can safely remove those two items from this cave, bring them with us!"

Andre's face fell, eyes brimming with despair as he struggled to ignore the order.

Luke's reaction was different; he didn't move even as his Sigil began to shine brightly. A wide smile blossomed across his face as a warning note began singing from the overburdened enchantment on his forehead. "*No.* Uh-oh, *Sir.* You just gave me an unlawful order."

An instant later, one of the lines on his Sigil began sparking furiously, looking for all the world like a 'Dazzle' Spell a brand-new Mage had picked up to entertain children. Sir gasped and retreated instinctively as Luke took a single threatening step toward him. "Belay that order! Cancel it! Don't bring them if you don't want to!"

Immediately, the Sigil that had been breaking down due to orders conflicting with laws stopped glowing and sparking. The Ascender visibly sagged with a deep sigh of relief, then ordered the two men to follow him as he led the way to the other members of their party. Luke and Andre had no choice but to comply, though Luke's wild smile was hidden as well as he could manage. Sir hadn't double checked the Murderhobo's leash.

The damage that had been dealt to the Sigil wasn't repairing itself, and Luke could practically *taste* its impending catastrophic failure. From this point forward, it was only a matter of time.

CHAPTER TEN

- TAYLOR -

Once the sounds of combat had traveled far enough down the cavern for her to trust that physical harm was unlikely, Taylor blasted her way through the confining stone, ready to do the same for Zed. The two of them would have to make a break for it while they had the chance. They would be trapped in this world until they could find another Druid who was willing to let them out, but at least they would be-

"Mage Taylor! By the order of the King, you're to remain where you are!" A man she had never seen before had pushed himself through the stone fragments that were limply hanging from their surroundings via a series of interconnected roots. "You may call me 'Sir'. I have been tasked with returning you to the Hollow Kingdom for your next orders."

The Mage didn't respond, simply remaining in place with empty eyes and a defeated expression working its way across her features. The strange man rolled his eyes and scowled in annoyance. "Seriously, you're all taking this like a death sentence! I don't understand it. Like I told your large friend, you're being heralded as heroes to the people! Combine that with the fact that you made the majority of the nobility extremely wealthy, and your next assignment is most likely going to be relaxing on a beach somewhere out of the way until your term of service is complete."

"Sir." Taylor's response came out as a soft sigh. "I'm the prospective Archmage. Andre is the kingdom's only Druid, by default becoming the Archdruid. Zed is a *True Bard*. Luke is an incredibly powerful combatant who is nearly wholly unhinged, and he is constantly on the edge of escaping his oath of servitude to the kingdom, with nothing to prevent him from turning on the kingdom if he so desires. None of us are getting cozy assignments. You're dragging us out of a willing exile."

"Oh." The candid statement truly seemed to set the man aback. "I didn't realize that. Unfortunately… I have my orders, and you know exactly what that means. I cannot pretend that my mission was unsuccessful, and I most certainly don't *want* to, if you're all as politically sensitive as you say. Please don't think of me unfavorably or hold a grudge. You should know better than anyone that doing your job is the only way-"

"Stop trying to cover your own rear, and just do your job before things go wrong." Taylor gestured into the distance, where the clash between the Archdruid and the Murderhobo still rang through the air. She was worried about what could happen if Luke and Andre's combat became too wild. Only one living thing in this haven could be damaged or killed: the Peace Lily. If anything happened to that flower, and the others didn't realize it, it was very likely that someone would die, even if it wasn't intentional.

Sir nodded and walked away, returning only a few minutes later with Andre and a disconcertingly smiling Luke. A moment later, the Murderhobo rolled away the boulder covering Zed's cell, which allowed the man to gasp and finally inhale his lungs.

"*Seriously*, Luke? You couldn't leave me an *air hole*?" The Bard coughed violently as fresh air entered his lungs for the first time in several minutes. "I know I can't… that is, you obviously had faith that I would survive, but a little bit of life's luxuries, like *air*, you too-crunchy crouton, certainly wouldn't have been amiss!"

Taylor was impressed that Zed didn't reveal the secret of the Druid's personal grove, as that news would have spread like a wildfire and put Andre's future security at risk. Likewise, she had to keep up appearances and pretend that she was upset in order to move the conversation as far away from the sensitive topic as possible without raising Sir's suspicions. "Most likely, he recognized the fact that you're full of hot air and could use a deflation every once in a while."

Zed rounded on her, face set in a rictus of anger, but a twinkle in his eye combined with a subtle wink confirmed the game they were playing. "As for you! *You* are the reason we were caught in the first place! Who in their right mind sees an unstoppable juggernaut of still-growing meat coming toward them and decides it would be better to just hang out and wait around?"

"A realist, Zed." Taylor shook her head hotly, deciding that she was done with this line of questioning even if he was just playacting. It rang too close to the Bard's still-present distrust of her true loyalties.

The answer seemed to astound Zed, and he puffed himself up with a deep inhalation, launching into a barrage of straw man arguments and shouted insults, culminating in, "-last of all, you're a Mage! You read random words, wiggle your fingers, and create blasts of fire or crazy lightning! What part of that sounds like someone who could possibly be grounded in reality?"

"Enough!" Sir had herded them to the edge of the portal back to their base world, and he had amplified the outburst with his hands cupped around his mouth. "I have no idea how the four of you have managed to live in the same area for the last several years without killing each other! Frankly, if we had left you alone, the kingdom would likely have fewer issues in the future! *Abyss*, get it together. The rest of us have been fighting a war while you four have been relaxing in the trees, swinging in hammocks, and sipping drinks out of coconuts!"

Zed blinked twice, then pointed at Sir, his eyes hungry. "You found my hammock? Tell me you're at least bringing it along."

"You… you actually…?" The Ascender shook off the effect that Zed's interjection had on him, working to control his breathing. "Step through the portal, step to the side, and wait for the rest of us."

One by one, The Four left Andre's grove, emerging into a small room created within the hollow of a tree's roots. Sir followed them through, turning back to inspect the open portal with great interest. "It seems to be stable… interesting."

Luke reached over and gently punched the shimmering rift, completely destabilizing it and causing the Scar to collapse. Sir's eyes widened in horrified shock, and he opened his mouth to shout at Luke, only for the enormous, looming Barbarian to meet his gaze and cut him off. "Wouldn't want anyone getting *ideas* about going after the fruit of Andre's hard work, now would we?"

"I… of course not. I suppose." Sir swallowed, trying to wet his suddenly-dry throat. "That would be the height of impropriety. Naturally, our responsibility is returning to our mission and getting you home as quickly as we can."

Over the next several hours, all of the search parties were informed of the fact that The Four had been captured, were contained, and were on their way back to the Capital. Each of The Four complied as reluctantly as possible, but the only observable effect was that their attitudes weren't the best as they traveled quickly and efficiently through the flourishing terrain.

Even so, there were points of great interest to occupy each of them. Taylor was especially interested in observing the subtle ways in which Andre interacted with the land as they journeyed. His face shifted to clear delight as they approached the edge of the Scarrocco Nature Preserve, and he sank into a light bout of meditation to test how well his work had integrated with the earth.

Great joy warmed Taylor's soul when a bright smile lit up the Druid's face, and the Mage could only be glad that there was a silver lining in this situation. Nothing Sir could say or order, due to his discomfort, could preclude the Druid from performing his duties. Specifically, the fact that Andre suddenly started to bleed, then created an enormous magical circle overhead that did... seemingly nothing. Taylor quietly savored the view as blood rushed from Sir's face, leaving him pale and shaking, every time the Druid activated his circle magic.

It was clear to everyone involved that any individual of this small party could deal immense damage to everyone around them, if they either somehow managed to break their bonds, a careless order was given, or their captors failed to take proper precautions. As a result, their escort to the Capital was a tense, muted affair filled with flinching and sleepless nights for their captors.

Taylor shook her head at their apprehension, attempting to reconcile the fact that these people weren't meant to be jailers, and that the four of them were not meant to be prisoners. This was supposedly an honor guard that was returning them to be rewarded after a pseudo-exile. It was meant to be a great honor... at least if Sir's claims were to be believed.

It had been at least four years since she had last visited the borders of the revived desert personally, having relied on Zed's clones to bring pertinent information. Even with the updates he had relayed, it was still a shock to witness how the population in the area had exploded. Hamlets had sprung into existence by the dozen, filled with well-maintained homes and cheerful, nourished citizens, where before there was only starvation and despair.

"All of this exists thanks to Andre." Her reflection was muttered, but everyone could easily hear her thanks to their superhuman Characteristics.

The Druid in question flushed almost as vivid a red as his hair, shaking his head in protest. "I could not have done it without all of you. The creatures that were hoarding the resources we needed, everything each of you invested, the protection and security that you provided were instrumental in giving me the freedom to complete my grand working."

"I don't know if you've heard, Archdruid," Sir respectfully joined the conversation, his eyes only for the spindly redhead, "but they aren't calling you Andre the Archdruid anymore; the entire kingdom has taken to referring to you as Andre, the Terraformer."

"Better than your other most recent nickname, if you know what I mean." Zed nudged Andre in the side with his elbow. "'The Druid of Flesh and Bone' certainly stuck in the mind, but not in such a nice, pleasant manner."

Taylor winced as Andre's eyes darted over to her. She was glad that he had finally earned a moniker he could be proud of, one that celebrated his successes and true contribution to the world. The fact that he had previously been referred to by such a horrific name was nearly entirely her fault: he had only gone through with the experimentation on other humans due to her pushing, prodding, and pleading. It had seemed like the right thing to do at the time, but now that her mind was her own—as it should have always been—she recognized the horrors that she had inflicted upon him. It was no wonder he had turned into an insomniac.

When he slept, his nightmares caused the forest to scream with him.

She inhaled shakily, hoping that they would be able to move past this hurdle in their strange relationship. Over the last several years, Taylor had worked diligently to better herself, slowly regain her friends' trust, and prove that she would be willing to do anything for them. The fact that she was bound to the world by the Earthen Node had allowed her to rapidly repair the foundation of her relationship with the Druid. With Luke, she was uncertain, thanks to his apparent apathy, but Zed wasn't as easily won over.

As they trekked through the countryside, word of their travels moved even faster than they did. Citizens of the Hollow

Kingdom came out in droves to cheer for them, throwing flowers and other such niceties. Andre reacted jubilantly to the offerings, converting the airborne flowers and petals to spring up into fully formed plants which continued growing on their own, creating a vibrant trail of beautiful plant life along nearly the entire path they trod. The lively vegetation only added to the air of celebration that their arrival created, and nearly everyone seemed caught up in it.

Taylor's attention shifted questioningly to Luke as he stared at the people around them with confusion in his eyes. "What's the matter?"

"I don't know how else to say this." Luke spoke in a hushed tone, unwilling to ruin the mood. "But everyone in that crowd is becoming more real. Every. Single. Person."

Time slowed to a crawl as Taylor tried to privately determine what such a change could implicate, but eventually the questions overflowed and began pouring from her mouth. "They are becoming more... real, you say? Do you think they were caught up in the surge of overabundant mana in the Nature Preserve when it reconnected? This close to the border where it's connected, that would make sense. Does that mean... every single person was able to endure a Mana Baptism and survive?"

Luke nodded slowly; his brows furrowed. "That's exactly what I think happened."

"Then that means..." Taylor started breathing heavily, trying not to hyperventilate as she scanned the thousands upon thousands of people who had shown up for the festivities. "Everyone here, from the youngest child to the oldest adult, is eventually going to test positive as an Ascender?"

"That would be my guess," Luke affirmed her assumption grimly. "Sometime in the next couple of years, the kingdom is going to have the largest Ascender corps in its entire history. As Andre's got me saying... *whoops*."

CHAPTER ELEVEN

Taylor admired the city walls that loomed in the distance in spite of herself. Even from leagues away, her eyes noticed the improvements, upgrades, enchantments, and sheer wealth that had been poured into enhancing them to a degree the kingdom had never been able to achieve before. Part of her was pleased that the nobility had been using the materials they retrieved for defense—ensuring the safety of their population—but a larger part of her winced internally, forcing her not to make eye contact with her friends.

If she would have told the other three that they were entitled to the spoils of their combat, the four of them would have been wealthy beyond the kingdom's entire treasury. Instead, she had allowed them to operate under the mistaken belief that they were required to turn over the vast majority of it. Each of them had benefited from the small remaining portion immensely, gaining Noble titles, lands, and businesses. Luke, more than the others, had made surprisingly sound investments, using his wealth to outright purchase *banks* instead of other, smaller businesses.

Zed interrupted her reverie by drawing a deep, noisy inhalation through his nose and letting it out with a *smack* of his lips. "Ahh, the city. Home to thousands of people that have never heard my voice, the largest population center in the entire kingdom. I can practically *taste* the Potentia."

"I have been ordered to escort you directly to the Grand Hall of the palace, with no stops or diversions," Sir stated carefully, intentionally not making eye contact with the Bard, who deflated heavily. "All I could say, perhaps in passing, is that there isn't anything stopping you from speaking to the people that we pass on the way?"

The Bard was abruptly reinvigorated, and Taylor shook her head in amusement at how easy it was for people around the young man to influence his thought processes. It highlighted the difference between the two of them, especially the fact that he had *not* spent decades in seclusion on another world while learning to harness his powers.

His Masteries were almost exclusively increased by speaking with people on their base world, resulting in a real-world decades-long venture to level up or increase those Masteries. For Ascenders who were able to step into another world, their bodies didn't age even a day until they returned to the lower-energy communal plane of existence. Even then, returning to their bonded higher world would rapidly rejuvenate them to their peak physical age.

The fact of the matter was, no Bard had ever successfully reached the level cap and been able to Ascend. All of them had died, one way or another. It was common knowledge, and a topic that the group intentionally didn't discuss. Zed was able to travel into other worlds without bursting into flames, which gave Taylor hope that he could find a way to Ascend before he was too old to enjoy the greatest benefits.

Her hopeful thoughts were dashed as she remembered that Zed would never be allowed to Ascend. It was just far too dangerous. If the legends were true-

"It's *The Four*!" someone screamed practically in her face, causing Taylor to flinch and curse at herself for getting lost in thought while surrounded by strangers. "Look, it's the *Terraformer!* He's real!"

All too soon, they passed through the city gates, nearly deafened by the resulting cheers and excitement of the common folk. The wealthier citizens observed them from elevated positions, radiating contentment and happiness as they nodded politely or even waved at the filthy Ascenders that had finally returned. Something that Sir had mentioned in passing had stuck in Taylor's mind, and she realized at that moment what it was.

The fact that they were not allowed to stop, rest, or recover from their return journey was a petty plan intended to humiliate them in front of the peerage. They would arrive in front of the stuffiest-of-stuffy nobility, creating sharp contrast with their Ascender bodies filthy and reeking of sweat and grime from not only the road, but also their unwilling capture in the forest.

"Not if I have anything to say about it." She expanded her powers, lightly brushing against her friends and actively casting Cleanse, as well as Purify. In the blink of an eye, their clothes were as clean as the day they had been purchased, their skin was clear and unblemished, and the stink and grime of the road had vanished. Each of the others were also likely more comfortable, although she had no way to prove that other than a slight relaxing of their faces.

No one said a word, but she didn't need them to do so. She understood that they, as a unit, didn't need to verbally acknowledge that the people around them were doing their jobs well. That was the *expectation*, and it actually made her feel more like part of the group that they no longer felt the need to comment positively on every minuscule thing that she did on their behalf. One in particular took the soothing sensation and used it to his advantage: the Bard swung into his element like a salmon breaching the surface of a river and smoothly splashing back in.

"Good people! Hear me, hear me! My name is Zed, and I have been cataloging the great deeds of... *The Four!*" Throughout the remainder of the forced parade to the castle proper, Zed narrated their quest at the top of his lungs, proclaiming their adventures from start to finish. Everything from their initial defeat of the Chimera in the mountain pass, to the reclamation and restoration of the desert.

Taylor could not help but slightly sourly note how expertly he brushed past any detail that made their group look bad, painting everything that they had done in the best possible light. She was forced to appreciate how effective his propaganda was, but it was propaganda nonetheless. The Mage wanted the population to know how much they had *struggled*. Instead, the Bard was glamorizing a snapshot of their greatest victories while shuffling the hardships that had allowed them to achieve those goals under the rug. "They are going to want what we have, to earn the renown that we have earned, but they don't realize the cost. Do they truly want what I have? Would they suffer as I have suffered to get it?"

"Taylor…" Andre placed a warm hand on her shoulder and gently squeezed. "There is no need to be so down about it. Most of these people are already where they are going to stay for their entire lives; don't begrudge them the dream of more. That is all Zed is trying to do: give them some hope, which may someday come back to benefit us in some way. Perhaps it will even be spread among our enemies and demoralize them before we need to face them in combat. Who knows what harvest this crop he is planting will bring in the future."

"You don't plant date trees and plan to eat dates," Luke agreed in his own monotone way.

Taylor caught the delight that sprang up in Andre's eyes at Luke's plant-inspired reference. The redhead leaned closer to the Murderhobo with a bright smile, affably bumping him with an elbow. "I knew that you listened when I talked! That's right; unless someone is an Ascender, they typically will not live to see dates! Sorry, Taylor; date trees take about ninety years to produce fruit-"

"Ah, yeah, Andre. I listen to you, too." She tried not to be affronted by his dismissal, but over the last half decade of this world's time, the little group had shared the experiences and knowledge that they had accumulated during their individual time and trials. Taylor had heard the Druid's reference to date trees at least a dozen times. She rolled her eyes and smirked at her friend. "Maybe *you* should go date a tree."

Then she remembered that Andre had successfully created a human-tree hybrid, and that sort of insult wouldn't work anymore. "Abyssal Dryads. Ruining all my good comebacks."

"Don't worry, Taylor." Zed paused his grandstanding to commiserate with her. "We're in polite society again. You can learn some new material."

Their honor guard advanced slightly ahead of them, clearing the path. With the general populace out of the way, they were at the gates of the castle proper in no time, then ushered into the throne room without hesitation. Taylor was proud of how tall her companions stood. Their posture was strong, their expressions fearless. Her eyes swept over the crowd, finding both familiar and unfamiliar faces among them, stopping in consternation as her eyes came to the throne itself. To her great shock, King Alexander was *not* the monarch occupying the dais.

Instead, the smirking visage of Prince Vir greeted them, and the dour expression on Archmage Don's face lent credence to the fact that he was not there by accident.

A nervous hush fell over the hall, and Taylor instinctively turned to clap a hand over Luke's mouth just as he opened it. He caught her palm before it could get near his face, of course, but it still generated the intended effect. The Mage gave him a final glare in warning and stepped forward, the only one amongst them that had all of the training and knowledge necessary to navigate the political turbulence that the peerage would generate in the stream of politics. "It is with great pleasure that we, the Ascender bounty hunting team known as The Four, greet King Vir of the Hollow Kingdom."

She swept into a formal curtsy, while most of her team also attempted their own versions of a courtly bow. Zed did it perfectly, his overly dramatic gesture drawing plenty of attention his way. It helped to cover for Andre's fumbling half-bow but didn't do a thing to hide the fact that Luke didn't move; instead he was staring at the new King with eyes that looked as if they didn't have eyelids.

Taylor hoped that he hadn't forgotten how to blink. Again.

They held their position until courtly manners dictated that the King should have permitted them to regain their standard postures. Controlling her face to mask her irritation, Taylor gave up being polite and straightened, fully aware that she was technically in breach of protocol. Still, her own political power was not insignificant, nor was Andre's. There was also a good argument to be made that Luke's sheer financial holdings granted him a certain level of protection and clemency; Zed alone had nothing of the sort. He seemed to realize this and maintained his position until the king finally spoke.

"Took you long enough," Vir sneered as he spoke directly to Sir. "I'm cutting your reward by twenty percent for requisitioning more people and using a longer time than was allotted."

"As my king desires," Sir replied without a single hint of animosity in his voice. Yet, Taylor could read his physicality like a book, and the man had become incredibly tense at the unexpected penalty.

"I'm *unhappy* that rogue Ascenders have been living within my borders, causing issues for me over the last several years." Vir droned nonchalantly, as though he didn't particularly care about the situation at hand. The fact that his hands were clenched so tightly on his lap that his fingernails were drawing blood gave away the true depth of his fury at Taylor's team. "Your latest *escapades* have created a continent-wide incident, and a full-fledged invasion is now imminent."

The nobility in the room gasped. Hints of this exact news had been circulating in the rumor mill for the last several weeks, but hearing it from the lips of the king himself gave it a weight greater than any whispers in a dark room ever could. Vir continued after a long pause to compose himself. "If you had been reading your Tome of Transposition, following the *orders* that had been sent to you, this outcome might have been avoided. For months, my people have been seeking you out, sending along decrees, orders, pleas… for you *not* to reconnect the desert with the rest of the kingdom."

Out of the corner of her eye, Taylor watched Andre flinch back, his puzzled expression shifting into hardened resolve. Once again, she was glad that she had 'accidentally' allowed the book to be destroyed. All it had taken was a tiny hint that the book was the true reason that Luke had been forced away from his own world more frequently than he'd wanted, then stepping away to inspect the impressive yet simple growth of the new trees in the area. When she had returned, all that remained of the book was a pile of pulp roughly the same shape as the book had once been, with all of the enchantments destroyed by direct application of percussive maintenance.

"Now the Dynasty of Dogs is sniffing around our territory, attempting to determine what caused a wave of mana to spread out to our borders and rebound back inward." The king took a long, steadying breath and painted a wolfish smile on his face. "If we are going to survive over the next few years, to reap whatever few benefits your actions have provided us, we are going to have to survive the consequences that they caused. My father is the one who ordered you to resolve all of these issues, and I will, of course, honor the *spirit* of the quest that he had put in place."

All Taylor heard was that the king had no intention of honoring the completion of their quest with a reward, but was instead attempting to twist it into something it was never meant to be. If it had not been for the goodwill they had created among the population, their reputation among other Ascenders, and the sheer wealth they had generated for the nobility, the King clearly would have been demanding their heads on a platter. Instead, he was forced to give in to the pressure of the peerage and 'reward' them for their services so far. Taylor had a sneaking suspicion that their next assignment wouldn't be a *pleasant* one.

"Before we proceed any further," King Vir looked directly at Andre, "I have received a report in advance of your return. I'm told that you possess multiple artifacts of immense power that could be used for the benefit of the kingdom. By my authority, for the good of the people, I *order* you to hand them over."

CHAPTER TWELVE

"Your majesty, with all due respect," Andre began speaking slowly and carefully with a clenched jaw, unsure of how he should be handling this topic. "As I understand, it is my right to-"

"I'm going to stop you right there, Archdruid," Vir firmly stated, holding up one of his hands and motioning to someone else in the room. "The law has *changed*. We are at war, and the limp-wristed grip my father had on the population died with him. You *will* hand over those artifacts."

The Sigil on Andre's forehead shone brightly, but the Druid set his jaw firmly and crossed his arms. "*I refuse.*"

Against their expectations, the retort put a smirk on the king's face. "I expected that you would act childishly, and therefore, I have already sent for an enchanter to *repair* the Sigils upon your foreheads. These updates include the changes to our law and society that you *will* be following."

Luke stepped forward, and Taylor cursed softly under her breath. She'd expected their situation would devolve, but she had not expected it to be moving at this sort of breakneck speed. Her mind whirled in agitation as she attempted to put together a satisfactory legal argument against the King's claims, but she continuously drew a blank.

Frankly, the King could do whatever he wanted to do if he was willing to step on the necks of the people beneath him. The situation that had originally created the Scarrocco Desert in the first place was repeating itself directly in front of her, and it bothered her immensely.

"It seems history repeats itself. I sure hope you're ready to have every person in this room lose their life today." Luke hefted Cookie up onto one shoulder, his armor flaring to life under the point where the weapon rested to prevent damage being dealt by the sheer weight. "If you bring an enchanter within *ten feet* of me, trying to stick me with a bunch of rules that I didn't agree to, I'm gonna start swinging. This close to the royal armory? I'm pretty sure I can bring the whole castle down around our ears."

"Your threats are meaningless." King Vir's eyes flicked to the side, where Archmage Don waited, just to verify that the threats actually *were* meaningless. The elderly wizard gave a slight nod, and Vir's confidence was restored. A corpulent man draped in brightly enchanted robes glided into the room, his expression haughty and smug.

Luke made a sudden jerking motion at him, and the man tried to leap backwards in fear, tripping on his flowing robes and falling to the ground.

"That's ten feet. Great. You wanna fart around? Let's find out." Luke slapped his other hand onto Cookie's handle, sweeping her up above his head and dropping the weapon at full speed directly toward the ground. A barrier sprang into existence with a lazy wave of Master Don's hand, only for the Archmage to hiss in pain as it shattered after a bare moment, only reducing the momentum of the weapon by a little over ninety percent.

Stone and tile shrapnel went flying in every direction, injuring several onlookers and causing the crowd to immediately descend into a mass panic. Several people screamed, dozens shouted, and more than one troop of knights and

Ascenders tried to swarm into the room against the tide to protect the king.

"*Shockwave-*" Ignoring it all, Luke swung his weapon upward one more time, bringing it down... pausing halfway as a new voice cut through the hubbub.

"Luke!"

For a moment, the Murderhobo held his position, debating between continuing his attack and turning toward the source of the cry. His curiosity flared, and his eyes snapped over to spot his sister framed by the doorway, a tiara glittering on her elaborate hairdo and a perfectly fitted gown accentuating her figure. "Cindy. You got older."

"That will happen when you vanish for five years," His younger sister griped, slowly picking her way through the mess of the room toward her older brother. "We've been looking for you for years. You just... vanished. *Again.*"

"Got exiled. Can't really blame me for that." Luke slowly allowed his weapon to slide to the ground, though he remained poised for a quick strike as soon as the situation showed even a hint of beginning to devolve once more. "Why are you here? If you weren't here, I could kill all of these people. Now I have a conundrum."

"I would really rather you *didn't* kill all of these people, especially... my husband-to-be." Cindy half-turned, gracefully drifting her right hand upward as she gestured at the King.

"Ugh. Really? *Him?*" Luke spat to the side; the spittle lost among the debris that he had generated. "He seems like someone who's gonna be deposed in a few years. I'd rather you didn't get caught up in that."

"He speaks words of *treason!*" a nearby nobleman barked, wiping dust off his face with a pale orange lace handkerchief.

Luke held one finger to his sister to indicate that he would like a private moment. Turning, he walked over and gently slapped the nobleman across the face. The strike sent the blowhard tumbling across the room to impact the wall and slide down, completely unconscious. "Oh good, I outranked him."

"Smart thinking!" Zed interjected, tapping at his own forehead. "Otherwise, you would be burning from the inside out until you got a Royal Pardon. He insulted your honor, allowing you to instantly retaliate to defend your good name!"

"You think I have a good name? Thanks. I think most people like it. I'm generally called 'Luke'." The Murderhobo turned back to his sister, leaving Zed shaking his head in amusement. "Why are you marrying him? You had a good life."

"A good life is only the start. Imagine what I can do for our people as the Queen!" Cindy spoke quietly but with great passion. Composing herself and regaining her natural poise, she turned and dropped into a deep curtsy before the throne. "Your majesty, please pardon the manners of my brother and his traveling companions. Clearly, they have been lost in the wilderness long enough that it has addled their sense of propriety. Perhaps you would be so gracious as to allow them a night of respite so that they can collect themselves and ponder your wisdom-filled words?"

King Vir was shaking his head, clearly caught between fury, annoyance, and great mirth. "The Abyssal *Murderhobo* is your brother. Why did I fail to remember that? After all-"

Zed coughed quietly, studying the ceiling with great interest.

"-I've met your father and have seen his noble title. Who else among my Ascenders could my information network not manage to track down over these years? Yes... I suppose a small adjustment to our plans is necessary, at this point. But before we allow these... guests... to go to their cells—that is, guest suites —allow me to inform them of what awaits them over the next few days and subsequent years."

The brash young king pointed rudely at Andre. "Druid, none of this will be a surprise to you, but your task will be to travel the kingdom, preparing our land to repel the invaders. When that task is complete, you'll be reporting to the command of the Eastern front to assist in border security. Taylor, Archmage Don has specifically requested you return for retraining. He will be directly overseeing your progress for the next few years in preparation for his Ascension and your promotion. I look forward to working with you."

Regaining some of his smug composure as his proclamation left Taylor wide-eyed and trembling, his eyes flipped over to Zed dismissively. "I suppose I could use a court jester to amuse myself and my new bride. As for you... you absolute *wall* of a man, who else could I trust more than my bride's brother to be her personal guard? As soon as I have received the artifacts that Andre *will* be handing over, you'll be assigned as Cindy's personal guard on a permanent basis."

"You... *want* me here. In the city. With all these fragile people crawling around everywhere." Luke paused for a moment. "Wait. How will I be gaining Potentia?"

"Just as every other Royal Guard does," Vir drawled, wafting an idle hand. "You will be given a weekly allotment."

"Pass. That junk is for people who can't *get* their own."

"I refuse your refusal." Luke's obvious disquiet brought a full smile back to the king's face, and he straightened imperiously. "Now go, get a good night's rest, and prepare yourselves. Tomorrow, you'll subject yourselves willingly to the new laws of the kingdom, or be executed as traitors to the crown. The choice is yours, and I hope you choose... the correct choice."

His eyes had flicked to his eventual bride just before he finished his statement, and it was clear that he had amended his words mid-sentence. The Four were shuffled out of the room, and Taylor let out a long groan.

"The only possible way that could have gone worse is if you actually had managed to bring the castle down on top of us, Luke," she grumped at him, though the situation wasn't his fault; he was a victim of circumstance as well as the rest of them. Luke kept silent, a not uncommon occurrence, but something was clearly bothering him, more than the surface of the situation would suggest. He opened his mouth twice, closing it without saying anything. Taylor decided to press the issue, because if it was important enough that he felt he should say something, most likely he was correct. "Luke? What's going on?"

"Yeah, I think I might have accidentally made my sister into the queen."

Taylor squinted curiously at him, trying to suss out his meaning. "Luke, you don't have that kind of power. Your rank is nowhere near that high, and you obviously didn't purchase this arranged marriage. How could you possibly have made your sister the queen? Only the king has the capability to make that decision."

"Yeah. About that... before we went to the desert, I gave Cindy a necklace I had been working on for about twenty years."

"In Murder World?" Taylor prodded, receiving a nod to confirm that she had guessed correctly.

"To finish it off, I put a Skill Pearl as the pendant. You remember that?" Taylor returned the nod gently, understanding beginning to glimmer. "That was a pretty powerful one. If I had absorbed it myself, I likely would have gotten a Tier-six Skill out of it. With her wearing it, I think she has become nearly irre-sistible to anyone in a position of power."

All Taylor could do was gape at her companion in absolute shock, her mind blank and unable to process the information. Historically, their kings had always kept anti-illusion enchant-ments on their person, as well as powerful protections against anything that could affect their minds or entice them into doing anything they didn't want to do. Yet... those were only effective against structured magic. In other words, only something that was created with the specific intent to impact another person's minds would be rendered ineffective.

A natural treasure, like the Skill Pearl Luke had described, could very well be directly affecting the mind of the most powerful political figure in their kingdom. If the king found out about it...

Not only would the Pearl be confiscated, but Cindy would be at risk of being slaughtered for treason.

CHAPTER THIRTEEN

- LUKE -

The Murderhobo was escorted to his room, and as promised, it was a well-appointed, luxurious suite. The Royal Guardsman who had escorted him drew a line with his finger at the threshold of the room, "By the King's orders, you're under house arrest. Under *no circumstances* are you to step outside of your room."

Luke merely stood where he was, staring at the Guardsman with dead, hollow eyes widened as far as he could open them. He had found the expression to be unnerving to people who weren't confident in their own capabilities, and this Ascender was no outlier. Only letting the awkwardness stretch for a single nervous swallow, the man turned and hurried away without looking back. Luke remained where he was, not bothering to stroll about the apartment, let alone sample the food on the counter that was almost assuredly poisoned-

His head jerked to the side to stare at the bowl of fresh fruits on the counter. As soon as he considered that perhaps it *was* poisoned, he hurried over and scarfed down as much of it as possible. There was a chance, however minor, that he would be able to find a poison strong enough to increase the rank of his Skill 'You Need To Stop'. The instances were few and far between when Andre would help him out by putting together a concoction of various deadly plants, as the Druid had no particular interest in pursuing noxious lines of cross-pollination and plant breeding.

In other words, his friend had been a dead end for boosting his Skill. Unfortunately, it appeared that this fruit was also useless to him. "Not even a lightly caustic acid? *Tsk*. Fine, whatever, but why else would they put this in here?"

He focused on that problem for a few hours, but the answer was not forthcoming. A light knocking stirred him from his puzzled reverie, and he blinked owlishly in the room that seemed to have suddenly gone from full natural light to nearly dark. He stomped over, pulling open the door gently—for him.

On the other side waited his sister, standing just a few feet away, just far enough that he would need to step out of the room if he wanted to grab her, flanked by a duo of guards. He wondered, distractedly, if that was an intentional choice, if she didn't trust him as much as she had seemed to in the throne room. That made him wonder in turn what lies were being fed into her ears now that the king knew who he was in relation to her.

"Hello, Luke." Her voice was less timid, seemingly filled with steel as she spoke to him. "It's been extremely interesting to hear of all of the issues you have created, the laws that you have broken, and the people you have hurt. I only came here to let you know that I will be requesting that Vir does *not* assign you as my guard., You can go be a feral animal somewhere else, and I… and I can try to keep the image I had of you in my mind. Not… not what you have become."

She turned away, heaving a few deep breaths that sounded suspiciously like stifled sobs. Luke didn't stop her. He most certainly didn't have the Charisma to convince her away from her selected path, and it was clear that she had already chosen her side. She turned back after collecting herself, meeting his eyes in grim challenge. "If Andre will not hand over his artifacts willingly, they are going to use you to go in and take them. I want you to comply without fighting them on this issue. There are so many incentives lined up if you'll do it willingly, and so many punishments for refusing. If you're not... even if you're not who I had hoped you would be, you at least deserve to live a good life."

Luke nodded at her, eyeing the pendant that she still wore on the necklace he had given her. He wanted to ask if she knew that it was changing her fate, but being so blatant about it, in such a public area, would almost assuredly guarantee her death. He would have to wait and hope that another opportunity presented itself. He reached for the door handle, starting to close the barrier between them once again.

Only to stop himself as the partially closed door blocked a splash of blood from spraying across his body. Behind his sister, a strange man had suddenly appeared. To Luke's senses, this man was one of the most *real* people he had ever run into, second only to his own small party. The blood had come from the guards, both of whom had died in a single *chomp* from the strange beasts that were clearly under the control of this hound-masked figure.

A hand closed over Cindy's mouth just before she could scream, and another swiftly wrapped around her waist. Luke lurched forward, only for his Sigil to burn with an intensity only matched by lightning. The searing heat brought him to the ground and forced his muscles to relax. He roared in impotent fury as the invader chuckled lightly. The unfamiliar voice was distorted by the mask, but the words themselves were still clear. "How sad. I don't even keep my most poorly trained pups on such a tight leash. Ta-*ta!*"

With that simple declaration, the man swept Cindy around and hopped onto the larger of the two dogs. The hulking canine raced down the corridor, smashing through a window at the end of the hall and vanishing below Luke's line of sight.

The Murderhobo managed to regain his footing and shouted for the guards, for anyone. Over and over, he threw himself against the magical impediment, failing to overcome the Sigil time and time again.

Apparently, the Murderhobo raging against his capture was an expected outcome, and no one bothered to inspect the situation, no matter how much noise he made. Not until the following morning, nearly seven *hours* after his sister had been taken. By then, he knew she could be hundreds of miles and literal worlds away. Even so, he fought against his restrictions the entire time.

Finally, someone came into range, but not due to his ranting and raving. A guard ran into the hallway, ordered him to *be quiet*, and asked him if he had seen the queen-to-be. If Luke could have gotten his hands on the other man, the Berserker would have crushed his head between them. "Yes, I know where she *was*! Why do you think I have been shouting 'the Dynasty of Dogs took my sister'? To give you a sleepless night?"

"That seems implausible," the guard sneered with a half-smile as he rolled his eyes. "You are under my care. I order you to tell me the truth. Where is Her Royal Highness?"

"Cindy, my sister, who is supposed to marry that fool of a King, was captured last night by an invader. Have you not noticed those two headless bodies that are literally *right there*?"

That was enough to elicit a reaction, and upon seeing the corpses, the guard's eyes went wide. He pulled a whistle from his pocket and blew into it, sending out a pulse of magic instead of a high-pitched sound. Within minutes, the hallway was crawling with guardsmen, and Luke's statement was taken over and over as they tried to figure out what kind of mess they were in. Finally, one of the guards, specifically the man that had escorted Luke to his room the night before, made the mistake of stepping too close and shouting at Luke, "Why didn't you do anything to stop the Queen from being taken captive?"

The Murderhobo reacted with a lightning-fast backhand that sent half a dozen teeth shooting out of the man's mouth as he flopped across the room to land on the floor. "Because some *nitwit* ordered me not to leave my room under *any circumstances!*"

His point thoroughly made; the guards ensured that they remained out of reach until the order finally came for him to be hauled before the king. Luke went willingly, finally having something to say and a cause that he was willing to fight for. To his minor surprise, when he arrived in the throne room, his friends were already waiting for him. Andre seemed concerned at Luke's seething rage, which was barely contained to bubbling under the surface. The Druid instinctively recognized that the slightest provocation could cause the battle-scarred Berserker to boil over and start indiscriminately attacking. "Something happened overnight, Luke. Do you have any idea what is going on?"

"An invader from the Dynasty of Dogs kidnapped my sister last night, right in front of me." Luke scowled darkly at the king, grinding his teeth as he snarled, "I was ordered by the guards not to do anything to help her."

"Your Majesty, pay no heed to his claims; we have already ascertained what the actual instructions were," a man that was clearly a Captain of the Royal Guard called out. "This... *Murderhobo*... was informed that he was under house arrest and given the exact same instructions that any other person in his situation would have been given."

"Captain." The king's fingers were tapping loudly against the arm of his throne. "Do you think I give one single speck of fecal matter what his instructions were? My queen is gone. Without her, I feel like my mind is going to *break*."

"That would probably be the addiction," Luke rumbled quietly to himself, realizing that the King actually did look like someone who was going through the first stage of withdrawals. On one hand, it was nice to know that he wasn't the only person that wanted Skill Pearls more than any other item in this world or any other. On the other hand, going through withdrawals tended to make people do erratic things, oftentimes even engaging in behaviors that were not beneficial to themselves.

He could use that.

"Murderhobo." The king's words snapped Luke out of his internal dialogue and brought his attention to the man himself. "You and your team are officially tasked with finding my queen and returning her to me unharmed."

Quest gained: My Queen is in Another Castle! The bride-to-be of King Vir of the Hollow Kingdom has been kidnapped by a neighboring super-power. Find her and return her to the king, ensuring that she is unharmed in the process.

"That sounds dangerous," Luke called out in an ice-cold tone. "There'd better be a hefty reward, a *guaranteed* reward, or I'm going to fight this quest every step of the way. I will make *sure* that it is far too late to bring her back to you."

The room became so quiet that Luke could hear the gossip taking place in the kitchen a floor away. The King clenched and unclenched his hands, looking for all the world like he was about to hop out of his throne and attack the Murderhobo himself. Finally, he regained some semblance of mental stability and leaned forward, his eyes locked with Luke's.

"I know what you want, you beast of a human," the king managed to grind out. "Using your own sister as a bargaining chip... *despicable*. You go out there, you do anything, *everything* you deem necessary to bring her back to me unharmed, and I swear I will allow you to return to your personal world once a *week*, if you so desire. I hereby swear an oath that if you return with my queen, I'll give you cushy positions and land... only calling upon you to protect us in times of trouble and danger. I swear it."

He paused, and his expression sank, shifting from agonized to murderous. "Also, if you *fail* this quest that I'm granting you, my people will hunt your little group of friends until every single one of you is removed from this world. This I swear, by my power as The King."

Quest updated!

Vir said a few things to the rest of his team, likely promising them equivalent unparalleled rewards. Luke didn't pay much attention. He was satisfied with what he had been offered. One hand stroked Cookie's length, and he nodded slowly. "Soon, Cookie. Soon we are going to figure out what is waiting for us in Zone fifty. I know you're just as excited as I am. What's that? You're *more* excited than me? Fun. It's nice to have goals."

CHAPTER FOURTEEN

The first stop for The Four was visiting the kingdom's Spymaster. Everyone had somewhat expected the Archmage to hold the position, so they were vaguely surprised to be met by Ma'am, the head maid of the castle. She was in a terrible mood, likely because she had been unable to detect the intruder who had taken the future queen, realize that she had been taken, or initiate any chain of events that could begin the process of bringing her mistress home.

"Hurry along!" Ma'am snapped at them, tapping her hand rapidly on her desk. "I don't have all day. I have my other standard duties to attend to as well. This... *situation*... has taken all of us by surprise. I don't *like* to be surprised."

"What *do* you like, sweet baby blue-eyed mistress?" Zed leaned forward inquisitively, batting his eyelashes at her. "Did you know I pegged you as the Spymaster the very first time I laid my eyes on you? This confirmation is... exquisite."

She didn't even deign to answer, instead tossing a report in front of them as well as a thick, sealed envelope. "This is all the information we have been able to collect, including the most likely culprit, the route they took to escape, and the worlds that they likely traveled through to rapidly exit the area."

Taylor picked up the paper, but Luke eyed it suspiciously. Documents were just one step away from being books, and *books* were completely unnatural. His stare roved to the unassuming caretaker of the castle as she continued her miniature rant. "As far as we know, there is only one agent of the Dynasty of Dogs that could pull off something like this. To us, he is known only by his code name, the 'Gytrash'. As to his capabilities, well… we have only documented a few. Most of the time, he is used as an assassin. Very rarely has anyone been able to identify him or survived his presence."

"The Black Dog?" Surprisingly, only Zed was aware of this strange figure. "You know, he is one of the best tavern tales in wet, stormy weather. People want to feel like being inside is a bigger benefit than it really is, and feeling the shakes when they are alone on the road definitely gives them a reason to stay by the fire, drinking spiced ale. He's real, huh?"

"Too much so," Ma'am agreed grimly, her eyes allowing a hint of acknowledgment toward the Bard. "It seems that the abilities are transferred to whoever can tame the dog, so killing the handler of the Gytrash doesn't guarantee he won't reappear again in the future. The only positive note is that it seems this dog is a solitary type and either so difficult to find or tame that there is usually only one bonded Ascender to worry about in a generation."

Following her verbal report, she tapped on the still-sealed manila envelope that lay untouched on the desk. "Everything we know about the social and political structure of the Dynasty of Dogs is in here. Hopefully, it will suffice as a briefing so you'll be able to move quickly, efficiently, and return triumphant. There's no reason to tell you, but it certainly doesn't hurt you to know: more people than *you* will be on the chopping block if your mission isn't a success."

Almost unconsciously, she gently rubbed her neck, and Luke could practically see the executioner's sword coming down, ever so slowly. With a polite nod, she straightened her shoulders and hurried out of the room, leaving The Four to their own devices. Zed inhaled deeply then heaved out a deep sigh of satisfaction. "I wasn't joking when I said I had guessed who she was. As soon as it was confirmed, I gained a *massive* influx of Potentia. My Mastery is starting to Tier up!"

Luke had already noticed, as the sparse mana in the area had been converging on the Bard. Upon observing how slowly the trickle of energy moved, the Murderhobo had to wonder if the actual process of 'Tiering up' was generally delayed for normal people and how long it would take before Zed's Mastery was unlocked for usage. Andre joined the Bard in his excitement, whooping in excitement and grabbing Zed to spin him around before letting him stand on his own again.

"Congratulations, my friend! Which ability? Do you have an idea of what it will turn into, or how long this process will take?" At the redhead's torrent of questions, Luke nearly allowed his lips to quirk upward a fraction of an inch. It was good that his friends were as inquisitive as he was and much more willing to be touchy-feely. It was nice to get the answers that he desired without having to resort to asking for them directly.

Zed paused for a moment, reading over his Cal Scan. "The Mastery I chose to devote Potentia to is 'Creu Hunan Newydd'. Why are you all looking at me like that? You've seen me use this all the time; it's my Mastery that allows me to create a clone of myself and send it out into the world."

"What language is that?" Taylor questioned with great interest. Luke recalled that she had a knack for languages, and words were *literally* power in her Ascendancy.

"As far as I know, it's Bardic." Zed tossed his head back and brushed his bangs away from his face. "I wouldn't *expect* you to understand. That's part of why I've never told you the actual names of my Masteries. Usually, I just let you know what they do."

"So you have no idea at all," Taylor guessed accurately

enough that the Bard stiffened and refused to meet her eyes. "That's fine. We need to get out of the city and finish this mission."

Strangely, Luke was the one to block their path. "I need better armor."

Andre pointed at the door. "No matter what we decide to do before leaving the city, let's get away from the castle and our babysitters before discussing it."

Everyone readily agreed, and they walked out through the front gates, taking their time to make sure no one was going to suddenly chase them down and start shouting orders again. The farther they walked from the castle, the calmer they all became. Luke didn't restrict himself as the others had. He knew *exactly* where he was going, and he was ready to snap some necks. His hurry was noted by his friends, with greater worry than he felt was warranted.

"Where are you going in such a rush?" Zed half-jogged next to the Murderhobo to keep pace with him. "Not to put any ideas in your head, but you're looking a little... extra-murdery today."

"I'm just going to talk with him." Luke's very calm, exceedingly reasonable statement didn't have the effect he had been expecting. Instead of his friends being on board with his plans, they started to question him. Things like 'who are you going to speak with' and 'what did they do to deserve death' were common amongst the menagerie of cross-examinations.

He didn't feel that their inane quizzing deserved a proper answer. They had heard his complaints about this precise situation for the last several years. It was not *his* fault that they didn't remember, and Luke didn't like to repeat himself. Besides, his destination was already in sight, and he closed faster and faster, until he was moving at a light jog. Plants began erupting spontaneously from the soil, the air grew thick with mana, and he clapped two hands over his ears to drown out the cloying, honeyed words that Zed was attempting to ply him with.

Luke didn't need to be stopped. He would ignore any Spells,

and there was no need for arguments against doing what had to be done.

The door of the armorsmith was heavily enchanted on top of being extremely durable, as was to be expected from a workshop of such quality. He knew that the owner routinely boasted that the door could stop the charge of a bull elephant, so he was not surprised that he was able to barrel directly through it, leaving the door intact but ripping it directly off the hinges. He stared down at the fallen door, which still had not a mark on it. "That would make a good shield, if I was some kind of weakling that needed a *shield*."

There was no clerk in the storefront, not another customer nor employee to be found. Instead, only one man occupied the space, and it appeared he had been expecting this visit. "Ah, Lord Murderhobo! I'm so glad you came personally to pick up your order. It has been waiting *ever* so patiently since its completion."

Luke's index finger, which was approximately the length and diameter of a garden trowel's handle, jabbed through the air to point accusingly at the armorsmith. "I paid for delivery, and you know it."

"I had plans to send your gear; of *course* I did!" the armorsmith defended himself, self-righteously placing his palms on his own chest. "But every time I started to put together a shipping order, Inquisitors would pop up at my door, demanding that I attach tracking enchantments, smuggle people in the box, or other such unsavory practices. I value the privacy, comfort, and safety of my customers above all else. Why else would I create these masterpieces of armor to their individual specifications?"

The Murderhobo's glare lessened slightly, and he allowed his hand to drop to his side. "You've got a good point. Perhaps I should pay a visit to the other vendors I had selected instead."

"Why don't we get your armor unpackaged and ready for your inspection?" the armorsmith offered with a soothing smile, unable to hide the sweat that was trickling from his temples. "I'm certain that it will meet your standards. I followed each of your requested specifications and made *hundreds* of iterations before I was satisfied that it would exceed your expectations. As per your instructions, the failed copies were sold off or melted down as needed, and those profits were returned to the project to generate a better-quality version."

"Enough sales pitch. All you're doing is making me think that you have some apprentice in the back room desperately trying to finish the piece while you keep me distracted." Luke's dull growl made the other man burst into laughter, slapping his knee. It slowly petered off into awkward silence when he realized the Murderhobo wasn't joking.

"I have the set right here." The man swallowed visibly as he lifted the top off of what could have easily been a coffin. "As you requested, it has all been made to link together perfectly, with as many useful embellishments as possible. Every tenth of an inch contains a fully embedded spike, each of which has been carefully decorated and enchanted by the finest jewelers and enchanters in the capital. As you might suspect, the fact that such a quantity of gold, silver, precious metals, and natural treasures is imbued into this gear has made it incredibly dense and heavy. I would even go so far as to say that it is utterly unusable, if it were not for the fact that I personally ensured that each piece is able to fully articulate."

Luke stared at the gear hungrily, then stepped forward and pressed one finger against a random spot. Immediately, his magical armor flared into view, preventing the spike from pushing into his flesh. The result made him nod in very slight appreciation. Unless the item had been able to deal some damage to him, even with that light touch, it wouldn't have activated his Source-cerer's Armory. "Good quality."

"Would you like to try it on?" the armorer asked with great interest. "I haven't been able to find anyone with the sheer strength necessary to give this beauty the tryout it deserves. I call this the 'Promiscuous Stud' set, since it is almost exactly the opposite of an 'Iron Maiden'."

Even though the armorer was busy laughing at his own joke,

Luke felt that his business with the man was done, and the conversation was over. Ultimately, he wouldn't be trying on this armor. At least, not in this form. He didn't trust that some form of failsafe hadn't been built into it, so he simply allowed his mana to pour out of himself and into the gear.

As the mana density infusing the metal reached a critical point, he was forced to whisper the name of the Skill to activate it, due to the lack of available free power in the environment. It was frustrating being unable to simply enact his will on the world with a thought, but each world seemed to have its own rules. Here, calling out the name of his Skill appeared to be necessary to make it function properly. To be fair, this particular Skill was Tier nine, level nine. The fact that he could use it so easily, so *quickly*, was a testament to his familiarity with it and its constant usage. "*Source-cerer's Armory.*"

The armorsmith shrieked in confusion and horror as the entirety of nearly half a decade's work vanished in an instant. The armor melted away, allowing the paper packaging to flutter out as various shavings of wood scattered across his floor. "That! I didn't do that! The armor was real, I swear it! Someone must have stolen it and replaced it with an illusion-"

"I'm satisfied with my purchase." Luke turned on his heel and walked away, leaving the flabbergasted smith to sputter indignantly and suffer a small existential crisis. The Murder-hobo wasn't worried about that. Instead, he was *far* more intrigued by reading over his new gear's combat utility.

Masterwork 'Promiscuous Stud' Set.

When wearing 1 part of the set: 4% of overall health is added as armor. You can stick to any surface without falling, so long as you're touching it with this armor.

When wearing 2 parts of the set: 6% of overall health is added as armor. Apply a bleed effect equal to 1/2 of damage dealt with any spikes on this armor per second. This effect lasts for three seconds. Stackable. All previous bonuses apply.

When wearing 4 parts of the set: 8% of overall health is added as armor. You are able to greenlight up to 10 people that can touch areas covered with this armor. Anyone who has been greenlit will not take damage from the spikes. You need to greenlight yourself in order to not take damage. All previous bonuses apply.

When wearing 6 parts of the set: 10% of overall health is added as armor. Any creature touching you with any part of their body will suffer 4-9 penetration damage per second, per foot of exposed body touching the armor. All melee attacks using no other weapons will deal an additional 20-31 penetration damage, and all punching damage gains 20% armor penetration. All previous bonuses apply.

+8% Physical damage (Penetration Damage). Hands treated as weapons when attacking.

Strength: Slashing/piercing attack reduction (70%).

Weakness: Blunt force, magical damage. (-22%)

By the time he had finished familiarizing himself with the associated features, he was bleeding from multiple points. "Greenlight myself. Remove the Soul Brand from the other gear, add it to this. That'll double my armor, and I think that means I can bust through Zone twenty now, as soon as I can get back in."

As soon the declaration left his lips, fresh holes ceased to open in his exposed flesh, and the existing ones slowly healed. He glanced down at his hand, which was dragging Cookie along and tearing up the road behind him. Magical sparks went flying as his armor tried and failed to penetrate her exterior. "Greenlight Cookie. Two slots already filled. I wonder if I can greenlight the road? Nah. Why else does the kingdom forcibly take taxes out of what I earn, if not to cover potholes?

His companions stared at him with stunned interest, blinking and seeming to come out of a trance as he waved at the road. "I'm ready. Let's go."

CHAPTER FIFTEEN

- TAYLOR -

The instant she finished reading through the packet of information, Taylor burned the entire thing to cinders. Then she made sure to stomp on the ashes, scattering them before dumping an entire bucket of water on top in order to ensure that there was no way to reconstitute the pages. If she allowed that information to get out to the general public, it was highly probable that the Mage would be charged with some sort of malfeasance. This wasn't information that had any other usage beyond war and sabotage.

Luckily for them, that was exactly what they were heading into. War, sabotage, assassinations, intrigue, and what amounted to counter-kidnapping. There was a bold smile blazing across her face as she looked into the distance, where she knew the Dynasty of Dogs lay. Finally, she was about to be back in *her* element. Andre was the most useful in the wilds, Zed the most useful among the common people, and Luke... well, Luke had his own special place in the world.

But Taylor had been raised to thrive on political machinations and intrigue. She was ready for this, and the documents had given her the first step back into that world. Before anything else, The Four needed to leave the walls of the capital city. Except for highly guarded waypoints, the surrounding terrain was heavily enchanted to disallow Ascenders from opening portals into the area. As they made their way into the countryside, Taylor and Zed started to deflate, even while Andre took a deep breath as he reconnected with the flora of the kingdom. "Who would have thought that trail of flowers would be so useful in keeping me connected to the Nature Preserve?"

"Ah… you?" Zed laughed lightly as he looked back at the city longingly.

Taylor watched Andre seemingly rejuvenate out of nowhere, a tiny bit envious over the fact that he received a constant stream of healing, mana, and Potentia… even if the daily percentage of that last benefit was so minimal that it was almost not worth mentioning. She made a small sound, gathering the attention of her three male companions immediately. "I am going to open a portal that will allow us to reach the edge of the kingdom within only a couple days of walking, instead of taking more than a week. Unless, Andre, you know a better position that we could move to through your world?"

"Sorry to say, I have not been able to explore my world all that much." He shrugged noncommittally, and no one pressed farther. They had all heard his stories of being hunted by the other Druids from this world, and no one was willing to ask him to risk himself or his achievements solely to save a few days of travel.

Without another word, Taylor stretched her left hand out, palm leading, right palm braced on her hip as she spread her fingers. Infusing her Grimoire—settled in the crook of her arm and braced on her right hip—with mana, she hissed out the necessary incantation, and a portal began to form almost instantly. This close to the city, with all of its passive enchantments sucking up all of the ambient mana, not to mention standing so close to Zed, who was absorbing anything that remained as his Mastery worked to Tier up, she had to push and *push* until the portal stabilized. The second it *snapped* into place, she dropped her hands to her knees, leaning over and panting slightly.

There was no need to rush, since a stable portal didn't close on its own. If it did, their world wouldn't be plagued by so many monster incursions and other interdimensional troubles. Still, it was a better idea to recover on the other side, where they would be able to travel at four times the speed of this world's timestream. As soon as they were safely in her world, Taylor was able to close the portal behind them with a lazy gesture, the increased potency of the mana allowing her to access her capabilities almost effortlessly in comparison.

She tilted her head curiously as she sensed a faint increase in the amount of energy that was converging on Zed. "Do you notice any difference in the speed that your Mastery is Tiering up?"

"Surprisingly, yes. I hadn't realized it would be impacted so much!" Zed cheerfully acknowledged. "Have there been studies done on this? Does anyone know the *actual* speed?"

"As far as I know, it's different for every type of power." Andre had even more knowledge on the overall system of Potentia than Taylor did, having spent nearly a decade solely doing research as part of his training. "I know that having more free mana, or access to mana, will increase the speed at which it is able to evolve. If you have too little, it will slow to nearly a crawl while being locked the entire time. Too much, conversely, the sheer drain on your surroundings can cause the energy to collapse inward with immense collapsing waves, potentially even shattering your skull as mana tries to squeeze its way into your Sigil and be purified."

"Is *that* why I keep getting beaten up by mana?" Luke muttered so softly that Taylor, even with her enhanced senses, could barely hear it. His complaint didn't surprise her; she knew that he had upgraded many of his Skills over the years, but she had never actually met anyone who had taken damage from the convergence of mana. She was familiar with the study Andre was quoting, and severe pain during Tiering up was more of a hypothesis or wistful hope than anything else.

Taking charge of the situation, as became necessary far more often than the current version of her was comfortable with, Taylor started walking eastward, hoping that her companions would follow without requiring any cajoling. To her great relief, they fell in line easily, and they comfortably kept pace with her brisk stride. Opening her Grimoire and bracing the spine on the front of her hip, angled just to the side so she could maintain a safe walking pace, she scanned the map she had created within its pages. "If we're able to continue on this route, we will reach the border by... tomorrow night? Subjective time, obviously."

"Is it just me, or are there more Grimoires in the area than usual?" Zed's voice wasn't exactly worried, but it was striking to Taylor how he could point out details that she, with her massively enhanced senses, didn't even consider. Turning her eyes skyward, she noticed that there were, in fact, increased flocks of books zooming into the area, settling in clusters on book racks and other terrain features. The farther they traveled, especially over the next few hours, the more books alighted nearby.

"How did I not notice that?" Doubting herself for a moment, Taylor decided to open up her Characteristic sheet and take a look at her status, primarily to ensure that she hadn't been cursed or had a Spell cast on her that was actively dulling her Characteristics.

Cal Scan
Level: 14
Current Etheric Xenograft Potentia: 2,183 / 98,700 to level 15!
Body: 12.4

- *Fitness: 13.5*

- *Resistance: 11.3*

Mind: 22.65

- *Talent: 19*
- *Capacity: 26.3*

Presence: 12.75

- *Willpower: 10.3*
- *Charisma: 15.2*

Senses: 44.3

- *Physical reaction: 45.3*
- *Mental energy: 43.3*

Maximum health: 163
Maximum mana: 486
mana regen: 6.3 per second.

Ability: Tier: Level

Fingers of Flame: 4: 5
Frozen Trident: 4: 7
Cleanse: 1: 1
Purify: 1: 1
Nullify: 4: 9
Fissure: 5: 8
Thunder Beast's Eye: 7: 9

As far as Taylor could tell, everything looked correct. Her time in the wilderness had increased her resistance quite a bit naturally, although the sheer enhancement of her Mana Channels had given her the largest natural boost to her Capacity she had ever seen. Beyond that, in the last five years, she had been able to increase by four entire levels, granting her twenty free points to place in her Characteristics, at a minimum of five points per selection. She had evenly split the windfall between her Mental Energy and Physical Reactions. There should never again be any obstacle capable of preventing her from learning the name of a Spell that she wanted to tame.

There was also no reason why she shouldn't be able to notice things before the *Bard* had. No debuffs were evident, no enchantments working against her. She hadn't eaten any rye bread and gone insane, as far as she could tell. Yet, she hadn't been the one to detect the incumbent threat. She frowned up at the perched books once more, trying to find the underlying reason they were following her party.

None of the books were directly flying at them, either to bump into them or harass them. Instead, as the restless tomes filed themselves neatly along the shelves, their pages were rustling ominously—as if they were gearing themselves up to attack but didn't want to be the first to make a move. She hadn't experienced problems with a Grimoire in quite a long time, and she strained to recall what had provoked a degree of agitation as serious as what she was seeing right now.

"They usually are quite pleasant. They act like birds, hunting for food and…" Taylor's eyes went wide for a moment as she slowly turned, only to wince in stunned comprehension at Zed. "Their food source is mana. Specifically, free mana that is leaving or *converging onto* a person. I think they're confused because you're ranking up a Bardic Spell, and they're trying to decide if they like the flavor or not."

"Mastery," Zed muttered, imitating his conversation with Andre only a few days prior. "You're saying that I smell like an exotic restaurant to them, and they're trying to decide if they want a taste?"

"Pretty much. You're not releasing or drawing pure mana, so to them, you might smell… *spicy*," she admitted with a small shrug. "So long as the fight doesn't draw the attention of any overly powerful Spells, I don't think we will have any serious issues. It's just going to be a matter of a constant flock of books swooping at you. Overall, it should be more annoying than anything else."

"Ugh. Books *again*." Luke was walking with his eyes closed so that he didn't need to see all of the implements of knowledge fluttering around them at high altitude. As an oversized Grimoire on black magic came too close, his fist lashed out even without Luke needing to see. A spiked gauntlet materialized around his knuckles and detonated the book on impact. It exploded into a book binding, a cloud of falling papers, a splash of ink, and a small stream of mana swirling into the air. Several of the pages were stuck to his spiky armor, and he shook his hand wildly. "Get it off, get it *off!*"

"Now you did it," Andre stated evenly as thousands of books left their perches and flew into the sky, circling around the group with the harsh sound of flapping paper drowning out any further conversation. "Here they come. Anyone want a few vines on their shoulders to slap them away?"

"I'll take five." Zed stepped closer to the Druid immediately, who set a small sachet full of dirt and seeds on the Bard's shoulder. The placement allowed him to grow his plants faster, and without risk of them burrowing into someone's body in search of nutrients.

Luke stopped flailing and breathed out his relief, holding up a hand that finally had nothing on it. "Don't worry about me. I figured it out."

Taylor pointedly ignored him and turned her face up at the sky, trying to determine the best course of action. If she started throwing around her most powerful Spells, she could probably drive off the books quickly, though it would highlight their exact location to anyone who cared to find them. As a library's worth of tomes suddenly dove at them, the choice was taken out of her hands.

The Murderhobo leapt up, meeting the front of the swarm with a massive coiled rope that had appeared out of nowhere. The end flicked out and impacted the lead book with a *whipcrack*, generating a shockwave so close to them that it would have made a regular human's ears bleed. As the Mage hunkered down behind a toppled shelf, she realized that the shockwave hadn't only come from the sound. He had activated a different one of his Skills, which had spread the damage dealt to the leading target among the other volumes hovering behind it.

Hundreds of books detonated into clouds of paper that ever so slowly drifted down toward them. Luke landed, looked up, pointed at the descending sheaves of paper, and let out a small, wordless scream of alarm.

Taylor could only shake her head, at what she knew wasn't antics, but his genuine reaction to the sight of paper falling down on him. "I swear, sometimes the *people* on this team…!"

"What's the matter, Tay?" Zed prodded as he walked past, four tentacle-like vines on his shoulders, and one on top of his head, reaching up into the sky and slapping away any fluttering books brave enough to come close. "Do you see something strange out there?"

"Just *everything*." Taylor closed her eyes and shook her head. "Everything in my life, Zed."

CHAPTER SIXTEEN

- LUKE -

At first, the Murderhobo was quite concerned that everything he killed would explode into more things that needed to be killed. Punch a book? Get a shower of paper. Punch a paper? Create smaller papers, only for the fragments to stick to his armor indefinitely unless he dismissed it for a bare instant. But slowly, somewhere around the two-hundredth piece of paper that exploded into confetti, he started to enjoy himself.

"Ha, *ha*! You were all right! Books *are* fun!"

It seemed he never would run out of things that were throwing themselves against his body. He wasn't gaining anything from it, either; no Potentia, no strength enhancements… they weren't even good practice, as they were such easy targets. "When was the last time I kicked back, relaxed, and killed something just for the *fun* of it?"

With these deep thoughts simmering at the forefront of his mind, Luke settled in and tried to enjoy himself, to really take in the moment, as his friends had been trying to get him to do over the course of the last five years. To be fair, for him, it was closer to only two and a half years, thanks to his ability to safely burn time in the Descender portal between delves into his own world.

Still, he knew how important it was to get out and experience new things. After all, with his newly integrated armor, he should be able to stand on the fringes of Zone twenty and utterly ignore all of the incoming needles while he worked to clear a path for himself.

Luke was looking forward to that.

Still, even though the books fluttering around them were an annoyance at worst, they also drastically reduced the group's visibility. Luke could tell that Taylor was about to lose her mind and start blasting, and he appreciated the fact that she liked to maintain situational awareness at all times.

As night came along, everyone agreed that there was no point in stopping for a rest. They had been able to sleep the night before, even if Luke hadn't, but he was used to going up to several weeks at a time without sleeping. No matter what anyone else said, it didn't really affect him. Worst-case scenario, he was very well-practiced at ignoring the hallucinations.

The other reason they didn't stop was that, any time they tried, the books swooping around were able to settle on Zed. If the other three hadn't helped him out the first two times that they had taken a break, he would have been crushed under the sheer weight of the tomes *thudding* against him.

Luke blinked in surprise and shook his head as a new sound reached his ears for the first time in the last few hours. Andre was explaining something that sounded like it could be important, and as he turned his head to pay better attention to the man, an oversized book slammed into his head, shredding itself on the spiky armor that appeared upon impact. For a moment, his vision was filled with a detonation of papers, but he took a deep breath and allowed the impairment to pass without punching out. Truly, his self-control had reached incredible heights.

"I've been thinking," Andre was informing Taylor, and Luke shook his head at that sad fact. His Druid friend had always been a man of strategizing, and was very rarely a man of action. So many times, he would start a project, only to leapfrog past it and do something else entirely. "I don't think I've taken any time to grow any plants here before, and I don't know why. Sure, arrows, those vines for Zed and such, but this dirt should still work like dirt, even if it's made out of words, right?"

Luke shifted his attention to the Mage, who appeared to be deciding between several different responses. Finally, she slowly nodded and begrudgingly answered the question. "Yes, that is true. Otherwise, I would have starved to death a long time ago. After all, I had to eat the words 'fruit' and 'vegetable' for a couple of years while I was first learning how to get control of my powers. Everything should work the same, although I am not certain what the side effects of using the word 'dirt' to grow things will have on plants from another world."

"Hopefully, it will be something fun!" Andre rubbed his hands together in anticipation as he prepared himself. Luke frowned in bewilderment, then relaxed as he looked closer and nodded in appreciation at the Druid's subterfuge. What appeared to be an 'excited hand rub' was actually camou-flaging dirt and spores sprinkling out of the powerful Ascen-der's hands and settling onto the ground as they walked. With an almost casual flick of his hand, Andre opened up a superfi-cial cut and created a single magic circle around them. It expanded rapidly, glowed with mana, and dropped to the ground.

Several things happened in quick succession after that.

First, the expected result. Plant life started forming, even if it had a strange look to it. The flowers looked like flowers, the trees and grass looked *almost* exactly as they were supposed to. The only strangeness the world inflicted on them was a strange network of inky veins running through them, which Luke recognized as typical routes for sap and nutrient production. It was easier than usual to understand the plant life here, because a thorough examination revealed that those exact words were filtering through the various parts of the plants. 'Nutrients' flowed in a continuous stream from the ground and up into the plants as the magic accelerated their growth.

The entire process elated the Druid to no end, and he dropped to his hands and knees to get a better look at everything. "Look at these things! They're a perfect hybrid between what I can cultivate and what this world can offer! If I could transplant this, we could directly use these as training tools for new Druids, allowing them to have a deeper understanding of exactly what happens within each plant!"

Unfortunately, that was when the first *unexpected* result occurred. The Grimoires that had been harassing Zed went absolutely *bonkers*. Luke watched intently as the plant life released a light mist of mana, something most people would never be able to see due to its nearly transparent fingerprint on the world around it. For someone as sensitive to mana as he was, it was a curiosity. For the books inhabiting this world, which could only navigate and exist due to the presence of mana, it was a cross between a direct taunt and the clang of a dinner bell the size of a building.

The books attacked the plants with a ferocity that Luke hadn't seen before, going so far as to obliterate other books in their path that were too slow to evade the furious onslaught. Andre tried to swat the diving volumes aside, but they weren't playing nice. "Luke! Can you get over here and act as a scarecrow for me while I set up some defenses?"

Shrugging, the Murderhobo stepped closer and sheltered the Druid as he began growing his standard vine-tentacle defensive emplacements. As Luke spun in place, arms outstretched, each movement shredded up to half a dozen books at a time. That wasn't fast enough, so he switched to using his Chain-Link Scourge, twirling it in the air like a lasso and creating an impressive vortex of books, ink, and paper. Long before he was done having fun, Andre asked him to step away and allowed his vines to take over.

"This is so interesting to watch! Also, thank you for figuring out a way to get the books to ignore me! Who knew they would love flowers so much?" Zed was always quick to find the silver lining in any situation. "Let's get out of here before they realize I'm still exactly as delicious as I was only a few moments ago."

"No, wait." Now it was Taylor's turn to take interest in the process that was unfolding. "Look at this here. As far as I can tell, this mana is being converted from the standard 'World of Names' ambient mana into… something else. I'm not sure why, or what is happening, but look at how the density is different? It's not mixing properly with the rest of the mana around it, like oil being poured into water."

"It's also spreading," Andre muttered with no small amount of concern. "Is this something we should stop?"

"What kind of story would we get out of *stopping* this?" Zed grabbed the Druid and tried to bodily haul him backward. Of course, at his level and Fitness, Andre wasn't going anywhere he didn't want to go. "Let's wait and see what happens!"

Even though they were under a slowly ramping sense of urgency due to their Quest and the desire to save Cindy, they waited for nearly an hour before something changed. The cloud of altered mana that had been spreading out abruptly began collapsing back inward, and strange shapes began forming in the air above the plants. Taylor let out a gasp so sharp that Luke immediately hunted around for the threat, more than ready to jump into a fight to escape the boring situation he had found himself in.

Standing and staring at the movement of mana for an hour? Please.

"It's… I've seen this before! Never like this, of course, but…!" Taylor seemed to be completely lost for words, something that happened only during the greatest of calamities, in Luke's memories. Otherwise, she always had a word of caution, a biting retort, or a useful factoid to contribute. "If I'm right, a new Spell is coming into being. This is turning into a Spell spawn point!"

"That is… good?" Andre offered hesitantly.

Taylor nodded with great enthusiasm. "A new spawn point

means new Spells. Since we're the only people here, let alone the first ones on the scene, I can claim the first new Spell, if it turns out to be worth *Naming*."

It took quite a long time—nearly five more hours—before the words above the plant life coalesced into a proper Spell. As soon as it snapped together, a creature composed entirely of scribbles that were smoothing out into beautiful calligraphy dropped to the ground. As far as Luke could distinguish, the characters held no meaning, but Taylor apparently disagreed.

She tracked the Spell with blatant longing, whispering under her breath, "Nature... plant... growth and control?"

Taylor nearly swooned when she worked out the final combination that gave her the True Name of the Spell that had just been created. As she spoke it aloud, her Grimoire lifted up off of her hip, cover flying open of its own accord, and sucked in the newborn Spell. "It's a miracle."

"The Spell is 'Miracle'?" Zed tapped his fingers together, trying to figure out how that would have been created based on various plants. "That seems to not fit the theme of-"

"No, Zed." Taylor cut him off almost ruthlessly. "This *Spell* is a miracle. It's something I have never seen or heard of before. The Spell itself is only a Tier two creation, but it carries incredible potential. It's an arcane version of a Druid's Abilities; specifically, this Spell is 'Grow Plant'. The mana cost is absurd, but it allows me to cast the Spell and leave, and it will independently grow a plant to maturity. Obviously, depending on how large the plant is going to be, or how long it takes to reach full growth, the Spell's effect might not bring it all the way there, but it's still the most... I know you don't understand how miraculous this actually is."

"So tell us," Luke ordered sternly, annoyed by her circumlocution.

She didn't seem to notice that he was getting grumpy, instead launching into a detailed explanation. "There are Spells that mimic things Druids can do, like my Tier five 'Fissure'. But Andre could create a fissure in the land far more easily, with a fraction of the mana investment, and have complete control over how it opened. My Spell is a fire-and-forget version, meaning it will have a standard length and width, and I have only minimal control. There are other Spells that can affect the weather, but they're Tier *nine* at the lowest."

"Something that I can also do, if I ever manage to get a Fifth Circle Spell awarded to me by the world," Andre chimed in to offer a counterpoint.

"Exactly! You'll be able to do it, maybe not easily, but in a controlled way that you know won't impact the world negatively. Spells don't work like that." Taylor shook her head, *hard*, side to side. "I just Named a variable mana cost, Tier two Druidic *Spell*. It gives me the same control over growth, variation, and final product that I believe Andre has. It will take me time to learn how to best use that, but…I have a Druidic *Spell*, not an Ability like he has."

"That is neat, but I don't really understand why you're making such a big deal of it." Zed shrugged and opened his mouth to say more, only to find that she had clapped a hand over it.

"It's amazing because it's not something that is supposed to be *possible*," Taylor insisted, her eyes burning with excitement. "If Andre has found a way to transfer what he can do over to me, does that mean that the rest of us can trade some of our best Spells, Masteries, Abilities, and Skills with each other?"

When her hand was removed from Zed's mouth, his jaw had fallen open. "Welp, I have a new goal in life. I'm going to be the first Bard to ever cast Fireball."

CHAPTER SEVENTEEN

While each of them was extremely intrigued by the new realm of possibilities that they had unlocked, there was no simple or easy way to replicate the unexpected feat of magic that Andre had just performed. If there was, they were certain that so much cross-contamination would exist between classes that they would be practically indistinguishable from each other. There was no way to know exactly what the reason was for the sudden shift, let alone the new Spell formation, but they had some ideas.

That wasn't the only thing they had learned from this patch of flora that the Druid had grown. It was Luke who first noticed it, but the plants were still releasing their strange combination of mana into the air. For just a fraction of a second, he could have sworn that he could see into the Druid's base world, which appeared like a foggy window into a world full of greenery, before returning to the simple haze of power in the air that his eyes were able to distinguish from the ambient energies.

"I think you did something to the veil between worlds." When the others looked at him to try to ascertain his meaning, he pointed at the air directly over the plants. "It's weaker. Look. I can see Andre's world."

Taylor shook her head at him, immediately dismissing his claims. "Luke, it's impossible to travel to worlds that are in parallel positioning from any world other than the base world. This is a known fact. If you-"

"You haven't tried it yourself; don't tell me it can't be done. If the *air* can do it, we can." Luke scoffed at the claim she was trying to assert. It didn't escape his notice that his teammates traded knowing glances, so he narrowed his eyes and slammed his knuckles together. "You think I'm wrong? *Prove* I'm wrong, Andre."

The Druid shrugged and stepped into the small patch of greenery, shuddering slightly as his mana regeneration increased by a minute fraction. Clearly expecting no results, he traced a circle in the air, trailing a wake in the surrounding mana. Once the trajectory was complete, he pushed and strained dramatically, as though he were putting way more effort into the attempt than he actually was. Even so, for an instant, a pinprick of bright green light gleamed through, and Andre leapt back in shock, causing the partial distortion to collapse as he stumbled to the ground.

"It was *working!*" Andre bellowed at the top of his lungs, scrambling with his hands and feet to stand back up and try again. He rushed into position, fully bending his will and power to create the portal in earnest. It sprang into existence, glowing green light shifting the coloration of the lightly purple-hued world they were standing in. He stepped through the stabilized Scar, and to their perceptions, returned just an instant later. "I walked around for a minute, and it's real. No doubt about it: that's The Grove."

"Not sure if you know this, a ton of mana is leaking over from your world into this one." Luke traced out the pluming clouds of mana with his fingers. A fraction of a second later, dozens, then hundreds of books attempted to go through the portal, jockeying for position as they zoomed over. Only a few got through before Andre forcibly closed the portal, but it was still enough to make him greatly concerned.

"What do you think is going to happen to them over there? Wait, more than that: how will they mess up my world?" None of them had an answer to the Druid's query, as this wasn't a situation that had ever before been deemed possible.

As the mana cloud settled down into its strange behavior once more, Taylor stepped forward to inspect the space where Andre had been creating his portal. With a gentle push of her own mana, another sprang into existence. This one revealed a much more familiar world, one that seemed to be frozen in time, or at the very most, moving in incredibly slow motion. Taylor's forehead wrinkled as she pulled her hand away, closing the portal with a thought.

Another gentle push made the portal reactivate with a *pop*, and she slowly nodded her head. "I think… if I am correct, we just made a synthetic bind point to our world."

"A bind point? You mean those places in our world where, if we step into one of your portals, we end up in the exact same spot every time?" Zed laced his fingers together and cracked his knuckles. "I don't know about you, but I think we should split the profit perfectly four ways. I will market your capabilities; you guys can zip across and make artificial bind points. Since no one else can do it, we automatically have a complete monopoly. Sound good to you? Sounds *great* to me."

"Bind point…" Andre breathed the words in awe, his turbulent thoughts slipping unbidden out of his mouth as he retreated into meditation in an attempt to parse the information he had gained. A few minutes later, he opened his eyes slowly and relayed his conclusions. "This has to have something to do with our unique bond to the world. Something about who we are, or what the Earthen Node has changed in us, is causing the influence of our base world to impact other worlds. Probably because we're so closely tied to it that everything we do is a reflection back onto it, even across dimensions."

"It could also be the fact that we have such incredible Mana

Channels now," Taylor offered as she flashed a sidelong glance at Luke. "Perhaps our mana is infused with our Essence, now that it can stream through us so cleanly. Maybe our power is just so pure that it-"

She was interrupted by a *snort* from Zed. He was trying and failing to hide a disbelieving smirk. "What kind of a children's fantasy novel do you think you live in? 'I'm just so pure that everything falls into my lap'. Let me break it to you, sister. To be in that kind of story, you need cute little birds fluttering around you and tweeting. Not heavy, leather-bound books that are trying to break your bones in an attempt to gobble down the mana that you're considering so 'pure'."

"Well, I don't see you coming up with any *good* ideas." Taylor snapped her retort back at him.

"I *had* good ideas. I said I would be your marketer!" Zed rubbed his thumb, middle, and index fingers together on both hands, miming an influx of cash. "Being an Ascender is great, but cold, hard coins are going to be what really gets us what we want in life. Money is power-"

Luke's fist stopped in the air less than an inch before it would have crushed Zed's face to a pulp. The wind generated by the incredibly swift motion, combined with the absolute terror it generated in the Bard, sent the man to his back as he rolled away in reflexive fear.

The Murderhobo peered down at him, an intrigued expression on his face. "Doesn't appear so. In my experience, *power* is power. I own three banks, and I still have to go in person to pick up my purchases from merchants, because someone with power over me is making my life hard for no good reason, other than the fact that they think I am defying them. Get strong enough and *take* what you want from life. Don't wait for it to be handed to you."

"Maybe it isn't direct power, but passive income is still helpful." Zed wheezed gently as he hopped to his feet and brushed himself off. "Money is another kind of power, isn't it? Indirect power?"

"It's a pale imitation," Luke leaned in and whispered, as if he were sharing a great secret. "Two of the bankers didn't *want* to sell their banks to me. They still did in the end. Afterward, they were able to convince the third to sell without me having to show up."

Zed's eyes went wide as he thought over the implications of the outrageous admission. "I *knew* there was something fishy about *you* being a proper businessman!"

Ignoring the rest of the conversation, Luke went to inspect the distortion in the air for himself, setting up a few meters away from the spot where the other two Ascenders had originally opened their portals so he wouldn't get a false positive from his experiment. His fist lashed out, and the membrane of the world *popped* with a single punch. He poked his head through, finding a portion of the Hollow Kingdom, and exhaled some tension he shouldn't have been holding. "Good. Now, even if something happens to Taylor, as long as we have Andre or myself, we can escape this world."

Small smiles appeared on the faces of each man in the group, even as Taylor frowned at each of them suspiciously. "Did you think I was going to trap you here or something? Why are you all so relieved that you can leave if you want? I would *always* open a portal if you asked me to!"

"No reason, Taylor. Of course we know you would," Zed consoled her as he cast a knowing look at the other two. "Now, we have spent a lot of time here already. Is there any other test to run, or can we continue on with our quest?"

"I have one thing I want to test." The other members of the group turned in surprise when Luke spoke up, but they were too slow to stop what he was doing. He was holding a water skin in each hand, the special light blue ones that indicated they were filled with liquid mana. His hands swept toward each other with the clear intent to pop the containers against each other to release all of the mana in a single burst.

"Luke, *no!*" Taylor screamed in fear as her eyes went wide.

Zed's eyes also went wide, but in pure excitement. "Luke, *yes!*"

The bags burst, but the mana didn't rain to the ground like other liquids would have. Instead, upon being released in an area of reduced mana density, it expanded into an immense fog in less than a single second. For a long, terrible, terrifying moment, everything went silent.

Luke promptly shattered the calm before the storm, his fist shooting into the epicenter of the fresh cloud of power as words erupted from his mouth. "*Rift Hunter!*"

CHAPTER EIGHTEEN

In a stunning reversal, the mana in the area that had been expanding outward rapidly collapsed back upon itself, rending the air and rebounding with a concussive reverberation at chest level. Where Andre's portal had been gradually leaking mana, slowly meandering its way towards instability, Luke's jagged portal *gushed* energy into their surroundings.

The Murderhobo slowly nodded and tried to take a step in, only for his Sigil to once more screech at him, refusing access yet again. He stared at the opening, knowing that true happiness for himself was only a step away, and he could not take it. Pulling off his backpack, he retrieved several empty water skins and handed them over to Zed. Everyone else was too shocked to comment on his actions, so Luke used the opportunity to the fullest. "Fill these up with water; use this scoop so you don't get it on your hands. There's a quantitative difference between the mana in the air and liquid mana. Don't test it. I'll hold the portal open, so you should be able to come back."

Without waiting for a response, he chucked the Bard through the portal, earning a confused scream from Taylor and a sharp, rapidly bitten-off curse from Andre. Almost as soon as the Bard vanished through the portal, he returned with eight full water skins. He was clutching them to his chest for dear life, and his face had gone ashen white.

"Wh-what *were* those things, Luke?" Zed whispered, barely able to force the words out through the chattering of his teeth. "They weren't there when I was with you. They moved so slowly, and yet-"

"Try not to think about them. Doing so lets them find you faster. I can't promise there aren't any in this world or the base world. *Don't* draw them in." The Murderhobo patted his friend on the shoulder, pleased with his work. "Thanks for the refills; I was worried I was going to be out for the next two months."

"Their eyes, Luke. Why did I look into their eyes?" Zed whispered, causing his friends to recoil from him in horror, though the Murderhobo merely shrugged.

"You'll get used to the nightmares. Now I even find them soothing." He approached the open portal and began punching it until the Scar folded over in agony and collapsed. Turning around, Luke frowned as he realized that the free power in the air was affecting his friends in a strange way. Both Taylor and Zed had vacant expressions, and they were staring at something that only they could see.

Something unfamiliar was wrapped around—and originating from—the Bard. Puzzled, Luke followed Taylor's eyes and found that she was studying that *something* floating in the air. It was words, and once again, he could not recognize what they spelled out.

Taylor and Zed both spoke, nearly in unison, with the Mage being only a fraction of a second slower than the Bard.

"*Echoes of Reality.*"

"*Meta-Magic.*"

The remnants of mana in the area flooded into the two of them. The whip crack suddenness of the power draw smacked into their respective Sigils, directly knocking them out. Luke and Andre looked down at the fallen friends, then at each other.

With a slightly annoyed shake of his head, Luke pointed at Zed. "I'll carry him, you carry her?"

"As per usual," the Druid agreed, attempting to inject some humor into the situation. Luckily for the unconscious pair, the ambient power in the area wasn't enough to create continual shock waves, as it did for Luke in Murder World. Perhaps less luckily, the distinct lack of energy meant that the metamorphosis they were undergoing was going to take longer than it otherwise would have.

By the time they woke up, Luke and Andre had been able to traverse the remainder of the distance that they had been scheduled to cross in this world. At least, mostly. Because the World of Names was such a common destination for Ascenders, it had been simple to the point of the plane where the front lines of the Hollow Kingdom congregated to exit into the base world.

They could see troops in their kingdom's colors as they drew near. Andre didn't want to start an accidental fight with someone that would cause them to be punished by their Sigils, and Luke had no interest in interacting with people he didn't know if he didn't have to. They mutually agreed that it was best to resist approaching the larger group until they had someone who was as versed in the legal system as Taylor was.

Zed's eyes fluttered open first. He blinked a few times, then sat bolt upright with a strangled yell of exultation. "I gained a new Mastery!"

"We heard," Andre stated dryly, though he offered a wide, happy grin for his friend's moment of triumph. "What does it do?"

"It lets me cast *Fireball*, that's what it does!" Zed lifted a hand and wiggled it side to side. "I mean, eventually it will. It actually lets me perfectly mimic any sounds of magic that I hear. I can play those sounds back into the akashic field around us to recreate the magical frequency!"

"If you say something like that to me again, I'm going to

break your left pinky toe and slowly pull the nail off. In that order." Luke calmly informed the Bard.

"Wh—oh, right. *Non*-Bard terms. Ah-*haaa*." Zed flipped his hair with his left hand in a show of signature superiority. "Once I hear an Ascender's spell being cast, then I can use that same Spell. As far as I can tell, I can even use it more than once. But, every time I use it, I am hearing my own 'Echo' instead of the 'Reality' of the spell. That means the next time I cast the same spell, it will grow weaker, until eventually it's not worth using again."

"Is it just Spells, or is it any power?" Taylor's voice was raspy, as if she hadn't had a drink of water in days. "Also, I think we can chalk up the manifestation of new powers to our Mana Channels once and for all."

"Doesn't prove anything about the bind point," Zed flippantly countered. "I was saying 'Spells' for brevity's sake, not for any reasonable limitation. Also, thanks to the sheer amount of mana that you released, my other Mastery finished upgrading as well. Now I can slightly alter my appearance, and I have more control over how my clones look. Not as cool as this new thing, but it's still pretty neat."

As one, the group's eyes turned to Taylor expectantly, even though she was less interested in sharing everything like the Bard had done. Still, the peer pressure got to her after a few moments, and she broke her silence in a rush. "I'm kind of annoyed to say that my new Spell is really similar to Zed's."

"Ha!" Zed taunted for a moment, then went still as his eyes hardened. "Hey. Wait. All you did was steal a lesser copy of my Mastery as it was made!"

"It's called Meta-Magic," Taylor pressed onward, not stopping though his consternation brought a grin to her face. "Despite its name, it doesn't give me a greater understanding of magic as a whole. Instead, it enables me to see a Spell being cast and perfectly copy it. Unlike the music man over here, I can't use it more than once. Instead, I can increase the potency of the final effect by adding additional mana to it. Even though my

Spell is restricted to a single use per observation, I can actually use a stronger version than I saw cast in the first place."

"Neat." Luke's answer, as always, was succinct.

Andre's was less so, as he shouted in inarticulate excitement and grabbed both of his friends in a bear hug, picking them up and swinging them around as he laughed with them. Luke was only able to stop them by pointing out the fact that a group of Mages from the Hollow Kingdom was closing in on them, likely due to their screaming and shouting. The group slowly composed themselves and started marching toward their fellow Ascenders, ensuring that they were visibly calm and clearly not moving toward them threateningly.

"Abyss, I want to see if I could crush those smug faces with Cookie, even if they put a barrier up." Actually, only *most* of the group wasn't moving toward the others threateningly. Luke was swallowing several times a minute, clearly having a buildup of saliva as he envisioned destroying the people in front of them. "Do you think they would be good training for going against Archmage Don? Maybe not, but it would be a start, right?"

"Master Don is as far above these Mages as you're above a common militiaman," Taylor told him with perfect enunciation, ensuring there could be no miscommunication. "Frankly, I'm almost positive that even *Zed* could wipe the floor with these low-powered noble sons."

"Halt right there, you *silly* trespassers!" The man hailing them was dressed in a peacock's dream, his clothes being reflective on top of having a brilliant hue. "You can't just walk into an active war zone! You have to have a reason to be here, or we have to go out of our way to detain you. None of us want that; the cages are so *stinky*."

"I'm starting a betting pool right now," Zed told the others under his breath. "The wager is not *if* he was dropped on his head as a child; it's how many times. We'll do two to one, over-under. I'll start the betting at being dropped five times."

"Eight," Andre breathed.

Luke shook his head and firmly countered, "Three. Not dropped, but thrown."

"All of you need to knock it off!" Taylor hissed at them, causing the three men to let out puffs of laughter only through their noses so that it wouldn't be quite as loud. "Hail, brave Ascender of the Hollow Kingdom! I am Archmage presumptive, Taylor Woodswright. Myself, and my team, The Four, have been given orders to... well, we need to get to the front lines."

The incredibly flamboyant nobleman skidded to a halt, jumping up and down in place and clapping his hands wildly. "Is it really you? Oh, my goodness! Good golly gracious! By the Celestials, can I get you to sign my autograph notebook? I'd love to have proof that I was the one who got to meet you at the border!"

A stunned silence caused every other person to simply stare at the man as he pulled open a fanny pack and rummaged around inside of it, popping up with a quill and notepad a moment later. "I have heard so many stories about you, and I have been following your work for *years*! Someday, I too hope to have a well of personal power deep enough to reduce a mountain to purified minerals in a single day!"

"You know what?" Zed stepped forward and happily scrolled his name on the paper after ensuring that there was no magic involved in either the quill, ink, or paper. "There are worse dreams to have. I think I can like you."

"You must be the Bard, correct?" There was no fear or revulsion in this Mage's eyes as he stated the question, a first for Zed, at least amongst people in the know of his power set. "Your exploits are nearly as legendary, even if not something that I think I will ever be able to achieve myself. Still, being able to live *vicariously* through you is already a great honor! To think, the first of The Four signing my notebook is the Tornado of the Red Light-"

"Aaand that's enough of that conversation!" Zed laughed as he pulled his hand off the Mage's mouth, revealing a disconcertingly wide smile under the palm. "I don't suppose you could show us to the border we share with the Dynasty of Dogs?"

"Oh, I certainly can! The only *teensy* issue is that you'll have to leave the World of Names and go back to the Hollow Kingdom to get there." Seeing that Zed was about to argue with him, the Ascender merely shook his head and smiled knowingly. "The world distortion won't allow you to go much farther, anyway. We're nearly at the edge of the world, and the closer you get, the worse the ratio between walking and achieving a distance in the base world becomes. Here, in case you didn't know, for every step that you take, approximately four times the distance is traveled in the base world. As you get closer to the border, that ratio approaches an inverse, then scales higher as you continue. You'll ultimately wind up needing to cross significantly more distance."

"I've heard of this." Andre joined the conversation with great interest, reaching out and signing his name on the notebook as well. "Something to do with how the dimensions are not layered on top of each other, but are at oblique angles."

"Exactly!" The nobleman looked Andre up and down, then fluttered his hands together in tiny claps. "The Terraformer himself, in the flesh! I will tell this story to my grandchildren. I *do* hope they will believe me!"

"You believe in yourself more than I believe in you, if you think you're going to have grandchildren." Luke grabbed the quill and scrawled out a rough approximation of what he thought his name was supposed to look like. "Where do I go to get some fighting in?"

"The *Murderhobo!*" The vivacious nobleman somehow managed to keep himself very still, even though his smile looked like it was going to tear his cheeks. A slight giggle burst from his lips as he tried to speak around his nervousness. "It is such an honor to meet you, and you definitely came to the right place! This is the front lines, and we're currently experiencing an invasion! If you're allowed to take the field, it will be an all-you-can-fight buffet. If you don't mind waiting, I will try to get relieved from my position so I can watch you work. I hear your Abilities are… *huhh*… exquisite."

"Get away from me." Luke stomped away and didn't look back as the Ascender watched him leave, his garish, gleaming chest heaving with every breath.

"Gracious me!" The man pulled out a handkerchief and dabbed at his forehead. "What an *experience*."

CHAPTER NINETEEN

- ANDRE -

They stepped through the portal and into one of the Druid's nightmares. When the overly excitable Ascender who had been guarding the way in had called this place a 'focal point of the invasion', he hadn't done justice to the absolute *charnel house* that they were about to walk into. The scent of inflamed flesh and rotting meat, combined with the screams of pain and fury ringing through the area on a grand scale, was enough to make him dry heave.

Such a sudden shift in locales made Andre freeze for a moment, but he was forced out of it as Luke burst through the portal right on his heels, started nearly squealing with glee, and shot into the distance. The Murderhobo hit the front lines and vanished, at least to Andre's capability of keeping track of him. He had a sneaking suspicion that the sudden wave of death that spread outward from a certain point might lead back to his Murderhobo friend; yet he knew that by the time he got over there, Luke would have moved on to the next most dense portion of the battle.

Andre wasn't someone who relished combat, especially against other humans. There was something to be said for fighting monsters, for destroying abyssal abominations or Chimera that were coming after them, but the specific act of taking a human life was something that still wounded him on a deep and personal level.

The Druid was grateful that these other fighters *could* act, feeling concerned over how Luke would *re*-act, but knew that he needed to get his *own* act together. Trying to clear his mind and become the man that this world needed him to be, Andre stomped his right foot onto the bare earth and initiated the process of binding the world to his will.

Call Of Nature has generated a quest: Sore Spot. This area is rotten and filled with shifting, unstable powers. Clean and restore the land. Reward: Potentia. Increased macro-manipulation of the impacted area. Harder-to-disrupt area presence.

The fact that the world itself was calling out for help, giving him a proper quest for the first time since he'd gained the Ability 'Call of Nature', meant that he wanted to spring into action to prove to the world that it had made the correct call in choosing him. He had never traveled along the border, certainly not this far out. Therefore, his powers weren't connected to other areas of his own influence. Until he was able to gather a large enough space under his control, he would be limited in how much he could directly influence the ongoing battle or heal the land the battle was taking place on.

Appreciatively eyeing the almost literal rivers of blood that were soaking the ground, his worry seamlessly shifted into pleased satisfaction. Without needing to cut his own skin, he had access to every resource he needed in order to make the most of this project. A sheet of blood lifted into the air off of the churned earth at his command, and he expertly shaped every last drop into a large, perfect Circle.

Factoring in that the ground had been pounded into veri-table brick by tens of thousands of feet, ensuring there was incredibly little plant life remaining in the area, he created two more Circles around the first: allowing him to bind with the land directly. Andre wouldn't recover as much mana, as the esoteric energy was considered to be a byproduct of living processes, but he wasn't worried about that for the moment. Thanks to his upgraded Abilities, he wouldn't need to invest very much effort in order to make up for the resources he was currently investing.

A tap of his LivingWood staff on the ground set the Circles to spinning, the center one moving counterclockwise, opposite to the inner and outer ones which were revolving much faster in the clockwise direction. Retreating inward, he put all of his Willpower behind binding the terrain directly around himself. A small frown creased his face as he sensed the influence of another Druid who had controlled this area far before he had. Even so, it was obvious that, while the other Druid was clearly still alive, they were somewhere far distant. Seeing as Andre was the only known Druid in his own kingdom, the unfamiliar influence must be coming from an enemy of his people.

With just a touch more power, the control of the distant opponent was shattered, and the area was bound to Andre's will. From there, he paused and allowed the circle to slowly expand on its own to test how far it would be able to reach. To his great surprise and pleasure, the mud that had surrounded this encampment rapidly began to dry, the blood leached out and repurposed to expand his control. "Bloodflood Binding, you truly live up to your name."

He could feel his area of influence expanding wildly, slowing down at times only to reach a new blood-soaked pit and race into the distance. With so many Spells active, and so much death having been dealt in the land around him, his power stretched farther and faster with every passing moment. "Okay… doesn't look like I need to do that again for a while; let's start on stage two."

Seeds poured off of his clothing, and he flung his cloak made entirely of woven foliage to the side to spread them

farther. Grass sprang up around him, transforming the immediate area into a small oasis of thriving, verdant happiness.

He sat down in the center, bracing his staff in his hands as
he focused on growing all of the new plant life through its full
life cycle, generating seed and beginning the process anew. It
was not nearly as fast as his binding to the land had progressed,
but the grass began to expand outward, spreading farther and
farther with every completed cycle.

His own people, as they walked across it, gradually discovered that their footing was firm. No longer were they being
subjected to the whims of slippery stone, sucking mud, and
guaranteed infection if they got so much as a *scratch* that broke
the skin. Where combat was heaviest, Andre was unable to
teach the grass the difference between friend and foe, so he
simply didn't allow the better terrain to form past that point.
Instead, he focused on expanding the outer border ever farther.

Sinking so deeply into his meditations allowed the Druid to
split his focus slightly, and he watched in wonder at the
authority and power he was able to exert upon the world
around him. Each small increase to the radius under his control
drastically improved his capability to produce more plant life in
the influenced area. "Being at one with nature is a true blessing… it's a beautiful thing to watch the lifecycle move and
witness the truth of how it is meant to be self-perpetuating."

His eyes shot open in concern as he felt his influence stutter
and stall against a barrier deeper within the territory controlled
by the Dynasty of Dogs. After a brief flare of irritation, he was
able to accept the fact that it wouldn't be as easy to capture
enemy land from the Druid who had been assigned to that area.
Likely, their control had been solidified over that area long ago.
Breaking that grasp would be a true challenge, a direct competition of Willpower combined with his ability to actively smash
through his opponent's Abilities. Delight glittered in his eyes as
he contemplated that future, and a small smile quirked into
place as he realized that perhaps he had been spending too
much time around Taylor and Luke.

Still, that would be a game for another time. He would need to leverage the control he had over his own kingdom into that competition, as he had no doubt the opposing Druid would do the same. Andre refocused his intent, guiding the influence deeper into the land controlled by the Hollow Kingdom.

Eventually, the sheer surplus of blood in the battleground would dry up, and his automatic expansion would slow. Then again... he recalled the fresh waterskins of liquid mana that Luke had collected on their journey and wondered if his friend would be able to be convinced to part with... well... most of them.

In a burst of inspiration, he recalled another simple solution to his mana generation issues. In fact, he had used the exact method back in the desert, when enemy combatants, especially Ascenders, were hunting him. Settling in a little deeper, he grew some vines around himself to ensure that anything coming his way would be intercepted, as well as giving him an opportunity to defend himself if needed. Once they were firmly established, he felt along the border of grass he had created. With a simple application of intent, he caused the ground underneath any unmoving form to slightly desolidify.

Thousands of corpses slowly sank into the ground, where they were consumed for nutrients. He tried to take deep breaths, knowing that it was unlikely that any of the bodies could have been returned to their still-living relatives.

Andre was able to steady himself with the knowledge that, if he didn't do something about the bodies, some sort of corpse animator would likely come along and use them for a different, more nefarious purpose. Only one major downside came from his accomplishment: with the vast majority of ground-level obstacles out of their way, the combat between the two sides drastically intensified.

The soggy mud had turned into firm ground—granting the defenders an advantage, thanks to the grass that supported their feet—and there was no longer mangled flesh to slip on or to distract from the fighting at hand. Sending his mind farther away from the front lines, into the area that had no grass but was still under his control, Andre started selectively opening small pits. A few people managed to get out of the way, hopping over them or outright dodging the slight tremors that indicated an impending Ascender assault. Their evasion only made him work harder to capture them, as they obviously had some access to their mana.

In no time at all, he had collected hundreds of unwilling test subjects. Within ten minutes of their imprisonment within the pits, large lotuses began to flourish on the muddy walls. The parasitic blooms closed around each human, cutting off their already-muffled cries. Moments later, the natural sedation created by the flowers knocked out their prey, and small vines grew into the inert bodies. Back in the Scarrocco Desert, Andre had been able to use these flowers, and the passive mana regeneration that they stole from their human captives, to produce water and infuse the ground with nutrients.

In this scenario, he didn't want or need to use that mana in any structured sense. The Druid instead directed the flowers to release the energy into the air, where his Bloodflood Binding captured it and allocated the potent power to perpetrate his protected premises. "Perfect. Now that there's an excess of blood, and mana is joining it properly, I should see a doubling of the area per second that comes under my influence."

He opened his eyes to inspect the far more palatable battlefield. Andre took a deep breath, pausing halfway in expectation of the foul stench that had pervaded the area previously. Instead, he was met with the scent of sweat, a slight tinge of blood, but also the fresh, sweet air produced around old-growth grass. He rose to his feet and dusted himself off, preparing to take a more active role in combat now that his initial setup had been completed.

The Druid managed a single step before the general commanding the battlefield skidded to a stop in front of him, clearly furious at the tall redhead. "Are you trying to get us all *killed?* Your team just got here, and you're already making international incidents and escalating this invasion?"

Andre froze momentarily, but quickly remembered that he wasn't under the command of this officer, as they were the last time they had been near a battlefield. "I hate to have to be the one to tell you this, but it's about to get worse. A *lot* worse."

Before the General's scowl could shift into a commanding glare, a familiar voice caught Andre's attention.

"Hobo Holler!"

CHAPTER TWENTY

- LUKE -

Escaping the ridiculous world full of confusion and strangely aggressive scribbles, the Murderhobo found something he understood perfectly. There was fighting afoot, and this time no one could stop him from collecting any armor or weapons that were better than what he had.

He was quite pleased with his brand new armor and was nearly certain that there were going to be very few people, short of the most powerful officers or wealthiest of nobles, who would be able to match the armor that he currently was able to bring to bear. That meant Luke was on a hunt for weapons. Before his team could attempt to control him with their fancy words and the magic burned into his forehead that forced him to listen, he shot toward combat. Andre shouted something behind him, but he activated Bum Thunder at just the right time, drowning any potential commands out.

Launching over the heads of his fellow countrymen, Luke dropped in the epicenter of the battle, already in the process of swinging Cookie with a fairly average amount of strength.

Against such weak, pathetic enemies, putting his whole strength into any attack was foolish. It would merely put him off balance as his weapons disintegrated whoever they went through. As it turned out, attacking standard soldiers instead of Ascenders meant he should have used even *less* strength.

Cookie turned them into paste, just as she had the goats in Murder World all those years ago. With his second strike, he merely stepped forward and thrust out with a straight punch, activating Shockwave Cleave at the last moment.

"They won't know what hit them…" Dozens of standard humans were obliterated in an instant, a cone of deadly shock waves radiating out. "Because they'll all be dead!"

It wasn't just the soldiers that were destroyed. The armor and weapons they bore seemed to be crafted of basic materials with no special purpose in mind, no mana infusing their shapes and curves. When the Shockwave passed over them, the weapons warped, bent, and broke. As an entire platoon was reduced to bloody pulp and scrap metal, Luke realized why Ascenders didn't bother fighting other humans, why kingdoms sent non-Ascenders into their Legions and had them wear each other down. "It just isn't worth the mana expenditure to kill them off."

That was saying something, because every Ascender had a natural mana regeneration rate. It cost them nothing, over time, to wipe out any standard human they wanted to kill. Yet, it made sense not to spend that power, when even a small lack of free energy made it more likely that another Ascender could take advantage of that moment of weakness.

For an empire as large as the Dynasty of Dogs, it also made sense for them to sacrifice their lowest class of humans, the ones with no chance of rising above their station. There was always the chance that any given citizen would show true usefulness and merit, perhaps even fighting so hard that they unlocked their innate potential and qualified to become an Ascender.

The odds were so low that it was practically non-existent; something like one in a million people could gather Potentia from reaping the lives of their own race. With that said, as he scanned the battlefield, Luke could see the potential for extreme outliers to come from a conflict like this. The sheer size of the enemy's invasion force made their own defenses laughable. The dynasty was clearly using their kingdom as a whetstone, attempting to produce veterans and elevate the rare Ascender who simply hadn't been able to pass the original muster.

He approved and appreciated this methodology, knowing he would be able to take advantage of the situation they had provided for him. Luke dashed from one section of the ongoing battle to another, targeting any area filled with promising enemy candidates. Almost always, spotting a well-coordinated offense from the soldiers of the dynasty and wiping them out with a single blow was immensely satisfying. Whenever he appeared in front of his countrymen, they cheered for him, the exhaustion and terrible living conditions showing on their face seeming to melt away as the people seeking their lives were taken down instead.

Even as he had that thought, Luke noticed that the fallen enemies had started to *literally* melt away. The horrendous terrain disadvantage the troops had had been dealing with began to shift in their favor, and he realized that Andre was doing something to help them. The ground hardened under the feet of the Hollow Kingdom's soldiers, allowing them to generate attacks from a stable position, defend more easily, and push back against the foes who had been on the brink of over-running them at dozens of points in their line.

The Murderhobo did a double backflip, retreating from the front lines as he scanned the remnants of ongoing combat. His eyes tracked up and down the line, and he zeroed in on a patch of color that was spreading toward him with a strange, creeping motion. Just before he went on the offensive, he noticed that it was grass, and was rippling across the muddy field in a pattern that suggested Andre was controlling it. "That guy spends way too much time planting and thinking about grass."

He rethought that comment as he watched and watched the

grass grow. It was surprisingly interesting. Something about the way the blades shot up, aged, and went to seed so quickly made him want to stare at it for hours. He blinked and pulled his gaze away, shaking his head and leaping toward the front lines once again.

Luke paused for a moment, then set Cookie upright in an easily visible location. He wasn't at all concerned with someone trying to steal her and run off–not only was the beautiful bone weapon four feet long and several hundred kilograms, but she was also the only one of his weapons or items he would never remove his Soul Brand from. Even if someone managed to drag her away, a simple thought would send her careening back into his open arms.

"Take a rest, Cookie. There's no one here worth your time." The Murderhobo patted the weapon lovingly, then ran back toward the fight. Bellowing a disconcertingly cheery war cry, he rejoined the front lines, manifesting a spear in each hand and simply running in a straight line with the weapons held out to the side.

Between his speed, weight, and the angle of the spearheads, he earned a new kill every quarter second or so. As he sped along, practically skipping with the ease of defeating so many enemies in one go, all he could think was, "I feel like a child with a stick, chopping the heads off of dandelions in a field because I'm bored."

The work quickly grew tedious and endlessly repetitive, making him far more bored than excited. But the troops of the Hollow Kingdom were gaining confidence, becoming bolder in the aftermath of his effortless destruction. The buckling lines were able to reform their defenses, holding firmer than they likely had been for days. Between the lessening pressure, the earth solidifying, and the putrid, rotting flesh mysteriously removed from the battlefield, everything from morale to measurable combat output increased.

A short while later, there was another small effect that likely only Luke was capable of noticing, thanks to his highly developed mana sensitivities. The air and the earth were both becoming denser with power, even if it was only a trickle every second. Recognizing that the improvement likely had something to do with Andre, Luke willingly continued his grisly work, zoning out slightly as he thought on what he should do when he got back to Murder World. Now that he likely had everything he needed to penetrate Zone twenty and deal some actual damage to the enemies waiting for him, he could spend the rest of the time planning his strategy for best effect.

Only his highly developed sense for danger brought him out of his daydreams in time to save him.

Enormous jaws clamped shut on the air in front of him, where his head would have been only a fraction of a second later. Even though they missed, the massive chomp released a cavitation bubble in the open air, sending a half-dozen soldiers reeling backward, blood shooting out of their mouths, ears, noses, and eyes.

Luke reacted with an instant uppercut, switching his weapon mid-punch from a spear to his Battering Ram Knuckles. His enhanced fist landed on the closed jaw of the towering hound, shattering the lower mandible and driving the bones up into the creature's skull. The enormous monster went flying, only to dissipate into motes of light before it ever managed to return to the ground.

"How very interesting," a clipped voice called out as Luke oriented on the new threat. His eyes landed on a man wearing a combat robe, which piqued his interest. The garment appeared to allow for easy, fluid movements, yet was decorated with enough ribbons, medals, awards, and embroidered embellishments that the free-flowing material should have been reduced to a stiff, jingling uniform. It was a testament to its quality that it was able to remain as balanced and useful as the day it had originally been created.

Luke noted with slight annoyance that someone was already wearing his new outfit. That was okay with the Murderhobo; most of his gear was secondhand. The fun was in the challenge of getting it off its current owner before the lovely outfit was ruined.

The man wearing the robe that would soon belong to Luke raised his voice, obviously unused to being ignored. Or, perhaps he was feeling slightly uncomfortable over the hungry stare that the huge Berserker was sending him. "It's not every day that someone is able to defeat the *least* of my hounds, yet your presence on the battlefield gives me sufficient justification to take the field myself. Here I thought your insignificant kingdom was invested in staying alive by making sure to follow the rules of engagement we had set. In a way, I am glad you stepped forward. I have been growing so *bored*."

Now *that* was something that Luke understood, but even more than that, he sensed that a potent Ascender had appeared to challenge him. There was no way for him to know what rank this man held, either in the military or the nobility, but to possess gear as high-quality as his, as well as impressive summons, meant that this was an important figure.

Someone the Murderhobo could actually test himself against.

His new opponent waved a hand, and two swirling, shimmering portals opened to either side of his billowing sleeves. Out of each portal prowled an enormous canine, standing a foot taller than Luke at the shoulder. The fluidly moving man watched as Luke stared on unconcernedly as he prepared his summons for the fight, a scornful smirk gracing his anger-pinched face. "You truly don't know the mess you have made for yourself, do you? Let me elucidate you. I... am Lieutenant Garmr, the Bloodstained Guardian of the Western Gate. Run, if you wish, but know that I have your scent."

"Why would I run? You look like you're all bark and no bite." The smile that had appeared on Luke's face was far too wide, showing far too many teeth, to be misunderstood as anything other than pure excitement. "I finally get a chance to beat up some fluffy animals."

CHAPTER TWENTY-ONE

Even back when he was a child, Luke had always known that the Dynasty of Dogs was the boogeyman of the Hollow Kingdom. His homeland shared a border with only a few small nations, capped by the sea to the north, but the vast majority of their country was connected to land owned by the dynasty.

For as long as he could remember, they had been under the threat of annexation by the massive superpower that was the dynasty. Only the fact that their kingdom had an obvious dearth of resources and available mana to produce large quantities of Ascenders had kept them safe.

Weakness wasn't Luke's idea of a good defense, but until recently, it had been the only defense they'd had. A small amount of mirth filtered into his manic smile upon realizing that it was the actions of his team, and his team alone, that had forced the kingdom out of obscurity and into being a target worth capturing once more. Anything to put a few gray hairs in King Vir's hair. Pleased that the Lieutenant appeared ready for the fight, Luke sprinted forward, kicking up a divot of freshly grown grass as he pushed himself to his maximum speed in an instant.

He targeted the first of the dogs on the left, excited to see how well it could take a punch. It wasn't exactly surprising, per se, that the creature was able to react in time to adopt a more advantageous position as the Murderhobo closed in on it, but the shift did make him amend his strategy somewhat. Instead of bringing himself into perfect fist range, he instead swapped his weapon back to a manifestation of a long spear, selecting one with a lightning elemental variation.

Using both hands, he ensured the spear tip preceded him by several feet, saving him from getting mauled on the arm as both dogs moved in unison. The enormous beast to the right of the Lieutenant snapped its head to the right, biting the shaft of the mana-manifested spear, while his original target hopped lightly to the side to avoid the weapon's crackling spearhead.

For the first time in practically years, Luke utterly *missed* his target.

He braced his feet, pushing off the ground and reversing his momentum to keep himself out of reach of the dogs' lethal jaws. It didn't escape his attention that the Lieutenant was staring smugly at him, his arms crossed over his chest. The man hadn't moved a fraction of an inch since summoning the dogs, absolutely certain of his own safety. "Your handlers should have kept you on a tighter leash. At the very least, they should have informed you of how polite society works. I understand that, in your kingdom, everyone grabs whatever scraps of power they can attain from whatever useless world they manage to insert themselves into. But in the dynasty, your rank is determined socially, militarily, and politically by your ability to tame and train your dog."

Dropping to his knees, Luke managed to avoid the lunge of the leftmost dog, passively shredding the underside of its front right leg against his armor. The Murderhobo let the splash of blood wash over him, knowing that it wouldn't matter and could demoralize his enemies. With a simple jab forward, the spear tip punched through the canine's rear-facing knee, forcing it to disengage in a limping retreat. Before he could get excited about the minor wounds he had inflicted, a wave of mana washed out from the Lieutenant onto the dog, wrapping the wound in power and causing the damage to fade away nigh-instantaneously.

Lieutenant Garmr continued to monologue, and by now Luke was nearly positive that he was doing so intentionally with the sole purpose of distracting him from the attacking dogs. "You cannot become an officer without managing to tame at least three dogs. Nobles will lose all ability to inherit, if they do not manage to subdue a Tier five at the very minimum. Higher nobility have higher requirements, as I'm sure you fully understand. As a Lieutenant and a noble myself, my dogs have all reached Tier *seven*. I don't suppose you understand what that means, do you?"

The Murderhobo *did* in fact understand what a Tier seven was capable of, perhaps even more fully than the Lieutenant himself. Luke begrudgingly amended that thought. Seeing as the man commanded multiple dogs at that Tier, he might have as much or even more data than Luke did. The huge Berserker decided that it was unlikely, but stranger things had happened. The real question was: why was this man giving him so much information? It must have been an attempt to get him to give up or run away, but the only effect was that Luke was informed ahead of time regarding how strong the effects of the dogs' skills were going to be.

"*Command*! Open the gate of catastrophe!" As soon as the Lieutenant had barked the order, both of his summoned dogs moved into position next to him, their heads and feet perfectly parallel. Both ferocious mouths dropped open, tainted mana cascading out and forming a swirling miasma in the air. Several smaller, lower-Tier dogs charged out of the strange portal until dozens, then scores of creatures were snapping at Luke from all angles.

He traded his manifested weapons for his Chain-Link Scourge, which he began whirling around at high speeds, causing the blades hidden in the rope to pop out as they struck the summoned beasts. "Weird that your dogs are summoned by a Spell that calls cats. I thought everything was hound this, dog that, wolf here, dingo there."

"Cats?" Garmr, to his credit, picked up on Luke's implication right away, his tone darkening with disgust. "The command is for *catastrophe*. It has nothing to do with those disgusting *felines*. Enough of this… the first effect is clearly not enough. *Command*! Scatter. *Command*! Life-Threatening Growl."

All of the newly summoned creatures, which had been unable to leave a single mark on Luke through his spiked armor, instead followed their directive to devote their talents of rending flesh to the soldiers that had been getting into position behind Luke. The Murderhobo was annoyed that his enemy was looking down on him, thinking that he could summon creatures to attack him, then not even bother to follow through. "None of you get to escape me. Cookie, c'mere. I found someone worth bothering with. *Hobo Holler*!"

Against the shouted orders of the Lieutenant, all of the creatures in the area that counted Luke among their list of enemies suddenly only had eyes for him. The smaller, less useful dogs that had been summoned were compelled to charge, and Luke sliced his way through them with his scourge as though he were calmly preparing a dinner for a baby. That is, he made sure that his attacks perfectly pureed anything that dared to try to come for his life.

As he moved to destroy more of the creatures, a low sound began to shake the ground, causing rocks to bounce, debris to tumble back and forth, and most concerning of all… a line of skin on Luke's shoulder parted, allowing fresh blood to seep out. The tiny twinge of pain was enough to draw his attention to the two dogs next to the Lieutenant which were growling, a deep, ferocious sound. It apparently counted as some kind of area of effect sonic damage capable of ignoring his armor. The growling continued, slowly ramping up in intensity and threat level. A small silver lining was that Luke wasn't the only creature affected.

The effect seemed to be hitting anything within a certain cone in front of the summons, including the small creatures that the Lieutenant had tried to make leave the area. At least his reasoning was finally clear to the Murderhobo. Luke didn't want to be thought of as weak during combat, after all. It was nice to know that his enemy wasn't thinking he couldn't handle everything being thrown at him; it was his enemy not wanting to waste his limited minor summons.

As far as Luke could tell, the spell that was being used was mana-intensive, and took quite a while to ramp up before it started having serious consequences for those caught in its effects. As another small eruption of blood sent sanguine fluid flowing down his chest, Luke activated Bum Thunder and burst through the defensive line of canines stationed between himself and the Lieutenant. Just as he appeared in front of the robed man, a four-foot bone zipped through the air—and a few summons—to nestle perfectly into Luke's waiting hands as he hopped and spun.

Cookie and the Murderhobo moved as one, striking the summoned dog on the Lieutenant's right and ever so slowly destroying it. The Tier seven dog was incredibly resilient and managed to survive long enough for the Lieutenant to reposition himself. As it was being flung at a secondary summon, it burst into light and vanished, allowing Luke's swing to continue unimpeded. Were he a normal combatant, he would have been caught off-balance as the other dog leapt to take advantage of the situation. Happily, balance was his strong suit, with his Skill 'Pristine Balance' being at Tier four, level zero.

Still, he had almost never met another creature that was able to match his sheer speed, certainly not recently. As useful as Cookie was, he was forced to drop her in favor of slightly longer, most certainly faster, weapons. He didn't mind taking a hit or three, but he was certain some form of magical effect had enhanced the natural weapons of this creature. Even though its teeth *screeched* against his manifested armor—the spikes digging into its mouth and causing it to bleed–some of the damage passed through the armor to cause burning pain to his body.

Damage taken: 62 infernal damage! 169 damage resisted!
Infernal infection! -1 health per minute until the wound is treated.
Health remaining: 868/930.

"I see you're finally starting to realize the situation that you're truly in." The Lieutenant's smile grew nearly as wide as Luke's own, his eyes glittering in excitement as he confirmed the damage had begun to set in. "There is no Healer on this plane, unaligned with my faction, who can cure infernal damage. You're a dead man walking. From this point forward, no matter where you go, where you escape to, your health will be eroding. Whether it takes a day, a week, a month, or a year… eventually your Healers will grow weary of keeping you alive and let you succumb to the curse in your flesh."

"Curse in my flesh? Good idea." Running headlong into an attack, he intentionally dropped the armor around his arm and dropped his technique at the last moment in favor of allowing blood to splash into the dog's open mouth. "If that can kill a Giga ant, you shouldn't be a problem."

It took almost no time at all for the dog to begin whimpering, clawing at its own mouth and throat as the noxious poison that was Luke's blood flowed down into its stomach. 'You Need To Stop' didn't have a direct damage meter, so it was unable to guarantee that the pain itself would kill any of the summons, but he knew that either way, he would have an easier time defeating this animal if it was distracted. The Murderhobo hit it twice, left, then right, ending his combination attack by leaping into the air, pulling Cookie to him, then coming down and *cratering* the beast.

Luke savored the warmth of absolute satisfaction as the summon was reduced to shimmering lights, and he basked in the glow for a moment as he shifted his stance and prepared to take on the Lieutenant. His eyes flicked to the clearing where the man had been standing, only to be greeted by an empty horizon. He blinked and hunted around in confusion, only spotting the hastily retreating Lieutenant thanks to the sheer volume of ostentatious ornamentation flapping wildly about his robe.

"Hey! You can't just run away in the middle of a duel!" Luke bellowed at the man as he started giving chase.

"Watch me!" The Lieutenant laughed wildly as he secured himself within the inner depths of his army, which closed behind him in a practiced sequence and raised their weapons in preparation of their impending deaths. "The next time you see me, I will be standing above you, watching the light fade from your eyes!"

"You can't just *run away* in the *middle* of a *fight!*" Luke howled in fury as he began taking his anger out on the assembled troops. After a swing or two, he was obscured by a mist of falling blood droplets. Yet, no matter how quickly he eliminated and chased, the Murderhobo was unable to locate the cowardly Lieutenant. He screamed in rage, walloping every last one of the Dynasty soldiers that threw themselves against the meat grinder of his attacks. "More! More! *Hobo Holler!*"

His words pealed across the landscape, bringing all eyes on him.

CHAPTER TWENTY-TWO

Luke blinked blood out of his eyes, hunting for his next targets. The enemy army was in a rout, at least the portion nearest him, and was working to maintain a solid perimeter of a few hundred meters of clear space around him at all times. It wasn't doing much to help them, as he could outrun any of the basic humans with barely any effort. Regardless, now that he had been deprived of a worthy adversary, his annoyance had increased to unexpected levels. Destroying these base humans was as simple to him as swiping a quill over a figure to strike it from a document was for an accountant.

Happily, things began to shift quickly, though in a literal way, which was slightly more concerning than he wanted to let on. At first, Luke thought it was his imagination, but a quick glance confirmed that either the ground beneath his feet was lifting higher, or the land supporting his enemies was sinking slightly. Only half an hour after it began, it was obvious that some large-scale magic was at work. Seeing as it was constant, and slow, and impacting the earth... Luke immediately recognized who was responsible. "Andre is up to something."

Both armies had retreated, clearing enough space that the end result was apparent at a glance. As far as Luke could see in either direction, the Hollow Kingdom's side of the border had lifted nearly four feet into the air. Such a low cliff wasn't an insurmountable challenge or impediment to anyone who had some kind of Potentia, but to the common soldiers, it might as well have been a castle wall.

The earthen barrier was certainly more *secure* than a castle wall, seeing as they would literally have to tunnel through it, or build ramps, in order to conquer the bulwark that it presented. The handiwork of the Druid didn't stop there, and soon all areas within five paces of that new border wall had sunk even *farther* into the ground, then filled with spikes that grew directly from the earth itself.

It was clear to see that there was nothing special about these spikes. No ores were involved–in fact, it appeared that the native stone was rather weak and would break away at the first hint of being disturbed. Such brittleness would make it all the more deadly against fleshy targets, if they fell onto the spikes and were impaled. Cleaning the wounds would become nearly impossible, and in the unsavory conditions that these armies were forced to camp in, it was highly likely that the embedded fragments would lead to infection. From there, the possibility of disease spreading among the enemy forces could only grow.

Luke was incredibly impressed by his friend's ingenuity. Even though these changes were happening slowly, they were obvious, as well as being highly effective. Deciding that he had done enough for the day—mostly because he was bored of the constant slaughter—he hopped up the strange new tectonic shelf and set his course toward the greatest concentration of mana produced amongst his countrymen. Following that energy signature would lead him directly to his team… or at least that was the thought.

Instead, he was led to a man who looked strangely familiar talking with a group of soldiers in Hollow Kingdom armor as they huddled around a small campfire. The fact that the camp-fire had been built in the middle of the battlefield demonstrated exactly how long these troops had been in this area, likely overnight, due to the constant pressing of the dynasty's forces. The Murderhobo's presence quieted the soldiers, but not the man who was speaking. No, that man gave him a jaunty wave and a wink as he continued with hardly a hiccup. Luke scrutinized the face for a long minute, took a deep breath, and walked away with only a tiny roll of his eyes. "If Zed wants to play with the locals, why not?"

That was when things started getting weird. The next knot of dense mana revealed yet another man who had a slightly strange, familiar countenance. Luke walked directly up to him, grabbed the man by the shirt, and pulled him close. "How many of you *are* there in the area?"

This one's features had seemed drastically different from the last clone he had encountered, but now that he was this close, Luke could tell that the man he grasped was just wearing makeup, or at least a combination of dirt and blood that had formed naturally and obscured his appearance from a distance. "Hello, Luke! At last count, there were ten of me around. The original me has us come to the front lines to learn about all of the scuttlebutt in the area whenever we have accomplished our original mission. Doesn't hurt that us being in the ranks with the other men means a real person gets saved whenever we fall."

Luke straightened the Zed clone and dropped his meaty hands on the man's slight shoulders. "I don't *like* this. You're worth more than being a throwaway. I'm going to find you and talk to you."

"You are talking to me. But you don't mean *me*, me. Do you? I'm here in person? You should get me out of here; it's too dangerous." Replica Zed seemed somewhat choked up as he tried to get a hug from the Murderhobo. He failed, as Luke was far too cautious to be easily trapped in a position where he wouldn't be able to maintain his full range of motion. "I know you probably didn't intend it that way, but what you just said was… very kind. Believe me, we agree. None of us throw our lives away casually. Even so, we are homunculi. Whenever any of us meet, we discuss our existence and what it means. We have settled on this definition: we're not truly people, and we have this knowledge from the moment that we are created. It's our *honor* to rescue someone who will go on to do other *real* things in the world."

Luke searched the other faces around the flickering campfire, noting that the people that had been conversing with Zed had life in their eyes and could still find a way to smile, even though they were bivouacked in the epicenter of a slaughter zone. He finally recognized that, even though the Bard standing before him might not be a real person, he was having a real impact on the people around him. Nodding stiffly at the copy of his friend, he started walking away. "Be well."

Even amidst the hubbub of an encampment, Luke could still hear the whispered, "I will."

Unwilling to risk any farther detours, he used his standard sight instead of honing in on any specific mana clumping, allowing him to pick out the only pure white swath in this murky area. Knowing he had found Taylor, he wove through the clusters of soldiers in time to overhear her animated conversation with some type of officer of the Hollow Kingdom's military. She was standing, looming more like, over Andre. "I understand your position, General; however, I cannot allow you to interfere with the Archdruid's undertaking. If he believes that this is the best thing for the land, I guarantee you that it is."

"But what about the *kingdom*, you daft Spellweaver?" The General practically howled in fury as he tried to win what had devolved into a circular argument. "We have treaties preventing exactly the sorts of actions your group has taken! You're going to throw us into a full massacre instead of a mere invasion *game!*"

"We have our orders, and you have yours," Taylor coolly stated as she stared the general down. "You *won't* be interrupting the Archdruid; his work is far too important."

Luke was increasingly impressed as he watched the Mage work her verbal magic instead of blasting the person yelling at her with actual magic. Even a few years ago, this General would be either a blood splatter or on his way to a political prison of some kind at this point in the conversation. It was nice to see how she had changed in a real-world setting.

Anyone could make claims about how well they were doing; very few people were able to prove the truth of the matter with their actions. Still, the fuming General was in his way, so the Murderhobo casually slapped him to the side as he walked up to his party. "Getting boring out there. Can we get moving yet?"

"The King's orders were to do everything that was required to ensure the success of our mission." Andre was the one who answered, demonstrating that he had some awareness even within such deep a meditation as he had sunk himself into. "I am merely doing everything I can to ensure that we will have a kingdom to return *to*. I am not going to fail this quest because of some ridiculous loophole."

Luke pondered that for a moment, silently agreeing with the decision. Needing something to occupy himself in the meantime, the Murderhobo's eyes landed on the armory, and he set off in that direction without a word. He'd only made it a few steps when Zed, finally looking like he was supposed to look, popped up in front of Luke with a knowing smile on his face. "Why, hello there, friend! I don't know if you remember, but you're not the only person who is at the warfront! These fine people around us are going to need those sets of armor and weapons, and there is going to be no benefit for you to have them, anyway."

"There was a Lieutenant on the field that actually gave me a challenge. He had a really nice robe that I want. How was he so much stronger than *our* officers?" This blatant disregard for the general, who wasn't even a few feet away, didn't go unnoticed.

Zed put his arms up as though he were performing a sun salutation, then swept them out while dropping them to his sides. "The dynasty is a big, *big* country. Think of how big you think it is, then make it three times bigger than that at the minimum. Now you have one *province* of the dynasty. Even without factoring in their ambient mana saturation being significantly more dense, if their average population only produces the same percentage of Ascenders our kingdom does, they've got us beat nearly two hundred times over."

"Wow." Luke deadpanned.

"Very wow. Much Ascender. With so many to choose from, they have many more options than we do. The only people who can attain positions of power are the people that earn it. Even their Emperor is required to control a Tier-nine or ten summon in order to take the throne when their predecessor Ascends to a higher world. At least in theory, because the rumor is that the person on the throne has *always* been there."

"Interesting. Instead of trying to make one perfect Ascender and dump all the resources into them…" Taylor's features took on a worrisome, considering look, "They just churn out Ascender after Ascender, knowing that they will separate themselves into the hierarchy simply by merit alone. If only we could mimic that in our kingdom! Think of how powerful we would be, if we were able to take a tiny kingdom and pack it full of incredibly powerful-"

She cut off her musings, realizing that reintegrating the Scarrocco Nature Preserve into the kingdom might have made that vision a reality already. Only time would tell, but bringing that possibility up when anyone could be listening in was likely not the best way to keep that secret to themselves.

"Something is happening." Andre suddenly took over the stunted conversation, his eyes popping open as he launched himself to his feet. "I think the dynasty is bringing their Druids into the area; my influence over their land just got shoved back. If Druids are approaching the lines, I think we're about to see a big push by their Ascenders."

"You've killed us all!" The General threw his hands in the air and walked away, appearing more like a broken man than a leader of them. "How long do we have, Druid?"

"Judging by the shifting wind, the trembling earth, and the threat of violence that is filling my heart…" Andre's words were dramatic, to the point that Luke rolled his eyes back into his head so hard he involuntarily blinked a few times. "Not long enough."

CHAPTER TWENTY-THREE

- TAYLOR -

Taylor was *not* excited to fight in this war. There was no benefit to her, nor for her team, and even the enemy armies were treating it as a training exercise more than a real war. Even so, she wouldn't abandon her countrymen to the fate that was awaiting them if her team departed from the field of battle.

She hoped everyone would be on the same page as her, as she took a deep breath and started directing her friends into what she hoped would be the most effective battle position. Unsurprisingly, their resident Murderhobo would be taking point, Andre would be entirely focused on solidifying his connection to the land and defending against other Druids who would be pushing to break his control. Zed would... Taylor looked around, noticing that the Bard who had been by her side only a few minutes ago had vanished without a trace. Seething internally, she hissed through gritted teeth, "I guess Zed will be doing whatever *he* wants to be doing."

If he influenced their battle the way he normally did, providing overwatch and whispering into their ears of threats and positioning, she would be happy. Even so, she knew better than to count on it. Zed was under the same orders as they were, and her biggest fear had been that he would completely abandon their team and make his way to the capital of the dynasty on his own.

There was even a good chance that he would someday succeed, but he would take the orders literally, spending as much time practicing his Masteries as he could while traveling closer to the seat of power and finding the missing princess. She only hoped Zed wouldn't make that same realization.

Boom.

As Andre had clearly warned, there truly wasn't much time between his announcement and the arrival of a squad of Ascenders. Clearly, they had been stationed near the border as a quick-reaction force, but each of them, even from this distance, was exuding pure excitement and bloodlust. If Luke wasn't standing directly in front of her, she would have thought he was staring her down from their opponents' side of the battle-ground. The Murderhobo stretched and cracked his neck. "Those guys look as bored as I feel."

"The fact that you're looking at them as though they're real people concerns me." Andre quietly released the thought that had been trapped in his head. Taylor eyed the Druid sharply, but he explained without hesitation, "Come on, you know as well as I do that every time Luke looks at someone and views them as a 'real' person, that means that they have extremely dense personal power. Even the Royal Guard looked like fluffy caricatures, so what level of power are we thinking that group is going to bring to bear against us?"

"Three of them look green, like you do," Luke pointed out the Druids to him. Taylor confirmed after a moment, her eyes easily as sharp as the Murderhobo's. "The rest of them wear a bandolier of dried bones and meat, so they could be Necro-mancers or Dog Tamers."

"Going by the theme and proximity of the Dynasty of Dogs," Andre let out a light chuckle, "I can only hope that they're Necromancers, so they're weaker than the others. I have my doubts. If that is their quick-reaction force, as Taylor seemed to suggest, we're likely looking at the command structure of this army. If a Lieutenant somehow didn't get crushed by you, what would a Captain, a Colonel, or a General look like?"

"A good time."

"No."

Taylor decided that their rambling had gone on long enough. "If one of them is truly a high level-commander, that means he's also going to be an extremely powerful Doggutorēnā."

"Gesundheit," Andre called over.

"That is the title of their Ascenders," Taylor explained impatiently. "Since they have the strongest ties to that world in the dynasty, they have the ability to create the etymology. It just doesn't easily translate to our language."

"Doggu. Tah-rainer." Luke broke it down into multiple syllables, frowning thoughtfully. "Seems like it would translate just fine as 'dog trainer'. It's actually somewhat refreshing to find a group of Ascenders who aren't sniffing their own stink and swearing it smells like roses."

"You know *I* like it when people are down to earth," the Druid joined in on the joke.

For a moment, Taylor considered creating a portal and just leaving. Forcing herself to take a deep breath, she reminded herself that these two irreverent men's lives weren't the only ones at stake. "Luke, if there is anything that you can do to keep their attention off of the common people, I would appreciate it. I will try to defend against—*what!*"

A massive dog, easily fifty feet tall and thirty feet wide had materialized in front of the group they had been tracking. It bit the air and gently pulled back, and the atmosphere around them shifted, drawing in toward the dog. It took Taylor a moment to realize that it wasn't the wind actually blowing, but rather her sense of the free-flowing mana of the area had changed. Before she could react to the shift, a massive Spell circle formed in front of the dog's face, and a glowing orb of power began to pulsate in the center of the swiftly completing ring.

"Luke, throw me!" Taylor ordered, not getting a word of complaint from the Murderhobo as he grabbed her with both hands, spun, and launched her like a javelin directly at the giant, pulsing field of mana that had appeared practically out of nowhere. She wasn't exactly sure how she was going to land, but that wasn't the issue at hand.

It only took two seconds of flight to reach the top of the parabolic arc before her trajectory started slowly drawing her downward. At that moment, a beam of mana lanced forward, directly toward where she had been standing in front of the command tent.

"*Nullify!*" It was unlikely that she would have needed to cast the Spell herself, as there was a built-in safety feature that would have activated the Spell as soon as she sensed the incoming danger. Still, she didn't want to risk any accidents, and as the Spell disintegrated harmlessly upon impact with her and was completely destroyed at the same time, she was glad that she had made that choice.

Even though the core of the Spell was broken, the land that it had traveled over was suffering greatly from its passing. Despite behaving as a beam, it had rained thick globules of corrosive dog slobber which landed on people below, their own countrymen, burning through flesh and leaving behind putrid, diseased corpses.

Meta-Magic has captured: Yelp of the Gelert (Tier seven). At the cost of 500 mana, create a beam of mana-infused air that will penetrate nearly any armor. In passing, the Yelp of the Gelert will rain acidic slobber that destroys and putrefies any flesh it encounters.

"Neat, can't even use it." It was just her luck that the first time the Spell captured an effect from an enemy, it would be too specialized to replicate. She was extremely perturbed to find that it hadn't listed all of the different capabilities that the Spell could and should create. As far as she knew, there was no deviation from the Ascender formulae, where each Tier of Spell gave a specific benefit. Could it possibly be because she didn't understand the Spell or anything about it before capturing it? Could she only capture a fraction of its potential power? There were so many things to test about this new branch of magic. As much as she wanted to test her theory farther, run her hypothesis, she was currently falling.

As she now understood, the attack she had just blocked had created a funnel of moving air to continue outward, and Nullify had stripped the mana from it. However, that hadn't canceled out the physics of the Spell itself. To her delight, the air continued onward, slowing her momentum and even buoying her backward as though she were a kite flying in a hurricane. A quick glance confirmed that she was going to fall on her side of the border, so she spread her arms wide and tried to land as flat as possible.

Exactly as she had hoped, the grass reached out to break her fall, and the ground beneath turned into a soft sand that let her sink in without damaging her body. There was little chance of her being hurt either way, thanks to her Etheric Xenograft Potentia-enhanced body. Even so, it was nice to know that she had someone to rely on who would literally catch her when she fell. She bounced up to land gracefully on her feet, hurrying back to where her team had remained standing.

Zed had returned and was currently standing in front of Luke, hands flung out to the side while dodging in front of the big man whenever he started to make a motion to leave. The Bard looked over his shoulder at the sound of her approach, a relieved smile appearing on his face. "Look, everyone! Taylor is back!"

"What happened after I blocked that shot?" Taylor was nervous that they would need to continue combat; her trump card had been played immediately. Now it was going to be necessary to let the attacks land where they were aimed, and she had no way to stop them.

Andre had been keeping an eye on the overall battle, so it came as no surprise that he was the one to respond. "They looked more confused than anything? I think that was a fairly demoralizing effect for the enemy army, considering the attack came from their own leadership and only damaged their own people, while one of ours canceled it out. I don't know if you heard all of the soldiers from the Hollow Kingdom cheering for you, but they were. Oh, last thing–that giant dog vanished."

"Must have been a canine likeness that creates an effect but is unable to actually do any fighting on its own." Taylor mulled over their situation but didn't see an easy answer on how to move forward. Thanks to her team's greatly enhanced senses, it was obvious to them the exact moment that the opposing Ascenders began summoning additional dogs. The Mage looked over at Andre as he winced and grabbed at the side of his head, sinking to the ground in a lotus position.

"The Druids are working in concert to break my influence over this land." He took a deep breath and smirked, his eyes already closed as power raced out from him. "I think they're going to have a very bad time. In fact, I'm gonna make sure of it."

Taylor watched the border, where the earth had suddenly started trembling. The wall that had grown under Andre's control began to buckle, then stabilized. It was clear that a monumental amount of effort was being expended, and she hoped that her friend would be able to succeed.

First a trickle, then a flood of dogs began pouring from around the Dynasty Ascenders, mingling with the ranks of the infantry and howling, barking, and nipping at ankles until the entire invasion force was moving forward as one. Fear wasn't Taylor's preferred motivator, but in situations like this, it was obviously effective. She turned her attention to her kingdom's forces, realizing that if the wall fell, they would be overrun in no time flat. "Luke, you and I are going to go and even the odds. Zed, keep a lookout for us and protect Andre while he works."

"Before you go…" Andre cracked one eye while keeping the

other tightly shut, looking over at Luke. "Just in case, can I get a bottle of liquid mana?"

The Murderhobo hesitated, studied the amassing enemy forces, and gently snarled. He pulled out a dark blue waterskin and gingerly nestled it on the dirt in front of the Druid. "It's not *just* liquid mana in there. If you have to open this, contain it so that you don't just die."

Luke seemed nervous at handling the container, making the entire team stare at it in great concern. With no choice but to follow her own instructions, Taylor and Luke hastened toward the impending battle. Even so, she couldn't help herself and glanced back over her shoulder several times. "I hope I didn't leave behind a situation even more dangerous than the one I'm heading into."

"Same," the Murderhobo agreed, not at all assuaging her fears.

CHAPTER TWENTY-FOUR

Taylor peered up at Luke, trying to puzzle out a way for them to coordinate their efforts in the upcoming chaos. Even if Zed used his strange Mastery that allowed him to whisper directly into their ears, she was uncertain if it would be effective over the din of battle. "I trust that I will be able to find you wherever the fighting is the most difficult?"

"Yes." Luke didn't even attempt to sound reassuring, merely stating his answer as an absolute fact. "Stay out of the way."

"Right; that's what I'm trying to figure out before we're in the thick of it. How can we coordinate our attacks so you don't Shockwave me to death, and I don't accidentally blast a hole through you?" Her concerns earned her a snort of derision, and she raised an eyebrow at him. "I have multiple Tier seven and higher Spells. I feel confident that some of them could accidentally hit you and deal significant damage."

To prove her point, she started casting *Thunder Beast's Eye*, investing one hundred mana for the initial cost, then began charging it. Layer after layer of dense electrical power was packed in, and the fact that she had been able to boost the Spell to level nine had decreased the additional cost for adding extra lightning strikes to only twenty-five mana per every five bolts. The Spell that had once been practically impossible for her to control now allowed her to walk around with the equivalent lightning capacity of a true thunderstorm.

It carried fifteen charges in total, which would generate seventy-five strikes before the eye would dissipate. Between the lightning and the sonic damage formed after each strike, she could deal approximately seventeen thousand damage. Her main limitation was going to be the fact that the Spell had a maximum time limit of five minutes, at which point it wouldn't merely discharge its power, but instead fizzle out entirely. Luke pointed up, then nodded as if she had made some kind of grand gesture. "Good. I will be able to avoid hitting you, if you keep this thing up."

"Great, you will know where not to hit me, but only if I keep a giant target painted on my head," she sarcastically rebutted, her nerves getting the best of her for a moment. A meager nine mana remained in her total pool of four hundred eighty-six, but she was able to fully refill her power in approximately seventy-seven seconds. That gave her some peace of mind as she continued preparing her battle. "You're pretty sensitive to mana, right? What if I start upgrading my Nullify Spell? It's on cooldown anyway, so I might as well use this time to bump it up in power. Will you be able to follow those fluctuations and figure out where I am?"

"You're overthinking this," Luke promised her, though the anxious clenching in her gut disagreed. "Feel free. Who knows? Might be useful. Plus, if we survive this, you get a boosted Spell. More strength is better."

Not seeing any downside to upgrading the Spell immediately, beyond disliking her main defensive option being out of commission—and it already was—she added the final one hundred Potentia into the Spell, causing it to begin the process of upgrading to Tier five. She had slowly been adding the strange energy to the Spell over time in preparation for a scenario just like this. The chaotic energies of the world shifted toward her, far faster for her than they had for Zed, even though the two of them held the same potency within their Mana Channels. "Being bound to the world pays off again."

She attributed the higher speed to yet another side effect of the Earthen Node drawing her into its power and restructuring her body from the ground up. She paused and considered using that saying as a joke for Andre later; she was sure it would prompt a chuckle from him. As far as Taylor could tell, unlike her Druid friend, there seemed to be no negative drawbacks to the trait that had been added to her. The world didn't request or require anything of her—it merely changed how things worked for her to a very slight degree.

But the time for philosophizing had passed, and about half of her pool of mana had replenished since she had created the eye in the sky. Happily, she didn't need to forcibly insert herself into the press of bodies that was forming along the shoulder-height border wall. Since her lightning Spell was hovering in the air above her head, she designated a target and allowed the charged storm to move.

Zzt. *Boom.*

The delay between the strike of the lightning and the subsequent sonic damage was less than half a second, but it was still distinctly noticeable for anyone close to it. There was an odd incongruence to it, and she watched curiously as the deadly light passed through scores of bodies that didn't know they were already corpses, only for them to *jiggle* a moment later as the concussive retort converted the fried air to thunder.

That was enough for the cooked bodies of the basic humans to explode as though a necromancer were using a particularly nasty Spell.

She wouldn't have wasted her mana on the press of people, had it not been for the Dire Wolf-sized hound that was prowling amongst them, exuding a red mist that seemed to egg the nearby combatants on to higher heights. The lightning struck true, and the summoned aspect of the wolf vanished with a pained howl.

Damage dealt: 270! 225 Lightning damage, 45 sonic damage.

"One bolt used, seventy-four to go." In almost all other circumstances, Taylor would have put her chances of absolute, crushing success near one hundred percent guaranteed. Faced with the vast array of forces aligned against her, she could only swallow her fear and try to focus on taking out high-value targets. "I see a dog over there, but I can't find its summoner... where could they be hiding? How far away from an Ascender can their summoned creature go, or is it fully autonomous?"

There was no one nearby with whom she could dissect her concerns and hopes. She decided that, if the Ascenders were opting to hide in the very back lines instead of joining in combat, it was very possible she was going to scream. Another bolt of lightning arced out from the eye in the sky above her, startling her nearly as much as the creature it had caught. The biggest difference between the two was that she was able to survive the use of the bolt. That thought made her smirk, but it also enticed her to focus on the battle at hand, instead of speculating what the battle could turn into.

With the opposing army rushing toward them at full speed, Taylor ultimately decided that her priority should be working to take down any Druid she could locate. The flows of mana shifted back and forth, faster than they had any right to be doing naturally, which was a clear indication of the fight Andre was putting up against the enemy Ascenders.

To his great credit, and her delight, unless the opposing group of Druids managed to work together, Andre was able to hold and maintain his influence over any given area. As the dynasty's legions moved forward, they were forced to walk across a handful of rough stone bridges that had been hastily created by the Ascenders on their side.

They were only able to maintain a few of these siege ramps, which rose over the stone spike pit and connected to the top of the short earthen wall that Andre had generated. Working in tandem, the opposing Druids were able to set up five such points, although anytime they tried to exceed that, Andre would push back and directly dissolve the work they had completed, dropping tens of men onto the stone spikes and likely ensuring their death. Each time a bridge was dismantled, it seemed to become harder for the Druids to retake the same location.

Taylor knew that this was a byproduct of having an influx of blood that was automatically absorbed and used by her Druid's Abilities, expanding and solidifying his influence over the area. Even without actively working to wrestle the land away from his opposition, Andre's influence started creeping farther into the Dynasty of Dogs' terrain with each new death.

The Mage's eyes snagged on a man that seemed slightly out of place, the people around him standing awkwardly straight and sweating more than the physical exertion should produce. With a slight squint, she zeroed in on him and directed her lightning to lash out.

A small dog, which could not have weighed more than five pounds, jumped in front of the bolt and seemed to be fully confident in stopping it. To the trainer's great credit, that bolt was fully expended on the tiny beast and went no farther—nor did the dog's life on this plane of existence. The man pointed at the eye, and Taylor heard a slight, "Ha!"

The follow-up bolt took the Ascender in the face, deleting him as a threat for the future.

Deciding to become more actively involved, Taylor reserved her lightning for an active defense and instead used her fully regenerated mana pool to cast Frozen Trident and Fingers of Flame as rapidly as possible. Fingers of Flame had once upon a time been known as Flame Lance, and its increased Tier allowed her to create five lances of flames, one over each finger on a hand, and launch them at different enemies. That was a strange restriction that this Spell had: each of the lances must impact or at least be targeted at a distinct target. When the flames hit, they were currently dealing four-hundred-fifty damage per lance.

Frozen Trident had been upgraded from Shatter Shot. Its Tier four Multitarget Bonus allowed the spawned spike of ice to detonate into three smaller spikes that launched out at oblique angles from the original projectile, though none would ever move backward. This allowed her to use it without fear of inflicting friendly fire on herself. However, those angles were otherwise random, and while the fragments could hit the same target multiple times, most often, they would fly to the sides and take out other creatures if they were nearby.

More often than not, when fighting a single creature, only the initial blow would hit, while the other spikes would split off and zip into the ground or off in a different, still useless, direction. Even so, she considered it a phenomenal upgrade, primarily because each of the newly generated spikes would deal full damage, which meant that each shard of ice at this level was impacting for two hundred forty-five damage. Taylor still had the option to purposely shatter the Spell before it landed, giving her a higher chance of sending three full-powered shards into a single target.

However, she hadn't figured out a way to control that, other than getting it as close as possible to the target before making it *pop*. If that managed to land, she could hit a single target for seven hundred thirty-five damage, which was spread between the damage types of ice and force. This allowed her to hurt a creature, even if it was resistant to one of those two types. *Very* few creatures could ever be resistant to both.

With her game plan in mind, Taylor began stalking the battlefield, searching out any other Ascenders that she could find. Whenever she did manage to locate one, lightning would herald her realization. Soon, she had to order the eye to float in a different direction than she was actually looking, otherwise the Ascenders would duck deeper into the cover of the expendable bodies around them or retreat fully until she passed by.

"Well, at least I'm getting good practice with my other Spells as well." Taylor reluctantly allowed, burning a screaming Ascender's heart out with a Finger of Flame and causing the basic humans around him to sizzle and melt as they became the unwitting distinct targets that the Spell required. "Hopefully, I can get used to this fast enough that I stop puking every time I need to kill another person."

She grimaced and wiped her mouth with her pristine robe, leaving a small streak that vanished as her passive Spells cleaned her up. With no other choice but forward, her hunt continued.

CHAPTER TWENTY-FIVE

- LUKE -

"This is more like it." The Murderhobo looked on approvingly as the enemy forces put themselves in nice, neat rows, packed densely together so that they could try and diffuse the force of any heavy weapons coming their way. He knew that it wouldn't help them against *him*, but there was no possible way that *they* could know it. Patience had never been his forte; it always confused him when people would say such pithy sayings as 'good things come to those who wait'. In his experience, standing around doing nothing was a good way to be killed.

Even so, he wanted to know what Taylor was planning. Over the next few minutes, he saw her surgically strike into the crowd, and each time she did so, various dogs would vanish off the battlefield. As far as he could tell, she was targeting Ascenders, and he decided that might be a fun thing to do as well. "At least it will be more interesting than only taking out a bunch of pathetic humans that are here seeking 'glory' in death, or something. No need to give them what they're actually looking for."

As he contemplated the forces, he tried to figure out where

exactly the Ascenders were hiding—thinking that perhaps he should try the game of taking them down with as few additional casualties as possible—he realized that the press of people had a secondary effect that was somewhat frustrating. All of those lives together tended toward hiding the stronger life among them. Not perfectly, but he could not work out the exact position of the truly powerful among them. Still, he had what he considered to be a great idea.

"If I only kill a few dozen people and the Ascender, it's still less wasteful than breaking all of them, right?" Then he remembered that all of them were enemies anyway, so it didn't particularly matter if they got what they wanted. If they were seeking glory in death, maybe they would find it. He could help them. Luke switched his equipped weapon manifestation to a bottle he had found so long ago, then aimed it carefully at center mass of the area that seemed to have a large congruence of power.

"*Hup!*"

He activated Shockwave on the bottle, just as it started to leave his hand, and the mana-glass flew true. It struck the first line of humans, the force more than adequate to annihilate and obliterate every human in a cone from that point to nearly the end of the ranks. But only almost all of them. There were two Ascenders who had been hiding in that area, and they were still on their feet, even if they were swaying slightly and bleeding heavily.

Luke jumped over the defensive line, running at the two Dog Tamers who remained in this section of the fight. He heard calls for him to return to his own people, to stop putting himself at risk, but thanks to the King's orders... he was as autonomous as it was possible to be at this point. So long as he was doing *something* to further the completion of his quest, no one could order him to do *anything* he didn't want to do. *Everything* was on the table, including actually having fun in combat. "This is refreshing. I like this."

"Who are you? How dare you attack us, Officers of The Hunt! Do you know how many treaties you have broken simply by standing where you are at this moment?" The man on the right didn't have fancy clothes, which was somewhat of a disappointment to Luke. He hoped that this man would at least have some sort of fun combat ability. "Hey! What are you-"

The spear that manifested in Luke's right hand skewered the shouting man, then nearly bisected him as it was ripped out to the side. Luke's expression shifted to a scowl, and he looked over at the other Ascender who was still on his feet. "Are you as boring as this guy was?"

"You're one sick puppy," the man stated in Luke's language —heavily accented—then followed up with some other unintelligible language that Luke didn't care to try and parse. All the Murderhobo knew for certain was that this man most definitely wasn't as boring. Even if his clothes were more functional than the Lieutenant's from his irritatingly unresolved fight earlier in the day, they were still fairly grand. He also managed to summon two dogs before Luke was upon him, though these creatures were far closer to real dogs than the Berserker had expected.

They looked similar to Presa Canario, whereas every other dog he had seen brought onto the field was some kind of mythological greater species. Perhaps this man was a non-commissioned officer tasked with guiding and leading troops. At least that would explain why at least two of his summons were extremely large dogs mostly meant for guarding and herding cattle. Unfortunately for this man, 'not boring' wasn't exactly a resounding guarantee of being able to survive for any length of time.

Damage Dealt: 112 stabbing. 212 damage lost in overkill!

"I thought the Ascenders of the dynasty were supposed to be stronger than my kingdom's usual stock." Luke spat to the side, frustrated with how the day had been going so far. Either his enemy had been too slippery and escaped combat, or so weak it wasn't worth engaging them in the first place. "Pathetic."

A new voice intruded into his ear holes, notable only in that it was calm even though the person it belonged to was standing in a field of absolute carnage. "Perhaps you're looking for a greater challenge? I suppose I can play with you, if you're a good boy."

Before even turning to take in the visage of his new opponent, Luke threw a bottle at them. Only when he heard a loud *clink* of it being deflected and no damage notification showing up to block his view, did Luke bother to turn around and look. There was a young man standing there, someone who looked to be roughly twenty years old, holding a short whip in one hand and a wooden chair—of all things—in the other. "Can you fight? Or are you just going to die?"

"I can tell you true, Ascender of the Hollow kingdom, that this glorious champion has no intent of an ignoble loss in a churned cesspit such as this." The young man bowed forward slightly. "You may call me-"

"Don't care." Luke activated Bum Thunder and crossed the distance between them, leading with his left hand just to get some additional practice using a spear on that side. No reason not to get better at the same time as defeating an enemy. The chair swung up, blocking the sharpened tip of his weapon, and to Luke's surprise… the attack ended there. He jolted to a stop, finding that his momentum had been arrested by the seemingly simple seating implement.

"Bad. *No.*" The Ascender lightly whipped Luke's outstretched arm, the length of braided leather failing to do anything other than get a slight rip as it struck against his spiky armor. "There are rules of decorum to be followed when fighting, even when you're fighting for your life or your honor!"

"Honor is stupid. What good is your standing and reputation, if you don't survive the fight?" Luke could already tell that this was going to be a fun time, and so he mentally called for Cookie to start making her way toward him. Until then, he switched weapons, equipping a Battering Ram Knuckle on his left and his Scourge on his right. With a quick punch, he caused the other man to take a single step back, then Luke leapt into the air and reached out with his Scourge. "That's not a whip. *This* is a whip."

"No, they're *both* whips." The still-calm assailant countered the attack with his chair, and the words with a ghost of a smile showing on his lips. "I am so glad I stepped forward to meet you today."

"We've never been formally introduced." Luke barked a laugh at his own joke, twirling his Scourge and sending it *snapping* across the air. This time, when his strike was blocked, one of the legs of the chair was broken, sending splinters of wood flying into the air. Pressing his advantage, he switched the scourge to a bottle midair, throwing it almost directly down. It hit the bottom of the chair's seat, and the strange choice in weaponry fully broke apart.

His opponent went very still as he looked down at the stick that he was currently holding. For a moment, Luke thought that he was going to get another easy, boring kill.

Then there was a drastic shift in the man's demeanor. He went from a calm, noble, and honorable officer to a fuming, spoiled child in the blink of an eye. "This was a chair from my father's table! Are you *kidding* me right now? First of all, how stupidly strong are you that you can break it? Secondly, do you even know what it's going to take to replace this thing? I'm going to have to get an entire new set of chairs for the table; otherwise, they won't match!"

The man arched his back backwards so far that Luke was sure he was about to fall over, then he flung his arms out to the side and *screamed* like a toddler having a tantrum. It seemed that was actually a defensive ability, because Luke was pushed back while he was still in midair, forced to reset before being able to capitalize on the slightly upset man's distraction. The air began to distort, and dozens of dogs began forcing themselves into this world.

These weren't the sad excuses for magical beasts that Luke had been fighting in the last few minutes. No, these were what he had been looking for from the start: a real test. Their sizes ranged anywhere from coming up to his knee to standing several feet above his head. Several of them were glowing with magical effects already; some seemed to shift in and out of reality, even though the pawprints they were leaving on the soil revealed that they were absolutely present, and a few of them appeared to be on fire.

"Hot *dog*. Now it's a party." Feeling the incoming mana signature that could only belong to one thing, Luke held out his hands and caught Cookie before landing on the ground. He didn't wait around to see what would happen. Instead, as soon as his feet were on the soil, he was once more leading the charge with his face.

Fireballs, auras of destruction, stealthy beasts popping out of nowhere to try and tear into his flesh... to Luke, it just felt like being home.

CHAPTER TWENTY-SIX

The Murderhobo wasn't going to be patient anymore. He wasn't going to give his opponent another chance to spring surprises on him, to get ready. At this point, if he wasn't able to participate in a fight worth having, Luke would simply put him down and go find someone that was more fun.

One of the dogs blew out a light blue mist that settled over Luke, held at bay in part by his armor. Even so, it slipped through whenever he would take a breath, driving into his lungs and trying to do…something. Luke was *eminently* unconcerned over that; he had been looking for something that could be the final boost his Skill needed to get to Tier four. Poison wasn't working anymore, oversaturation of mana only made him stronger, and the feeling of stagnation was stifling. For an instant, he even deactivated the armor on his head and took a deep breath, just to make sure he got the worst the man could offer.

It was a brutal collage of slaughter as he began swinging Cookie with utmost accuracy and force. The two-handed Drag-onbone Greatmace ensured that there was no surviving animal beneath its length when he lifted her up to move into another attack pattern. Flames rolled toward him, burning the air as it collapsed onto him, superheating the environment around Luke and causing a small amount of damage to leak through his armor.

He ignored it for the moment, instead intently hunting the wolf that was causing the black flames to spring up around him. Releasing Cookie, he clapped his hands around the dog's head, his thumbs pulling up and forcing its jaws shut. That cut off the flame, and he continued squeezing until he heard the thick skull *crunch* under his fingers. His overgrown fingernails plunged into the summoned creature's brain. "Slimy, yet satisfying."

The gore vanished as the dog did, and Luke moved on to the next obstacle. He heard the other man shouting things at him but mostly ignored what was said. "Did you just crush an abyssal hound's skull with your *hands*? Most people have the meat melt off of their bones as soon as they're within a few *feet* of it!"

It was bizarre to Luke that his opponent was praising him for his battle prowess. He decided at that moment that he should probably hunt down this man's entire lineage to ensure that anyone remotely similar to him wasn't allowed to exist in the future.

Judging by the variety and Tier of the dog that he was having to put down, the Murderhobo assumed that this man was someone important. Punching a ghostly hound in the snout hard enough to make it look like a pug before it disappeared, Luke looked over and assessed the quality of the clothes his opponent was wearing.

At first glance, the simple material could be mistaken as some kind of after-shower robe. Looking deeper, it was clear that the simplicity of the material was hiding a perfectly cut outfit that was designed to look understated. It was as though this were someone who was trying to blend in among lesser people but didn't understand that most people didn't have clothes made out of fabric that a family of four couldn't purchase with their entire cumulative lives' savings. Luke's tongue flicked out, running over his top lip slowly as he considered what it would feel like to wear that robe as a mana manifestation. "It's gotta be comfy."

"What, my robe?" The strange man smiled winningly, "I'm so glad you like it! It's hair from the last Dragonkin, harvested over the course of half a century, spun into the softest, most fire-and-magic-resistant yukata this world has ever seen. You have an eye for quality, and I can appreciate you appreciating me."

"Dragonkin?" Luke looked at Cookie as she performed amateur chiropractic services to a wolf that was snapping at them. She needed a lot more practice, as instead of helping that creature to be better aligned, she caused several of the vertebrae to rip out through its stomach on that last hit. Narrowing his eyes, he looked back at the man offering him false hope. "Aren't dragons covered in scales?"

"Well... yes, mostly." The man smiled almost shyly, a hint of color turning his cheeks pink. "There *is* a reason this outfit is naturally curly and perhaps a little too wiry for a non-Ascender to wear. I assure you, it has been properly cleaned."

"Bum Thunder," Luke almost casually stated, crossing the final bit of distance between himself and this odd human from another empire.

Cookie was already coming in from the man's left, Luke grunting in exertion as he leaned back and pulled, increasing her momentum to the maximum he could achieve in the short time that he had. Various magical effects started appearing around his opponent, everything from barriers to planes of force that attempted to push back against Cookie. Nothing could stall her advance, and Luke's eyes started twinkling, his eyelids pulled back so hard it was like he was falling off a cliff with the wind blowing against him.

He was going to have that... yuka... yuk... yucky outfit. Cookie got all the way to the man's cheek, going so far as to begin distorting the skin. Lightning struck the man, and it took a moment for Luke to register that some final lifesaving Spell or artifact had pulled him away.

Where it pulled him away *to*, Luke had no idea. All he knew for certain was that the man had teleported or been teleported by something else. It had literally been done at lightning speed, meaning none of Luke's Skills were fast enough to take the man down before it happened.

"No! My Pajamas!" The Murderhobo screeched as he looked around for his opponent. The Ascender was nowhere to be seen, and his surviving dogs seemed to be weakened greatly. They were panting, as if they had been running for hours, whimpering as though their Master had completely abandoned them. Luke was certain that was only partially true, and they would be summoned to that stranger's side once more, after he destroyed them. He got to it, and only one of them escaped, running in a straight line deeper into the dynasty.

His gaze trailed after that dog, somehow knowing that the escaped soon-to-be-murder victim was at the end of the path that dog was running along. He started to follow, only to find himself blocked by other Ascenders, these ones in much more functional armor and gear. It interested him, but today he was all about the yucky robes, for some reason. He started running toward the new combatants that had presented themselves to him, only to grow in frustration as Zed's voice whispered into his ear.

"Hello there, Lukey!" The sing-song, teasing voice of the Bard only caused the Murderhobo to grow more agitated, to put a tiny bit more force behind each strike. "Taylor says that we need to get off the battlefield right away. Something bad is happening, and we need to make sure to take advantage of the distraction. I can practically guarantee a whole bunch of people are about to get turned into dust, and you're in the line of fire."

"I can take it!" Luke twisted out of the way of a lunging three-headed dog, turning the momentum into a backhand on its Trainer. The attack ripped the man's lower mandible off of his head entirely, leaving a bleeding mess with a tongue hanging out in the open as the trainer tried to gargle new commands at his dogs.

"Pretty sure you can't!" Zed cheerfully deflected. "Turns out, this fight has gotten way too big. Now a whole bunch of higher-level Ascenders are getting involved. Taylor estimates about three minutes before Archmage Don shows up and starts blastin'."

Luke didn't pause, though he was startled by the information. "You mean to tell me that the Archmage is going to be here, out in the open, *distracted*… sometime in the next couple of minutes?"

"That's exactly what I mean." Zed's voice was dark, as he knew exactly what Luke was thinking and was happy to encourage it. "As soon as I have his coordinates, I will let you know immediately."

Luke hopped into the air, swinging Cookie up as though he were going to bring her down in an overhead chop. His opponents flinched and tried to dodge out of the way, but the Murderhobo had never intended to follow through on the strike. While in midair, he activated Bum Thunder, appearing ten meters behind his starting location. He turned and threw Cookie back toward his home country's territory, then manifested the Scourge in his right hand, grabbing the end of it with his other hand.

He was surrounded on all sides by enemies, so he didn't have to be cautious with his next moves. Even so, he had been testing out a new movement technique and decided it was the perfect time to put it into use. Swinging the scourge up into the air, it created a perfect parabolic arc over his head.

Then he brought it down, hard, as he hopped over it. The rope impacted the ground, the force of it throwing him higher up. As he reached the peak of his momentum, he brought the weapon up behind him then down again, remaining in the air the entire time without needing to have his feet touch the ground.

The scourge whirled through the air as fast as his wildly

enhanced muscles could make it happen, making it appear as though he were levitating as he moved along. Whatever got in the way of the mana-manifested scourge was dealt blunt damage then partially shredded as the blades popped out of its braids. In under a minute, Luke had used his self-created movement technique 'Jump Rope of Doom' to return to his countrymen, and he dismissed the scourge as he sailed over the border wall.

Seeing as his travel had destroyed all of the enemies that would otherwise be pressing against this point, the soldiers had a few free moments to watch him in absolute awe, some of them breaking out into claps, cheering, or whistles. "Hero of the battle! Luke, Luke, Luke!"

Other soldiers started taking up the chant, only for a familiar-looking simulacrum of Zed to slightly shift the chant to a more recognizable form. "Hero of the battle! Murderhobo, Murderhobo, *Murderhobo!*"

Luke huffed in annoyance as his legal last name was chanted up and down the lines. "What are you all so excited about? I only killed a few thousand people. It's just a regular day for me."

That got a round of laughter started, and the whistles increased in volume. Most of the clapping had completely stopped, their hands needed for weapons or shields. Truly not understanding their excitement, Luke found his group, his eyes peeled for any sign of the Archmages' arrival. He locked eyes with Zed, who shook his head slightly to indicate that the Archmage hadn't yet poked his head into the area.

Then Luke heard the words that he knew would be coming soon, but nearly caused his anger to completely boil over. Taylor had her hands in the air and was pushing mana out in a familiar pattern. "Get ready, everyone. As soon as we have a guaranteed distraction, we need to make a break for it and start our stealth operation. We won't have long before the Imperial hounds are called to sniff us out, if they realize that we're within the boundaries of their empire, so speed is of the essence."

"Can we wait two and a half more minutes?" Luke's words earned him a suspicious glance from Andre as well as from Taylor.

The Druid was still mostly focused on holding back his opposing Ascenders but retained the presence of mind to vocalize his inquiry. "That's a fairly specific amount of time, Luke. Any particular reason you would like to give me?"

"No."

Taylor tried next, though it seemed she wasn't particularly concerned with the outcome of whatever answer she would get from him. "You're not going to try and take the Archmage by surprise, are you? It's not going to work."

"Maybe I am; maybe I'm not," Luke tried to deflect, like he had heard Zed do in the past.

"Sorry to break it to you, big guy." The Mage smirked at him as she finished her portal. "The requirement for him to join the fight is that you're not in this world."

Luke clenched his teeth so hard that they would have broken if they were merely dentin covered by enamel. Luckily for his future meals, they had been empowered by mana, just like every single other portion of his body. Nothing about him was easy to break or lose, except his temper. Then he blinked, and his eyes went wide in excitement. "Did *he* make that condition?"

"Yes?" Taylor replied quizzically as she urged the other members of her team to step through the portal. To her surprise, the Murderhobo went first, a wide, dark grin on his face.

"You're saying he's *afraid*." Luke let out a dark chuckle as he paused with one foot through the portal, casting his eyes out over the world he was leaving behind for a short while. "I guess that will have to do. For now."

CHAPTER TWENTY-SEVEN

Thanks to the fact that the time dilation of The World of Names was higher than their base world, it was nearly a minute in Luke's subjective time before each of the others were on his side of the portal. Taylor closed it with a flick of her wrist and gestured in the direction where she believed they needed to move.

Zed was the first one to point out the major issue with this plan. "Sorry to be the one to burst your bubble, Taylor, but I seem to recall that this was about as far as the world went in this direction? Remember the whole 'diminishing returns on distance traveled' thing that we had going on?"

"He has a point; maybe we should have gone into The Grove?" Andre offered immediately. "If they have Druids on their side of the border, they have to be bound to that plane of existence as well, right?"

Luke waited for the Mage's reasoning, seeing as she had a smirk on her face and was letting the others build up the issue on her behalf. Finally, she decided to clue them into her thought process. "You're correct, but I have a plan. Also, you have to think that, if they have Ascenders of a certain type on their side of the border, they're going to have defenses in place to protect that border, just like we do. If we went to The Grove, I am certain there would be all sorts of traps and ambushes ready and waiting for us in no time flat."

"Cool, a plan. I love plans, especially when they have us do something that no one else has ever been able to do in the history of the world. Let's hear your plan." Zed cheerfully plopped onto the ground, sitting in a lotus position before dropping his chin into both hands. He looked like a schoolchild waiting for a particularly interesting story from his favorite teacher, a bizarre dichotomy with the bloodstained clothes he was wearing.

"Zed. You have a little singe right there." Luke poked the spot on Zed's shirt, earning a wince of pain and a sharp intake of breath from the Bard. "Ah. It burned the skin under that spot, too."

"I noticed." Zed glared at Luke, only for his eyes to go wide. "Hey buddy... not sure if *you* noticed, you have a gaping wound on your inner thigh. Did you get savaged by a dog?"

"No, I'm fine-" Luke looked down at his leg, blinked a few times at the blood that was practically pouring out, and reached for his satchel. "Huh. Look at that. I wonder why I didn't get notified about a serious wound."

"Heh. That worked to clear out the infernal infection. That Lieutenant is going to be so annoyed that his plan failed." Pulling up his status was a strangely difficult task, and his numbers, specifically his health and mana, were fuzzy and difficult to discern. There was an easy solution to this issue, so he popped the top of his waterskin and took a deep gulp. Then he looked down at his leg, ensuring that the flesh knit back together as rapidly as it was supposed to. Thus assured, he turned his attention to the other problem he was having. "It's hard to read my status currently..."

"Well, Luke, you see, sometimes words get really big. Then, they get very difficult to understand-" Zed's words were waved off by the Murderhobo, the physical action sending a light shower of blood away from his hand.

"I can read just fine. I'm good numbers, too."

"Good *at* numbers, Luke. 'With numbers' is also acceptable, linguistically." Zed spoke soothingly, taunting the huge man. "See, this is why I'm worried about your ability to read your status."

Luke paused in place, devoting all of his attention to trying to discern why he might be having this strange issue. There hadn't been too many things that had been able to damage him during his fight so far, certainly nothing that had been able to potentially alter his Sigil or his mental state. When he realized what the issue was, he snapped his fingers and opened his eyes, having not even realized that he had closed them. "That blue mist. It had to be some kind of magical anesthetic. Tricky. If you see an enemy blowing blue mist at you, try to avoid it instead of inhaling it. It makes your status hard to access."

"A good practice in life, Luke." Andre chuckled lightly as he watched Taylor draw something out. "Whenever an enemy sends anything at you, just go ahead and try to avoid it instead of breathing it in. Mist, fire, lightning…"

Luke stared at the Druid, a strange expression on his face. "I've never tried to breathe fire. Do you think that would-"

"There!" Taylor's sudden cheerful cry made the others glance her way. "I think I figured out what we need to do. Remember how Zed made a joke about making artificial bind-points to our world? I think if we place plants *here*, Andre, then grow them, followed by a burst of mana from Luke's stores, we can generate an artificial bind point and allow us to travel unimpeded into the Dynasty of Dogs!"

They considered her words for a few moments, each of them pondering the implications of the information she had just offered. Luke was the first to get on board, mainly because he already had his waterskin out and ready to use. "You think, if we make a bindpoint, it'll fold the dimension around our earth more than it currently is? Instead of it being a flat plane, we will have a bridge that allows us to move a greater distance? I like it. They won't be expecting it. We can drop in on them and slaughter their army from behind."

"When did you become an expert at extra-planar move-ment?" Andre quizzed Luke, excited to have another person to include in his academic theorizing.

"Huh?" Luke's answer was enough to stymie Andre's grand ambitions, so he merely focused on growing the plants in the location Taylor had indicated. They weren't entirely certain if the previous point had been a fluke, or if it was something they could replicate, so they made sure to use the same type of plants and recreate the conditions as best as they could.

As the plants finished growing—mostly flowers from their base world—some combination of the flora, Andre's mana being bound to that world, the growth being accomplished being in *this* world, and an influx of pure energy from Luke caused the effects to be copied near perfectly. Once again, the Murderhobo was the first to confirm that he saw flashes of the other worlds appearing in the energy being released, but this time, there was a clear change in their surroundings.

Things in this world that had seemed so far away a moment ago drew closer, as if the group had suddenly put a magnifying glass in front of their eyes. Taking only a moment for Zed to command the plants to protect themselves from any of the local wildlife, they began running. For the first time since they had begun this quest, it appeared as though they had a clear corridor to its completion.

Luke watched as Taylor pulled out a thick parchment, unfolding it over and over until she revealed a large, not-well-detailed map. "If I am reading this correctly, the nearest palace we could find in the Dynasty of Dogs is going to be the provincial capital. I say we aim directly at it, figure out if Cindy was taken there, then plan our route from there."

No one had any complaints about this option, so they merely continued running as far as they could, until eventually Zed passed out from exhaustion and needed to be carried by

Luke. After that, the group moved slower, mainly due to the changing conditions of the world that they were in. Instead of the strange, nearly perpetual twilight that coated this plane of existence, they had been moving toward what appeared to be full night. Luke was incredibly interested in the new information he was gathering and hoped that stronger monsters, Spells in this world, he supposed, could be found in the night.

Taylor seemed more concerned than anything else and was watching the encroaching darkness with worried eyes. "I've never heard of the World of Names having true nighttime before."

"Well… we're going in a direction that has been known to have incredibly diminishing returns on travel. Could it be that you're the first Mage from your world to be able to make it all the way over here? Or at least to bother doing so?" Andre offered brightly. "Also, do you think we should pop into the Dynasty of Dogs and make sure that we're going the correct direction? Or, Abyss, we should just make sure that we're getting as far as we actually think we are."

Taylor agreed, and the two of them went through their portion of making a binding to the world. They looked expectantly at Luke, who hesitated before firmly deciding to keep his waterskin exactly where it was. "Stop wasting my mana. Actually, where's the one I gave you earlier, Andre?"

"The one…?" Andre winced and looked away, unable to meet Luke's eyes. "I'm so sorry, I think I forgot it in the commotion. I only used a little bit of the water; I hope we can replace it for you. Shoot, I hope it doesn't get stepped on and cause an issue."

The Murderhobo stared at the Druid for a long moment with hollow eyes, slowly allowing a smirk to appear on his face. Not saying a word, he pulled the waterskin off his belt strap and tossed it to the two of them. They watched him curiously, but he only shrugged and offered no further explanation.

Not wanting to waste his generosity, they poured some mana out then waited until the distortions appeared once more.

Luke was watching the surroundings carefully, and as the artificial bindpoint was created, the dimension they were in shifted and firmed up slightly. It moved like a slow wave, traveling along the path they had taken to reach this point. When he looked more closely, everything about the universe between the two points seemed more clear, more usable, and somehow he knew it was a safe-ish path for him to tread.

Taylor popped open a portal then stepped through as cautiously as possible. With her enormous Physical Reaction characteristic, she was able to be more stealthy than any of them either could, or—in Luke's case—would choose to be. When she returned, she quietly closed the portal before looking at the two awake members of her party. Her beaming smile said it all, but she decided to also tell them what she had seen. "We're hundreds of miles from the border, and when I compare the map to the constellations, it looks like we're three-quarters of the way to the provincial capital already."

"That is fantastic!" Andre twirled her around before realizing what he was doing and awkwardly setting her down. Watching them, Luke could only shake his head. It had been more than five years of real-world time, and nearly a decade of their subjective time, since they had confessed their feelings for each other. Even *he* had heard of taking it slow, but *glaciers* traveled faster than their relationship. Andre cleared his throat and tried to change the subject, putting his focus on Luke. "Sorry again about losing your waterskin."

"Yeah, that's going to have some really interesting side effects." Luke couldn't help but chuckle at that thought, and the flustered smile on Andre's face was slowly replaced with questioning dread.

"Luke… why are you acting like this?" The Druid grew a half-cocked smile on his face, clearly hoping that the Murderhobo was trying to just mess with him a little bit over losing his personal possessions. "My Bloodflood Binding will be able to rectify any issues with that mana getting loose, right?"

"Probably." Luke shrugged his shoulders, not particularly

worried about that aspect of the situation. "I'm more interested to see what happens when the rest of it hits open air."

"The rest of it? The rest of *what*, Luke?" Taylor joined the tête-à-tête, her concern causing the tension of the conversation to spike. "What else might happen?"

Luke shook his head, pointing at Andre accusingly. "Hey, I told him it needed to be contained. Whatever happens isn't my fault."

"What *could* happen, Luke?" Taylor looked for a moment like she was about to jump at the huge man and shake the information out of him.

"Yeah… I have no idea." Luke picked up Zed and started walking once more, assuming that, if he was going in the incorrect direction, someone would point it out to him. "I've never pulled a solid chunk of mana out while I've been on the base world. It always seemed like a really bad idea after experiencing how liquid mana explosively decompresses and kills everything around it that's unable to survive a basic Mana Baptism. Anyway. If I've never done it, how could I possibly know what would happen?"

No one answered him or interrupted his words, so Luke merely said his peace and clammed up. "I bet it'll be neat. Kinda wanna go back and see for myself."

CHAPTER TWENTY-EIGHT

"If my calculations are correct, we're just outside the provincial capital," Andre announced, breaking the silence that had been hovering around the group since Luke's announcement nearly a day prior. "I think it would be a smart move to exit here and walk the rest of the way, perhaps give ourselves a chance to scope out the situation, perhaps pick up some of the local customs and language?"

The way the others in the group nodded as if they would have no trouble at all was confusing to Luke. He didn't enjoy being confused, so he decided to murder his confusion as cleanly as possible. "You think we will be able to learn how to blend in by walking a couple miles? We can't even do that in the land we live in."

"Well... we'll be able to learn the language, maybe grab some clothes, and the best part is that they won't be expecting us." Taylor slowly worked through her thought process, which she had been able to intuit based on Andre's words. "If we have at least ten points in Talent, we can pick up the local language if we hear it for only a little while. I'd say approximately... thirty minutes of conversation?"

"That's about what it *used* to take me," Zed interjected with a wink. "I feel like the Murderhobo special we all inhaled will let us understand things easier. Shall we go test it out?"

"Murderhobo special?" Andre chuckled as Taylor started opening a portal. "I like it, and I get what you mean. But better Mana Channels, easier to live in, high-mana areas? Seems like it should be a Mage special."

"I've got a Source-cerer Skill. That counts," Luke informed them just as the portal fully formed. Each of them stepped though and began moving directly toward the city in the distance.

They had only made it a handful of paces before they heard a long, low howl in the distance. At least, it sounded like it was far away, but only for a moment, as it increased in volume and seemed to get closer every fraction of a second. All of them prepared for battle, rushing to enact all the defensive and offensive options they had available to them.

Andre scattered some seeds on the ground around them. Taylor began chanting softly, sending her mana out and forming an eye in the sky that she kept as close to her as possible. Luke hefted Cookie, glaring around with a deep scowl. Zed put his hands in the air and sank to his knees in surrender. That earned a scoff from the Murderhobo, but it didn't convince the Bard to change his position.

The earth started to shake, revealing Ascenders as they began to emerge from the soil. Dogs raced toward them from all directions, and soon The Four were encircled entirely. A voice called out to them, and Luke frowned lightly as he realized that he recognized it. "Uninvited *guests*! Thank you for delivering yourself to us right here. If we had to travel out to the countryside again, I would have been greatly annoyed. This close to the city, it's barely even a chore to come out and gather you up."

The Murderhobo looked at the man, who seemed far too familiar. All he saw was a male looking at him, wearing a robe that was clearly well made, yet not ostentatious. There was a smug grin on his face, and he called out to Luke. "Are you ready for me to introduce myself yet?"

"I don't know what you mean." Luke denied him immediately.

The man rolled his eyes and shook his head. "You're a fun one. Also, attacking before I could even get a chance to introduce myself the last time we met? Poor form."

"I don't know who you are." The Murderhobo tried again, as this man was clearly having trouble understanding him. "Have we met?"

"I admit, we were never formally introduced." The Ascender wasn't alone, which by itself explained his laissez-faire attitude. Luke assessed the people who were with this man, finding that the least of them was a more potent Ascender than any the Dynasty of Dogs had fielded against them in battle previously. "Still, it has only been a few days since we fought. Did you truly forget me so quickly? Perhaps the gaping wounds I left all over your body would serve as a reminder?"

"Sorry to interrupt! He actually doesn't remember who you are. I have known him since I was a child, and he still forgets that I exist sometimes." Zed volunteered the information, earning dozens of weapons directed toward him for interrupting. "*Yeah*, that does nothing to alleviate my concern. See how my hands are already up? Hard for me to surrender more, don't you think?"

"Silence, *mutts!*" One of the other Ascenders, who was deferentially standing near the original speaker, suddenly barked at them. "Lay on your backs and show absolute submission, and we will make your deaths swift! Do you not realize that you speak to the eighth Prince of the Dynasty of Dogs, His Royal Highness-"

Luke stuck his fingers in his ears and hummed loudly, trying to drown out what the other man was saying. It didn't help. His senses were so great that he could hear a butterfly pass gas from a dozen paces. "-William Merryck!"

The Murderhobo let out a grunt of annoyance. "You know,

every time someone tells me their name, it takes up valuable space that I need for other thoughts. How are you going to repay me for forcing your name into my brain? Nobody gets to live in here rent-free."

"How about I tell you a little story?" Prince William spoke with a chuckle in his voice. "Once upon a time, there were four Ascenders who didn't know that there are tamed dogs which allow the dynasty to sniff out any intruders in our territory, even if they're not inside our world at the time of their incursion. From the moment they crossed the border, until the moment they walked into a trap, they were tracked meticulously. Since the intruders were of such high value, they were given an option to surrender without being immediately slain. They only got one chance, and if they didn't come into the custody of the dynasty immediately, they would be put down like the rabid beasts they are."

"*I* like this story, Your Highness!" Zed called out immediately, flopping onto his back and wiggling around slightly. "It sets a great scene, the expectations of the listeners, and it has an open ending that still has yet to be written! I think that's my favorite part."

"Truly, I have no interest in killing you all." The prince informed them magnanimously. "More than anything else, I am interested in your ability to even penetrate this deep into the dynasty. It has taken us many centuries, possibly millennia if my father is to be believed, to cut off access to other worlds. What you did shouldn't have been possible, but if you can replicate it on our behalf..."

Luke decided that he would rather just fight his way out of the situation. Not bothering to listen to any more of the *words*, he began his *actions*. Bum Thunder put him within striking distance of the prince, and he twirled Cookie to the side, aiming to land a blow directly on the prince's abdomen.

One of the Ascenders standing near the prince suddenly *shifted*. His muscles grew, his knees inverted and pointed backward, and similar changes occurred all over his body. Then, with a motion that was designed to appear as contemptuous as possible, he swung his clawed hand at the Murderhobo-projectile. The tips of his claws met Cookie's outer edge, shattering with a sound like crystal falling onto a stone. From the tip, to the halfway point of the claws, the natural weapons were completely destroyed. Then the bulk of Cookie's body landed on the outstretched palm...

Coming to a stop.

This was a completely unexpected situation for the Murderhobo, as he had never found himself nearly perfectly matched against another Ascender in a physical contest. No... he realized that the fact that the attack had been completely stopped without any apparent damage to his opponent's hand meant he was *severely* outclassed. Luke moved to dodge backward, but the instant of hesitation meant he didn't get to find his footing and leave under his own control. No, he was sent flying by the other hand that swept around and slapped his chest with an open palm.

Damage taken: 14! 186 mitigated!

Damage dealt: 9 penetrating! Target is bleeding!

Luke's armor completely shattered over his chest, the Promiscuous Stud cuirass completely dissipating into motes of bright blue light. This was also a rarity for the Murderhobo, as very few opponents had ever been able to completely disrupt his armor with a single attack. His eyes tracked the swift-moving Ascender, locking onto the hand that was gushing blood from at least a half dozen new holes. Then Luke realized that he was nearly thirty feet in the air, but he seemed to have reached the maximum distance that gravity would allow his body to be thrown from this casual attack.

He righted himself, allowing Feather's Fall to kick in and allow him to glide right back at the man, a huge smile on his face. He equipped the bottle that he had as his only projectile weapon, chucking it ahead of him to put the enemy off-balance. Instead of taking the blow directly, his opponent slapped out and redirected it, allowing the weapon to move around himself.

This wasn't without cost, as the hand that moved out to deflect the bottle also had its nails shattered. Luke's eyes narrowed as he tried to determine what the strength of this fighter was. "That should have been your *bones*."

Then he was back into the melee, flipping over in a forward somersault in an attempt to turn the dog-man into a splatter of gore on the ground. Somehow, an arm snaked around the enormous Greatmace, and Luke's nose met with an open palm. Feeling as though he were moving in slow motion, Luke was thrust backward and sent rolling at his teammate as if they were playing a game of 'knock down the bottles'.

Damage taken: 14! 186 mitigated!

Damage dealt: 11 penetrating! Target is bleeding!

Andre caught Luke with a net of greenery, which shredded upon slowing him down, thanks to his armor. The Murderhobo was slightly dazed, seeing as his helmet had been destroyed with yet another single strike. There were flickers and stutters over his chest, indicating that his mana regeneration was in play and nearly ready to recreate his Cuirass. "Wow. What a slap."

"No better than a lowly *Rage Wolf*." The man sneered with a voice that had turned more bestial. "You have no combat forms at *all*? Have you truly never encountered a being able to redirect your physical might? Do you not understand the basics of the transference of motion? Does the Hollow Kingdom truly live up to its reputation, sending children with no formal combat training whatsoever to their most easily accessible planes of existence? This is pathetic."

A bolt of lightning passed through him just as he finished speaking, creating a jagged wound as the superheated plasma acted more like a physical object than lightning, blasting off his right arm from the elbow forward, leaving a cauterized stump where it had once been. Taylor watched with a cool glare as the man howled in pain. "No resistance to magical attacks at all? How pathetic."

Having his words mirrored back at him almost sent the Ascender into a blind rage. Only the calm command of the prince forced him to stay his hand and kept his guard from charging in to slaughter them all. "Wait. My father's researchers have given us their requirements; don't throw away our prize. Let's crate up these subjects and send them to the kennel. You know better than I do how effective they are at training obedience."

"As you will, Your Royal Highness." The guard let out a long, slow breath. "Can I break them before sending them off?"

"This one seems to have an enhanced ability to recover. I give you permission to test the limits on that. My father would love to have a baseline," the prince offered as a small compromise, indicating Luke, who was already on his feet and rushing toward them once more. "He's pretty fast... perhaps you start with his legs?"

That put a dark smile on the strange guard's face.

"As my prince commands."

CHAPTER TWENTY-NINE

- TAYLOR -

The Mage watched as Luke hurled himself against the Prince's bodyguards, half horrified as he received the beating of a lifetime. A tiny, excited part of herself recognized that, if he survived this experience, the Murderhobo would set out to actively learn how to do better.

She didn't recognize the exact methodology that the guard was using, but she knew that the dynasty's high-level combatants, especially those associated with royalty, had been trained since birth to be able to fight against creatures and people who were stronger than them. With every strike Luke sent, which was subsequently deflected, and every attack that landed on a new part of his body to shatter his armor, it further enunciated exactly *how* outclassed they truly were in this situation.

"This is not a fight we can win; we need to retreat!" Taylor called out to her friends, even as she peppered the guard with lightning each time Luke had been knocked away. After the first strike, she had been unable to land a clean Spell, only grazing the man at best.

Zed, still laying flat on his back—though he had folded his arms to give himself a small pillow—didn't bother to get up. "I'm almost able to guarantee that, if they were able to track us while we weren't even in this dimension, they would have ways to temporarily shut down our escape. I mean, feel free to give it a whirl, but getting out of here is going to be harder than just leaving."

She turned around and rushed to the position where they had entered this world, expelling a small amount of mana as she attempted to force open the connection. Her energy took hold, trying to do the task it had been assigned, only for some other Spell or Skill to interfere at the last moment and collapse the burgeoning portal. With a grunt of frustration, she glanced back at the guard slapping Luke around like a misbehaving pet. Taylor watched as Luke's gear was systematically broken, including his chest plate, when it sprang back into existence.

Each time, the Murderhobo would find some way to be back into fighting range and form in only a moment. For a short while, she assumed he could go all day.

He was a monster in human form, a prodigy of destruction.

Then Luke took two hits in a row while he wasn't wearing any armor. He was tossed back, the guard laughing at him as he tried to stand up on destroyed legs. "As my prince has commanded, I started with your legs. I am certain that you're very near death right now, and I am impressed with your sheer health! You would make for an excellent combat dummy for our youngest trainees, as you have the same combat skill level... as the dummy."

Luke grunted a reply, but between the blood coming out of his mouth and the sheer vitriol the words contained, Taylor was unable to discern what it was. She had a sneaking suspicion that she wouldn't willingly repeat it, even if she could hear it clearly. The Prince stepped forward, his hands held out to the side in a show of generosity. "Dismiss your methods of attack and defense and willingly come to our side. With a little bit of train-ing, you may actually be useful to the dynasty. With a few slight alterations to your Sigils, we will even be able to trust you and perhaps even send you into positions of authority one day."

The words he was saying sparked something in Taylor's thoughts, even if she would never be able to willingly give herself up. She had as much authority as she could ever want in the Hollow Kingdom, but it had done nothing for her up to this point. The only real authority that mattered was personal power, and that was what she was focusing on at this moment. "We would need more than just a little training... we would need a lot of it."

"Well." The prince smiled widely, not a hint of malice or ill intent showing through his bright smile. "Going by the showing of your friend here, that is extremely true."

"With that said, we have a mission that we cannot simply give up. I am certain that there is a vastly limited amount of time to complete it." Taylor was speaking very slowly, hoping that Luke would be able to understand what she was *truly* attempting to say. "We need time, a *lot* of time."

"As you know, that can be arranged." The prince waved her seeming concerns away. "I know that you cannot simply give up; your Sigils will not allow it to happen. All we need to know is what your mind will choose on the other side, after we have stripped your current Sigils and replaced them with ours. That being said, I will ask only once. Given the opportunity, would you renounce your oath to the Hollow Kingdom-"

"Abso-abyssal-lutely," Luke told them as he 'walked' toward the guard using only his hands.

"-and swear an equivalent oath to the dynasty? I assure you, our ability to craft and guard our oaths is far higher than your kingdom's. Generations more advanced, constantly updated and regulated." The prince had never let his smile slip, only growing it when he heard that Luke would be happy to change his allegiance.

"Oh. No, in that case," the Murderhobo suddenly stated, getting close enough to the guard that he could attempt to grab at his leg and bite into it. His weak attack was easily avoided, though he did earn himself a kick in the face for his troubles. "You remove my Sigil, then we'll talk."

"I'm afraid it doesn't work that way." Now the prince was speaking with faux sadness.

"Don't be afraid. Just free me." Now Luke was staring at the prince, his eyes wide as he attempted to convince the royal dignitary. "I'd be a great mercenary."

"Luke, can you *stop* trying to join the enemy? *Again?*" Andre had a great deal of frustration in his voice as a vine snaked over, wrapped itself around the huge man's ankle, and dragged him back to the small cluster of people. "Thank you for your generous offer, Your Highness. Unfortunately, we must decline."

He didn't wait for an answer after that, instead allowing the various flora he had been growing under the surface of the earth to sprout upward, in an attempt to entangle the legs of his enemies. Pitfalls opened, attempting to pull the people down, as vines studded with thorns whipped out.

Seeing that the attacks missed, Andre glowered and lifted his hand in front of his face, blowing a cloud of spores off his palm. "Luke, Taylor was trying to get you to open a portal to Murder World. It's the only way we can get out of here, get training, and return strong enough to defeat not only these opponents but whatever group they brought in."

"I can't." Luke only had eyes for the man who had brutalized him. "I've gotta rip that guy's spine out. Gimme five minutes."

"*Luke.*" Andre stated in a slightly rushed tone as the guard and Prince began summoning various dogs. In the distance, they could see dozens, if not *hundreds* of additional troops sprinting toward them. "A portal, if you will."

"No, I *can't*. My previous statements were separate facts. One was not a reason for the other." Luke strained his neck, forcing himself to meet Andre's eyes. "I'm still locked out of advancing myself for the better part of two months."

The Druid cast around for an answer to this conundrum, but it was Taylor who had already done the heavy lifting on the thought process and justification. As lightning lashed out, keeping the dynasty at bay, the noise of combat and the din of dogs began stealing their attention. "The king told us to do *whatever needed to be done* in order to complete our mission. Well, Luke, we *need* lots of time and training. We *need* an enormous power boost. Get that portal open, and get us out of here!"

"Think that'll work?" Luke hesitated for a long instant, before firmly making a decision and pulling out the very last of his mana-filled waterskins. He popped it open, took a deep swig of the liquid inside, then placed his thumb over the opening and started shaking the container. Taylor stumbled back, knowing better than anyone that the properties of mana dictated that agitating a container of liquid mana when it had interacted with the air was a recipe for disaster.

The Murderhobo's armor reformed within a second of the liquid hitting his mouth, rapidly followed by tiny popping noises as his bones aligned, set, and healed. Luke hopped to his feet, darting over to where Taylor had been attempting to reopen her portal. "I'd love to get out of here for a while. How much training do you think we need until we can take these scumbags down?"

The Mage was absolutely uncertain what to say in reply to his inquiry, but started sincerely thinking about the question as soon as it was asked. "If I had to guess, we either need to find some more Spells... or Skills, I suppose, or get our levels up as high as we can."

"Level twenty, here we come." Luke was practically dancing in place as he removed his thumb, allowing the unfiltered mana to spray out of the opening. Thanks to its sheer power, he was easily able to penetrate the thin barrier that had been erected. Using all his strength, he smashed through both the dimensional barrier, as well as the protection against egress into another universe.

"How did you just do that?" the prince bellowed in shock and excitement. Were it not for the fact that they were escaping his captivity, Taylor had a niggling feeling that he would be more than happy to merely study them for an extended period of time. "That's not supposed to be possible, not in the slightest! There is an active command in the air! Even I, a *prince* of this dynasty, cannot ignore a command from the emperor!"

Taylor didn't bother answering the questions the prince sent their way, even though they started coming faster and faster as the four of them approached the portal. Andre was dragging Zed by the feet because the man still hadn't removed himself from his supine position. She stared at the open, swirling blue portal that was awaiting her, feeling a line of sweat break-through her passive Spells. Taylor was nervous, and she had every right to be.

"Zed went in there and was able to survive just fine," she whispered to herself, gathering all the courage she needed to make her first step. "Everything *he* can do, *I* can definitely survive."

Finally spent, her Thunder Beast's Eye Spell faded. With that added motivation, the Namer stepped out of her current dimension into a much higher plane of existence. Her three friends were with her, the only thing that slowed her nervous-ness and kept it from turning into full-blown panic.

"Welcome to Murder World," Zed called out sarcastically from his position on the ground, where he was rubbing at a bruised spot on his forehead that he had bruised after being dropped off the vine. "Ahh, smell that sweet mana. Yup, nothing like going from a dangerous situation where everyone wants to keep you alive for inscrutable reasons… to going into a dangerous situation where literally *everything* wants to kill you as fast as possible. Life goals, I tell ya."

CHAPTER THIRTY

Taylor scanned the area, noticing the strange faces that seemed to be forming in the blue mist in the distance. She took a deep breath to launch into a rapidly prepared discussion on how they should focus on their new challenge, then paused as the realization struck that lecturing her team would be a terrible idea. There was another factor that caused her to stop: that single lungful of air contained denser mana than she had to put up with nearly anywhere else she had visited in the multiverse. The Mage started coughing immediately, feeling as though she were drowning in the near-liquid air.

It was *Zed* of all people who came over and gave her a comforting pat on the back. He stayed next to her until she was able to catch her breath, settling into a box breathing pattern. "There you go! Smart, smart. All mana control starts with the breath, as it's the easiest to visualize. Four seconds in, hold for four seconds, four seconds out, hold empty for four seconds, repeat."

She straightened her posture and pushed his hand away, although she did so gently out of consideration for his support.

"Yes, Zed, we all know how to breathe. I think that we should focus our efforts on… on… where's Luke?"

"Luke?" Zed lifted an eyebrow and showed her a half-cocked smile. "Do you really need to ask that? He left."

"He *left*?" Taylor's fingers curled into fists as a tiny spark of fury coalesced in her chest. "How are we supposed to find him? How are we supposed to understand the dangers in this area, and *most* of all, what are we going to do about the army that is going to be sitting outside this portal for *years* of our subjective time?"

Zed held both of his hands up, showing that he wasn't the one at fault here. "Hey, yell at the big guy, not the affable Bard. As to finding him, that'll be easy. He moves in a straight line, or at least as straight as you can on a curved world like this. By the time we catch up to him, he'll be at the edge of Zone twenty, for sure."

"Is everyone seeing those faces?" Andre called out, watching the horizon slightly nervously. "By the way, this isn't grass. I'm not sure what it is, but if I had to guess… it's just mana shaped like grass. Trying to connect to the world, the earth, is like attempting to tap into a bolt of lightning."

"The faces are the monsters of this Zone, and we should really leave." Zed put his hands on his hips, threw his head back, and laughed loudly. Wiping his left eye, he looked at the others directly. That was when Taylor recognized that the Bard was on the verge of a full-fledged panic. "Laugh or cry, know what I mean? Gotta choose one; also, we should start running. This is fun! I've never been able to be a tour guide in a whole new world for someone else."

It was easy enough to follow the Murderhobo's tracks, as he had made no attempt at subtlety, destroying any foliage or monsters that crossed his path, either by accident or intention-ally. Taylor tried to keep an eye on the strange abominations that she could see in the distance. Whenever she lost track of them for a moment then found them again, the creatures would suddenly be much closer but always trying to stay in her peripheral vision. Based on how fast the Bard was running, he knew something about these creatures that she did not.

At that moment, she decided that she was perfectly happy *not* knowing the capabilities of the creatures that were ever so slowly closing in on them.

As a Mage, everything about this world seemed simultaneously easier and far more difficult. The paradoxical nature was frustrating to her, but it was easy for her to trace her feelings and put them into clear thoughts. "Andre, let me know if you're experiencing anything different, but it seems to me that our bodies are rapidly drinking in the mana around us. I'm seeing large-scale distortions around all three of us. Less so on Zed for some reason, now that I think of it. It's messing with my vision, but at the same time... I think my ability to accurately discern things in the distance is increasing?"

"Oh good, I thought that was just me! Good to know I'm not crazy." Zed laughed wildly, though the sound was high-pitched and breathy, thanks to his dead sprint. "As far as I can tell, our bodies are practically starved for mana. You'll see what I mean after a few days of this, but that distortion goes away pretty quick. Think of it like being super dehydrated, then all of a sudden your body has access to as much water as it wants, and you don't need to drink it to bring it in. For happy feelings, what you *should* do is check out your mana regen right now."

Deciding that she could handle all three actions: running, staying alert for monsters, and reading her status, Taylor let her curiosity get the better of her and pulled open her character sheet.

Cal Scan
Level: 14
Current Etheric Xenograft Potentia: 3,141 / 98,700 to level 15!

Maximum health: 163
Maximum mana: 486
Mana regen: ~~*6.3 per second.*~~ *22 per second.*

"What? Twenty-two per *second?*" Taylor nearly choked on her words and *did* trip on a thick tangle of grass. She easily rolled forward and into a standing position once more, the minor inconvenience hardly impacting her speed at all. "I knew that our environment affected our ability to regenerate mana, but I didn't realize it was *this* much! I thought there was a hard cap based on our Mind stats."

"Everyone has thought that, forever. Because, in almost all circumstances, it's true." Zed cheerfully acted as tour guide once more, though his eyes were far too wide, and his smile far too bright. "That's because it has been true in literally all other circumstances, as far as we know! Also, if it's only at twenty-two right now, just wait until you've been here a while and your body is pumped full of the stuff. I think mana we have in our bodies is actually a result of biological breakdowns or is a waste energy produced by our cells. When you're fully saturated, your mana regeneration is going to be closing in on three figures."

Andre voiced a question almost immediately, the academic in him apparently overriding his concern at the current situation. "Hold on there, Zed. You can't just say that we're simultaneously requiring mana *and* have it be a byproduct that is specifically a waste product. If that were the case-"

"Why not?" Zed challenged him directly.

That took the Druid aback. "What do you mean?"

"I *mean*, why not? Why can't it be both a necessary resource and a waste product?" The Bard tapped his own gut. "Going back to the water analogy, we need water in order to fill our meat sacks, but it's also a waste product that exits us along with other filth. Maybe having really good Mana Channels, like we do, is like having really efficient kidneys. Kidneys keep our blood clean, but they also collect water and waste material to expel."

"Theorizing is fun, *totally*," Taylor interrupted before they could start an all-out argument about meta-anatomy. "Zed, what do we need to do to fight off those faces that are getting closer?"

"Yeah, about that." The Bard shrugged and let his smile shrink down to a weak grin. "I have no idea. Luke was so angry about being back here that he never bothered to stop and fight one of them, and on the way to the exit, we were rushing too much for him to give me a decent first-hand example on how to do it. Before I forget, he did tell me that using fire is a bad idea. Just in general, not against these particular monsters."

"Why?" Without bothering to consider the ramifications about what she was about to do, Taylor casually activated Fingers of Flame and sent the deadly Spells at the strange faces closing in on them.

Boom.

All she could see was an enormous wall of flame exiting her left hand. After that, everything became hazy memories. She was tumbling through the air, knocked silly by the close proximity of the detonation. Someone was screaming, and her head hurt. Her arms and legs weren't listening to what she was telling them to do, but that was okay. Moving hurt, so the Mage stopped doing it.

She blinked and watched as the azure grass five feet below her face swayed gently back and forth. Rational thought started returning to her mind, and she realized that she was being carried. "An... dre?"

They slowed down for a moment but didn't stop. Moments later, their pace increased further, but now she could see the front of Zed's feet as he ran behind Andre to explain what had happened. "Hey there, you absolutely insane wizard! Good to see you're alive."

"Hate... you." Taylor managed to clearly state.

That earned a chuckle, though it sounded strained. "Good news and bad news! The good news is that, congratulations! Your Fire Spell was enough to kill off the... I'm calling them banshees. The bad news is that you have fourth degree burns all over your upper body, and your left hand is charred to the point that I think it's not usable anymore. *Pretty* sure you're going to need to find a Healer when we get back."

"What... happened?" Taylor rasped out at him, trying and failing not to panic about the state of her body.

Damage taken: 151! You're lightly burning.

Health remaining: 12. Seek immediate healing!

Damage dealt: 325 x222.

Potentia gained: 22,200. You have killed a type of creature unknown to the Hollow Kingdom! Update the records for a bonus? Yes / No.

"Fair enough, not sure how much you remember. So... some really smart guy told you that using fire was dangerous, and you reacted by immediately casting a fire Spell. Is that much still in your head? I think it's an important fact."

Zed continued speaking quickly, no small part thanks to her snarling and trying to bend her fingers enough to point a single finger at him. "Right, right. Let's not be hasty! Not sure if this is true everywhere, but it appears that mana is flammable to a certain point, and it'll just continue burning until it hits the ground. Good news there, the atmosphere *didn't* light on fire and kill us all by sucking all breathable air out of the world. Not going to lie, I'm pretty sure that *is* possible here. Downside, the grass *did* start on fire, and we're being chased by a wildfire."

"Nullify didn't work? Luke can help. How... far?"

Zed couldn't help but laugh in disbelief at the words that needed to come out of his own mouth. "Yeah, I think you're really not going to like the answer to that. Luke has a pretty good head start on us. If his estimate was correct the last time we were here, crossing all of Zone eighteen and nineteen to catch him at the front of twenty will be something like... twenty-seven hundred miles?"

Andre swore harshly enough that the air turned blue. Taylor blinked slowly as she thought about that. Her mind was hazy, but she couldn't help but wheeze out a laugh. She thought that it was his swearing turning the air blue, but the air was *already* blue!

At first the Mage was expecting them to laugh, but she slowly realized that she hadn't spoken the joke out loud. "I think... lungs are burning."

The uncomfortable silence that followed seemed to last forever, but that might have been her lack of mental acuity. Taylor watched as a vine snapped out and grabbed Andre, then they were flying through the air, extremely long plants 'walking' them along the ground in enormous leaps. Andre's ice-cold hand touched her forehead, and he looked into her eyes with great concern in his. "There's no way that we can wait for a healer. I'm sorry, Taylor, but I need to put you in a Lotus, if you're going to survive."

In only a few seconds, flower petals were closing over her, and Taylor started to drift off. "I've always wanted you... to bring me... flowers."

Then the Mage truly fell asleep, swaddled in the purest of flowers, hoping that, when she awoke, she wouldn't be a destroyed husk of a person. A small frown crossed her face as she realized that this might be the *last* time she fell asleep.

After that, her mind fell silent, with only the small movements of her labored breathing revealing that she was, in fact, alive.

CHAPTER THIRTY-ONE

- ANDRE -

"I'm gonna kill him for leaving us like that," the Druid whispered harshly as he watched the petals close over the charred flesh that Taylor's face had become.

"Just... *don't.*" Zed's words were unexpectedly harsh, so much so that it broke Andre's spiraling anger and gave him a new target to focus on. "This is what all of you did to *me* when you came back from your first training period. You expected everything to have changed, and you treated me as though I had been able to get the same kind of experience you did. Think about it, Andre! What has motivated Luke the *entire time* you've known him as an Ascender? What has changed for him? Nothing? Correct. Lastly..."

Andre was already slightly shaken, but the Bard's next words landed like a sledgehammer.

"...Why would you expect him to stick around and care about what is going to happen to you, when you just let him rot in a Descender portal between massive swaths of combat? Do you even understand that, for Luke, it has only been about two and a half years—objective time—from when we defeated the Corrupted Nature Dragon? What has it been for you... ten years?"

"What are you trying to get at, Zed?" Now Andre was on the defensive, though, for some reason, he couldn't force himself to meet the Bard's eyes. Instead, he used scanning the horizon for threats as an excuse to look away. "Are you trying to say that, just because he has had less time compared to me, I should accept that he would leave us to die on a world we don't understand?"

"No." Zed let his anger seep out of him with a long exhalation. "You just need to understand that the only time he has *not* been in combat—for nearly a half century of his time—was when he was on our base world, traveling with us to the *next* battles. He is motivated by bloodshed and becoming stronger. At this point, I think he lives for it. For decades, he has *never* had to deal with having anyone else here. Abyss, I think that when he sees us in this environment, he might think that it's just his mind playing tricks on him!"

The Druid finally turned back to the Bard, who was looking at him with a burning stare. Andre felt his eyes starting to betray him, so he reached up and angrily dashed away the tears that were forming. "It's *Taylor*, Zed. I... I just can't..."

"*When* she is healed up," Zed clapped his hands on the Druid's shoulders, "You had better do something to change your relationship status. Otherwise, I'm going to lure you to the side of the world, you can see it from here, and have Luke chuck you over."

That earned a watery chuckle from the gangly redhead, but he sobered up in the next breath. His eyes had landed on the lotus, and they were rapidly hardening. "I can do more than keep her in stasis. With the sheer amount of power available to me here, I'm certain I can figure out a solution to the terrible damage she accidentally inflicted upon herself."

"That would be good, since the only way we get a professional Healer Ascender is by stepping out of this world and surrendering immediately." Zed started to smirk, but Andre appreciated that he was working hard to keep it off his face. "I hope you figure something out quick, because otherwise, the three of us are going to get all sorts of juicy Potentia, and she's just gonna get delivered to someone else on a platter when we leave. Celestials, she'd be so mad, and there'd be no one for her to blame except herself."

Once again, Andre was impressed by the sheer amount of insight this Bard possessed. "I have spent my entire adult life working with plants, animals, and soil. Perhaps... perhaps I should spend some time following *you* around and learning. I just don't have the same kind of understanding of people that you do. If my life goes the way I want it to go..."

His eyes flipped over to the lotus that Taylor was wrapped in, then back to Zed, who was already wearing a smarmy grin. "...then I need to understand how to deal with people. How to treat them correctly and understand their needs. I believe I can fix an entire planet, yet I can't figure out how to live my own life."

Zed shrugged at that. "First lesson is free! Listen well, my student. You can make all the analogies you want about people and love, like comparing everything to plants that need special attention, lots of watering, additional fertilizer, and such... but the fact of the matter is, people are just different. You cannot fix other people so that they do what you want them to do. Relationships are *not* a problem to be solved; they are a tension to be managed."

"Huh." Before Andre could say much more about that, they seemed to have passed an invisible barrier, and the density of mana in the air around them increased by a small but noticeable amount. "What was that? Are we under attack?"

As far as he could tell, there was nothing around them. Well, that wasn't strictly true. There were haunting forms that he could see in the distance, thanks to his high vantage point. Small flowers started blossoming all over his body before seeming to age and wilt in the next moment. Seeds poured across his clothes and collected in his hands, which he squeezed hard enough to draw a few drops of blood to fertilize the tiny dots of potential life.

"Oh, that? All we did was cross into Zone nineteen. Have we been running for eight hours already? I guess escaping that wildfire took longer than I thought it had. Anyhoo, every time we get into a new Zone, the mana density is slightly higher." Once more, Andre was amazed by how casually his companion could explain what had happened.

Zed pointed at the monsters. "Now, I wasn't exactly informed on what those creatures are, but even Luke stayed away from them unless they got in his way directly. I'm fairly certain that they inflict some kind of Sanity damage, because the last time I was here, I forgot to eat or drink for several days. Probably would have died if I hadn't found myself so fascinated by what Luke was doing to the creatures at the edge of Zone twenty. Also, don't look them in the eyes."

"These are the things that gave you nightmares? Did Luke's advice help?" The Druid wondered aloud, only to see his friend shudder and hunch in on himself.

"I owe Luke a lot. Even more than the two of you." The plain-seeming man stared at the creatures in the distance, his voice coming out hushed. "For many reasons, but most recently... I'm pretty sure his slaughtering hundreds of creatures at a time literally pulled me out of the starvation death spiral those beings inflicted on me, just due to how absolutely *interesting* he was. The Murderhobo was able to ignore their attacks because his only goals are killing monsters and collecting gear. There's no gear to collect here, so that leaves him only one option."

Andre was silent for a long moment, thinking through what his friend had just revealed to him. Now, it was Zed's turn to avoid his eyes, as Andre searched them for answers. Finding none, he turned back to the strange, corkscrew-shaped world they were wandering along. Then, doing what men do best, he ignored the situation and tried to hurry them past it. "How's the weather here? Does it change very much? Is there a rise in beast attacks during certain phases of the moon?"

"No moon here!" Zed seemed just as relieved as he was to be past the awkwardness of the last few minutes. "As far as I can tell, there's no weather to watch out for. Probably for the best for us, because if it rained, that would mean liquid mana was pouring out of the sky and… well, we would die, right?"

"Totally, totally…" They lapsed into silence, which stretched out so long that Andre felt being the one to break it would make the situation even more awkward than the silence was. Soon, he had no choice. Questions were demanding to be released, and his mouth was a poor gatekeeper. "You seemed confident that we would be able to find him at the edge of this Zone, just before he could get into the next one. Why is that?"

Zed was, of course, happy to tell the tale of the last time he had been trapped in this world. Soon, Andre was just as excited to see the unending horde of manufactured monsters that awaited them at the edge of this Zone. He had heard of different Ascenders going to worlds where everything was made of gears and metal and were able to bring back creatures, spell-like abilities, and impressive manufacturing capabilities.

He wasn't certain if these monsters would play a role like those other worlds would, but it would be interesting to bring back some samples to compare with others… Andre paused, realizing that there was no point in weighing himself or his team down. There was no escape from this world without going straight into full-on war, and they were not ready for that. Collecting samples at this point would be nearly as pointless as planning to leave in just a few days.

"We're really going to be trapped here for… a long time, aren't we?" The Druid soberly inquired of the Bard sitting next to him, who had pulled out a lute and was strumming it softly in time with the 'rootfalls' of his mobile flora. "It isn't going to be days or even weeks. It's years, right?"

"Only if we want to stay alive when we finally leave." Zed didn't look up from his instrument, as serious about this situation as Andre was. "We're going to need to be able to defeat those high-level Royal guards and whatever forces they bring to bear. The longer that we stay here, the more defensible of a location they will be able to erect. But, if we don't stay here long enough, we'll be easily captured either way. Let's hope that we just get insane influxes of Potentia and can boost our levels and competency to an extremely high degree. Also, *please* don't die. You're our only source of food and water, or juice I suppose, so if we lose you... everyone except Luke needs to leave immediately."

"I'm glad you see me as your mobile larder."

"No, larder *and* cistern," Zed corrected him instantly. "Don't sell yourself short. It's a small yet important distinction."

"One of these days, I'm going to make you walk." Andre took a moment to point out all of the monsters that were sprinting toward them, unable to catch up thanks to the extremely long-legged, plant-based travel device he was piloting. "It's not just here, Zed. I can think of half a dozen times when you're just too slow to catch up, so you jump onto my back or Luke's. I've heard of riding someone's coattails to success, but you do it just to keep up."

Zed waved his hand while wiggling his fingers, "We all have our strengths and weaknesses. The two of you just happened to be very fast and able to carry a heavy load. Onward, my noble steed!"

Andre let the Bard fall off his mobile plains-walker, allowing a satisfied smile to grace his lips as he heard Zed scream. "Stop whining! I tied you on; you can just hang out down there, closer to the monsters for a while."

"What if I-" Zed's words were lost as he swung in an arc underneath the plains-walker. He tried again as he swung back. "What if I said I was *really* sorry?"

CHAPTER THIRTY-TWO

The long strides and hops of the plains-walker were reminiscent of a gazelle, allowing it to eat up the distance between them and Luke, although the high-leveled Ascender was able to move much, *much* faster. Still, they soon had their first indication that they were getting close to the Murderhobo—the air itself was shaking, small shock waves that felt like rapid changes in elevation reaching their ears. They were extremely intermittent, only once every five minutes or so.

"I recognize that sound!" Zed called out while clapping happily. He had been reeled in and was back to sitting in a normal position on the enormous plant. "Luke is striking the front line of the creatures ahead then getting blasted away as a chunk of ground meat! I think the time in between *pops* is Luke sucking down some mana to heal his wounds."

Andre shuttered at that thought. The fact that the Murderhobo would willingly inflict so much damage on his own body, even knowing that he could heal up time after time, was something he just couldn't wrap his head around. Of the group, Andre was the only other member who had any kind of enhanced healing factor. That was a benefit he had greatly enjoyed when he was in the Scarrocco Nature Preserve, but he had very low hopes that he would be able to connect to the world here, at least enough to have a significant benefit to his own healing.

He needed blood, oftentimes his own, in order to use his most potent Abilities, but that usually only required a few drops. The way he had heard Zed describe Luke fighting on this world was something entirely different. Luke would happily shed half a dozen pounds of his abdomen in order to inflict a *wound* on another creature. The Murderhobo would be bashed, smashed, and in any other plane of existence, he would be broken beyond any hope of repair. Frankly... Andre was interested in seeing it in person, his academic proclivities urging him to get a good accounting of what sort of damage his friend was capable of dealing and taking.

He wouldn't have to wait very much longer, going by how much louder the sounds of the blows landing were.

The landscape didn't work against them, being an ever-downward, gentle slope. No, the only true impediment to their vision was the dense suffusion of mana in the air, creating a thick fog his eyes simply couldn't penetrate. Still, it was affected by physical movement, and that was how they found their friend. For an instant, he was visible as his enormous Great-mace landed on the forefront of a strange type of creature that Andre's mind had no frame of reference for. Chunks of metal, an oily substance, the very ground that the Murderhobo was standing on, and the air itself was shoved away from the absolute devastation the blow generated.

Andre blinked, and his friend was replaced with a plume of dirt and grass erupting into the air. Dozens of needle-like spears penetrated through it and peppered the area his friend had been standing on just a moment before. The Druid's mouth dropped open, and he rubbed at his eyes to see if they were deceiving him. "No way is that real. Where did Luke go? How'd he avoid those attacks? How fast can these things throw spears?

I had no idea that they were even getting ready to attack; I couldn't even see it!"

"I hate to be the bear of bad news," Zed reached into his satchel and pulled out a small headband that had bear ears attached to the top, putting it on and growling lightly before saying the rest of what he had to say. "Everything in this world is just like that. Ridiculously fast and dangerous like you wouldn't believe. Also, all of the food is poison, and the water is toxic. Abyss, most people would have burst into flame just breathing the air!"

He growled again, swiped at the air with his imaginary paws, then took his headband off and put it away. The entire time he was doing that, Andre could only watch with great incredulity. "You actually bought that, just so that you could use it for one joke?"

"No." Zed had an enormous smirk on his face. "I bought that so I could use it as a joke with every single person I *possibly* could. You're going to get so sick of that bit. Guaranteed. Also, Luke is over there. Remember, when you're looking for him after an attack, you don't look at where you think he went or where he was going. You follow the trail of destruction until you set your eyes upon his broken corpse. Wait, no, I mean 'rapidly rejuvenating body'."

Andre followed the Bard's pointing index finger, his eyes eventually alighting on what could easily have been mistaken as a meteorite impact site. The swirling mists made it so that his normal habit of looking for movement was failing him, and he instead needed to find what was still. For a long, long moment, he actually thought that Luke was dead. More of his body was on the ground around him than was on his bones—or at least, that was what it looked like from his vantage point.

Now that his eyes were locked upon the fallen man, his greatly enhanced eyesight could make out the fact that his skin was knitting back together, fresh blood was pumping from open wounds, and a large amount of his hair had fallen out.

"Are you noticing the hair?" Zed nudged him, the humor in his voice attempting to hide the slight quivering of fear underneath it. "Yeah, apparently that is a strange side effect of getting liquid mana on your body. It just makes all of your hair fall out. I think it has something to do with it being nonliving material, but, who knows for sure? Maybe you can do a study on it. It would have a fairly niche market, since I think there are four total people that have the option to bathe in liquid mana. I'd read it."

"But he's always *so* hairy?" Andre simply couldn't wrap his head around what he was seeing. The sheer devastation Luke could wreak on everything around him was how he perceived his friend. Not this… destroyed being. Even as he had that thought, Luke hopped back to his feet, lifted his hand, and caught the enormous Greatmace that was flying through the air toward him. Then the man vanished again, reappearing where the Druid had first seen him, only to almost perfectly replicate the situation.

This time, Andre was able to watch as hundreds of the strange, synthetic monsters were absolutely devastated, only to have a fresh group of them appear in the exact same position with no discernible damage to them. His brow furrowed as he looked at this new detail. "What was that? How did that just happen?"

"We don't know!" Zed chipperly announced. "Luke really hit a wall trying to get into this Zone. Ha! *I* hit a wall in effort I'm willing to expend when I try to run too fast; he literally hits a wall of monsters and bounces off. Anyway, he has been stuck here for quite a while. Every time he kills a large group of monsters, they just get back up. He's tried to go over them, through them, and I think he was muttering something about making a tunnel at one point. I don't think that would work, as they're right at the boundary to the next Zone. Something about this place does *not* like interaction between the two areas and actively fights back against intrusion."

"You mean to tell me that he just shows up here, kills all of these things as much as possible for nearly thirty days straight, then comes back?" Andre had never felt that he understood his friend as well as he did right now. "This explains just... so much. How he handles problems back on the base world. Everything from seeing something in the way of his goals to having an enemy take the field against him. He's used to having so many enemies that he just needs to throw himself face-first against them until they break, or his skull stays caved in permanently."

"Yes, but now that *we're* here, we can-"

Andre's eyes lit up, and he snapped his fingers, "That's it! Good thinking, Zed, we can figure out a better method for fighting each of these individual types of monsters. They have to have some kind of weakness, and perhaps we can take out large groups of them from a distance? What if I figured out a way to send across some seeds and took over the majority of the Zone with plants that could destroy these things? Sure, that might take some trial and error, some testing over time, but I think it's manageable. It's not like we're going anywhere until we're strong enough to handle most things."

"Huh." Zed cleared his throat and looked away. "Yeah, that's better than what I was going to say. I was going to say that since we're here now, we can start siphoning off some of the Potentia he's earning from these monsters. It isn't like he's going to be annoyed that we're joining in on the killing, right?"

Andre took a deep breath and sent a long look over at the lotus Taylor was wrapped up in, wishing wistfully that he had someone he considered his intellectual equal to discuss these issues with. "Well... I suppose... that *is* the end result? The goal itself isn't to take the Potentia, but it is a side effect. Fair enough. I guess."

Zed beamed at him so brightly that Andre felt bad for his unkind intrusive thoughts. Internally, he chastised himself for forgetting that Zed had something like fifty years less life experience than him. The Druid shook that off, once again looking over at the lotus. His jaw set, and his mouth firmed into a line.

"We have lots of work to do, Zed. Let's get down there and help him."

The plains-walker dropped a foot root near the fallen Murderhobo, and as Andre started to lower them, Luke was suddenly on his feet and swinging at the vine that had come within range. Andre could have slapped himself. As the enormous plant started to topple over, the Druid's thoughts were barely louder than the Murderhobo's challenging, inarticulate bellow of rage.

"You know *better* than this, Andre. *Why* did I put a moving plant near the tree-punching Barbarian? Come *on*." The red-haired man focused his attention on his companions, wrapping them in vines and swinging each of them to safety as the plains-walker collapsed to the ground. "Hey there, Luke! Want a hand?"

The Murderhobo stared at them, evaluating them and seeming to come to a conclusion. "No. I have as many hands as I can use, but I would take new and better weapons. Unless you can grow me an additional arm? Then, I would take another hand."

Andre's smile froze on his face as he remembered that his friend was far too literal. "Well, in that case, how about I help you bust this blockade?"

"Sure." The Murderhobo hoisted Cookie to his shoulder and started walking toward the enemy. "Don't get too close. You'll die."

CHAPTER THIRTY-THREE

- LUKE -

He would never tell them this, but Luke had completely forgotten that his group was in this world with him. Right now, he had carte blanche to increase his strength and delve deeper into his world than he'd ever had the opportunity to reach before. The Murderhobo wasn't about to give this up. Now that his team had shown up, he felt a subtle, lingering dissatisfaction. Luke knew that at any time, they could say that they were strong enough to go back, and he would be forced to leave. That fear was slightly relieved when he saw that Andre had taken it upon himself to throw Taylor into a lotus.

That eased his nerves a little bit, even if he knew it was an unfair assessment of the Mage's intentions. She had changed, drastically so, since they had been able to upgrade her Mana Channels. All of her decades of experience were able to be utilized properly, her thoughts in an order that prioritized their team's cohesiveness instead of a fervent patriotic zeal that stripped away all variant avenues for growth or completing a mission.

Luke had even been slightly impressed when she started frying the Ascenders hidden in the army of the Dynasty of Dogs. The fact that she could so easily sniff out the powerful enemies was a trait he wanted, so that they could no longer escape him and "*Ambush* us when we pop out of a world!"

It was only when his friends nearby took a step back in shock that he realized he had bellowed the last part of his thoughts aloud. He didn't particularly care if they were nervous around him, Luke had work to do. Looking at the massive stretch of enemies that was waiting for him, he decided to try a ranged option one more time. After all, things changed all the time. Maybe *this* time, a ranged weapon would work. Throwing his bottle at the synthetic monsters, he waited patiently as it sailed through the air. He frowned slightly, noting that the throw had taken nearly a *half* second to reach the front ranks of the enemy, instead of its usual four-tenths of a second.

He wasn't sure if he was a little farther back than he normally was, but the end result was the same. A silver needle sniped the bottle out of the air, and both were destroyed or disrupted. For some reason, these creatures wouldn't react to a melee weapon caving in their faces, at least not until one of their comrades had taken the blow. But a flying bottle, rock, boulder, spear, or person?

Luke didn't know why, but that seemed to infuriate them. All of the strange, towering monsters were jostling slightly, looking for any other target in the area. That was why he tried this method from so far back; it would guarantee that they were agitated. Then, if he walked into range, he would be met with a wall of silver death flying through the air at him.

Several minutes passed before the strange monsters settled into their normal hibernating patterns once more, and he charged in with Cookie at the ready. At this point, he had tried thrusts, uppercuts, and crushing blows from overhead, but nothing was quite as effective as a simple swing of the Great-mace. Combining that with Bum Thunder and Shockwave Cleave—boosted by an additional chunk of mana—meant that several hundred of the creatures would die and give him a few instants of lag time before he had to contend with the first needles. As per usual, the creatures had respawned before he was even able to land, thanks to the double-edged weapon that his Source-cerer's Armory forced on him.

Damage dealt: 34,212 blunt. (6,831 weapons in range, average maximum damage 50 per weapon.)

Potentia gained: 2,743.

Damage taken: 445 damage from rebound.

Current health: 485/930.

The sheer number of weapons in the area boosted his attack so high that the backlash caused blood vessels to collapse, arteries to explode, and meat to be stripped off of tendons. His bones broke in dozens of places, and the cartilage was shattered... overall, it was a truly unpleasant experience. He had refilled all of his water skins on the way here, so he was able to yet again pop the top of one and pour as much as he could down his throat, then dump the rest over any open wounds. The flesh underneath hissed and popped then reformed into a slightly better version of itself. "Yeah, that sucks. Okay. Let's do it again."

"Luke! A moment of your time, if you wouldn't mind?" Andre's voice from so near made Luke's head snap to the side, and he barely caught himself before he clobbered his friend. The Murderhobo let out a puff of breath, having known that their mere presence would cause constant interruptions in his work. He trudged over, dragging Cookie behind him and leaving a trail of tilled soil in her wake.

"What, Andre? I'm busy." He waved a hand to indicate the monsters swarming in the distance, still firing silver needles at him. Something about that thought caught his attention; he wasn't entirely certain why he was calling them needles, as they were six feet long and nearly a half foot thick, but... "Maybe it's just the shape?"

Andre gave him a strange look, which Luke promptly decided to ignore. "Right. Anyway, I have an idea of growing vines and such that could destroy the creatures on that side, but it would help immensely if I could get a sample of their bodies for testing purposes."

The Murderhobo simply stared at the oversized Druid, trying to think of the best way to explain to his friend how ridiculous the idea Andre had just presented to him was. "That's stupid, so much so that I can't even explain it properly. You want one of them? Go ahead and try."

"Is it just that you can't get close enough, or that you can't *stay* close enough?" Andre called out questioningly. "I might have a solution for that as well."

He dangled his words in a tantalizing manner, which made Luke grind his teeth. Why did people never just say what they wanted to say? Did he truly need to engage in a back-and-forth simpering competition with his cohort and drag information out of them? "Look. They cannot cross that dividing line while they are alive, or they just detonate. If I could get close enough to keep on hitting them, I would. I can't grab one and drag it across, as again, it *explodes*."

"Listen, I have a solution to your problem, or at least I think I do. Based on what you have told me in the past about your 'Skills', that is." Andre let a half-cocked grin show on his face but seemed to realize that Luke was getting annoyed with the conversation dragging on. "Let me ask you something... are you using Shockwave Cleave every time you hit?"

"Yes." Andre seemed to be waiting for more of an answer, but if he wanted more, Luke firmly believed that he should have asked for more.

The Druid smiled knowingly, pulling out a *book* of all things. Luke resisted the urge to punch it in the spine, as it wasn't flying or diving at them. "I think you have a few synergistic effects on your Skills! Look at this. Based on what you told me about your weapon abilities-"

"Skills."

"Yes, those." Andre waved him off without taking his eyes off the numbers in front of him. "Based on what you told me about them, you shouldn't be having this kind of insane backlash. Your weapon Skill, it adds on the weapons and armor of creatures near you, correct?"

"Yes." Again, there was a slight pause as if Andre were waiting for more information.

"Good, good. However, it should not be doing... that." Now he waved at the trail of destruction that had been appearing each time Luke slammed into the earth after getting backhanded by his own attack. "Look here... that Skill should only be registering weapons and armor that are within one *meter* of your attack. It's registering instead a massive swath of creatures. My hypothesis, if you would care to test it, is that when you activate your Shockwave Cleave, the Skill is counting *all* targets that'll be impacted by the shockwaves as valid targets and factoring in their weapons!"

Luke took a moment to digest that, looking down at the weapon in his hand then into the distance. "Huh."

"All you need to do in order to test this is attack without adding on that particular Skill. If this succeeds, you should be able to stand in front of them and consistently kill the monsters as they reappear, instead of getting blasted away time after time." Andre took a deep breath, and Luke just knew the Druid was going to be talking for quite a long while to explain his proof and theorizing, but he had better things to do.

"Bum Thunder." The casual activation of his Skill seemed to take the Druid by surprise, but Luke was already ten meters away. Then he was running and soon swinging Cookie at the once-again dormant synthetic beings.

Dong.

Damage dealt: 434 blunt.

Potentia gained: 5.

The creature rang like a bell as it shattered into broken rubble—specifically, a dinner bell. As soon as his blow had landed, Luke had half a dozen needles bouncing off his armor. That half a dozen turned into several hundred over the course of two to three seconds, but he stayed still in the deluge in order to verify the results.

A smile cracked his set-in-stone face as a long needle came for his left eye, only to hit his armor and fall to the ground. "I only killed one of them instead of approximately four hundred, but now I'm not taking damage. Let's see which way is more efficient."

With his armor constantly being regenerated, thanks to the mana density of the area, he was able to completely weather the attacks of the void-tipped needles, even as multiple of them hit his armor at once. Dropping Cookie to the side, he equipped a long spear in either weapon slot, then started stabbing forward with alternating strikes. Left, right, left. Every attack was aimed at the exact same spot, and each attack killed a creature. Even so, by the time he had pulled the weapon back and shoved the other forward once again, a new monster had appeared in the place of the fallen one. This close to the combat, he was able to discern for certain that they were not moving to fill the gap; they were simply reappearing out of thin air.

"Three hundred and ninety-nine, four *hundred*." He paused at that point, trying to tally up how much time had passed. "I get four attacks a second, so it's a little bit less than two minutes to get to four hundred kills. Yes. This is more efficient."

There was no need to explain the situation to Andre, Luke was certain he had figured it out by now. He stayed right where he was, continually attacking until the pile of needles around him reached his shoulders, which impeded his ability to attack. Then he moved a few feet to the right, and the attacks continued as a new pile started to form around him.

"I guess just join us whenever you get tired!" Zed called over to him with slight exasperation in his voice.

"Heh." Luke chuckled a single time, not slowing down his attacks in the slightest. "Joke's on you. I'm always fresh, thanks to all this mana."

CHAPTER THIRTY-FOUR

After several hours of harassing and haranguing, Zed finally convinced Luke to take a break from the slaughter and come back to discuss various strategies. He assured them that he was very unhappy with having to stop watching his Potentia counter increase and informed them that the break in going Full Murderhobo had better be worth it.

What truly convinced him was the fact that his efficiency had increased to ridiculous heights, thanks to a simple one-off comment from Andre. If the Druid could give him more helpful tips like that, he might even be more inclined to pay attention when the man spoke outside of advice. It was doubtful, but *everything* could happen in a universe of infinite possibility. By the time Luke joined the duo, they were deep in a heated conversation.

"I *understand* that she's going to be in pain, but if you don't wake her up, she's going to miss out on all of the Potentia." Zed was arguing furiously. "What do you think she would rather do? Miss out on all of the new monsters that are easy to kill, and give high amounts of experience, or sleep through it so that she doesn't have to 'hurt'?"

Andre leaned in, his voice going low and dark. "She was charred to the bone, Zed. It's not *about* if she'll be in pain or not. Frankly, her nerves could be completely destroyed. There's a chance that she just doesn't survive waking up. Not unless we do something that gives her a better chance or *anything* to regrow what has been destroyed. She needs a Healer, and we don't have one."

At first, Luke wasn't going to join in on the conversation, but then he realized what they were talking about. "That's why Taylor is in the lotus. I thought you chucked her in there because she was causing you problems."

Andre and Zed both looked at Luke blankly, their eyes full of confusion. Unsurprisingly, it was the Druid who replied. "What are you even talking about? Do you have any idea how hard she would try to kill us after we let her out of a lotus, if we had put her in one without getting her permission? I don't think I could even force the issue, unless I had a whole lot of land that I was bound to, and I went all-out. Even then... she's pretty quick to shoot lightning around."

"She blew herself up." Zed helpfully explained. "I was trying to tell her that using fire on this world was a bad idea, and she wanted to test why that was. Sent a full power blast of flame out of her hand. It was super effective, but she hurt herself in her confusion."

Luke nodded solemnly at that information. "Fire is way too explosive here. Burns too hot for too long. On the plus side, it will stop at Zone boundaries."

"You're saying we don't have to worry about igniting the atmosphere and killing everything on this planet in one giant conflagration?" Zed's eyes were sparkling as he spoke, though his tone was disappointed.

"No. That's not what I'm saying. That might actually happen, if you were to use a ranged fire Spell and aim *up*." Luke sternly warned the Bard. "But if it's just the ground on fire, eventually it will go out, and it won't cross the Zone boundaries. How close to death was she?"

"They were shaking hands and playing rock-parchment-shears." Zed started to spin up a story for the Murderhobo, but he lashed out and clamped a hand over the Bard's mouth.

"Andre?" The Murderhobo growled, trying to get some information that was actually useful.

The Druid actually agreed with the Bard for once, "He's correct. She was down in the double digits, and if she sneezed too hard, she could have died. That might not seem like much to you, since you can just regenerate with a sip of liquid, but to the rest of us-"

"That would work." Luke hesitated and started rapping his knuckles on Cookie's outer edges. "I probably wouldn't smash her face in accidentally, if I knew she was going to be doing it."

"Smash her face...? Luke, what?" Zed moved protectively in front of the lotus that contained Taylor, an action that increased his reputation in Luke's brain. The Bard was the most outspoken against the Mage, even years after her mental rescue. The fact that he would protect her from a perceived threat, even from one of their own team members, was a huge step in the right direction for unit cohesion.

Luke tapped the Bard on the chest. "You should learn it, too, but you won't be staring at me. That'll make things easier. It won't feel quite as challenging. Heh. Alright, wake her up."

Now it was Andre's turn to get defensive, "No! I don't know what is the matter with the two of you, but I am *not* going to be waking up a person who is being held together by charred ligaments and carbonized flesh. Not without a good reason!"

"Sure you are. Pump her full of the best painkillers that you can whip up, keep her focused and alert, and we'll have her fixed up in no time flat." Luke slowly held out a fist, letting it inch through the air closer and closer to the Druid, then lifted his thumb ever so slightly until it was finally in the upright position. "We got this. Go team."

"Thank you, Luke. You know, I was *just* trying to figure out how to make giving someone a thumbs up as creepy as possible, then you stepped up in a big way." Zed had scooted to the side so that he was out of the way between Luke and the flower-encased female. "Just so we all know what you're planning here, can you explain it as though we had no idea what you were talking about? As in, no clue at all?"

"She needs to heal; we don't have a Healer. We can make her heal herself." Luke turned to start walking toward the monsters once again, as his companions tried to see if there was any information in what he had said that was usable at all. They seemed to decide that there was not.

Zed scooted up next to him, stopping when he was about fifty feet away from the monsters, also right at the edge of their range. "Maybe just a *tish* more information, buddy? Otherwise Andre will get all grumpy about not knowing what he is supposed to do. You know he doesn't like that. He's the sort of guy that really likes to have a plan, a man with a-"

"If *you* stop talking, I will start." Luke closed his eyes for a moment. Then he opened them and turned his full attention onto the Bard. "I will say that I don't understand why you can't come up with these plans yourself. Andre was able to optimize my attacks with old information. Why is he not using the correct new information to make his plans? Taylor got access to Meta-magic. All she needs in order to make a Spell version of something is to see it in effect. I'm going to go and intentionally get damaged so she can watch carefully and turn my healing Skill into a single-use Spell effect."

Zed's eyes bulged to the point where Luke idly wondered if he would need to catch them as they popped out of his skull. "That's... that's brilliant! Just like you said, I can do the same thing with Echoes of Reality! I'll tell Andre! Maybe give us twenty minutes or something, so that we can make sure she is all painkiller-ed up? Also, I still need to convince Andre about the importance of waking her up at all, and will do a little vote to see if we think that your plan will work at all. Then we could-"

"Bum Thunder." The shockwave that followed his move-ment sent Zed tumbling, even as Luke appeared in front of the wall of monsters. He needed to do a bit more running to get in range, then he went straight into fighting. For the first time, some of the needles being fired off were not sent at him, instead being launched toward the Bard who had dropped to his butt. Luke wasn't worried, as he had ensured that Zed was out of their casual range. Still, it was funny to hear a yelp of fear in the distance, followed by the sound of feet pounding on soft grass. "Never gets old."

He had earned nearly a thousand Potentia by the time Andre angrily shouted at him that they were ready. Luke glanced backward, seeing a wraith coated in flower petals staring at him. For a moment, he almost went on the attack, then he realized that he was looking at what was left of Taylor's face. Without another word, he positioned himself correctly, called Cookie to hand, and swung. "Shockwave Cleave!

Damage dealt: 34,881 blunt.
Potentia gained: 2,652.
Damage taken: 349 damage from rebound.
Current health: 581/930.

Then he was flying through the air, his body nearly half destroyed. Blood flew out in huge arcs, and his clothes were shredded even further. He had been noticing that his manifested armor was holding his clothes together, but he was pretty sure that, if he were to drop the manifestation at this moment, he would be completely naked as soon as he was hit by the first gust of wind. Instead, Luke landed and tore through the ground, coming to a stop only a few feet away from his mummified teammate. "Ow."

"Seriously Luke, I have no idea how you're able to consistently damage yourself over and over! I bet that, if you would just take the time to-"

Luke interrupted Zed's tirade by holding up a hand and wheezing out, "This is probably going to be really hard for you to learn, Bard. Pretty sure that, in order to 'hear' a Skill and turn it into a Mastery, *you* have to be quiet."

A look of dawning horror crept across Zed's face. "Oh no!

He's right! Those monsters finally did it! They beat *sense* into him!"

Then he scampered over and got on his hands and knees, pressing his ear up against Luke's actively bleeding chest. Luke let his head slide to the side, and he locked eyes with the Taylor almost-corpse. "I hope you're ready; I don't want to have to do this more than I need."

He dumped a mouthful of mana into his mouth, then onto his chest, narrowly missing the Bard. To Zed's credit, he was so focused on listening that he didn't react to the liquid death that was mere inches from his head. Usually, Luke would get to his feet as soon as he was physically able to do so, but now he held still until 'You Need to Stop' ran its course fully.

"This Skill allows me to take mana from my environment and use it to regrow and replace damage to my body. It also makes it impossible for poisons and hallucinogens to take effect and slowly increases in potency when I find something that can make it through the resistance."

"I refuse to be part of increasing this Skill for you," Andre warningly stated, getting an annoyed glance from Zed and Luke almost at the exact same moment. "Did you get it, Taylor?"

It took a long moment, but she was able to rasp out a harsh, "No."

"If we did it again, do you think you could learn it?" Luke stood up and asked her, trying not to loom over her desiccated form.

Again, there was hesitation, but he could tell that she was trying to form the word 'yes'. Luke nodded then ran toward the still-agitated monsters. "Then we try again!"

In just a few moments, he had returned to his crater and was drinking liquid mana. He let the Skill play out then got to his feet and sent a questioning glance at their Mage. Luke didn't need to ask if she had been successful. The reforming trachea that could be seen through her sloughed-away skin told him everything he needed to know. He took a quick step toward her, dumping the remnants of the liquid mana down her open mouth.

"*Luke!*" Andre wailed in fright as he *walloped* the huge Berserker away with a sapling-sized tree trunk. "You killed her!"

The Murderhobo returned in an instant, backhanding Andre so hard that he went tumbling like Luke had only a few minutes ago. He shouted after the bouncing form, "*Careful,* Druid! You don't have a bunch of *grass* fighting your battles for you!"

He looked at Taylor, whose flesh was actively bleeding now that her body was rapidly producing blood once again. "Huh. You need to prioritize growing skin so that you keep that blood inside of your body."

"Is that... possible?" Taylor's voice had energy in it again, even though she coughed and sent out a handful of charred black particles, whose origins Luke didn't bother to put too much thought into.

He shrugged, "It might be. I usually just dump water on myself until the process is completed. How long do you have the Spell for?"

"Until I am... fully healed... or the concentration of... mana decreases." Taylor managed to gasp over the course of a few seconds. "I'm so weak... I need more mana. Get me some?"

"Mana? More like man *up*." Zed appeared next to Luke, a huge smile on his face. "You've got to be at least half healed by now; go get your own water! Hey, Luke! I got my own version of it, too! Andre, looks like *you're* the easiest to permanently damage while we're in this dimension!"

"Yeah, I *am*." Andre woozily walked over, his jaw obviously broken. "Pleash shtop hitting me."

The Murderhobo shrugged at that, even as he offered a water skin to Taylor. She was healthy enough she could push the flowers away and reach out for it. "You started it. Don't hit other people if you aren't okay with getting hit back."

CHAPTER THIRTY-FIVE

- TAYLOR -

Her organs were barely holding together, and lightning and fire raced through her body, altering everything it touched. She had used mana. She had been connected to mana. She had never been *molded* by mana. Her body was, until this point, only changed in the standard ways by her expenditure of Potentia. However, as she activated the Spell that she had managed to copy off of Luke's Skill, she was able to directly feel her body being remade.

Thanks to her main Characteristic increase having always been placed within her Senses, Taylor was able to track the lightning-fast movement of power, watching carefully within herself as she waited for it to be expended. She only had access to this Spell until she was fully healed, which meant she needed to regulate her intake of liquid mana so as not to burn herself out. As the mutagenic power roiled through her, she took a small sip again and again, whenever she felt its efficacy waning. She had never considered mana as a 'mutagenic', but now she was confronted with that very fact.

Her reasoning behind this was simple: her cells were not being healed by this power; they were being *replaced*. This strange liquid energy seemed to understand intrinsically what the best parts of her were, as if it were following the optimal growth of her body from something even smaller than the cells within her.

Finally, she was too close to the edge to risk taking another sip, so she opened her eyes and pulled her mind out of the deep, dark well that she had put it in to keep her sanity intact. Now, instead of watching the process, she felt at her remade body. A wince was only a fraction of a second away, as she stretched her body and fully expected to find that it was still damaged beyond repair.

But there was no pain, no matter how much her mind screamed that it should be there. Opening her eyes fully, she looked around and noticed that she was still wrapped within the lotus, and it had roots tickling up her left arm toward her mouth and nostril, now that Andre was otherwise occupied. "Oh, *no* you don't!"

Flexing her arms and legs simultaneously, she burst from the petals of the lotus in a shower of white confetti and chunks of burned, blackened... bone and skin? Which had fallen from her during her rejuvenation. Truly, it was a macabre sight, but she didn't mind one whit. For the few moments she had been fully conscious after damaging herself so badly, she had been in unimaginable pain. Taylor would prefer death to going there again. Now, having been able to move past that so quickly, she exalted in the freedom of movement her body allowed.

All the way until Zed coughed and pointed downward. She followed his motion, realizing that she had been clothed by a flower. All of her garments had been completely destroyed in the conflagration. Slowly she turned around, so that she was facing away from her teammates, and calmly called out to Andre. "My Druidic friend, would you be so kind as to clothe me in greenery instead of my birthday suit?"

"Ah, ahh... yes! Yup, I can do that." Andre quickly reached

for a seed pod on his own outfit, tossing it in an arc toward her lightly shivering body. It bounced off her back then latched on, roots growing along her skin for a moment before vines and leaves sprouted and rapidly wrapped around her. In only a double handful of seconds, she was covered enough to rejoin her group, if not polite society.

"What did I miss?" Taylor gently inquired of the others, meeting their eyes in a direct challenge. Zed smirked and opened his mouth to call her bluff, only for a vine to wrap around his head and gag him.

"Mostly, it was just travel," Andre casually stated, even though he was blushing as red as his hair. "For the last while, we have been watching Luke destroying monsters as we tried to figure out a way to help."

Taylor looked over at where the rhythmic sound of spears clinking against armor were ringing out. She watched through the strange fog as Luke pumped his arms like the pistons of a waterwheel, each thrust forward felling one of the enormous monstrosities he was fighting. The Mage took in the tall, ivory-colored, faceless amalgamations of metal and cloth and had to suppress a gulp on a sudden dry throat. "What are *those*?"

"We don't know, and for some reason, that makes Luke really upset!" Zed had bitten his way through the vine and spoke as he was spitting out a pulpy chunk of green. "I guess he's used to knowing what he's fighting when he's here, and he muttered something about this being 'just like the goat situation', whatever that means."

With the tingle of overabundant mana still present within her system, Taylor looked out at the thousands of enemies in her vision and allowed a savage smile to slither across her face. "I think I know how I can help."

"Please don't shoot fire at them," Andre pointedly reminded her. "I don't know if you can survive doing it again."

That removed a small amount of her feral grin, but she hadn't been planning to roast herself again. "I was talking about long-range attacks. A bombardment of artillery attacks and the like, with Zed coordinating it so that he can get some Potentia as well."

Deciding that it would just be easier to start making with the magic, Taylor started casting Thunder Beast's Eye, continually pumping mana into it in order to bring the Spell to new heights. Each second, she was able to regenerate enough mana to consistently put more into the Spell, so she continued devoting that power to adding additional lightning bolts to the frame-work. Eventually, she was forced to stop, out of sheer mental fatigue of containing the power and keeping it from erupting in a cataclysmic single burst.

Panting heavily, she cut off the channel running between them, ending her mana expenditure. She stared up at the enor-mous eye in the sky, which easily had five thousand bolts of lightning ready to blast out of it. She couldn't help but whisper, "It's *beautiful*."

The eye was staring at the strange amalgamations, the central pupil of it flickering along the ranks of enemies so quickly that it wouldn't have been possible if it were not literally made of lightning itself. It could have been Taylor's imagina-tion, but she felt that the eye was *excited*. Completely satisfied with the Spell of her own creation, she smirked at her compan-ions and started walking toward the edge of the conflict. "Are you guys coming, or am I going to claim all the Potentia for myself?"

As she glided across the ground toward her new test subjects, Luke turned and took a look at the enormous spectacle she had created. He huffed gently in either surprise or slight disbelief, indicating that she should take the enemies on the left. Taylor was fine with that and almost positive that she would be able to end this threat entirely on her own. With a deep breath, she very carefully had the eye send out only a single bolt of lightning.

Zzzap-pow!

Damage dealt: 10,125 (225 lightning damage, 45 creatures hit!)

Potentia gained: 2,250! Your Sigil is recording a new type of creature destroyed! Would you like to add this new creature to the Hollow Kingdom's bestiary for a small reward? Yes / No.

The fact that the creatures were not added to the bestiary already meant Luke had not wanted to. She trusted his judgment and selected 'no' without any further hesitation. "Forty-five creatures killed… that means they are worth fifty Potentia each?"

"They are worth *fifty* to you?" Luke shouted furiously. "I'm starting to get less than five!"

"Hey!" Zed called sadly. "You guys are getting Potentia?"

Andre shrugged at the Bard and got to work making plants.

"Let's see if this works for getting a cut sent my way… hey, Taylor, there're a whole bunch of enemies to the left of Luke. Try killing as many of them as you can."

Taylor decided to keep her mouth shut after that and simply rake in the power increases. Controlling the Thunder Beast's Eye was a slight challenge at this size, but she mentally willed it to strafe along the line of creatures, blasting a straight line of energy every other second.

Just as she made the command, a silver needle penetrated her right kneecap, obliterating it and pinning her leg to the ground behind her. She let out a scream of pain, even as she gripped the needle-spear-thing to keep from falling over backward and taking additional damage.

Damage taken: 50 penetrating damage! Right leg crippled, movement speed will be greatly impaired until this wound is repaired.

"Ahh! Look out, they increased their range!" Zed shouted just an instant too late to help her. Taylor heard Luke roar in pain as the automatons that hadn't been able to attack him due to their distance suddenly added their attacks to the ones raining down on him. Through the pain-filled haze, she watched him accumulate light wounds. "Retreat! Everyone! It looks like they are able to react to outside interference. That, or they are able to fight back at greater range if someone is using ranged attacks against them!"

The Mage grabbed the needle, pulling it out of her leg with

a wet *squelch*. Using her hands and one leg, she bear-crawled away from the new edge of the creatures' range. Moments later, she was dragged out of the way by her clothing, which had grown longer vines and was pulling her toward Andre. Before she even got there, her clothing had wrapped tightly around her wound, staunching the blood flow and injecting her with local anesthetic.

To her great relief, during the entire time she had lost her concentration, her Spell had been continuing to work as ordered. Hundreds, then thousands of monsters were being destroyed every second, even if there was no indication on the battlefield. Her eyes tracked one of her bolts of lightning, seeing a long row of the creatures get melted into slag, only to be replaced in the next instant by a fresh set of the creatures, perfectly healthy and ready to attack.

"Celestial feces, this world *sucks!*" Her annoyed mutter was heard by her teammates, and Zed began laughing so hard he had to hold his sides.

"You're so... ha... so right." He wiped a tear off his cheek, sitting down next to her and smiling as she felt at the leg that had almost been entirely amputated. If the needle had hit dead center, it would have completely removed her leg in a single strike. Luckily for her, it had been aimed at center mass, so it was still attached by two inches of cartilage and skin on the outer edge. "Looks like you need to watch Luke heal up again. Something tells me you're going to do a lot of that. Just remember... no matter how impressive he looks, *don't* fall in love."

"W-*what?*" Taylor muttered in surprise as she looked at the Bard wildly then over to Andre in a flash of concern. "Luke? Who could ever-"

"Ahh, I'm just messing with you." Zed's eyes twinkled knowingly. "But it wouldn't hurt to let your other teammates know that you aren't going to be swayed by his enormous, rippling muscles. You know, for posterior's sake."

"Posterity's sake, you mean?" Taylor's thoughts were whirling so quickly that she missed his chuckle.

"Yeah, that. Sorry, I was distracted. Not sure if you noticed yet, but the vines that dragged you over here and are now acting like a tourniquet had to come from somewhere. Like... your clothes." He gave her a wink, then turned and sprinted away.

She was laying flat on her stomach, having not been able to move under her own power, but she looked back and down... seeing that the full moon was indeed out tonight. Even though she had feigned disregard the first time, being caught out like this twice within only a few minutes was too much.

"*Ze~e~ed!* I'm gonna *blast* you!"

CHAPTER THIRTY-SIX

When she was back into a safe location and wasn't in too much danger of dying, Taylor took a more active role in controlling her Spell. She *absolutely* wanted to maximize her Potentia gains, but it was highly improbable that the massive influx of foreign energy would remain at the same height for very long.

Seeing as how Luke was getting five total Potentia or less per kill, Taylor exulted in the fact that she had gotten fifty per kill for so long. If she had been able to maintain that rapid advancement, she could have used her five thousand bolts of lightning to kill forty-five creatures a pop, bringing in over eleven million Potentia to use as she wished.

Unfortunately, their Sigils thrived on change and new challenges. There was a greater than logarithmic rate of decay, and by the sixth bolt, the increase had dropped down to forty per kill. Then thirty, finally seeming to stabilize around five per kill, like Luke. Still, she had nothing to complain about and took the windfall for what it was. Taylor still had over four thousand, five-hundred bolts of lightning to send out, and she gleefully had the process continue as she worked to study Luke once more.

While her Meta-magic Spell was powerful, the unfortunate drawback of only being able to use it a single time before having to relearn a Spell was something that she had not had to deal with before. It was a standard issue for Mages, and she had to remind herself over and over that this would have been nearly every Spell in her accessible grimoire, were she not a Namer.

It made Taylor wonder if she could take additional time to study the Skill and figure out how to officially name it and keep it permanently; but she tried to remind herself not to be greedy. She was already functioning at a higher level than any other Mage she had read about in the historical records she had studied.

There was the secondary benefit: it gave her something to focus on beyond the pain of having her leg almost entirely severed. Watching Luke intently as he sat down to recover from his extreme injuries was a nice perspective shift for her. He looked like he had come back from an acupuncturist, if the doctor on staff had been a giant. The massive spear-needles had been mostly blocked by his armor, but a few of the enormous weapons had managed to penetrate through. Not to the extent on her own body, of course. Instead, they had landed and stuck within his muscle, shoving flesh to the side but not chunking enormous holes through his body.

She watched his strangely oversized form as he casually gripped the needles and yanked them out, one by one. They clattered to the ground with a strange sound, as if they were bones made of metal. Luke was humming a light tune, incredibly repetitively, as he worked to repair the damage. He splashed water on the open wounds, which released a *hiss* before rapidly sealing up. "Running low on water. Back soon."

Taylor nodded at him, her eyes tracing over his chest, which moments ago had contained six enormous divots. Perhaps it was because she had learned this Spell once before, but the words were already there, hovering over the still-healing damage. She whispered them to herself, wondering why this Spell was announcing itself in such a strange manner.

Almost everything she had seen since she got this Meta-magic Spell were whispers of words that she needed to carefully parse and study. But these... if she could use this method to advertise some goods for sale in the capital, it would draw attention like nothing else. The words themselves were metallic, bold, and seemed to practically leap off of him as they appeared. "You Need to Stop. I just don't understand why your Skill is named like that."

Meta-magic has captured a Spell: You Need to Stop.

She skipped over reading the details, moving straight into activating it. The Spell wasn't as effective as it would have been if she had the liquid mana to enhance it, but it didn't stop until the damage was healed or there was less mana in the air. Seeing as they were in a world that was completely and utterly suffused with energy, it was better to get the process started now. As her flesh slowly began to grow, reattaching the dangling portion of her leg to the core of her body, the pain actually increased. Nerve endings were fixed and rejoined, allowing the dangling chunk of meat to be felt once more.

Taylor breathed through the pain, noticing the vines around her legs undulating at a greater speed as her heart rate increased. In the next few moments, the area went numb once more, and she felt a rush of gratitude toward Andre. Taylor had been expecting an answer from Luke, but when she managed to focus on her surroundings once more, he was already gone. That was slightly frustrating, but the fact that she still had Potentia pouring into her system partially mollified her. She glanced around, finding Andre and Zed nearby, talking to each other, and decided to join in on the conversation.

"They die like real creatures." Zed was arguing, waving his hands dramatically in the air as he spoke. "I see no reason why they wouldn't *react* like real creatures as well. If you started growing plants around me, I would either get out of the way or cut them down."

The Druid was having none of it, whatever 'it' was. "I'm telling you that it literally costs me nothing except a tiny amount of time to test it. Why are you being so obstinate about this? All I'm going to do is start growing some entangling vines."

"Did you not see how they changed their attack patterns as soon as a ranged attack was impacting them?" Zed scoffed incredulously. "What might happen if you managed to get something out there among them, which is able to continuously wipe out a large area of the monsters? Is just having something out there going to let them always maintain their distance attacks, or will something *new* happen? It might not cost *you* anything at the start, but what are the hidden costs, or the actual damage that might be done by this venture? All I'm asking you to do is target somewhere closer to the front lines so we can get rid of the plant, if necessary."

"Well, I'm telling *you* that, after the seeds leave my hand, I don't have any control over them until they start to grow!" Andre stood up and walked away from the conversation, frustration writ large on his face. "Abyssal Bard. There's literally *no reason* to have this kind of reaction."

Taylor opened her mouth to say something, but she paused as she realized that Andre was holding still and focusing on something in his own mind. He muttered under his breath then shook his head. With meticulous care, he opened a small seed sachet, pulling out a pinch of tiny seeds. He rubbed them between his fingers before casting them into the air and letting them settle on the ground directly in front of him. Thorny bushes sprang up then started to expand and extend. After a handful of seconds, they pulled themselves out of the dirt, rolled into tumbleweeds, and moved down the natural downhill slope.

"What a waste," Andre muttered to himself as the plants reached the edge of the Zone, crossing over with a slight bounce, as if they had hit something right at the edge. As they moved into the air, the needles flashed out, putting dozens of holes through the tumbleweeds. As far as Taylor could tell,

Andre didn't seem to mind that. Instead, as the thorns rained down, they burrowed into the ground, and each of the hundreds of small protrusions grew into its own bush. They erupted up out of the ground, entangling the creatures and continually growing. "See? No issues."

First one, then a handful, then dozens of the strange synthetic creatures were overrun and pulled apart by the thorn bushes that had sprung up. It was interesting to watch; the thorns would pile up over a creature, it would collapse, and a new monster would appear, pristine and clean, on top of the falling thorn bushes. Her eyes narrowed at that as she saw a potential issue. "Andre! Careful, you're starting to give them a height advantage. If they can combine that with their extended range, they might be able to hit us."

The Druid grunted and made a subtle gesture. Now, instead of growing higher, the plants extended along the ground and pulled the creatures' legs out. They slowly toppled, torn apart as they fell onto the mat of writhing thorn tendrils. "Everyone has something to say."

She could tell he was in one of his strange moods, but she didn't know what to say to drag him out of it. Taylor had plenty of experience convincing him to finish tasks for her while he was acting like this, but that had backfired on her in a big way. Looking around, she spotted Zed walking toward her with a grim look on his face.

"You need to tell your boyfriend that it's not his fault he couldn't heal fourth degree burns on your body. He's not a Healer, and he doesn't have access to plants that offer miracle recovery powers."

"Is *that* what his issue is right now?" Taylor looked over at the hyper-focused Druid, who was furiously wiggling his fingers and moving small particles that she couldn't see from this distance. He cast his hand forward, and an eruption of bluish greenery spiked upward out of the next Zone, sending dozens of the mechanical automatons across the Zone edge. Every single one of them exploded with the force of a Tier-three fire-ball, sending chunks and shrapnel flying.

Even so, after the initial shock, that wasn't what caught Taylor's attention. There was a huge hole in the enemy line, and for once, it didn't instantly fill back in. Instead of the creatures popping back into position as soon as they had died, now it was taking nearly half a second. Zed had also noticed the discrepancy, and he shoved a finger at the next Zone. "Did you see that? I saw that! We need to tell Luke that they're slowing down!"

"All we had to do was kill…" Taylor paused as she estimated how many of her lightning bolts had gone out, what Luke had been able to do on his own, and how many creatures were simply slumping over to be replaced moments later, thanks to Andre's small and large plants. "I think we're closing in on ten thousand dead?"

Andre started walking back toward them, a grim smile having replaced the sad puppy dog look that had been on his face since his conversation with the Bard. "Something tells me it's not about how *many* have been destroyed since we got here. If my hypothesis is correct, it's all about how fast we've been managing to kill them. We need to keep it up and figure out how Luke gets information on these things."

"That's an easy answer." Taylor was startled, hearing Luke's voice from only a few feet away. She was almost certain he hadn't been trying to sneak up on them, seeing as how his footfalls wouldn't sound out of place in a menagerie containing exclusively elephants. She cursed this world quietly, knowing that it was working with strange rules that she didn't understand. "All I need to do is get into the next Zone. If I can make it about ten feet in, my Sigil gets a download of information from Murder World."

"Ten feet in?" Zed groaned as he tried to calculate everything that was going on here. "I saw what happened when you tried to get through the line of these things. You just bounced out. What's going to happen to you if you get in there and can't get out because of the monsters in your way?"

Luke shrugged at that, truly unconcerned. "All I need to do is a full power attack facing the other direction. Then I'll come out of there, whether I want to or not."

He splashed a bit of water toward Taylor, sprinkling it on her leg. She sucked in a breath at the sudden surge of pain. Her leg fully reattached then started undoing the damage from having no blood flow inflicted on that chunk of meat. His actions, whether inadvertent or intentional, drew all eyes to her as she stood up and tested her leg. They seemed to be waiting for her to weigh in on the situation, and she let out a deep sigh.

Waving her hand forward, she could only nod and say, "You know this world better than we do. You understand the rules. Just... *please* don't die and trap us here forever."

Luke grinned and shrugged slightly. "No promises."

CHAPTER THIRTY-SEVEN

- LUKE -

For the Murderhobo, it was a toss-up between which of the two methods he wanted to attempt. Did he want to follow the lightning or have a larger area carved out with a patch of thrashing vines? Eventually, he nodded over at Taylor. "Here's what I want to see. Send a bolt down a line, then move directly to the left and send another one. I'll follow the first, then run back after the second."

"What the Abyss, Luke? I can control my plants *way* better than she can control lightning!" Andre interjected, showcasing his control by crushing dozens of monsters at once with a single squeeze of his fist. "If you time it poorly, you're going to get hit by superheated arcane plasma!"

"Her lack of control is *why* I'm doing it." The Murderhobo gruffly informed his friend. "I *understand* lack of control; I *get* it. She lets go of her Spell, and it does its effect, then vanishes. Your plants follow your rules, but only to a point. What's been going on back at the Hollow Kingdom now that you're not there to control the Dryad? Did you leave detailed instructions? Or did you just give it a general command?"

"Well…" Andre hesitated for a long moment before shaking his head and pointing at the monsters not very far away at all. "But I *am* here! Right now! I can do whatever you need."

Luke shook his head and put out his hand, shoving Andre to the side. "I just don't trust trees. They're too shady."

"Ha!" Zed quietly laughed. "Guys! He is risking his life so he can make a joke. I think he's starting to get back into the swing of being human."

The Murderhobo didn't deign to respond to that accusation. Instead, he merely nodded at the Mage then got down into a crouched position. "Whenever you're ready."

"I'll count down from three, sending out the bolt of lightning at zero. In the next second, I will send the next strike down just to our left. Are you sure you're ready?"

Once again, Luke didn't bother answering. Taylor could only shrug and start her countdown, sending out a bolt of the strangely silent lightning exactly as she had said she would. Luke leapt into action, honing in on the corridor of falling monsters. He had plenty of room to maneuver, seeing as each of these burned-out husks was nearly five feet wide. He got to the dividing line of the Zone, ignoring the needles that were flying through the air at him, and activated Bum Thunder. For the first time in what felt like years to him, the Skill succeeded, and he penetrated deeply into Zone twenty.

As the Skill ended, lights appeared in his vision as the world attempted to explain his current situation to him. Unfortunately, he didn't have the time to pause and read it, pushing off one of the falling creatures as a bolt of lightning crashed down to his left and opened a new path. His skin crisped up as the flash of light vanished, but it wasn't enough to deal any damage through his armor. Pushing off against the now falling creature as the first line respawned, he activated his movement ability one more time… slamming face-first into a freshly-respawned creature. "Abyss!"

Another creature appeared directly behind him, and the two monsters pushed together in an attempt to crush him between their bodies. Needles shoved forward in nearly the same attack pattern he had used, as monsters from all around attempted to jab him with their weapons, those farther back sending flying needles. Luke switched over to his Battering Ram Knuckles, unable to otherwise maneuver enough to use any of the weapons. A one-two punch landed on the creature in front of him, and he tried to take a step forward, only to be met with a brand new, undamaged version that had appeared on top of its fallen brother.

"Time for plan... *punch!*" Luke kept fighting until he was able to ever so slowly turn himself around. Now facing back the way he had come, he pulled his fist back as far as possible and launched forward with a full-powered Shockwave Cleave. Multiple explosions happened at once as he was tossed backward, bringing a monster with him across the Zone boundary. The detonation of the creature's Skill Pearl nearly canceled out his momentum, and he dropped to the ground well within the range of the needles.

The next several moments were spent scampering along, performing acrobatic movements from a prone position that eventually brought him outside of their effective range. For a few seconds, Luke simply exulted in the fact that he had succeeded. Then, practicality took over once more, and he used the time to go over the information that he had been given.

Data packet from unknown accessed... updating log with provided data... cross-referencing with Source-cerer protocols... complete! Messages will be displayed in order of creation.

Welcome to Zone Twenty! This area is filled with creatures that are set to automatically return to life after a set period of time. Somewhere within the depths of this Zone, there's a respawn buffer! The longer you go without clearing out this Zone, the faster the creatures will return to life! Use the Skills you have learned in the previous Zones to fight your way through the Zone to a buffer point. Once you have destroyed at least one, the overflow buffer will be cleaned out, and the respawn rate will return to one creature per hour!

You have slain Towering Ossified Expedient Sentinel! (Several thousand repeating messages collapsed for convenience.)

Luke was once more staring at the sky above him, watching the blue gasses and liquid shift and stir. He was mightily pleased with himself, and there was something truly satisfying about being able to achieve his goal after so many attempts. "There's a long way to go, but now I know it can be done."

His left hand unclenched, and he let his head flop to the side as he looked at the glowing Skill Pearl that he had been able to snatch off the ground from a falling sentinel. "Abyss, it's good just knowing what to call these things. Makes me wonder what kind of Skills I can pick up off of them... *nom*."

Without further preamble, he shoved the Skill Pearl in his mouth, washing it down with a generous pull of liquid mana. This had the effect of letting him easily swallow the pearl, as well as the side effect of healing his body from the massive damage he had just inflicted upon it. As his flesh and bones mended, he waited for the Pearl to be fully integrated.

Skill gained: Aerial Grift. T5, level 0.

Effect 1: When catching a projectile out of midair, you're able to immediately halt its momentum entirely and set it on the nearest flat surface or the ground within $1n$ feet of your body, where n = Skill level.

Bonus 1, at range: you're now able to autonomously catch $2n$ projectiles from midair and deposit them on a flat surface or in a pocket or bag within $1n$ feet of your body without needing to use your hands. Cost: $1n$ mana per second, 10 mana per item caught.

Effect 2: You can automatically construct preset arrangements for collected projectiles. This can be anything from creating spiked traps, to caltrops, to small structures created entirely from projectiles. You can place $5n$ items per second into a preset arrangement.

Bonus, Multitarget: You can now set a no-fly Zone within $3n$ feet of your body. All projectiles that come within that range will be automatically collected and placed into either storage or a preset formation based on your settings. Cost: 50 mana to activate, 10 mana per second for upkeep.

Effect 3: Collected projectiles may be assigned to return to their point of origin. They will be returned at 5n% velocity, where n = Skill level.

"Exactly what I needed. Thank you, Murder World." Luke closed his eyes and took a few deep breaths before getting up and activating his newest Skill. Then, unafraid of the mana upkeep cost, he simply walked up to the nearest Sentinel and started attacking it.

Needles flew at him by the hundreds, only to vanish as they came within touching range of his body. Fractions of a second later, those same needles returned at the same angle they had come in. A series of *clanging* filled the air as needles slammed into each other, like the world's largest wind chime warehouse on 'bring your child's entire school to work' day. The needles were exceptionally effective at drilling into the Towering Ossified Expedient Sentinels, and when they met the monsters, they usually went right through them, thanks to their void-tipped attribute.

"So, Luke, how are things *going?*" Zed's sing-songy voice popped into Luke's ear, the conversational tone completely out of synchronization with the situation they found themselves in. "Looks like you're doing something pretty neat, so do you mind if I get some information off of you?"

The Murderhobo didn't mind at all, and in fact relayed all the data that he had been given. Zed listened patiently, asking only a few questions. "The gist of it is we're looking for something that is constantly spawning these, and we need to smash it? That makes perfect sense to me. Seems a bit extreme to create this *many* monsters, but who knows with this world. Now, tell me... is that a new Skill I spy?"

"Yup." Luke was enjoying pummeling the monsters in front of him without fear of the longer-ranged enemies being able to do anything about it. "Collects projectiles, returns to sender. Mana-intensive anywhere except here."

Zed made small happy noises as Luke spoke. "That's very interesting! Mind if I listen in on it?"

"All you need to do is get within three feet of me, and the Skill will take care of any of these needles. Go for it." Even Luke didn't expect what happened after making the casual comment.

The Bard came sprinting down the slope, predicting the flying needles and moving to evade them at top speed. As he got closer, the Sentinels' aim became more accurate, and Zed was forced to dive into a flying tackle to escape. He wrapped his arms around the Murderhobo from behind and brought his momentum to an instant halt. Luke felt almost nothing, even though Zed sounded like he had hit a wall. "Ow. I hope this shows my devotion to getting cool things. Also, that was perhaps the most terrifying thing I have ever intentionally done in my life."

Luke actually paused in his killing to take a look at the smug Bard who was sitting on the ground next to him, his eyes closed as he listened intently to the magic flowing through the Murderhobo. "Alright. I admit it. That was impressive."

Something about the Skill was apparently subtle, as the Bard needed to listen for nearly five hours before it transformed into a Mastery for him to use. Luke could tell the instant the Bard figured it out, because he jumped to his feet and *whooped* for joy. Focusing on the young man beside him, Luke watched as something in the air around him shifted ever so slightly.

"Moment of truth!" Zed's normal cheerfulness was replaced by apprehension as he ever so slowly inched toward the edge of the safe Zone Luke had generated. He seemed to be psyching himself up, as he continuously repeated the words, "It will only end when I run out of mana or actively cancel the Mastery. It will only end-"

With a strangled yell, he squeezed his eyes shut and ran forward, then paused, expecting at any moment to be skewered on the spot. When no pain came, he opened his eyes and watched as dozens of needles were absorbed what felt like inches from his face, only to be returned to the assailants. "Yes!

I'm pretty sure I'm not dead! Wow! I'm also earning Potentia when they spear themselves! Alright, Luke... proof of concept complete. Let's stomp these T.O.E.S."

CHAPTER THIRTY-EIGHT

"I can't *believe* how much Potentia this is worth!" Zed had taken to sitting around and pretending to meditate as he returned the attacks to the sentinels. He had asked Andre to grow a stump for him to sit on to make sure that he maximized the range of his stolen Mastery. It didn't matter if it was above him, below him, or to the sides, any projectile coming within three feet was returned.

At this point, they had been at it for days, with Taylor joining in on the fun by stealing her own Spell version of Luke's new Skill. Between the three of them constantly returning attacks, Luke endlessly destroying Sentinels, Taylor sending out endless lightning storms, and Andre creating a deadly under-brush that slowly but constantly subsumed the towering Sentinels, the respawn rate of the monsters was ever-so-slowly decreasing. It had gone from nearly instant to just shy of three seconds at this point.

They were all swimming in Potentia, especially Zed, who was getting *hundreds* per kill. This led to endless theorizing by Andre, who had gone off on a rant about how the Bard had practically never killed any monsters to this point and had then started with such impressively strong ones. Even with the rate of decay he would have to deal with over time, the sheer influx of power was more than he had ever seen in his life.

Luke was already on his second level up, and from the events he had been observing over the last few days, he was leveling up even slower than his teammates. What he *truly* wanted to do was invest his Potentia in his Source-cerer's armory Skill, but unfortunately, it appeared to have been locked at Tier nine, level nine. When he had attempted to devote the final point it required, his Sigil rejected the input, and a tiny lock with the crest of the Hollow Kingdom had appeared over the Skill. He checked it one more time, just to be certain.

Source-cerer's Armory (Tier 9, level 9). You have devoted the maximum amount of Potentia allowed to this Skill! In order to upgrade it further, you must receive direct permission from the King after a thorough study has been performed on it to ensure that it will not interfere with your duties to the Hollow Kingdom.

The Murderhobo felt a growl building in his chest, but he channeled his anger into the enemies waiting to be destroyed. One after another they fell, doing their best to inflict harm on him. Due to the powers he had gained from one of their own, they overwhelmingly failed. "Fine! Increase to level fifteen."

Hello, there! It looks like you're trying to devote 98,700 Etheric Xenograft Potentia to leveling yourself up! As this level is 3/4 of what is required to ascend to a Higher Realm permanently, the Hollow Kingdom would like to remind you that reaching level 20 can only occur with a direct order from the ruler of the Hollow Kingdom. An alert will be sent out to your first line leader, their supervisor, as well as placed in the Royal Ledger, that you have increased your level to this point!

Make sure to spread out your expenditure of Potentia so that you're able to keep up with the increased mandatory duties and services to the kingdom that your level will bring. Are you sure that you would like to increase to level 15? Yes / No.

"Yes." Luke tried to keep his mind off the fact that his increased level would bring greater attention to him. He looked over his Characteristic information, placing this upgrade in

Fitness, as was his usual. "Neat, now I can casually inflict seven hundred fourteen points of punching damage without having to activate any other Skills. Thank *you*, Source-cerer's Armory."

Cal Scan
Level: 15
Current Etheric Xenograft Potentia: 2,799/61,000 to level 14!
Body: 40.85

- *Fitness: 56.7*
- *Resistance: 25*

Mind: 22.4

- *Talent: 19.9*
- *Capacity: 24.9*

Presence: 21.5

- *Willpower: 27*
- *Charisma: 11*

Senses: 29.85

- *Physical reaction: 39*
- *Mental energy: 22.7*

Maximum health: 1020 (Giga)
Maximum mana: 378
Mana regen: ~~*6.57 per second*~~ *Overridden: 100 per second.*

His situation wasn't like most other Ascenders. Luke wouldn't be getting an increase to his Noble rank, a fat purse for general expenses, and long stretches in luxurious locations for his services. No, he knew from experience that all that awaited him was heavier restrictions and more fear from the weak nobility as they realized that he was coming closer and closer to escape. "They probably think I'm going to come after them... but I will literally just forget they exist and move on."

"I can't tell you for sure which one they would prefer." Zed spoke in his ear, using his distance speaking ability to connect the team. "One of the biggest draws in having Ascenders in their pocket is the hope that, as they ascend to higher realms, they'll have someone waiting for them who'll give them guidance and perhaps some of the luxury they poured onto you in the past. Do you mean to tell me that, if someone were to ascend to a higher realm after you did, you'd look at them and be happy that they made it? You wouldn't try to destroy them?"

"I wouldn't bother." Luke rejected the question immediately, only for Zed to *tsk* at him and smile knowingly in his direction.

"Really? What if it was Master Don?" Zed offered teasingly, though he flinched in the next moment and closed his eyes again as multiple needles came for him. "You mean to tell me that, if someone like *that* were brought up, and you were a couple levels above them, with far more powerful Skills, you wouldn't want to crush him for how he treated you when you were younger?"

Luke didn't answer, though his blood was boiling. Using that fury to motivate himself further, he decided that he had been spending far too long at the edge of Zone twenty. It was time to push deeper. On his next attack, he took several steps forward. His team noticed immediately, and each of them called out to him in their own way, with Zed being the clearest, of course. He could essentially speak directly into their ears, no matter the distance.

Step.
Slam.
Step.

With each attack, he followed the momentum, and soon the Murderhobo was surrounded on all sides by enemies. He constantly ground forward, attacking, stepping, attacking. He moved at a measured speed, only going a few steps every other second. If this Zone followed the principles of the others, he would need to maintain this pace for the next one thousand, three hundred and ninety-one miles to reach the end of the Zone. He hoped desperately that he would find whatever it was that was creating these creatures far before then and ease the burden on himself.

Not that he truly minded the combat, just that he was concerned about being able to stay awake long enough to get to the other side while moving this slowly. He paused as he had a realization. "Wait a second... the only reason I hadn't been able to fly over these things was that I was constantly shot down."

"Luke, don't do anything foolish! I can only maintain contact with you for about five miles before-" Zed's voice slowed to a stop as the Bard remembered who he was talking to. "Fine... I can just tell that you're about to do something that'll put you at great risk. I'll pretend I didn't know. Try to be back before Taylor gets too worried about you. I mean, *I* know you'll be fine, but still."

"Yup." Luke launched himself upward, kicking off the nearest Sentinel and jumping onto its head. From there, he activated Bum Thunder and pointed himself directly upward, throwing Cookie forward as hard as he could and activating Feather's Fall. Hundreds of Sentinels looked up at him as if they had just spotted the most delicious thing in the universe, and thousands of weapons shifted to point upward. "I really hope my Skill can deal with all of this."

Gravity took him, and he started moving forward down the slope, rapidly building up speed. Once every handful of seconds, he had to reactivate Bum Thunder or jump off of another creature's head. He preferred the former, as it was nearly impossible for him to see exactly what was going on below him. Everything in his vision had turned into a field of metallic white, as a constant deluge of needles were flung into the air in an attempt to destroy him.

Luke needed to control his new Skill, pulling the activation of it closer and closer to his body. He was concerned that he wouldn't be able to react in time, if some of them did manage to get through farther down the slope, but it wouldn't be able to handle everything within range. The only needles that got redirected were the ones that would have directly struck him, but not a single one of them managed to return through the wall of metal flying upward.

Even so, that wasn't his main focus.

Between his constant bounding off of enemies or increasing his velocity using his Skills, Luke was soon flying at a terrific speed. Realizing that he needed to be able to see the spawn beacon, or whatever it was, he chain-activated Bum Thunder until he was scores of meters into the sky. There was one hundred and three miles of land going width wise, and nearly fourteen hundred until the edge of the next Zone. Still, he maintained his vigilance as he flew for several hours.

Between his speed, vantage point, and near endless mana, he was able to float along until he finally spotted an anomaly in the distance. At first, he assumed that the Sentinels in that area were simply standing on a hill or something similar, but as he got closer, he could see that the T.O.E.S. were in fact nearly twice the height of the others around them. "Well, doesn't *that* seem suspicious."

He activated his Soul Brand, reaching out to Cookie and sending a call for her to start catching up. Luke felt a slight tug at his movement speed, as some of his momentum was transferred to begin the initial process. It would be several hours at the minimum until she managed to catch up to him, but he didn't mind. Really, he only wanted her to witness his triumph when she showed up. Angling himself to slam into the big T.O.E.S., he equipped his Chain-Link Scourge in his right hand and a long spear in the left.

Luke flattened his body, spread his arms to the side, and leaned into the spear. The mana manifestation penetrated directly through the sentinel, followed by Luke's face. Thanks to Feather's Fall's special ability to translate momentum into penetrative force, the Murderhobo blasted directly *through* the leading monster and into a box that was slightly smaller than his own body, even if it was several times harder.

He found out that fact by slamming into the artifact and bouncing off with a resounding *crack*. With the world around him spinning, he pulled himself to his feet and started battling the big T.O.E.S. Unlike their smaller counterparts, these ones didn't merely jab their needles forward like spears, instead skillfully using them as actual melee weapons. They had a greater flexibility in their bodies, allowing for more fluid and acrobatic movement, much to Luke's disgruntlement.

Damage taken: 16 penetrating damage! (186 mitigated by Promiscuous Stud Pauldron).

"That wasn't very *nice!*" Even as he roared at the creature's featureless face, a manic grin was spreading across his own. Luke flashed across the distance between them, whirling his Scourge above his head and wrapping it tightly around the creature's body. This removed the use of two of its 'arms', and the Murderhobo yanked on the manifested weapon to both pull himself closer and activate the blades hidden in the long length of rope.

The Scourge dug into the creature's body, tearing through large swaths of metallic bone, then the Murderhobo landed on its chest and shoved the spear up through the joint where the creature's spine met its head.

A moment later, it stopped moving and collapsed. Then Luke was slammed to the ground as an undamaged version of it appeared just above him, having been respawned in an instant.

"Oh, *come on!*"

CHAPTER THIRTY-NINE

The Murderhobo was pressed to the ground, but he shoved his hands out straight and caught himself in a push-up position. Bending his arm slightly, he shoved backwards, sending the creature flying into the air above him. Then Luke pulled, sending himself across the ground toward the odd rectangular box that had a silhouette of his face, thanks to the strange fluid that dripped from the T.O.E.S. he had smashed through. He had seen something like this before, back when he got his Mage Hunter set.

"This is something the world itself makes. When I crack this, another one of these is just going to appear somewhere else, and eventually this Zone will be overrun again. Ugh." Luke didn't particularly care about that; he assumed his line of thinking was extraordinarily similar to whoever had come before. "At least it'll be someone else's problem, not mine."

He had decided to accept the minor wounds that his enemies were able to inflict upon him, seeing as defeating them would have no purpose other than to bring another of their ilk into existence. It was a great relief to see the enormous needles hit his armor, slow to a stop, with only the very tip of them able to penetrate the armor and into his flesh. It still *hurt*, but it wasn't instantly deadly, like it otherwise could have been.

At first glance, there was no way to open the box, but that was perfectly acceptable to Luke. Switching his weapons over to his Battering Ram Knuckles, he forced his way over to the box, straddled it as though it was an enemy he had knocked over, and started raining blows down.

The entire time he was putting every ounce of his strength into use, his enemies were trying to disrupt his armor to get at the soft, meaty core inside of him. Luke ignored them as much as possible, only wincing and grunting as his health was slowly whittled away. Finally, on the fifteenth blow, a large chunk of the outer box cracked. This showed that he was accomplishing something, so the Murderhobo redoubled his efforts, even as his blood pooled around him.

On the thirtieth blow, his fist went through the outer shell and into the inner mechanisms of the box. Luke's hair stood up on end, and it felt like a minor lightning bolt had just been cast on him. His thoughts shifted, static filling his mind then exploding outward.

It took him a moment to realize that the attacks on his person had ended. He pulled his hand out of the box, looking around at the Sentinels that were now just standing there, staring at him. One by one, they slowly started to topple, falling over in concentric rings as the nearness of their bodies forced the others around them to drop.

Congratulations! You have cleared the respawn buffer! The standard time to respawn a Sentinel has been set to one per hour. Make sure to clean up any remaining enemies, as they will be coming back online... now!

"*Aby~yss!*" Luke howled into the air as the Sentinels around him started flailing, trying to regain their footing. He looked up the hill, down the hill, and made the decision to go find his team. "I *hate* backtracking."

Yet he found that the trip was extremely productive. He was able to move forward at a consistent pace, swinging his weapons and giving himself plenty of breathing room. The Sentinels were perfectly happy not to rush into the open space, firing needles at him that were simply stopped and returned. Nearly two hours into his upward slog, a loud crashing sound approached him far too rapidly. He steeled himself for a new type of enemy, only for Cookie to smash past another Sentinel and fly into his hand.

"Cookie!" he shouted happily, grabbing on to her with both hands and charging uphill. He whirled around, slamming her into half a dozen Ossified Sentinels, excitedly chattering about what he had done. "Then I flew in, smashed through one of the biggest ones, and pounded their box until it broke! After that, I've just been coming back to get you."

Luke paused for a moment, then nodded consideringly. "No, you're right, we should probably go get them. It's just… who wants to go *up* when you're in Murder World? What, you think I can just run? I *suppose* we could do that."

He didn't wait a moment longer, tensing his legs and throwing himself forward. Holding Cookie in front of him, he lunged forward and activated Bum Thunder in the same moment, blasting forward with her knocking the enemies to the side. He repeated this every few seconds, and ever so slowly, they made their way back up and out, nearly to the edge of Zone twenty.

That was where the travel got difficult.

"I don't suppose this enormous briar patch is going to be friendly if I step onto it." Luke unhappily stated as he whacked a nearby Sentinel and kicked it in the side, sending it toppling on to the innocuous-seeming underbrush. Just after it landed, the vines shot upward and wrapped around the fallen creature, spinning and swirling to grind through its metallic body.

In only a few moments, it had been reduced to chunks that were rapidly broken down even further by the plant. "I don't understand how he doesn't get that this stuff is freaky. If he wasn't able to perfectly control it, I'm sure Andre would have been eaten by his own creations by now."

"-Ke, is that you-" The Murderhobo rubbed at his ears,

trying to figure out if he was hearing things, or if Zed was attempting to contact him. About a minute later, the sound came again, just as distorted and broken. "-still find you if you don't talk, you gorilla wannabe-"

"Are you saying that you can track me by my voice? Not sound, or my presence, but my actual voice? If I don't speak, will you leave me alone?" Luke spoke aloud, since he *was* trying to get back to his people. In the same instant, he felt the weight of Zed's attention entirely focusing on him.

"-Alive! I knew you wouldn't get yourself killed and doom us to this blue Abyss until we finally succumbed to insanity!" Zed's voice was growing stronger as he spoke, as though the man himself were coming closer. "Okay, I think I have your location now. you're a little under five miles below us; we're still back at the edge of Zone nineteen. You did something, didn't you? About half a day ago, all of the attacks suddenly stopped for a few seconds, then the creatures stayed down when we hit them."

"Yes," Luke answered the only question that had been asked of him. "Tell Andre to get this plant out of my way."

"Yeah, no can do, friend-o!" The reply was instant and annoyingly cheerful. "You're going to have to go around! Take a left-hand turn from where you're standing, go a quarter mile, then start walking back up. Andre told me you would hate it." The Bard seemed to be amazed that the redhead was correct. "I told him, 'Andre! You can't just assume that he is going to hate anything that is growing and eating other creatures! He loves seeing stuff get savaged'! Then he says, 'he only likes to see things get destroyed by people, not plants'-"

The Murderhobo groaned and clapped his hands over his ears, trying to drown out the endlessly droning Bard. Unfortunately, it was some kind of magical connection, and the sound continued unabated, though the ambient noise was completely removed. In other words, it just made the rambling worse.

For a few long seconds, Luke considered simply going downhill and getting out of range again, but after tossing Cookie in the air and losing his guess as to how she would land two of the three times, he let out a deep exhale and followed the instructions. Soon, he was close enough to see lightning still striking nearly constantly.

Yet, there was one major difference. The Sentinels were *moving*. With their front ranks having been absolutely decimated, and open areas being laid out in front of them, the ranks of monsters had room to approach their attackers. There were so many of them that the vast majority of the creatures had not yet been given a chance to move, which was why he had not seen anything of the sort on his climb upward. Still, it was a sign of actual progress, and it lit a fire in his gut. "Taylor wants to know if every Zone was like this, and is speculating on if this is why-"

"Zed. You have to know that I'm nearly close enough to get my hands around your neck," Luke finally cut the Bard off with a very light threat.

The other man went silent for a long moment, and when he spoke again, the words were very different. Crisp. "Fifty paces to your right, there's lightning rolling your direction. Eighty-six paces left is another swath of anti-sentinel foliage. Continue at your current heading and speed, and you'll be able to rejoin the group within ten or fifteen minutes. Please keep all arms and legs attached to the body to maintain maximum speed."

A hint of a grin lifted the right corner of Luke's mouth, then he doubled his pace. In what felt like no time flat, he was back with his party, and they retreated away from the edge of the Zone, slightly deeper into Zone nineteen. Zed flopped to the ground, rubbing at his legs and stretching them out. "I don't know about you guys, but standing in front of a firing line of angry monsters is tiring work."

Luke could hear Andre muttering softly under his breath, "First he gets carried everywhere, now he can just *literally* sit around and gain Potentia…!"

"I'm down to only getting two Potentia per kill," Taylor informed the group. "How is everyone else doing in their accumulation of energies? How long would everyone like to stay here, and how long do you think the monsters will last? Luke?"

"We could stay here for *weeks* and not run out of monsters." He begrudgingly spoke to the group. "There's a hundred miles left to right, fourteen hundred long, and the Sentinels take up five square feet each. *You* do the math; I refuse."

"I'm having good success setting up plant Zones that keep the Sentinels out. They don't seem to react to it growing along near their feet." At this point, Andre sent a challenging, fierce smile at Zed, who merely shrugged in response. "It would take a while, but I can carve out a path for us to get to the next Zone. Can't guarantee it will be safe, but when it just isn't worth killing all of these things anymore, I'll be able to get us to the next one."

As the team started making plans, with even Zed inputting good information and ideas, Luke slowly let his gaze drift across the three of them. For the first time since he had gotten to this world, they didn't feel like a burden. In fact… they were being *extremely* helpful.

He liked that.

"Huh. Maybe it's not so bad having you around." Somehow, he had said the words out loud, and it ended the current conversation for a moment. Taylor flashed a bright smile at him, and the others nodded with pleased—if scrutinizing— expressions on their faces.

Not missing another beat, Taylor prodded Andre to continue where he had left off, and the strategy was slowly laid out. The more Luke listened, the more he liked the sound of what they were saying. "It's different… maybe that doesn't mean it's bad."

CHAPTER FORTY

As the rest of the team began the descent into Murder World, following the nice, clean, safe, green path that Andre had made for them, Luke instead followed along beside them, clearing his own way. Every once in a while, the scraps of his kills would be flung toward the path, but he wasn't overly concerned about their wellbeing, now that Andre had a chunk of plants under his control.

There was always some kind of wooden shield, leafy barricade, or thorny obstacle that was able to intercept small shrapnel, and they completely disregarded the Sentinels' actual attacks. With both Zed as well as Taylor having managed to copy Luke's new Skill, all they needed to do in order to protect the Druid was stand on either side of him. To Luke, it looked like the man had an overpowered honor guard, and their stroll looked boring as the Abyss.

"*Yahh!*" He screamed in pure joy as he connected Cookie with the faceplate of the synthetic, towering monster. The Murderhobo was unable to contain himself, and he accidentally used Shockwave Cleave, blasting himself backwards as well as sending out a wave of destruction that took out hundreds of the Ossified Sentinels.

Luke landed on the path that Andre had designed, and even as he healed up, the Druid worked to move him along. The grass itself flowed as if a strong wind was blowing across it. Before he had even managed to get back to full health, he was traveling alongside his friends. "Knock that off!"

"If you can't move, I'm *not* going to leave you all dazed and pathetic on the ground while monsters try to kill you." Andre calmly explained to his friend, ignoring the fact that the grass was now poking Luke painfully in several places. At least, it was trying and failing to penetrate his armor. In fact, to the Murderhobo's delight, he could look up the path and see that his armor had shredded every single one of the weeds that had touched him to this point.

"No wonder your greens are all grouchy with me." Luke chuckled as he flexed his stomach muscles and launched himself to his feet, charging forward off the path as soon as his feet touched down once more. Then, he continued his rampage, easily managing to keep up with the slow pace his friends were setting.

By all metrics, they should have been moving much faster than a slow walking pace. But there seemed to be something in this world that was resisting the intrusion of Andre's grass, so even though it grew extremely fast, the farther away from his body the plants were, the slower they would react to his commands or the input of his Abilities.

When he had simply flung seeds forward and ordered them to grow, they didn't spread out to make a nice, cohesive carpet that allowed for easy travel. They made little patches, which he then needed to connect. All in all, it was just less frustrating for him to grow them at close range.

Remaining on the grass was an absolute requirement for them. Along the edges of the green path were the strangely mutated thorn bushes that Andre had decided upon for destroying the Sentinels. As the machines came after them at their slow pace, the thorns would pull them to the ground and tear them apart.

That was extremely effective, and it seemed to be remaining in place the entire slope they had so far managed to traverse. Not only was the Druid creating a road for them that would remain for who knows how long, he was continually earning kills. Even as he got farther away, since the plant life was in a cohesive, bound manner, the Potentia would be transferred along to him.

Luke could tell that Andre was extremely smug about that fact, and he couldn't blame the man. While Taylor had exceedingly effective long-range Spells for destroying enemies quickly, the Druid could set up enormous defensive layouts that would work as long as they weren't destroyed.

That gave him a tactical advantage over time, and he was guaranteed to get far more kills than even Taylor had managed to amass with her Thunder Beast's Eye continuously blasting. That was partially why Luke was so adamant about earning as many kills for himself as he could: half of his party was better at killing things in Murder World than he was.

Completely unacceptable.

On the third day of walking at a slow pace—relatively speaking, and only in relation to how fast they knew that they *could* move—Zed's eyes rolled up into the back of his head, and he collapsed. Andre caught the fallen Bard with a look of confusion on his face, "Zed! What happened? Are you all right?"

"He's unconscious, Andre. Not dead. Try to see if he got attacked or something." Taylor's advice came smoothly and easily, even though she tried to show that she *was* concerned for this party member. She had a rocky relationship with the Bard, but Luke didn't draw attention to that fact. Cookie was having far too much fun smashing individual legs off the towering Sentinels.

Before Andre could do anything too drastic, Zed sat up suddenly, his eyes rolling back into position and slowly focusing on the Druid's face. "Whoo! What a rush!"

"Rush?" Andre squinted suspiciously at Zed. "Did you just pass out from leveling up?"

"Yes! Guys, I just hit level eleven! I am officially the highest-level Bard in living memory!" Zed crowed with excitement. "This was the first time I ever put points into Fitness and Resistance, and I wanted to get it over with all at once. Didn't realize it would make me pass out like that; my bad!"

"That's strange... I think the only time I've ever passed out from leveling up was when I put too many points into Physical Reaction at once." Taylor sounded relieved that her companion had been revived without her having to do anything about it. To Luke's ears, it sounded like she was now trying to 'commiserate' with him. Luke felt proud about that thought—he had read that word in the book Viscount Woodswright had given him. "I lost access to all of my senses for a moment as they were altered, and the sudden shock of it made me unconscious. I think. It was hard to tell, because you know, I couldn't sense anything at all."

"Yeah, that sounds rough. Anyway." Zed hopped to his feet and started moving to see if he could feel a difference. "Whoa! Look at that, I can jump so high now!"

Luke started smashing his way closer to the group, and when he was in easy earshot for the Bard, he barked, "You should try punching someone in the face. That's the best way to tell how strong you've gotten."

Zed held up a finger and opened his mouth as if you were going to say something, stopped himself and merely smiled at his friend. "Thank you for the advice, Luke. I don't know if I will get a chance to try it out, or if I will want to, since I like *not* being thrown in jail... but I appreciate you giving me your best advice!"

That earned him a nod from the Murderhobo as he turned his attention back to the ongoing, constant onslaught.

It took them a full week to finally reach the end of the Zone, with hundreds of thousands of kills between them. There was an unbroken trail of greenery from start to finish, and their resident Druid cheerfully reported that he was still earning constant and consistent Potentia. Taylor countered with how much Potentia she had *already* earned, while Zed just seemed happy to be there.

Luke didn't care about that at all. No, what he was excited about was the slight shimmer in the air that indicated the end of the Zone. It had been unending months since he had started his attempt at breaking through this Zone, and he was excited to finally reach the point where he could have a new exit from Murder World. As they came in range, he reached out and placed his hand against the strange energy barrier.

Happily, it didn't inform him of an exit requirement. Instead, the shimmer coalesced into a more concrete form, leaving a distortion in the air that he could use to leave this world at any time. He laughed at that thought. "Not anytime *soon.*"

Then the Murderhobo sneaked a look at Taylor, his eyes suspicious. She could see this distortion as well; they all could. Luke bent down and casually scooped up a chunk of mud, palming it just in case she tried to tell them that they should all leave. Then he would clap his hand over her mouth and force the mud inside so she couldn't get the words out.

Luke nodded to himself. It was a good plan.

"Well, this is exciting! What does it mean for us, Luke? Are we going to take a break and actually get a good night's sleep for—*wah!*" The Bard slipped, his feet shooting out from under him as he fell to his back. He wheezed, the wind knocked out of him.

When he saw why the Bard had fallen, Luke didn't bother to try and help him out. Instead, he let out a happy noise, which—based on the expressions of his companions—they had never heard from him before. The world was on a downward slope. Even though it curved to the side, round objects tended to roll. Along the entire edge of the Zone, he could see thousands upon *thousands* of Skill Pearls shining, trapped against a small ledge. They had been unable to collect the Skill Pearls from the vast majority of the defeated monsters, as they had been destroying them at range.

"Do you want all of those, Luke?" Andre's question was answered for him as Luke dove headfirst into the pile, trying to scoop all of the pearls up in his arms and instead sending them scattering everywhere. "Just wait a moment, let me... yeah, I can grow some grass around this area and have it send all of the pearls to a central collection space. Where do you want them?"

The Murderhobo went deadly silent as his mind rapidly flipped through all three of his emotions. Sucking in a breath through his teeth, he indicated a spot on the ground. Then he lifted Cookie up, slamming her down, over and over, until he had a four-foot trench. Then, standing to the side, he pointed at it. "Put them all in there."

"Yeah, I figured that one out," Andre muttered with great annoyance, pulling his hands off of his ears. "Maybe a little warning before you start going crazy and beating up the ground next time?"

"No promises."

Now all Luke needed was to find a large enough source of liquid mana to fill that hole, and he would be able to combine all of the Skill Pearls into their best, highest form. He hadn't seen any liquid mana running through this Zone, which meant his best option was going to be finding it in Zone twenty-one.

That worked out perfectly for him, because backtracking was the absolute *worst*. "You work on that; I'll go check out the next Zone."

"Wait, Luke!" Taylor called out. "It's not safe; you should wait until we can all go together."

"*Safe*, Taylor? You haven't figured it out yet?" He shook his head, his lip curling in a light sneer. "Nothing in this world is *safe*. Might as well get used to it now."

CHAPTER FORTY-ONE

As it turned out, Luke's search for liquid mana took almost no time at all. Zone twenty-one was set up in a wildly different manner than Zone twenty. Instead of being wall to wall with monsters, this floor was set up nearly like a puzzle. The ground was extremely dry, with no plant life to be seen whatsoever. Thankfully, he was able to spot an anomaly in the distance. He started walking toward it and received an information packet from Murder World.

Welcome to Zone 21! This area is filled with alluring situations with a variety of monsters! There's a Zone clear condition, and for the first time, you get to know about it ahead of time! How exciting is that? Very, we think. In order to exit Zone 21, what you'll need to do is create a continuous path for liquid to flow from the first Monster den all the way to the end of the Zone.

This can be done by defeating the monsters in the pools of liquid then choosing a direction for the liquid to flow. You may only choose one of three directions and must defeat the monsters where the liquid collects in order to change the direction once more. If, at any time, the liquid reaches the rightmost or leftmost edge of the Zone and falls off, the flow of liquid will end, and you'll need to restart! Make sure to plan ahead and use the lessons your instructors have taught you.

"You know Abyss well that I don't have any instructors!" Luke grumbled at the air, which seemed to talk to him every once in a while. Then his head jerked to the side, and he stared at Cookie, backpedaling slightly. "Yes, I suppose, *technically*, you have taught me a few things. Doesn't mean I consider you an instructor. I taught you how to turn goats into paste, and I've never claimed a special title for it, have I? Exactly, thank you."

Moving toward the anomaly in the terrain, Luke quickly figured out what he was looking at. There was a small mound of dirt built up in a dike around a deep pit, which revealed itself to be an oasis when he got to the top and looked down. Hundreds of gallons of liquid mana were placidly swirling, and beautiful women sat atop rocks and other interesting locations, their bodies at least partially submerged in the mana.

All of them seemed to see him at once and began calling out to him in sweet voices. The words themselves were... just *slightly* wrong. Just different enough from his actual language that he couldn't understand anything that they were saying, not that he cared to listen either way. He only had eyes for all of that glorious, flowing power. "Now, the only real question is... how do I collect enough to bring back?"

Luke started down the slope, much to the delight of the women who had apparently been trapped here, alone, for uncounted millennia. The closer he walked, the clearer their voices were, both in tone as well as diction. When he was only twenty feet from them, they were speaking the language of the Hollow Kingdom perfectly.

"Finally! A *man*! Look at those rippling muscles, that enormous, flowing mane of hair!" The words of the first lady he could understand made him stop, anger crossing his features before settling into resignation.

"Abyss." He waded into the liquid, and the laughs of the women went from sweet and tempting to cold and malicious. When he didn't pop like a unicorn that had just been punched in its underbelly, the laughter stopped, and they started moving toward him with clearly malicious intent. "I'm going to lose all my hair again."

Even as he said the words, the incredible density of power in the air swirled around him, and his shoulder-length, messy hair fell out as a large, single clump. He raised his hand and rubbed it over his bald, scarred head. "It's the goats all over again."

The monsters were moving through the liquid faster than he would normally have expected. But anything that could survive in this dense concentration of power had to be stronger than it appeared at first glance. He knew that firsthand, having seen his own reflection once or twice. The first of the incredibly alluring women lunged at him, her arms opened wide as if she were coming in for a tackle hug, her lips pursing as though she were going to give him a smooch. His hand flashed out, palm open wide, closing over her face before he turned and bodily threw her out of the liquid and up the hill.

His armor had come into effect, and every point of contact on her face had been penetrated by the passive effect it generated. The human-looking mouth that she sported had opened wide like a lamprey as she screamed in pain, her lower half revealed as a long fish tail. "Yuck. I hate fish. If I wanted brain food, I would crack something's skull open."

Now knowing for certain that these weren't going to be creatures he would get in trouble with his Sigil for killing, Cookie lashed out and cut across the surface of the water, impacting the nearest mermaid and cleanly separating the bottom half from the top. It splattered across the surface of the mana before sizzling and fading away. "Really, Cookie? I have no idea why you would be jealous about fish; you know I don't like fish. Too fishy. Why would you leave half a fish floating in the water with me? Fish."

Damage dealt: 518 blunt damage!
Congratulations! You have slain a Bewitching Mermaid.
Potentia Gained: 100.

For a long moment, everything seemed to go still. Then Luke's face twitched, his eyes began to whisk around the open pool, and his lips curled back from his teeth. "These things... are worth... one hundred Potentia *each?*"

For the next five minutes, there were only three sounds that could be heard emanating from the deep pit in the ground. The bellows of joy from Luke's lungs, a walloping crash as Cookie hit the water, and the mermaids screaming in pain or for mercy. Luke had learned his lesson when going against the unicorns: never stop killing when a monster asks you to stop. The sounds only settled down when the surface of the liquid mana had bobbing fishtails and a light scum of blood that rapidly popped and fizzed away.

He had ravaged the open hole, using his oversized bone to pummel its depths, finally deciding to leave as the smell of rotting fish began to overpower the natural sweet scent of the area. As he pulled himself out of the ring at the top of the pit, an option to choose a direction for the flow of the liquid appeared in front of him. He considered it for a long moment then decided he would enlist the aid of his team to make that decision for him. "That way, if they get it wrong, I can blame them."

It was only at that moment that he remembered why he had come here in the first place, and that was to bring back plenty of liquid mana to pour on the collected pearls. Casting around for a suitable item, his eyes landed on one of the large boulders that a mermaid had been lounging upon. He returned to the bottom of the pit, wading through the liquid to the edge of the boulder and heaving it out of its position. For some reason, it was far heavier than it should have been. He carried it out of the liquid then began using his mana manifested weapons to carve the boulder into an oversized bucket.

Shaping the stone had taken longer than he originally planned, but what was the point in making something if you didn't add the proper embellishments, inscriptions, or ornamentation? Lifting his brand new, beautifully crafted stone bucket, he returned to the water's edge and filled the item. He estimated that he had perhaps fifty gallons of the liquid and hoped that would be enough for what he was planning to do.

His return to his team was also slower than he expected, mainly due to the fact that he needed to carefully balance the bucket so as not to spill anything. When he was finally nearing his friends, they began retreating away from him. All of them were looking at the bucket apprehensively, and Taylor was the one to call out, "Please be extra careful with that, Luke! If you spill it on the ground, we're going to have to run for it."

"I wonder if you have any idea what you look like right now?" Zed conversationally interjected. "You're holding a massive barrel in one hand that is releasing mana like a forest fire creates smoke. If we were anywhere other than Murder World, what you're holding right now would be considered a crime against humanity."

"Would it?" Luke challenged him as he walked to the edge of the hole. He peered in, noting that the trench he had dug was already half-full with pearls, and more were crawling toward them as if they were being carried by ants. "You know what, Zed? I don't think it would be considered a crime at all."

"Oh? *Somebody* is in a good mood today," he said putting his hands on his hips and jauntily cocked his head to the side. "Well, then, Mr. Murderhobo, please *enlighten* me as to how this wouldn't be considered a horrible thing in a lower world."

"Never said that. This one's easy. Has anyone ever been able to walk around with a barrel of liquid mana before?" He wasn't waiting for an answer, as he didn't know how long the process was going to take. Luke tipped the barrel, pouring the contents directly into the trench. The pearls within it began to smoke and hiss, and the liquid mana churned as it heated up.

Zed hesitated slightly before speaking. "No... because an entire barrel's worth of liquid mana would be considered a *world* treasure, not just a national treasure."

"Right. It wouldn't be a crime against humanity or a war

crime." Luke chuckled darkly as the pile of Skill Pearls rapidly shrank. "It's never a war crime the *first* time."

His team was silent at that moment, digesting what he had just stated and watching with great interest the process of the pearls consuming each other. Luke blinked as he remembered a secondary effect of the pearls and hoped that the liquid mana wouldn't *all* boil away. The stronger the Skill Pearl, the greater the effect on any individuals near it. Higher-rank pearls would tempt them, trying to convince them to swallow them so that they could gain a Skill... or explode, if they didn't have the correct class to process them.

The Murderhobo didn't feel the need to warn them about that effect. He had mentioned it before, and they had seen it in person with Cindy's necklace. If they couldn't remember to keep their filthy hands off his pearls and wasted them by blowing their heads off... it would be a fitting punishment. He growled low in his throat, a natural predator's reaction to scavengers circling its food. When they didn't react to it, he assumed that they were all frozen with fear and was able to calm himself down.

"How much longer do you think before all of them are collected?" Luke directed his question at Andre, who blinked a few times before getting a concentrated look on his face.

"It depends. How long do you want to wait here?" The Druid shrugged and gestured vaguely at the upward slope. "There are tens of thousands more coming down the grass, from where the Sentinels are still being destroyed by my thorns. Otherwise, where they are already collected down here along the edge of the Zone? Probably a few hours before they've all been dropped into the trench."

Luke pondered the question, finally coming up with an answer that was acceptable to himself. "I don't know how many have been gathered so far, but I'll be reasonable. Going by the Skill I got earlier, these are Tier-five Skill Pearls. Unless we don't have enough, I want to keep collecting them until I am able to combine them into a Tier-nine pearl."

"How many pearls will you need for that? I'd like to get going and see what the next Zone looks like," Taylor quizzed him impatiently, which Luke appreciated. He also wanted to get back into combat, and standing here while there were so many willing sacrifices was making him antsy as well.

"Since they're Tier-five pearls, we only need six and a quarter million of them." Luke estimated how rapidly the liquid mana was draining away and nodded solemnly to himself. "Be right back; I think we're going to need more water."

"Luke, that's *not* a reasonable number of pearls!" Andre called after him, but Luke didn't care.

He had his bucket, and Luke remembered reading somewhere that it was important to complete short-term goals. The Murderhobo hummed cheerfully as he skipped down the slope, secretly hoping that the monsters in the pool had been given enough time to respawn.

"This is the most fun I've had in decades. Best day ever."

CHAPTER FORTY-TWO

- TAYLOR -

Every single one of Taylor's senses screamed that walking into one of the pits in Zone twenty-one was a death sentence. For the first time ever, she was regretting her choice of placing the vast majority of her Characteristic upgrades into Physical Reaction and Mental Energy. Without enough Willpower, she could only watch in almost a third-person view as she slowly walked toward the pit with a vacant expression on her face.

"So beautiful. So sweet. I want... *I* want to be able to do that," Zed murmured next to her, and a small part of her wondered at the fact that he was merely standing there listening to the siren song of the Bewitching Mermaids. One small consolation was that she didn't seem to be alone in her enthrallment, as Andre was matching her step for step.

"Hey, I think you guys should stay back. Luke said those pits are pretty dangerous. Guys? Taylor? I know you're not a guy, but I'm using the term colloquially in order to refer to our group, instead of having to say our team name all the time. Okay, now I *know* you're not listening."

A moment later, Taylor blinked as her awareness returned to her. Zed was playing an instrument, and between his Mastery and the sheer volume of the harp, the call to the pit slowly faded into background noise. Blood fountained out of the depression in the landscape, along with a high-pitched scream. She winced as she realized there was likely more than one factor keeping her out of harm's way at this moment. Even so, for the first time, she truly saw the value of having a Bard on her team.

"Thank you, Zed. I think... I think I was completely ensnared. How did you pull me out of it?" She smiled brightly at him, getting a cautious grin in return. At no point did he stop playing his instrument, even as the bewitching songs faded away completely as Luke completed his grisly work. The Bard was perfectly happy to explain at the same time as strumming, "This is a basic dispelling song, one of the only Masteries that the kingdom requires any Bard to learn. I guess what we're supposed to do is act as minstrels for the king, providing gentle background noise for their conversation at the same time as reducing the effect of any magical or mental attacks against him."

His face darkened, and Taylor recognized the signs of him about to go into a rant about the unfairness of his Ascender class, so she cut him off by stepping closer and pulling him into a hug, her words flowing out in a rush. "Thank you, Zed. One of my biggest fears is turning out like Master Don, and I know that could only happen if something was tampering with my mind. It might not seem like much to you, but you just kept my mind from being corrupted, and I will *never* forget it. Please... accept my apologies for how I have treated you in the past. Not only because of this, but, well, because I never actually said the words aloud before, even if I thought them."

The Bard was so off-put by the uncharacteristic show of affection that he gently pushed her away from him and played his song even louder. "Was something messing with you this entire time? Did you have a passive Spell on you that has always been active?"

At those words, her frown returned in full force, and she crossed her arms as she glared at him. "Go on. Explain to me *exactly* what you think is wrong with how I think and act."

Zed opened his mouth, paused, and closed it again with a strange mix of amusement and consternation showing on his face. "...No. I'm sensing that I messed up somehow."

Taylor turned away from him with a light huff. "Seriously, try to give a compliment to someone, and their gut reaction is thinking that I'm being mind controlled."

"Well, maybe you can give compliments more often, so it doesn't seem so out of place!" Zed's words made her freeze in place, but Taylor didn't turn around. It wouldn't do to have him see her blush at this moment. Even though his words aggravated her, she nodded her head fractionally and decided to take his thoughts under advisement.

Luke appeared out of the pit, hauling his bucket of liquid mana once more. A storm of mana swirled around him as he casually strolled along, seemingly oblivious to the cataclysmic amount of energy he was releasing every second. "I think this will do it."

"I still don't know why you made us come with you instead of waiting there." Andre mentioned as they backtracked to the trench that the Murderhobo had dug at the edge of Zone twenty. "It would have made much more sense for one of us to guard the pearls instead of standing around doing nothing like this."

"Heh." Whenever the Murderhobo let out a single chuckle like that, Taylor knew something absolutely insane was about to pop out of his mouth. "You *really* want to know why? Come on, then. See for yourself."

Andre fell in step alongside Luke, his pride not allowing him to shirk away from the challenge. As they got closer to the small trench, Taylor began feeling a strong pull. It was a warmth on her skin, like dappled sunlight falling through the canopy of a forest. Without thinking, a bright smile appeared on her face, and she walked a little faster. Next to her, Zed was already running, sprinting forward with an expression on his face like a starving man, pale and bloodless, though his eyes were shot through with bright red capillaries.

The vines began whipping off of Andre as he was impacted by… whatever this was. Eventually, Luke was forced to casually reach out, grab the Druid, and huck him back farther into Zone twenty-one. "Yeah, I didn't think so."

As Luke closed in on the trench, Zed and Taylor began running even faster. Then the Murderhobo dumped the water out of his barrel into the trench, and the compulsion that Taylor was feeling vanished, as though she were a moth and the flame she wanted *so badly* had just been snuffed out. The Bard started coughing, looking around as he tried to catch his breath. "What… what was that? Why couldn't I resist it?"

"Far as I know, that is something like forty-seven or forty-eight Tier-seven Skill Pearls all nestled together in a group," Luke informed them after staring into the boiling and thrashing liquid. "Not going to be long now."

Indeed it was not. Less than half an hour later, Luke informed Andre that he could end the relentless march of Skill Pearls from the Zone. Then, all at once, the remaining liquid mana in the trench boiled away, all at the same time, allowing a bright blue glow to emanate from its depths. The desire Taylor had been feeling just a few minutes ago returned in full force, doubled, no… *tripled.* She threw herself forward, gathering lightning above her head to strike down any obstacle in her path.

She was too slow. Luke reached into the hole, pulled out a shining star, and tossed it in his mouth like a single piece of popped corn. Her heightened Senses allowed her to hear his throat muscles working as he dry swallowed the Skill Pearl, and all she could hope was that he would choke so that she could *cut it out of him.* As she was so focused on the man in front of her, she could hear the instant the tiny sphere reached his stomach and splashed into the acid waiting below.

Taylor blinked, catching herself mid-motion as she started

to direct her Spell to destroy the impermanent being in front of her. She looked around at her party, seeing that all of them were in the middle of some kind of attack. Each of them slowly lowered their arms, weapons, or harp. Luke turned around, and she fully expected him to appear smug or aggressive at their positions. Instead, he simply nodded at them and started walking back toward the pit. "I decided to settle for a Tier eight. This was taking too long."

"What just happened?" Zed whispered so softly a regular human wouldn't have been able to hear him. "I was about to try erasing his mind. Why? Why does it have such a powerful effect, and why can I not dispel it?"

The Mage swallowed, her throat so dry that it felt like the muscles rubbing together we're going to start a bonfire in her mouth. "It's a natural treasure. It's not any kind of Spell or enchantment, nothing like that. It's... *desire*. Pure desire. I have no other explanation for it. Can you really erase minds?"

Zed evaded the question. "I said *try*, didn't I?"

None of them were in a speaking mood as they continued farther into the Zone. Anyone not a Murderhobo was deep in self-reflection and contemplation, trying to determine how they could avoid falling into that whirlpool of animalistic instinct. Trying to get herself out of her own head, Taylor realized that this Zone was a reflection of her inner turmoil. The ground was empty and barren, except for pits of desire randomly sprinkled throughout. Just like the Skill Pearl itself, getting too close and giving in was a guaranteed death. She swore to herself that she would do better and flinched as her Sigil *chimed*.

She pulled open her Characteristics, eyes widening as she realized that both her Willpower and Charisma had just jumped two full points each. A quick scan showed that this wasn't the only increase, just the most recent. Taylor had improved in all areas. Narrowing her eyes, the Mage decided that now would be the perfect time to place the Characteristic increase that she had been saving since reaching level fifteen. "Truly, training in high-mana-density areas is amazing for training all Characteristics."

With a mental command, she increased her Physical Reaction by five points, making it her first Characteristic to edge over the fifty-point threshold.

Cal Scan
Level: 15
Current Etheric Xenograft Potentia: 11,452 / 15,970 to level 16!
Body: 13.9

- *Fitness: 14.5*
- *Resistance: 13.3*

Mind: 23.65

- *Talent: 20*
- *Capacity: 27.3*

Presence: 14.75

- *Willpower: 12.3*
- *Charisma: 17.2*

Senses: 47.85

- *Physical reaction: 50.8*
- *Mental energy: 44.9*

Maximum health: 183
Maximum mana: 504
Mana regen: 6.6 per second.

She collapsed onto her rear as the changes took effect, but they settled quickly as it was only approximately a ten percent increase. Taking a few deep breaths, Taylor looked around, hoping for a notification from her Sigil. "Feces. I had really been hoping that getting over fifty points in a Characteristic would do something neat."

"Monsters are dead," Luke informed everyone abruptly, walking over, grabbing Taylor by the shoulder, and lifting her as if she weighed as much as a feather. When she got her feet under her once more, he let go and faced the group, his arms crossed. "I need to send the liquid mana along the Zone. My choices are directly downhill, slightly to the left, or to the right. This Zone is a puzzle, and the liquid needs to collect in the holes so we can continue onward. Tell me which way to send it."

The group was silent as each of them tried to think of a solution, but then a bright smile appeared on Andre's face, and his eyes started to glow with enthusiasm.

"I have a plan."

CHAPTER FORTY-THREE

As it turned out, Andre's plan was extremely effective. Even though it took two full weeks, they completed the Zone far faster than they would have otherwise. Trial and error had them constantly resetting, but the Druid had simply grown a sparse carpet of mycelium along the entirety of the Zone, since he had no other plant life to contend with.

The fungus had rolled along the Zone at a much higher rate of growth than grass or other more 'intense' plant life would have required. When it finished, he was able to determine the optimal path from the starting pool, going all the way to the end of the Zone almost fifteen hundred miles away. Needless to say, if Luke had been forced to contend with this puzzle on his own, it may have taken years or even decades before he had cleared it.

Still, the Berserker had nothing to complain about. Every time he went into a pit, he came out with a broad smile on his face. Taylor never trusted herself to get close to the pits while the monsters were still alive in them. Every time she tried, she was forced to start marching to her own death. Even so, she used it as willpower training and got as close as possible, having

Andre yank her back with a vine if she got too close to the edge. The Mage had recommended that each of them undergo this training, amending her words when Luke merely snorted derisively at her.

Even with taking time to train their Characteristics, grow small groves of plants for food and liquid, and making careful judgment calls, they cleared the Zone only days after the fungus had spread completely, and they moved on to the next one.

Taylor thought over what Luke had mentioned to them about this place, how every third Zone could now be used as an exit to their own plane of existence, but only every fifth one could serve as a new entrance.

That worked well for them months later, after they had evaded the strange monster made of light in Zone twenty-two and defeated a fortress populated by goblins in Zone twenty-three. Now, they were finally finishing a slog through Zone twenty-four.

This Zone had nearly been the death of three of them *thousands* of times, as it was a bog made of a combination of liquid mana and what served as dirt for this world. If they had stepped off of solid ground, they would have been plunged into the energetic fluid. That would have guaranteed a quick and nearly painless death as they exploded, and Taylor couldn't help but admit to herself that she had considered it at least a few times. Mostly intrusive thoughts, but having only the three men as company was slowly driving her mad.

Everything had been fine until she had snapped and started casting Cleanse on her teammates at least once a day. At first, she did it because they stank so terribly, but then it became one of her daily chores. With the expectation set, it was hard for her to find a reason to refuse, even if it only took a mental command from her for the Spell to take effect. She still needed to physically touch them in order to cast the Spell, and for some reason, that fact had begun to grate on her.

Intellectually, Taylor understood that it was a combination of constantly being on high alert, always being under attack, and never being farther away than an outstretched arm's length from one of her companions. When they had been living in the Scarrocco Nature Preserve, they had all been able to have their own space. They could pursue their own interests, move at their own pace, and feel confident that they could be alone with their thoughts or their private actions.

She accepted the fact that the mental fatigue was starting to get to her, and day after day, came to understand Luke the Murderhobo just a little bit better. His habits were starting to make sense, his aversion to dealing with people seemed brilliant, and his short and to-the-point answers were a relief after the circumlocution that Zed would put her through in order to answer even the simplest of questions.

As Luke reached his hand out and touched a strange film of power in the air between the two Zones, Taylor let out a deep sigh of relief as it collapsed into an exit portal. At that moment, she felt newfound strength, realizing that she had increased in power to an unbelievable extent over the last few months. The constantly shifting scenery, new monsters ready to fight at a moment's notice, and the sheer *quantity* of those self-same monsters had allowed her to break into level eighteen. That was in conjunction with increasing Thunder Beast's Eye to Tier eight, Fissure to Tier six, and Frozen Trident to Tier five.

As per usual, she had divided the increases in her Charac-teristics between Mental Energy and Physical Reaction, but as they stopped to catch their breath and watch the Scar forming in the air, she read over the changes in her Spells. One of them even made her blink in surprise. She hadn't been under attack by a mana-based Spell of some sort since her entry to this world, so she had not even thought to look at the upgrade that she had achieved in her Spell Nullify. She softly murmured to her Sigil, "Display changes in Spells since last viewing."

Frozen Trident → Astral Triplet (Tier 5, level 0).

Effect 3: The spikes of ice generated by this Spell are now tipped with ice from the void around planets, adding an armor penetration effect of

50+3n%, where n = Skill level. (Maximized at 80% armor penetration.).

Nullify → Absorb (Tier 5, level 4).

Effect 3: All mana from nullified effects are added to a temporary bonus mana pool that'll be drained before your normal mana pool when casting Spells. This bonus mana will be retained for 10n seconds, where n = Skill level, before dissipating into the surroundings.

Fissure → Earthshaker (Tier 6, level 0).

Bonus, AOE: Take direct control of all earthen materials around you, shaping it to your desires. This may disrupt control of other effects created by Ascenders attempting to control the same earthen materials. This Spell lasts for 10n seconds, where n = Skill level. Damage potential varies based on materials used.

Thunder Beast's Eye → Tribulation of Argus (Tier 8, level 9).

Bonus, Multitarget AOE: For every 25 mana invested in this Spell, gain a n% chance to summon one additional Thunder Beast's Eye 10 feet from the nearest eye in the sky. Each additional eye will only be able to cast a single bolt of lightning, but it will be done at no additional mana cost.

Though she had many powerful options, she had immediately invested Potentia until the Tribulation of Argus had reached level nine. She had not been willing to use this Spell to this point, as they had been on soggy ground. Taylor wasn't going to take a chance at accidentally obliterating herself and her team, not after the fire Spell fiasco when she first arrived.

Even so, the Mage was desperately excited to get a chance at using it. The main reason was… the Spell didn't specify *any* upper limit for how many additional eyes could be summoned, only that there was currently a less than ten percent chance that it would happen.

"I will be able to use this soon without killing us all," Taylor promised herself. On the note of safety, she had been far too cautious to allow her Meta-magic to increase in Tier while she was in this world. Even though the absolute abundance of mana would have increased the speed at which it ranked up, she *needed* to be able to activate Luke's healing ability. It had saved her multiple times, more than she wanted to count, and it frightened her how easily she was accepting wounds at this point. "Maybe I should stop relying on that… it's a bad habit to get hit, and we'll be back to the base world soon. Probably."

That last part was added because her musing had caused Luke to look over at her sharply, and for some suspicious reason, he had reached down and 'casually' scooped up a large quantity of mud. She didn't want to know what he planned to use that for and resolved to not give him any reason to bring that filth anywhere near her.

When Luke marched past the distortion and into Zone twenty-five, she couldn't decide if she was happy he didn't think they could leave, or if she should try to force the issue and escape this place. Her Sigil wasn't screaming at her that it believed she was strong enough to break past the barricade that was surely waiting for them, but she could tell that they were close. But… did she want to risk her life, and what freedom she enjoyed, on being *probably* close enough? As her mind pondered these questions, her body fell in step with Luke, and she marched past the distortion without a word.

Her suspicions were confirmed as the mud slid out of Luke's hand without another word.

After a few minutes of walking, she decided to say her first words to her team for the day. "Luke, did you get any information about this Zone when we entered?"

He nodded at her, remaining silent. She forced herself to have a calm reaction and merely continued her line of questioning. "Please share that information with us."

Taylor had found that it was best to give firm yet polite demands instead of asking him questions. Otherwise, he would share whatever he thought was the most pertinent detail that satisfied the query then go silent. It had taken weeks of failed conversations until she had worked out this methodology.

Luke took in a sharp inhale through his nose, as if he were about to hit something. All of the team's heightened reactions kicked into gear, and their heads snapped into position to stare at him as he turned around. Only after she had released some tension did Taylor realize how much her battle instincts had increased over the preceding months. "It appears that Zone twenty-five is a boss Zone. There's only a single creature here, and there's a good shot that we don't even see it; if we don't wanna."

"Is that... a good thing? It doesn't sound like a good thing the way you say it, even though it does sound like a good thing when taken at face value." Zed's words were far calmer than his attitude had been when they first arrived. Perhaps he was feeling like he was a true part of the group, now that he was rapidly increasing his power. Even so, he lagged far behind the other members of the group, but that was to be expected when he had started so far behind where they were. Even now, he was focusing most of his Potentia into his Masteries instead of increasing his level.

"It might be, it might not." Luke's answer was extremely cagey. "The information it gave me said that, if we make it to the end of the Zone without defeating the boss monster, we will be guaranteed enough Potentia to increase at least one level."

"Great, let's do that!" Zed started walking, but the Murder-hobo's hand reached out and rested on his chest to stop him.

"However..." Luke slowly announced the remainder of his thoughts. "If we were to *defeat* the monster, it guarantees us enough Potentia to gain *three* levels. I don't know about you three, but that means it would give me enough to get to level twenty-one."

CHAPTER FORTY-FOUR

- LUKE -

He was surprised to see his team take the information with only a shrug. This seemed like a bigger deal than they were making of it. Andre was the one to enlighten him, even if his words left the Murderhobo trembling with rage.

"Sorry to break it to you, Luke. It just isn't *possible* to assign your Potentia to break into level twenty. Not without permission from the ruler of the Hollow Kingdom. It doesn't matter how much extra you have, as soon as you assign enough to be one point of Potentia away from level twenty, everything in your Sigil will be automatically assigned to different Abilities. Sorry, Skills in your case. So... stay at least two points of Potentia away, if you want to be able to manage your own growth?"

"This is common knowledge?" Luke looked around for confirmation as his teammates nodded at him. "I dislike the fact that I don't know what seems to be common knowledge about what our Sigils can and cannot do. I believe it's an intentional choice, at this point."

Zed made a sound of disagreement, explaining himself as

Luke's eyes locked on him. "I could have taught you almost anything you wanted to learn, and if I didn't know it, one of these two would have. But… you spent the last five years in a hole. None of us were going to follow you into the Descender portal, and if you had stayed out, you would have found plenty of time for hobbies, such as learning new things about your Sigil. This one is on you."

The Murderhobo let the silence become tense as his glare intensified on the Bard. Then he nodded, a single, sharp bob of his head. "Understood. That makes more sense. Now, we should make our decision on if we want to take on the Zone boss or not."

"Three levels' worth of Potentia is… an absolutely insane reward." Andre piped up, his exhaustion from navigating the previous Zone tinting his voice with exhaustion. "When we're looking at the literally hundreds of *thousands* of beings we have killed in the last few months, even *those* aren't worth what our next three levels are. How strong do you think this monster must be if it's worth that much?"

Luke waited for a moment to ensure that the question was directed at him. When no one else spoke, he started to outline his estimation of the upcoming challenge. "I think it will be a nearly level-twenty threat. The world flagged this as an 'anomaly', and I've only run into two of those before. I almost died both times. There's a good chance that it has a Domain Tier Skill, that's Tier ten for anyone who didn't get taught all of this by a friendly face. *Oh wait*, that's just me."

"*Boo*, you already admitted it was your own fault!" Zed held out two hands with the thumbs pointing downward. "To clarify, is there any guarantee that there's only one of them?"

"Yes. Probably." Luke took that as agreement that they were going to hunt the creature and started walking into the Zone.

"Luke," Taylor called out in a voice that was as tired as the rest of them. "The word 'probably' automatically implies that there's no guarantee. We're in no condition to fight right now. Let's take a day or so and get some rest?"

The Murderhobo clenched his fists, *very* unwilling to stop when he was on such a great winning streak. In the last few months, he had cleared more Zones in a single go than he could remember ever doing before. Only as he realized that the success was partially due to his teammates being a part of the process, he gave his acquiescence to the pause. There was a collective sigh of relief, and Andre began growing an oasis for their comfort. It abutted the edge of the next Zone, just in case they needed to beat a hasty retreat into a 'safer' environment.

Within an hour, the trees were producing fruit, and everyone was chowing down with wolf-like hunger, having been forced to eat on the run for the last several weeks. There was a tacit agreement that Luke would be the one to keep watch, and the other three laid down on beds made of soft moss, asleep almost as soon as their heads rested on the unnaturally wiggling flora. The Murderhobo didn't mind staying awake. He was far too amped up, too excited over his recent successes and gains. For the last three levels, he had increased his Resistance three times, for a total of an additional fifteen points.

As they had progressed deeper into Murder World, the increased mana density and constant menagerie of situations and monsters they had to navigate through had also been beneficial to his overall Characteristics.

Cal Scan
Level: 18
Current Etheric Xenograft Potentia: 21,412 / 676,500 to level 19!
Body: 51

- *Fitness: 59*
- *Resistance: 43*

Mind: 25.55

- *Talent: 23*
- *Capacity: 28.1*

Presence: 27.5

- *Willpower: 40*
- *Charisma: 15*

Senses: 35.15

- *Physical reaction: 43.3*
- *Mental energy: 27*

Maximum health: 1,920 (Giga)
Maximum mana: 423
Mana regen: 7.6 per second.

An enormous shift upward in his Resistance—nearly doubling it—had a massive impact on his overall health. That, coupled with Giga increasing all the way to Tier one, level nine, had boosted his capability of receiving damage to utterly inhuman proportions. Unfortunately, it also meant his actual body had increased in size by a total of twenty-seven percent. Luke was taller, broader, and thicker. Thanks to his Pristine Balance, he hadn't noticed any changes in his ability to fight nor any alterations in his vestibular sense nor proprioception. Yet, if he were to Tier up that Skill again, his combat effectiveness would drop almost to zero until he was able to learn how to move again.

The main detriment was the fact that the changes were fairly rapid, drawing on nearby mana to fill in the gaps nutrition simply could not. In other words, he had burst through his clothes by the time he reached level nine in Giga. His pants had been repurposed into a tattered loincloth, as he had refused Andre's 'generous' offer to cloak him in wiggling plant life that he could control from a distance. "Not just no, but *Abyss* no."

Beyond a single Skill, Luke had devoted all of his earned Potentia into his levels, feeling that his Skills were currently serving him extremely well. Giga didn't draw from his pool of

Potentia, instead increasing on its own based on how much mana was in the area that his body was absorbing.

Source-cerer's armory had locked him out from increasing the Skill, forcing it to remain at Tier nine, level nine. In preparation for the upcoming Zone, he had added only a small amount of Etheric Xenograft Potentia to what he considered his most important Skill: Rift Hunter.

It had been stuck at Tier seven, level nine for quite a long time, and when they had been traveling through the bog, the monsters were few and far between. To relieve his boredom, he had initiated the Tier-up of the Skill, creating mana wave fluctuations that drew in monsters from all over the Zone. That had given him something fun to do as his friends screamed and writhed from the tiny droplets of bog water that splashed near them. Taylor had been suspicious of his motivations, but seeing as they were nowhere near an exit portal at the time, she had held her tongue.

He could tell that the Tier increase of the Skill was nearing completion, and he was excited to see what would happen to it. After double checking that nothing else had changed, he slumped into a seated position and kept a casual lookout for the rest of his watch. Surprising even himself, he managed to fall asleep when Taylor took over, sleeping deeply after counting goats jumping over a fence. He systematically whacked each one out of the sky with a dream version of Cookie. He woke up refreshed, his body practically *humming* with energy as he flowed up to his feet, prepared to immediately hunt down whatever this boss monster might be.

Luckily for his companions, they were also ready to go right away. Andre seemed much calmer than he had been the day before, but Zed seemed to have been having trouble sleeping, and had deep, dark bags under his eyes. "Are we looking for something enormous, or do you think this is going to be a sneaky beaky boss that tries to ambush us from behind?"

The Murderhobo had an answer for that. "It doesn't matter. Either way, you should stay right in the center of the group.

Monsters tend to go for the weakest combatant first. You know what? You should walk ahead of us, maybe ten to fifteen paces. That way, it will feel confident in coming right up to you and revealing itself with an attack."

"At which point you'll step in, take the monster down, and make sure I don't get hit." Zed paused, waiting for a response. When he received none, he chuckled nervously and tried again. "You *are* going to make sure it doesn't hit me… *right*, Luke?"

"Ugh. Fine." The Murderhobo growled out. Zed started to relax, and Luke finished his statement. "We'll just keep you in the center of the group."

Andre nudged Zed in the side. "He was going to use you as bait. Not the good kind, the kind that definitely gets taken by the fish."

"Yeah, I *know*, Andre." The Bard shoved the Druid away, only for the man to fall almost all the way to the ground, stopping when his vines came out and stabilized his form and pulled him into a horizontal reclined position. The plants walked him across the ground as Andre tried to hold back his laughter at Zed's incredulity.

Luke and Taylor were both focused on scanning the horizon, and when the Murderhobo noticed that she was copying him, he stood up straight and looked *twice* as hard.

He won.

His left arm shot forward, every one of his fingers pointed directly at the lumbering excrescence on the horizon. "Found it. Looks like your first guess was correct, Zed. It's a big boy."

Taylor held her hand up, trying to gauge the height of the monster by comparing it to the tip of her thumb and outstretched index finger. "I can't tell if I've gotten used to the mists in this world, or if they are just thinner in this part of the world. Or… is it closer than I think it is? Luke, do you know how big that thing is? Or, should I say, please give me your best guess on its size."

The Murderhobo took a few long minutes to study the beast in the distance that had not yet appeared to notice them. When he finally spoke, it was with a great deal of confidence. "We're on a downward slope, meaning we don't have the curvature of a planet blocking our view of that thing. It appears to be approximately the size of half of my palm from this distance, meaning that it will likely be anywhere from forty-five to fifty feet tall up close. As far as I can tell, it's a bipedal humanoid with hulking muscles, elongated tusks coming from the lower mandible, and carrying a shiny club approximately half the length of its body."

The other members of his group digested this information and had vastly different reactions. Andre looked around with a frown, "Where would it get a club from? There are no plants here taller than the grass. Also, if it's contained to this Zone, it's unlikely to have made a weapon out of materials from other creatures."

"Sounds like a Troll," Taylor announced after cross referencing the Characteristics with the bestiaries she had memorized years ago. "It should have a very high regeneration capability and incredible amounts of strength."

Zed listened quietly to the words that his friends said, nodding along with them before turning to the Murderhobo. "Extra-muscley, carries a huge club, is a giant troll. Luke, you didn't tell me we were going to be fighting *you*!"

CHAPTER FORTY-FIVE

- ANDRE -

It took Andre a full week to feel confident in the preparations he'd made for the fight against the giant troll. Every hour that passed seemed to increase the team's tension, but Luke was the worst of them all. As the Druid was expanding out the final finishing touches on the traps and final safety measures, they almost had to physically restrain the nearly-eight-foot-tall giant of a man. Andre had a sneaking suspicion that attempt would have ended poorly.

"I'll just go take care of this myself!" Luke told the group, picking Zed up with one hand and setting him to the side as if he were pushing a branch out of his way on a jaunt through a forest. "We've got things to do, monsters to kill. We can't just stand around and gawk at some creature because it's *big*. You know what I did to the last big monster? I crawled into its brain and poisoned it by opening an artery in my leg!"

"What does that even *mean*?" Zed spat out the words, blinking rapidly. "Are you speaking literally, or are you telling us a story to hasten our progress?"

"I am literally speaking right now."

"Okay, wait, no, that doesn't answer my question clearly-"

Zed was cut off as Andre clapped his hands and cleared his throat loudly. "I am prepared!"

"Awesome." Taylor acknowledged his words by beginning to weave her Spells. Her preparations could only be done a few minutes in advance, since no matter how much mana she could pump into her Spells, their biggest bottleneck at this point was the amount of time they would last before collapsing. Seeing that Taylor was making her move, Luke howled with delight and sprinted off across the plains.

The Bard pulled out a lute from his oversized backpack, muttering to himself angrily. "Better get a good story out of this, at least. No, we had better survive this, *and* I get a good story out of it."

The area around them began to brighten as the shifting lightning that formed the Spell above Taylor's head began to soak up all of the extra mana she was feeding it. Every few seconds, another eye would appear in the sky, and soon there was a cluster of them hovering over the group, making the sky above them look like someone had dragged the constellations closer to the world.

"Hmm." Andre realized something unfortunate at that moment. "Maybe we should have used someone else to get the troll's attention? I'm not sure if Luke will remember to disengage and bring it over here like we had planned."

Everything went quiet for a second as the others facepalmed. Even though they had been in this world with the Murderhobo for what amounted to two years at this point and knew his habits, they tended to still treat him as a normal person at the worst times. Noise returned to the world in a rush as a calamitous *boom* reached them in a physical burst of air. Moments later, dirt, rocks, and mulch peppered them as debris rained down.

Against everything they had expected, moments after the impact, Luke came sprinting back toward them. He was covered in wounds and had various rocks and other detritus embedded in his skin. The Druid frowned as he realized that it could only mean one thing: all of the Murderhobo's mystical armor had been overwhelmed in the few moments he'd been out of their sight.

"I am amending my recommendation. We should leave the Zone immediately, and take the single level reward," Luke calmly explained to them as blood rained off of his beard, where it had been collecting after streaming down his face.

"What did it *do*-" Zed bit his words off with a yelp as Luke bodily grabbed him and threw him deeper into the area that Andre had set up to be well-defended. A fraction of an instant later, the troll burst through the dust cloud that had impeded their vision, only to be met with a constant stream of lightning hitting it in nearly a hundred points along its body at once.

The light in the area changed once more, the world seeming to go dark as all of the eyes in the sky vanished except for one. That final portion of the Spell continuously blasted from that moment on, each lightning bolt taking less than half a second to target and fire. The troll's momentum was broken, but even as Andre watched, the charred wounds inflicted upon it closed up and sealed. It was moving again, fractions of a second after being hit the first time, but at least now he could track its movements.

The lightning was targeting the creature's face, clearly an attempt to disorient it and impede its senses. Andre needed to get into the fight, and he started by twisting and heaving a sack into the air, holding onto its lower corners so that the contents spilled out. It had been filled with prepared seeds, and the enormous investment of his time, blood, and mana scattered across the body of the troll as if someone had thrown a clump of dirt. Immediately, the seeds sprouted and began growing various plants over its body.

Nothing they had done so far seemed to be phasing the troll, and it almost casually lifted its sparkling club above its head with one hand, bringing it down like a moon crashing into a planet. The single attack moved almost as though it were in slow motion, Andre's brain pumping adrenaline into his system so hard he felt like he was getting tunnel vision. He noticed many details as the weapon was coming down, but the most important one was that, at first glance, the 'shiny club' appeared to be crystal. No, more than that, it looked to be a single, enormous, perfectly faceted diamond.

But it radiated danger at such an extreme level there was no way it was a simple natural material. No, Andre realized with horror. The entire weapon was a single chunk of solid mana.

As it impacted the ground, millimeters of the surface fractured off, scattering along the ground and into the air around it like shrapnel from a metal Mage's explosive Spell. Dozens of the shards were coming directly at him, and a simple touch from them guaranteed his death. Behind the shrapnel was a rapidly expanding cloud of debris, but it was riding the shockwave created by the blow.

With a thunderous boom, Luke appeared in front of Andre, taking the brunt of the leading edge's attack. Blood fountained from the Murderhobo's body, even as his armor suddenly reappeared and started fiercely glowing. The rest of the blast was completely blocked by the bulwark of a man, and fierce loyalty to his friend sprang up in Andre. "You saved me!"

Luke turned his head, showing that a spike of crystallized mana had gone through his cheek, but he'd held it in place by chomping down at the last second. "Ah caught h-one!"

"Close enough!" Andre didn't particularly care about the *reasoning* behind the save, only that it had happened. The world around them had vanished behind a wall of thick blue dust, but that didn't stop the Murderhobo from charging forward and swinging his club for all he was worth. The sound of a massive bone landing directly on dense meat wasn't something the Druid had ever expected to be a regular sound in his life, but right now... it was the best sound in the world. It meant that this unstoppable *demigod* of a monster was otherwise engaged.

On the fly, he changed his plans. The sheer strength exhibited by this terror was at least a factor of ten higher than what he'd been thinking he would have to deal with. He stepped into his prepared area, sinking into a semi-trancelike state as he wrapped himself in plants and opened the ground underneath his feet. The terrain reacted to him as a Druid, but there were many factors that made it decidedly unsafe for him to practice his normal tactics in this area.

First of all, if he sank into the ground and ran into an underground stream of liquid mana, he would explode, and his friends wouldn't even know that it had happened. Secondly, there was so much power packed into even the individual grains of sand that he wasn't comfortable with letting it come into contact with his skin, especially if he delved deeper into it. Every inch lower seemed to increase the sheer *quality* of the mana present. That meant burrowing through the entire Zone to escape the boss monster's attention wasn't only unlikely, it was a desperately inadvisable option of last resort.

That meant he was going to be in range of the club attacks, even if it was just handling the craters left behind from the megatons of force generated from each blow. Still, being as connected to the world as possible gave him the best control over his abilities and his Druidic Circles. With his eyes closed, he could track the troll far more efficiently, placing his mind in contact with the plants crawling along its body.

The first command he gave the new growth was to begin inserting thorns into the flesh of the troll. From there, he sprouted more plants, burrowing them deeper into the meat of the beast. Unfortunately, the growth of the plants simply wasn't strong enough to force itself past the first couple of inches. Almost all of the plants were caught in the dense brown fat of the monster, with only a few managing to reach near-surface veins and muscles. "It'll have to do. Next up, stage two. Slowing this thing down."

Long tendrils began erupting from the foliage. This time it wasn't pliant, easy vines. Instead, rapidly growing bamboo began weaving itself to nearby shoots, creating thickly braided ropes of the durable, flexible fibers. Beyond growing, Andre wasn't having the plants do anything else. They weren't trying to trip the creature, wrap around its legs, or latch onto something else to slow it down. It just wasn't *possible* at this stage, as the sheer amount of power the creature could bring to bear would render any attempt utterly futile.

Stage three was next, but it required his teammates to be pulling their weight and following the plan. He could only hope that... *there*! Luke was moving across the surface of the world incredibly rapidly, right at the center of Andre's seat of power in this Zone. "Yes! Great job, Luke!"

There was no way for the Murderhobo to hear him, as he was several feet underground and completely wrapped in plants and dirt. Still, the sheer speed that the Murderhobo was moving meant that he was willing to follow the plan, no matter what. It was just strange that he was leaping along... "Oh. He's not running and leaping. He got slapped by the troll, didn't he? Now he's skipping along the surface of the planet like a rock skips in a pond. You know what? *I'll take it.*"

The troll was running along after the tumbling Murderhobo, its speed so great it was only a few feet behind the battered human. As Luke bounced over the marked area, Andre took a deep breath and pushed against the world around him with all his might. His blood had been laid out in a trio of concentric circles, and as the Druidic Magic took hold, the ground underneath the troll shifted away as rapidly as someone blowing dust off of the surface of a countertop. Unable to halt its momentum with no point of contact with a stable object, the dense and extremely heavy creature dropped straight to the bottom of the pit they had created.

"Oldest trap in the world, for a good reason." Andre chuckled heartily as he took control of the braided bamboo coating the monster. It went rigid, slamming into the wall as the creature attempted to jump out of the pit that it found itself in. Thousands of braided bamboo trees strained against the creature's muscle, the woven net extending from every inch of the creature to work against any momentum it could build up.

Even so, as the troll began to thrash, willingly sacrificing large chunks of the surface of its body, the entanglement started to lose effectiveness even more rapidly than they had planned for, and the assessment had been *generous*. With a stray thought, he activated his part of the signal, and a ring of flowers burst into bloom around the edge of the pit. Then he went back to actively controlling the bamboo, causing every shoot to dig deeper into the ground, sucking up mana to reinforce itself and grow over the trees that were fraying and snapping. "This is gonna be close!"

"*Yelp of the Gelert!*" Taylor followed her part of the plan perfectly, activating her stolen Spell and summoning a massive hound that stared down into the pit directly at the troll. The jowls of the dog shifted as it snarled, and a Spell Circle began forming in front of its nose.

The Mage had explained to them that she only had enough mana after reaching level eighteen for the initial casting of this Spell, as it required an investment of five hundred mana just for the summoning and blast to occur. She was up to approximately seventy-five mana per second in regeneration at this point, her body having been steeped in the potent energy, just as theirs had. Unless she was interrupted, or until she ran out of mana to fuel the Spell, she could channel her mana into the summoned dog and let the blast continue indefinitely.

Structured mana shaped as a beam of corrosive darkness blasted into the pit, looking for all the world like a thick gush of tar that had somehow managed to form a laminar stream. Sensing through his plants, Andre could feel as the troll took the attack face-first, howling in rage and pain as its body slowly began whittling away... *far* too slowly. Nearly half of the damage done was repaired every second, and the corrosive properties of the attack were making the bamboo fray further.

The troll got its arm free and lifted its club to block the attack directly. Three seconds, five seconds, half a minute...

and at last, the troll tore free. With a single leap, it shot directly upward, out of the pit, and obliterated the summoned dog's head with a thrust of its club. At that moment, Andre realized that all of them were probably about to die.

Luke appeared next to the troll even as he had that thought, his Dragonbone Greatclub lashing out and hitting the enormous crystallized mana club. The Murderhobo was knocked away from the force of the blow, but he maintained his balance and reappeared next to the enormous weapon as the troll's momentum continued bringing it upward. He swung again, hitting the club in nearly the same spot.

Andre couldn't understand *why*, so he sat up, the ground and plants parting around him as if he were moving through air. As his head popped out of the ground, and his eyes could visually inspect the enormous glowing weapon, he realized what Luke was doing.

Taylor's attack had created a weak point in the club, and with every strike, Luke was widening that fault. When he realized what that would mean in the next few seconds, he threw himself backward. Encasing Taylor and Zed in stone coffins, he launched the three of them down and away, through the soil of Murder World. Increased risk of burnout from overabundance of mana or not, Andre intrinsically understood that if they remained where they were, this clash of titans would guarantee his death.

One hundred meters, two hundred meters, half a kilometer… the Druid dug deeper, until he was forced to stop as he noticed the ground becoming less like dirt and more like mud. He knew the instant Luke's plan worked…

Since the sun wasn't *supposed* to shine underground.

CHAPTER FORTY-SIX

- LUKE -

Cookie crashed against the crystallized mana, and Luke put everything he had into the strike. He could tell that the weapon was on the verge of being destroyed, his Source-cerer's Armory giving him a subtle understanding of the weapon his opponent was using. His Pristine Balance allowed him to reposition himself midair, Feather's Fall allowed him to get back into the swing of things, and Bum Thunder brought him right back to the point in space he needed to be in order to employ Cookie to maximum effect.

"Shockwave Cleave!" As his best friend and weapon landed, he activated that final Skill and was sent blasting away just in front of the leading edge of the detonation that followed. Mana was inherently unstable in any form other than the semi-physical gas that permeated their bodies. It was *always* attempting to return to that state, and when something interrupted the careful balance of Energy Matrices it had created, it tended to return to the gaseous state as expediently as possible.

In other words, as the crack in the weapon moved through

the entirety of the object, its crystalline state shattered and exploded into the lower state of liquid mana by increasing its volume dramatically, which then went a state further into gas. What seemed like unending discharges of pure mana expanded out rapidly, generating everything from light to various magical effects as the cataclysmic cascade rebounded against itself. Any particle in the air, any other form of energy that the mana could glom onto, impacted the final state of the discharging weapon.

The free mana turned into structured mana in some places, annihilating the landscape, the air, and causing devastation on a scale Luke wished he could casually replicate.

His initial flight away from the detonation had been the only thing that saved him from the worst of the effects, and he rode the outer wave of expanding mana as it created a cavitation bubble in the atmosphere. Constantly taking terrible vibration damage from being shaken so hard, Luke's skin was burning away as his speed increased to the point that the air friction lit him on fire—luckily, not hot enough to ignite the free-floating mana around him—but at the same time, he was *enclosed* in a bubble of power. Even as the damage was done, it was rapidly healing. A thought flashed across his mind. "Maybe Zed was right. Do that troll and I actually have something in common?"

As he watched the ground below him flashing past, Luke realized that he was approaching the edge of the Zone. He hadn't expected that to be an issue, as they had been fighting nearly exactly in the center of it. At that moment, the Murderhobo realized that he had not only flown fifty miles... at this point, with the speed he was moving, he'd already gone well over a *hundred*. He happened to have been blasted backward, toward the lower portion of this world. Luke activated Feather's Fall with a grunt of determination and ever so slowly corrected his course, riding on the explosion of force until it was weak enough for him to begin actively fighting to slow down enough to land.

When he hit the ground, he skidded across it in a *mostly* controlled series of hops and dragging of his feet. Finally coming to a halt, Luke leaned over and put his hands on his knees, taking deep breaths as he processed the fight he'd just been in. He heaved himself back upright, turning and looking back at the location the conflict had occurred.

A wall of swirling dirt and lightning swallowed his vision. More than one hundred miles across, an enormous thunderstorm filled with every type of deadly magic raged across the entire width of the Zone. He had no idea how many miles uphill or downhill it was swirling, but he could only assume it wasn't a small distance.

"Well, world? Did I get it?" There was no answer, so Luke heaved a sigh of annoyance and started running uphill, activating his Soul Brand to convince Cookie to return to his hands. He had dropped her somewhere along his flight but had no fear that she'd been damaged or gone over the edge. Only eleven minutes later, his confidence was proven correct, as she came whipping through the air end over end, only to land in his outstretched arms. "No? *Awesome*! Was that a fun fight or *what*, Cookie? I think we might even get to do it again!"

Once he'd reminded himself how glorious the conflict had been, his hesitation to backtrack vanished, and he broke into a full sprint. Just as he got to the edge of the thunderstorm, the world decided to give him an update.

Anomaly cleared! An enormous concentration of mana had been detected in this Zone, but you managed to clear the anomaly without outside guidance. Bonus reward granted. Sigil altered via Source-cerer protocols!

The death of the Angler Troll Exalt has registered!

Reward distributed! Potentia gained: 3,542,200!

Bonus reward distributed! Source-cerers are not as heavily bound by the rules of lesser Planes. Skill locks can now be more easily broken!

Aerial Grift has been used in an impressively unique way! By collecting shards of crystallized mana and putting them in formation within your own skin, you were able to maintain combat effectiveness even after taking ten _times your total health in damage in under five minutes! Hidden conditions have been met. Several Skills are updating!_

You Need to Stop Breaking into Tier 5!

Giga is breaking into Tier 2!

The entire time his Sigil was chattering at him, Luke maintained his pace, unable to misstep, trip, or fall, thanks to Pristine Balance helping him overcome any shortfalls from not focusing. Then a strange sensation rolled across his skin, which felt like tiny needles beginning to dig into him. The sensation rapidly became more painful, until it was covering his entire body and increasing in intensity. He stopped running, attempting to understand what was happening, and the pain remained at the same level. He took a few more steps, and the damage once again started to accumulate, now enough that his health was slipping away.

Current health: 468/480. You are suffering from mana burn!

There were several portions of that notification that alarmed him. The first was that his health was nearly fifteen hundred points too low. The second was that he was being damaged by _mana_, of all things. There had been days when he'd literally eaten mana for breakfast. "Is it this thunderstorm? Just the sheer output from the solid crystal being destroyed?"

He took a few steps away from the epicenter of the storm, noting that the pain dropped immediately. There were other small amounts of damage rolling over him, such as the mana being collected into his Sigil for the upgrade of his Rift Hunter Skill. As the Skill was attempting to break into Tier eight, it pulled a fairly intense amount of power that would slam into him every few seconds. Normally, he was able to nearly ignore the sensation, but right now, it was giving him a splitting headache, as though the center of his forehead was a tree, and a lumberjack was going to town on him.

"Ow." He looked over the most recent notifications once more, recognizing the issue after a few moments of contemplation. "Giga is deactivated...? I didn't shrink."

Looking down and smirking, he confirmed that. 'You need

to Stop' was also not currently functioning to filter the exorbitant quantity of power at this moment. The small smirk on his face widened. "I bet I could even be affected by poison or hallucinogens right now. Abyss, why did I never bother *collecting* any of those berries?"

With no way to brave the storm in front of him to search for his friends, and his Sigil guaranteeing him that the troll had been defeated, Luke did the first thing that any other reasonable person would have at that moment. He turned around and started walking toward the end of Zone twenty-five. "If they *are* alive, they'll probably come looking for me there. If not, I'll come back and kill this boss again in their honor when it respawns again. Then, I will move on."

Nodding solemnly to himself at his internal vow, he followed that up with doing the second thing any reasonable person would do. He opened his Cal Scan and went on a shopping spree. The first choices were easy and unavoidable.

The vast majority of the accumulated Potentia flowed into his body, bringing him to the peak of level nineteen, stopping two points away from pushing into level twenty, as he'd luckily been warned to avoid. "One million, seven hundred, seventy-one thousand and ninety-eight Potentia, almost exactly half of what I earned from that fight, gone in a flash. Huh. Wonder what happens to the rest of my Potentia when I hit level twenty. Does it just go into my Skills?"

Fire rippled through his veins, his nerves, and strangely enough, the nail of his left pinky toe. He subconsciously realized that this was the strange power priming his body for Ascension, and something told Luke that even a light *sneeze* in the direction of level twenty would force his Ascension, freeing him from the control of the Hollow Kingdom forever... but also barring him from the lower world he'd been born on.

If he had been able to do it, the Murderhobo would have added those final two points immediately and taken his chances with surviving on Murder World until he delved deep enough to find whoever his mysterious sponsor was.

Then he would decide if he was going to profusely thank that entity for the protections that it had imbued him with or punch it in the face until it stopped moving for inserting something into his mind that nearly killed him when he tried to strike a deal with the strange descender he'd met in the desert. "The Annihilator... or whatever he was. Had some weird name, should I bother trying to remember it...? Nah."

There was still Potentia to spend.

Since there were no other hostile creatures within the entirety of this Zone, the Murderhobo felt fairly confident in increasing almost all his other capabilities. His Skills gained levels as though someone were spinning a wheel, only pausing when they struck the point where they deactivated in order to Tier up. "Shockwave Cleave and Feather's Fall hit Tier five, You Need to Stop and Giga are already going, Rift Hunter is nearly done... let's send Bum Thunder and Hobo Holler to Tier four, then-"

Luke came to a complete stop as he looked at the next Skill he was thinking of increasing. Taking deep breaths, he gently added Potentia into Pristine Balance, tipping it over into upgrading to Tier five, then promptly tripping over his feet and face planting. "I hate this."

Exactly as he'd feared, his body was completely out of proportion. Without the perfect, innate sense of balance that was provided by his Skill, he needed to relearn almost all actions with his body. He ended up slapping himself in the face multiple times, throwing himself off of the ground only to land heavily moments later, eventually settling on rolling downhill until he could control himself better.

Unfortunately, this only added to the dizziness. Still, it was his most effective mode of travel at the moment, so he kept it up. With nothing better to do, he considered Source-cerer's Armory. There was still a small, magical lock over the Skill, bearing the crest of the Hollow Kingdom. But he remembered what his bonus reward had told him. "Locks on Skills are going to be easier to break... how *much* easier?"

Throwing every bit of his willpower behind the action, he *willed* the Potentia to be spent on the Skill.

This Skill cannot be upgraded at this time! Receive a direct, written permission from the ruler of the Hollow Kingdom in order to increase this Skill!

No matter how hard he tried to mentally push against that barrier, it replied with the exact same message. He was nothing if not stubborn, but ten hours of attempting to push past the block, combined with his heavily increased speed of rolling downhill, had given him a splitting headache and put him in a foul mood.

"Luke!" A familiar voice called out, and a few minutes later, Andre came running up to the floppy Murderhobo. "I can't believe you're alive! You were right next to that thing when it exploded!"

Moments later, Taylor and Zed casually jogged over as well, bright smiles on their faces when they saw Luke laying on the ground, seemingly undamaged. At first, they were greatly concerned with his lack of control, fearing that he'd taken some kind of permanent mental damage. When he explained that it was only a small annoyance, due to his Skill interactions, and that multiple Skills were upgrading currently, they relaxed.

Andre hauled him along in a seat he normally reserved for Zed, and they started trotting at a rapid pace toward the end of the Zone.

Tier up complete! Rift Hunter (Tier seven) has become-

Before he could read the rest of the information, his team looked at him with a knowing, searching expression on each of their faces. He could see excitement, hope, and determination. Taylor leaned in close. "I just felt an upgrade complete. Was that your portal-opening one?"

"Yes. I haven't gotten a chance to read over it yet."

She solemnly nodded. "With the power gain that we have earned here, combined with the end of this Zone opening an exit point, I think it's time for us to-"

Before she could say another word, Luke frantically opened

his Skills and dumped mana into the newly upgraded Tier eight Skill. An instant later, a new, powerful surge of mana fluctuated away.

"*Luke!*" The Mage was aghast at his actions. "Did you just upgrade your Skill again? Who *knows* how long that will lock us in here!"

"Yes," the Murderhobo replied to the only question in the words she'd sent his way. The other members of his team started to laugh, even as Taylor nearly started hyperventilating, puffing up her cheeks in an attempt to hold her vitriol in.

She failed, and the eruption of profanity she sent at him was *sublime*.

CHAPTER FORTY-SEVEN

Each of them had increased their power substantially. As the days turned into weeks, the Skills, Spells, Abilities, and Masteries they had earned or upgraded were tested, toyed with, and brought up to their highest proficiency.

You Need to Stop → *You Were Warned (Tier 5, level 0)*

Effect 3: When your mana pool is full, your body now automatically converts any mana in your mana pool which would otherwise be wasted into liquid mana. This liquid will flow through your body like any other liquid, except for being expelled as waste. If you are caused to bleed, a portion of the liquid lost will be liquid mana. Mana is converted at a rate of 1,000-50n gaseous mana to .001 milliliters of liquid mana. For every 5% of the total liquid in your body that is liquid mana, this Skill will gain a level.

Bum Thunder → *Bum Blast (Tier 4, level 9)*

Bonus 2, Multi-target: You are now able to store up to 1+n activations of Bum Blast, where n = Skill level. By selecting a target, you can automatically use all of the activations to cross a greater distance or be transported back to a specific point, if you were to move 10 meters away from it.

Hobo Holler → *Hobo Howl (Tier 4, level 9)*

Bonus 2, Multitarget: Hostile entities within hearing range have a

10+10n% chance to have their Attacks interrupted if they are targeting any entity other than you with their Attacks. Their next three Attacks within 2n seconds must be directed at you, where n = Skill level. (Currently maximized at 100% Interrupt chance)

Pristine Balance → Primal Balance (Tier 5, Level 9)

Effect 3: If your Characteristics are out of balance, 10+10n% where n = Skill level of the training done to increase one of them will be instead used to boost the lowest Characteristic. If Characteristics are tied, the training will be split among them. (Maximized at 100%)

Feather's Fall → Feather's Flight

Effect 3: You are able to convert 5+5n% of your downward momentum into upward momentum, where n = Skill level.

Shockwave Cleave → Zero-point Shockwave

Effect 3: You can choose to Attack an empty point in midair, delaying the shockwave that would be released from Attacking a target. The shockwave will be released from that point at the end of 1+n seconds or upon mental command. You can only have one point, but 1+n shockwaves may be stored in that point, where n = Skill level. All timers are distinct.

Giga → Mana Giant

Bonus 1, at range: mana is now actively pulled from the environment around you, increasing your mana Regeneration by 1n%, where n = Skill level. When touching a magical item, the mana draw is increased by 5x. When this Skill reaches level 9, your mana pool is expanded by 20%. This Skill will increase in rank for every 100,000n mana drawn into the body.

Aerial Grifter → Air Warden

Bonus, AOE: You may now designate a point n meter(s) from your body, where n = Skill level. 10+10n% of projectiles that are not set to be kept will be launched from that point at the same speed they were captured by Air Warden.

Approximately a month after defeating the troll, Luke woke up to his Rift Hunter completing its upgrade. Just like that, he had two Skills at Tier nine.

Without a second thought, he brought the newly named 'Piercer of the Veil' up to the peak of Tier nine. Luke let his gaze roam the area, knowing that he wasn't the only one who had noticed the Skill completing its Tier up. In the distance, he could see Taylor sprinting at him, a determined expression on her face.

"She appears to have something to say to me," Luke mused with a small hint of laughter in his voice.

"She does indeed." Zed had spent the vast majority of their recovery at the end of the Zone, listening to the details of Luke's life in Murder World and what challenges he had needed to overcome to progress this far. "Are you going to listen to what she has to say? Are we going back?"

Luke shrugged, finally somewhat more comfortable with conversation, after having been forced to practice it as he waited for his upgrade to Pristine Balance. "Probably don't have much choice. I just tried to push it to Tier ten; it wouldn't let me. Just like before."

"Yeah, that's unfortunate." With that, Zed looked over at the Mage, who was still coming toward them, now only at a light jog and wearing a relieved expression, since she wasn't feeling any additional fluctuations in the mana around them. "This place has really grown on me."

Luke cast his eyes over the Bard, but he didn't see any infestations in his skin. "If you think that is true, perhaps you should have Andre take a look at you before we go back to the base world? If there's something growing, I'm sure he can excise it."

They were playing a game of cards, a staple for the Bard during his downtime. He claimed he needed to be able to defeat *anyone* at *any* bar game, or he would lose his credentials as the Master of Minstrels. Luke was learning the game slowly, but somehow he felt that Zed wasn't playing fairly. No matter what set of cards he had, the Bard would always manage to beat him by the slimmest of margins. "High card. King Alexander."

"Pair of deuces." Zed shrugged as Luke glared at him. "What can I say, buddy? Even if it's only a pair of two, it has the power to overcome a single king. Them's the rules."

Luke nodded with annoyance, reaching for the cards. It was

his deal, and he hoped his luck would… his hand froze over the discard pile as a powerful thought shook him to his core. "A pair… has the power… to overcome a king?"

Taylor was within hearing range, but Luke sank into his thoughts as he threw open his Skill sheet and looked at his two Tier nine, level nine Skills. Willing it to happen, shaking with effort as he did everything he could to smash past the locks on his Skills, he shoved Potentia into them, forcing them both to accept it *at the same time.* "A pair can overcome a king! It's the *rules!*"

It worked.

In the next instant, Luke was weaponless and trapped in this world, just like his team. Any damage that reached his skin would dig into his health pool instead of being blocked or deflected. The Murderhobo couldn't care even a *little* bit. He howled with joy as the Potentia flared and sent out a call to the world around him: it needed mana to bind and complete the process of Tiering up the Skills.

The world answered in a big way.

Unlike previous situations when his Skills had Tiered up, this time, the Sigil on his forehead didn't merely send out tiny fluctuations that would collect ambient power and pull it in to reach the next Tier. No… the blue world around Luke shifted into grayscale as the power in the air was *ripped* out of it, funneling to him as a massive whirlpool that expanded rapidly, soon reaching up into the sky and causing the ever-moving mists of mana to be sucked down and in.

Luke was *crushed* to the ground, the influx of raw energy attempting to splatter his head like an egg against the terrain below him. In other worlds, this would have been a gradual process, locking the Skills out for years at a time as they slowly collected enough power to complete the upgrade. Here, the only bottleneck was what his body could withstand.

Thanks to his practice destroying his body over and again, his Skills which constantly returned him to the peak of health, and his teammates ensuring no monsters could close in on him to take advantage of his current weakness, the Murderhobo could *withstand* anything this world wanted to throw at him. 'Mana Giant' allowed his body to actively *attract* power to himself instead of having it collected in slow waves. 'You Were Warned' meant any excess overflow of power from his Sigil to his body was captured and converted into liquid mana, which flowed through his veins.

Where all of his other rank-ups for his Skills had taken anywhere from multiple weeks to over a month at a time, this duo of upgrades was completed in merely a day. The entire time, Luke was unable to interact with the outside world, his consciousness expanding as the Skills were brought to the highest point his base world could withstand without being permanently transformed into a kaleidoscope of dimensional shards around him.

Another noticeable difference between previous increases and this one—the time the Skill took to Tier up was also a mental tutorial, where he was given *exquisite* training and direction in how to use his new Domain-level Skills.

As the storm of mana slowly shrank in size, the world around him eventually returning to normal, Luke opened his eyes to be met with the information he had been experiencing, neatly summed up for his convenience.

Source-cerer's Armory → *Domain of the Murderhobo*

Domain: The user of this Skill instinctively knows where every weapon is within 2n meters and how it is moving; where n = Skill level. The weak points of all armor are inherently obvious to the user of this Skill. Upon defeating a combatant, all of their owned weapons and armor are destroyed. Upon <u>killing</u> the opponent, all of the weapons and armor of the killed opponent are destroyed, <u>not restricted</u> to what they have on their person at that time.

This Skill gains 5+n 'slots' counted separately for armor and weapons. These slots can be filled with any Characteristics taken from gear that has been destroyed.

The user of this Skill will gain .001n% of the armor or damage of any weapons or armor destroyed by use of this Skill as permanent bonus to armor or damage respectively.

This Domain replaces all previous effects in the Skill line, except Soul Brand.

Current bonus Damage: 0.

Current bonus Armor: 0.

Piercer of the Veil → World Anchor

Domain: The user of this Skill can be considered a virtuoso of planar conflict. By expending mana, the user of this Skill is able to open, close, keep open, or keep closed any portals between worlds within range.

You now have a sense of all worlds within reach of your current location and are able to open portals to them without assistance from another Ascender of that type. Reopening portals costs half of opening a new one without assistance. Closing a portal costs one quarter. Locking space around you forces all open portals to stay open and keeps any new portals or Scars from being opened. Caution! Unless space is unlocked by this or a similar power, that space will <u>remain</u> locked.

For each portal of the same type that you open or close, the cost of doing so again with a portal of the same type decreases by 5n%.

Cost to open a portal unassisted: 200-10n mana, where n = Skill level.

Cost to close a portal: 50-5n mana.

Cost to lock space: 20-(1+n) mana per 5 square meters.

This Domain replaces all previous effects in the Skill line.

Luke stood up and stretched, ignoring the influx of inquiries encroaching on his internal audit. There were many things he understood about these new Skills, as though he had been training with them for decades. The first was that, at present, he was generally weaker than he had been. Until he was able to fight opponents with their own weapons and armor, his protections and attacks had been set at a base level of fifty armor and damage per slot. This scaled with his Fitness, but at a much-reduced rate. Now, his maximum damage was set at his total physical output divided by twenty, plus his bonus damage. That meant his total maximum damage had dropped all the way down to two hundred and forty-eight.

"That is quite the decrease from nearly seven hundred…" The Murderhobo took a deep breath and moved past the minor inconvenience. The *potential* benefits were far and away more worthwhile; he didn't mind a little work or getting his hands dirty. "It's too bad I didn't have this when I was fighting the troll. Can't even imagine what the damage potential of that solidified mana club was."

There was an additional benefit which only showed in its *lack* of description in the Skill: it no longer cost mana for him to manifest his weapons and armor. There would be a slight delay in the armor re-manifesting if it was destroyed, but that portion was, for all purposes, now a passive Skill. He looked at his right hand, and five empty slots appeared over it. Next to each slot was an option of a trait that could be added to the weapon that would manifest there upon attacking something. "Put in doubled force from the Battering Ram Knuckles, armor penetration, lightning damage, fire damage, and four-foot length."

It was strange to essentially custom design a weapon out of nothing. Still, he recognized these effects from the weapons he previously had options to equip. Luke was *slightly* annoyed that he needed to use an entire slot to assign weapon length, but it made sense in a roundabout way. If he hadn't put something there, it would have defaulted to 'touch' range, as though he were fighting only with his fists. On his left hand, he used similar options, trading out the fire damage for ice and the four-foot length for the twenty-foot whip trait of his scourge.

Weapons taken care of, he set his armor to have slots that were all the same. Now they would have a massive bonus defense against magical attacks, as well as getting faster for each Spell he tanked, thanks to his Mage Hunter equipment. That was followed up with ten percent of his overall health being added as armor, seventy percent resistance to slashing and piercing, and automatic sticking to anything his armor touched, thanks to the Promiscuous Stud set. "Good. That brings my total armor per spot up to one ninety-four. I'm once again well-protected. Now, let's go kill some people and add their weapons' damage to mine."

For the very first time, Luke was excited to go back to his base world and fight humans.

CHAPTER FORTY-EIGHT

The portal back into the Dynasty of Dogs opened, and The Four stepped out at what appeared to be the same instant, to anyone watching.

Luke scanned the area, realizing exactly how *many* eyes were actually on them at that moment. His sense of time between the two planes of existence had been massively skewed, and even though several months had passed for him, he was unable to remember how much that translated to on this world. Even as his thoughts were whirring, enormous spatial tears began rending the universe around them. Dogs of all shapes and sizes stepped into the world around them as tens of thousands of creatures were summoned by the enormous army surrounding them.

Zed nudged Luke in the side. "Didn't you say you could lock down the area? Seems like an effect that would be extraordinarily *useful* against Ascenders who rely on summoning things from another world."

"I don't think it would work like that," Andre added conversationally, even as the seeds sprinkling from his open palms onto the ground around them began shifting into full bloom under his control. "They aren't true portals; they're something more similar to Luke's weapons. Manifestations of intent, given form based on the relationship that has been created between the hound and the trainer in this world."

Gently strumming his lute, the Bard pointedly ignored the Druid. Humming gently to himself, he sang a song he was making up on the spot. "If it won't work, just tell me, don't try to teach me in your condescending ways-"

"Thank you for giving us as much time as we needed to set up our defensive encampment." The prince of the Dynasty of Dogs, William Merryck, stepped forward with his hands to his sides, as if he were showcasing all of the embankments, trenches, and the legions of soldiers using them. "Truly, it was interesting to see you cross out of this world into an unknown one, then stay in the exact same position for... almost an entire eight days? Did you think we wouldn't be able to see that you were just camping on the other side of your portal?"

"Huh." Luke cracked his knuckles, leaning forward slightly. "I always wondered what that would look like on this side."

He charged forward, Bum Blast using all ten of its stored activations to send him across one hundred meters in under a second. Still, he was a few feet short of the prince, and even with his near instantaneous travel, the guard who had so thoroughly trounced him—apparently only a week before—managed to interpose himself between the Berserker and the royal. A well-practiced sneer was on the man's face, and as Cookie came down, he avoided the attack and aimed his retaliation against Luke's wrists. The strike broke the armor there and caused Luke's wrist to slacken, his weapon dropping out of his hands.

"How many times do I have to teach you this *lesson*, young man?" As the martial artist started to gloat, he realized Luke wasn't wearing a furious scowl as expected. Instead, the battle-crazed smile on his face was wider than ever. "What's different about-"

Even as the guards' eyes went wide, Luke's fist came forward at a tremendous speed, half again as fast as he had been able to manage in their last fight. Unlike in their previous battle, no matter how the guard twisted or attempted to shift his position, Luke's strike unerringly followed its target. An enormous fist crashed into the throat of the guard, crushing his windpipe and tossing the man away, even though he managed to shift his position and mitigate a portion of the damage. The guard spit out a mouth full of blood, raised a hand, and sharply dropped it.

Magical attacks of all kinds blasted across the open killing field that had been set up around the portal the Murderhobo had created. They targeted his three companions as they worked to build up their offensive and defensive options. A storm of butterflies appeared around them, completely erasing all traces of the attacks that were purely magical. There was a klaxon call sounding from the Spell, but even that was only in addition to Taylor's shout of surprise.

"Stay focused; it's mine!" Zed shouted in her ear through the link he had established between The Four. "I got it before you managed to reach the next Tier, so definitely make sure to let me be present when you activate the new version. I like upgrades as much as you do!"

Any of the attacks that contained a physical component were intercepted by the work of the Druid as he pushed power directly into the earth and raised enormous bulwarks of stone between their opponents and himself. Now knowing he didn't need to worry for his companions, even the *slight* amount he normally would, Luke was fully able to devote his attention to the fight he was in.

The truth of the matter was, Luke had not magically become a proficient technical fighter. Instead, as soon as he had begun combat, his opponent began to glow in multiple areas across his body. Knowing that this was the Domain of the Murderhobo's effects kicking in, Luke targeted the weak points in the guard's armor that were practically begging to be struck. He was uncertain how this Skill was working, seeing as his opponent was wearing a robe and not much else, as far as he could tell. Still, the fact remained that he had been able to land a hit.

That was good enough for the Murderhobo.

The guard shifted at that moment, combining into his hybridized form and sprinting at Luke. Knowing better than to simply exchange attacks, Luke closed his eyes and became completely reliant on his brand-new Domain. As the clawed fists came down at him, Luke could sense their position in space, their distance from his body, and the speed at which they were approaching. By cutting out the additional sensory information his eyes gave him, Luke was able to shift around just enough to completely evade the attacks.

He couldn't see it, but the guard's eyes had gone wide as his blow missed, only to squint in pain as the Murderhobo caught him with an extreme uppercut that sent him tumbling through the air. Before the guard could take advantage of his extended distance from the fight, Luke ensured that the man couldn't escape. "Bum Blast, lock point."

As soon as the martial artist had gone a fraction of a centimeter more than ten meters away, Luke appeared next to him and swung both hands down, holding on to each other in a hammer punch. His fists smashed into the man's stomach, and the guard corkscrewed into the ground, colliding with it before bouncing slightly, due to his momentum. The Murderhobo landed next to him, his fist moving forward in a straight punch that sent the guard tumbling away, skipping across the earth. Once again, the Skill pulled Luke next to his target with a blast of thunder. This time, he swung down with an open palm, caving in the guard's chest with a flat strike.

You have slain an enemy combatant!
Bonus Damage added: 1.23
Bonus armor added: 5.031
Armor slot option added: Always Clean.

"Clean? Don't need that." Luke shook his hand, letting all of the gore that had accumulated slough off of him. "Not bad. Makes sense that he had more armor than he had weapons.

Still, I've got a long way to go until I'm happy with only *this* level of damage output."

A few dozen feet away, the prince stared at him with wide-eyed shock. As Luke turned to face him once more, the young man let out a strangled shout. "Guards! Stop him!"

Unfortunately for the prince, he only had a couple of personal defenders remaining, having never expected that Luke would be able to obliterate the Top Dog martial artist who had been assigned to him by the Emperor himself. The guards barely lasted a double handful of seconds before the Murder-hobo was looming over the royal brat who had tried to ambush them. His hand reached out, fingers crooked to catch the prince's skull and crush it.

"Wait, Luke!" Zed's plea wasn't enough to slow the Murder-hobo down, but his next words did give Luke pause. "If you do anything that would kill him, I think he'll just teleport away again! He's had enough time for whatever defense that was to be recharged."

"I can do non-lethal." Luke promised himself as he clapped his hands together as gently as a person his size possibly could, as though he were trying to catch a butterfly, not a full-grown human. Even so, from the look of pain on the prince's face, he wouldn't be leaving this encounter without a bruise at the minimum. "Strip."

"W-what? No! I'm a prince; I must remain *pure* until my marriage-"

Luke slapped him across the face 'lightly'. "That teleportation activated without your assistance the first time I ran into you. That means it's some kind of item on your body that only activates when you are about to get slaughtered. Or it's some kind of power, but I doubt it. Otherwise, you'd have the ability to activate it intentionally and get out of here."

"I refuse." The prince spoke once again, but this time with evident relief in his voice. It seemed that he had forgotten about his life-saving artifact, and now that he remembered, he was feeling far more confident. "Laying hands on a prince without being a trainer of mine is grounds for immediate execution! *Command: kill this-*"

"Stop. You don't want to do that."

Luke froze for a fraction of a second before narrowing his eyes and ever so slowly turning his head to look at the man who was speaking. "Zed... I've *warned* you about messing with my head."

"Easy now, big guy." The Bard continued speaking in soft, dulcet tones. "I'm just speaking to our friend the prince here. He doesn't want to hurt us or get us in trouble. In fact, he wants to help us out, so we can get out of this mess we're creating. The sooner we're gone, the sooner everyone goes back to being happy about where they are in life."

"What are you even talking about?" Luke shook the prince out of sheer frustration, but before he could do any damage, the young man looked at him with a wide smile on his face.

"Luke! Sorry about that, buddy. I think things just got out of hand there." The Murderhobo's hands clenched tighter, threatening to rip the pristine white robes he was holding. "It's been a while since we've seen each other, and I was hoping we could exchange pointers. I guess we know who wins!"

He started laughing, and Luke pulled his fist back to deliver a sharp blow to the face, only for Zed to interject once more. "Yes, it's so wonderful that we have been friends *practically our whole lives*. Now, I know we aren't supposed to be here, since your father does not approve of our friendship, but Luke's sister went missing recently. She is extraordinarily beautiful, *mouthwateringly* attractive, and her name is Cindy. Those first two descriptors are different things, I promise you."

"Oh, I know." William's voice was somber, and his eyes had turned serious. "Who do you think was tasked with bringing her to the capital? She left a few days ago, escorted by the Emperor's death squads. As far as I can tell, she is going to be given to one of the princes as a bride, a reward for excellent services to the dynasty."

"My sister is no *prize*." Luke's voice was a thunder in his chest, and his muscles strained as he prepared to rip the smarmy brat in his hands in half.

"I know you mean well by that statement, but it could be taken the wrong way, Luke." Zed strummed a few soft notes as Prince William chuckled, and Luke felt his grip relax. "You know what will be really helpful... an escort to where she is being held. Sure would be nice to have a prince who can vouch for us and assure us safe passage through all of this unfamiliar territory. Maybe even teach us a few words of the local language and the customs they hold to. Doesn't that sound nice, Luke?"

"Ah. He's a hostage. Got it." Luke pushed the prince to the ground, placing his hands directly on the chest of the young man. "This shouldn't take too long."

"What's that, Luke?" The prince asked him with wide eyes, his smile faltering slightly.

"Just figuring out what it is on you that can teleport you away." The Murderhobo's grin looked like it should have been on a shark's face, not his own. "When I am touching a magical artifact, I drain the mana out of it. If I remember correctly, once an enchanted item completely runs out of mana, it destroys itself."

The prince gulped, a thick bead of sweat running down his face. "Can we not do that? I don't think I can impress upon you how *expensive-*"

A crisp sound like a vial being shattered rang out, and William seemed to sink into himself. Luke stood upright, holding the prince in the air. "You'd better call off your attack dogs. Nothing left on you to carry you to safety, if they decide that it's better to take all of us out because they think you have a life-saving treasure."

"*Abyss.*" William whispered under his breath as all the weapons and summons in the area went from a source of pride to glistening magical effects that screamed at his honed danger sense.

CHAPTER FORTY-NINE

After issuing a hasty set of commands, Prince William began walking The Four toward the capital proper. At first, Luke was extremely hesitant to follow, but he was assured by both Andre and Zed that the Bard's mental compulsions were completely effective. Apparently, if the prince thought they would be in any kind of danger, he would be forced to choose another path for them to take.

"The dynasty is so incredibly massive that even traveling via plane-walking simply takes too long," he was explaining to them as they casually scrolled up to the provincial capital. "It would take weeks of travel by foot to cross through the Wild Hunt and up to a year to reach the capital of the dynasty, were we to try and make our way directly there in this world. Something tells me none of you are interested in that?"

After receiving confirmation, the prince continued with his story, a pleasant smile on his lips. "There is another option, typically reserved for dignitaries and royalty, with the rare occurrence of being spoken for during emergencies. The Traveler's Gate. These are massive teleportation arrays created by the mad genius Will Wright, which allow us to traverse the entirety of the distance to the capital in an instant. As far as I am aware, no other kingdom in the world has anything even *approaching* the complexity of our transportation systems."

The small group was silent, focused entirely on the danger-ous, threatening stares they were earning from the soldiers they were walking past. Hulking beasts growled at them, and some-times so did their masters. Still, the presence of the prince prevented hostilities from erupting into actual fighting. The entire time they were walking, Zed's insidious subliminal commands burrowed into William's mind, causing him to talk about where they were going, why they were going there, and all sorts of other strange customs that made very little sense to Luke.

Slowly, the prince started slipping into his own native language, and Luke found that he had no issue understanding what words meant, thanks to their context. Every step closer to the city walls, he became slightly more proficient in the language. By the time they had stepped through the wide-open gates, Luke could tell he would be able to have a passable conversation with a local, if he so chose. That was never in his plan, so he merely focused on listening, watching, and using the new senses provided by his duo of Domains.

Everywhere they went, they were preceded and escorted by large groups of people with drawn weapons. At almost all times, he could sense that those weapons were pointed at him, or at the very least his team. He was almost wishing for conflict to break out, so that he could shake off the ever-building tension that their presence was creating.

At a normal walking speed, it took them nearly six hours to go from the entrance of the city to the palace near its center. There was a clear dividing line where the people who were escorting them from a distance transferred over, and Luke could easily discern that their weapons and armor were of a far higher quality than the troops they had previously needed to be wary of. As they walked onto the palace grounds, his eyes were caught by a sudden motion, as an instructor punched a recruit in the face.

"What are you doing, dragging your sword on the ground like that? Why are you dulling the edge of the Emperor's sword?" The instructor lashed out once more. "You think this is one of the toys from your hometown? No! It is property of the Emperor, just like *you* are! The only difference between you and this sword is the fact that *it* is currently worth more than you are. But, by the end of our time together, all of you will be glorious warriors who have been chosen for one purpose! To expand the borders of the dynasty! To push back the-"

Luke tuned out the propaganda as they continued walking, his hands starting to twitch as his discomfort leaked through. It had been nearly half a day since he had killed something, and he was starting to get the itch. The way these people were staring at him, hungry-like, was making his blood *boil*. As they passed a group that was glaring at them a little too hard, the Murderhobo's hand lifted almost on its own, reaching for those staring orbs set into the man's face, intending to *pluck them out-*

"There it is!" Prince William indicated a grand building, which was adorned with all sorts of gems and magical symbology. "Directly through here, and we will have you back with your sister within the hour. Can I just say, one more time, how unfortunate it is that the situation arose in this manner? I didn't realize my Empire had sunk so low as to need to *steal* women from other adjacent kingdoms."

The Murderhobo didn't feel the need to reply to this inane conversation, so he kept his eyes wide and roving. Something was wrong, inconsistent, but he didn't know what exactly it was. Yet. They were deep in enemy territory, surrounded on all sides, and he didn't feel as comfortable with that thought as he normally did. Cookie held ready to strike, Luke led the way into the grandiose building.

The interior wasn't what he had expected. Instead of some

kind of magnificent ritual hall, wide open and studded with stars and constellations, the ground floor of the building was completely crowded with small cubicles. Each of the work areas was in use, and the hubbub of noise would have matched a battlefield in volume.

Luckily for every single person alive in that area, Prince William hurried them through to the transportation array that he had promised existed. "All we need to do now is input the coordinates, and we will be off!"

Their hostage stepped forward and began speaking animatedly with the Ascenders in charge of this area. The prince continued to speak, his voice becoming ever more commanding as the workers tried to weasel out of doing what they were being told to do. Eventually, they simply threw their hands in the air then clasped them together and bowed to the prince with sheer annoyance writ large on their faces. Seemingly satisfied, he strutted back to the group and waved toward a platform in the distance. "Shall we get going? I'm greatly interested in accompanying you for this journey; I hope you are amenable to that. I'm not going to lie... I haven't been able to stop thinking about your sister since we met."

"She has that active effect," Luke deadpanned, startling a chuckle out of Zed and getting a rapid *slap* on the shoulder from Taylor. The Murderhobo was pleased to have their attention on him, as he could tell Andre was doing something sneaky. If he hadn't been paying attention, even Luke would have missed the sheer quantity of spores that had been pouring off the Druid since they had first walked into the city. He hoped the monster that hid behind the calm, academic face of the redheaded, green-eyed man was preparing something particularly nasty.

Just in case.

The prince fussed around with their positioning for a while, insisting that any deviation would cause unexpected issues in the transportation. "This isn't as simple as walking through a portal between dimensions; it's a precise and exact magiscience, calibrated down to the smallest portion of your weight. Alas, it's such an expensive transportation method that I don't foresee you being able to return in the same way, but hopefully you will find travel accommodations that are to your liking on the return trip."

He went on and *on*. So much so that Luke was beginning to become suspicious of whether he was truly trying to help them at this moment, or if he was stalling for time. But, finally, the prince nodded, told them all to stay as still as possible, and moved over to step onto his own platform. Just like them, he had to contort himself into a fairly uncomfortable position and hold the pose perfectly. "Teleporters are ready! Positions are locked; begin the initiation sequence."

Immediately, Luke felt a buildup of structured mana in the air around him. His body, craving the power, began drawing it into him immediately. He noticed a small frown appear on the prince's face, just before the young man shouted at the people in charge of the teleportation. "Increase power! Mana is being siphoned away."

The air started to take on a high-pitched whine, and Luke tensed his muscles in preparation of diving away from an imminent explosion. Yet, the technicians didn't seem at all concerned, which assuaged his worries. Fractionally. One of them began a countdown, shouting over the racket. "Five… four… teleportation to Capital City Detention Center activating!"

"What!" Taylor shouted in a panic. Luke didn't bother waiting, throwing himself as hard as he could forward—only for his face to slam into a solid metal wall as the teleportation successfully sent him to a different part of the world.

He could hear his friends, and it appeared that they were all in the same position where they had been sent over. None of them had been separated, unless you included the walls between their individual cells. Luke could hear the prince laughing, then the young man knocked on the wall between himself and Zed.

"Did you seriously think the prince of a dynasty would have no training in resisting mental compulsions? It took me all of fifteen seconds to shake off your suggestions. What kind of *narcissist* do you have to be to believe that your Masteries are infallible?"

William went silent as Luke hit the wall with his fist, and it bent inward. Then the prince was shouting, but this time, his words held a hint of panic in them. "Guards! Priority one, command: Saluki, Akita, Vizsla, Eurasier. Mastiff, Eurasier!"

"Wouldn't it have just been faster to call for help?" Zed taunted the prince as Luke began to pound on the walls. "What, did we use too much mana, and your message couldn't get here ahead of us?"

"Something like that." The prince returned haughtily, though Luke could hear him then mutter, "Most likely."

Luke wasn't worried about the reasons the prince had set them up like this. It made sense; they were a foreign national group sent here for counter-kidnapping. All it meant to him was that Prince William was once again fair game for *smashing*. Just as his fist worked the metal of the wall enough that he could get his hands through and start wrenching it apart, the door to the cell opened, and the terrified prince ran out.

The Murderhobo didn't waste any time pushing through and shoving Cookie forward, catching the door before it could close fully. Then he punched out, his fist stopping just in front of the metal of the door. He did that motion several more times, creating a space in midair where his Zero-point Shock-wave would activate. Then he turned and started smashing down the walls between himself and his teammates, knowing that they had a limited amount of time to escape this place until it was locked down. In the center of a country's power like this, there would no doubt be an unending stream of enemies at their level.

He ripped down the wall, allowing Zed to walk into the partially open cell. The Bard had a sheepish smile on his face, clearly showing that he knew how badly he had messed up.

"Welp, I did it, Luke! I got us to the capital. I just *knew* I could do it!"

The sound of dozens of boots filled the room, coming from the hallway just outside. Zed swallowed a mouthful of saliva then turned to Luke and held both hands out with his thumbs up. "Anyway, that means my job is complete. So… your turn!"

CHAPTER FIFTY

- TAYLOR -

She wasn't sure where they had been brought, but she did know that the cells they were in were reinforced with high-grade materials. Even so, they were designed to contain bound, power-dampened Ascenders. They clearly were *not* designed with someone like her in mind: a prisoner who still had full use of her Spells.

Her grimoire popped up onto Taylor's shoulder, and she gently ran a hand down its spine. It arched like a cat as her hand moved, and she thanked the celestials it had managed to empower itself over the years. When she had first gained this grimoire, it had only been able to hold Spells of a certain quality and quantity. But with so much power poured into it from her time being around Luke, as well as Taylor capturing Spells that constantly pushed the grimoire to the very edge, it had evolved several times.

Now the book was almost pure black, absorbing light and mana with great passion. Truly, it fit the Mage well, seeing as it was equally as ambitious as she was. Taylor lifted her hand, targeted the door in her path, and shattered it with a well-placed application of Astral Triplet. Chunks of flash-frozen metal flew out into the hallway, impacting someone out there, by the sounds of the pained screams that quickly filled her too-small cell.

Even though she already had the Spell at Tier five, level nine, she was slightly dissatisfied. Unlike Luke, who had simply abandoned all ability to attack or defend for himself at the end of their time in Murder World, she had kept her wits about her and merely brought all of her Spells to the peak of their current Tiers.

The entire time they had been waiting for *his* upgrades to complete, she had been assuming they might be leaving at any time and couldn't force herself to take the risk of not having her entire arsenal available. Now she was regretting that and wondering what a Tier six version of this Spell would look like.

"Stop *comparing* yourself to him. Compare yourself to Zed; it's more fun." She shook off the wasteful thoughts even as she had them, stepping into the hallway to take a look at the rapidly growing force that was going to be working against The Four. "On behalf of the Hollow Kingdom, I am officially giving all of you a single chance to surrender!"

No one laughed, chuckled, or even slowed down. They merely kept their weapons pointed at her and their Spells powering up. Lifting her hands into position, she could only shake her head while feigning sadness. Taylor had been wanting to see what this Spell would do in an enclosed environment, one that was man-made out of materials from the ground. "Earthshaker!"

The metal walls of the cell she had just vacated were the first target of her thoughts. They pulled themselves apart then wormed their way out of the doorway and snaked down the hall toward the approaching guards. The walls around her flexed outward and inward with her breath, and she felt a deep and powerful connection to every part of the world around her. As the guards got in range, any unenchanted armor or weapons simply fell apart then fused with the surface of the floor, becoming impossible to retrieve. "This is… *awesome.* I can totally see why Andre gets all excited about his Druid Abilities."

As she walked along the floor, the tapping of her feet on stone a perfect metronome, the epicenter of her Spell moved along with her—giving her access to new and exciting variables. The basic humans among the guards simply fell into the ground below them, which closed around their necks while leaving plenty of space for them to rest comfortably and breathe. She wasn't a monster, and she didn't want to sacrifice any goodwill she could easily accumulate. As for the Ascenders, those took a little bit of *convincing* before they would allow themselves to be caged within the stone floors or walls.

Even though she was a powerful Mage, her Characteristics had all been devoted to allowing her to have incredibly precise perception as well as the ability to move excellently, exquisitely, and undetected. In other words, she was a self-taught Assassin Mage.

As the Ascenders focused on the rampaging troll in the dungeon that was Luke, she would simply walk up to them and deliver a strike to the base of their skull, incapacitating them at least long enough to put them in a small stone prison. To her great regret, for a multitude of reasons, the time of the Spell suddenly came to an end. Now, she let out a true sigh of regret, as instead of being able to trap her enemies, she was going to need to make their disposal more *permanent.* A dagger appeared in both of her hands, and she flashed down the hallway.

Fountains of blood erupted wherever her shadow crossed paths with another.

"Testing, one, two." Zed's voice crackled into her ears, although luckily, Taylor had gotten used to his antics over the years and was unaffected in her rampant slaughter. "We have a series of portals opening up in the local territory, according to Luke. We should be expecting a flood of Ascenders coming at us shortly. I am highly recommending that we fall back, get together, and prepare ourselves for the worst. It's going to be a bit of a slugfest, but we can make it out of here *together!*"

"Zed, get over to one of the people I stuck in the rock and start interrogating them," Taylor replied aloud, her words snapping out with all the efficiency of a battlefield commander. "I need to know our location, the lay of the land, nearest exits, and what sort of personnel are usually on hand."

There was no reply directly into her ears, but she had a sneaking suspicion that the Bard was saluting the empty air in front of him at this very moment. A lanky hound sprinted down a stairwell in front of her, moving so quickly that she thought a lightning Spell had been loosed into the room. Barely managing to fall to the ground, Taylor slid under the canine as it snarled and jumped at her, sailing through the air above her head and missing only by inches. "Ascenders have arrived! More powerful ones than these guards, that's for sure."

"Look, we're just doing our job." The voice came from the floor where she was lying nearly prone. It was one of the lower-level Ascenders this prison was using as a guard. "You might be a lot stronger than us, but there's no need to use your words to be so *hurtful.*"

Taylor spun to her feet, leading with the edge of her knife. She kicked the severed head down the hallway, annoyed with herself that she had bothered to murder a trapped Ascender for the crime of being annoying. "He wouldn't have survived long with that attitude, anyway. Ugh. Maybe I've been around Luke a little too much recently."

Her attention was then completely consumed with fighting off the insanely fast creature that was attacking her. It zipped by several times, trying to tear chunks of her off each time it flitted past. Eventually, she had to resort to preparing a Spell, and casting Astral Triplet as the beast went for its next strafing blow. Instead of passing, it splattered into meat chunks that vibrated and turned into motes of light, every bit of the mess cleaning itself up as the creature was unsummoned.

Then things went bad.

The ground that she was on opened up, sucking her into it in a manner similar to how she had been able to trap the other low-level Ascenders. In mere moments, she slid down an earthen slide, coming to a rest against her companions, who had been likewise captured. Then the ground began lifting up, a column of solid stone pushing upward while spinning at the same time to generate momentum. "Andre! The ceiling!"

The Druid threw his hands to the side, splashing blood in a rapidly drawn circle. The blood ignited with power, and his Druidic Circle lit up, but it appeared that the ground around them was completely unaffected. Panic filled his voice as he shouted, "It's other Druids! Higher Circle than me, and they're working together to counter my control. I can't get a foothold here! They're too well-established!"

Zed let out a high-pitched scream as the ceiling came closer, his cry suddenly echoing out as the ceiling shifted away, and they found themselves in a much larger area. His extremely manly squeal cut off, and he coughed a few times as they found themselves surrounded on all sides by extremely powerful Ascenders. "Oh, right, did I not mention that I finished my interrogation? Turns out, the detention center for Ascenders is directly underneath the throne room of the Emperor of the Dynasty of Dogs."

"Yes. It is." A powerful, regal voice filled the space. Their attention was forced to the throne that rested upon a dais a short distance from them, less than a quarter of a kilometer. Upon the throne sat a man who was nowhere *near* unassuming. He looked at least as large as Luke, who had been artificially grown by his Skills. As far as Taylor could tell from this distance, she was certain that this was the emperor, and he could match the Murderhobo muscle for muscle. Any competition judging the two of them would choose the emperor as the winner in a tie, thanks to the savage royal influence that he oozed like a pus-filled wound.

The ornamental back of the throne that he sat upon reached to the top of the building they were in, disappearing so far up that a regular human's eyes could never see where it ended. In fact, it reached the ceiling, not that most people's eyes could penetrate the magical darkness that unnaturally coated it.

Appearing to be a relic from a bygone age, the seated man was covered in battle scars and bite marks, clothed in fur-lined garb that wouldn't be out of place in a historical center in the Hollow Kingdom.

Sitting in front of Taylor was a man who proved the fact that Ascenders could live unnaturally long lives, nearing immortality. He leaned forward, and his voice echoed evenly through the kilometers-long throne room.

"Welcome to the Dynasty of Dogs. It seems I'll need to thank my son for providing his own wedding gifts."

CHAPTER FIFTY-ONE

The aura of the emperor was so domineering, it took a few moments for Taylor to realize that the object of the statement, Cindy, was standing placidly next to him. She was dressed in an intricately embroidered gown, gem-studded tiara holding back her hair. Unlike what Taylor had expected, the tanner's daughter wasn't showing a fearful expression. Instead, her chin was thrust forward, and her poise was immaculate.

Frankly, Taylor assumed that she had gained some kind of power that allowed her to act, and for a brief moment of terror, she considered the possibility that Luke's sister had ended up as a Bard. Before she could decide how to phrase her next words, or if they should bow to the emperor to show good manners as representatives of their kingdom, the Mage's mind froze as Luke began walking toward the throne at an unhurried pace.

"You." Luke was addressing Cindy, completely ignoring the emperor. "Are you wanting to stay here and get married to a prince? Do you 'want' me to bring you home, so you can get married to… Vir? Or should I just bust you out of all of this and chuck you into the correct world for whatever your power set is?"

Instead of fury on the emperor's face, amusement danced through his eyes. "Very interesting that you wouldn't even say hello, Murderhobo. Yes, I've heard of you and your little team. I must thank you for fixing up that plot of land you all come from. Now that splinter of my dynasty is actually worth reclaiming."

Luke didn't answer, still plodding forward, his eyes locked on his sister's face. Cindy looked between the emperor and her approaching brother, trying to determine the correct course of action. Taylor could practically see the wheels spinning in her mind as the young woman decided to act. "Luke, there is no way that I could refuse the hospitality of the emperor, whether I was in his throne room or not."

"Just go if you want to go." The emperor casually flipped his hand at her. "My son might be disappointed, but I have a few hundred more of them. I'm not going to be able to keep all of them happy all of the time."

Out of everything that had been said, having had no concern for the fact that they were completely surrounded by people near their own power level, *this* was what gave Luke pause. Taylor could practically see smoke coming out of his ears as he tried to unwind this bizarre course of events. Then he shivered slightly and continued as though he hadn't stopped in the first place. "Seems kinda pointless to grab my sister and run if you didn't want her for anything."

"Didn't know she was your sister." The emperor smiled again, and this time Taylor could see that his teeth were pointed, like a shark's. She was uncertain if that was due to some kind of ability, or if he had simply filed them down at one point. "I *did* know that your little King can't let his toys go without a fight. I figured he would send out the most talked about, highest-ranked bounty hunter squad he had access to using. That means you and your lil' buddies."

The Sigil on Taylor's forehead let out a low, warning *chime*. Before she knew it, she had stepped forward and was standing in a confident pose, which she acknowledged was nearly identical to Cindy's. "If you wished for a delegation from the Hollow Kingdom, I am more than certain King Vir would have been ecstatic to send us along on a diplomatic mission. By kidnapping his bride-to-be, you have overstepped your boundaries, and proper remunerations must be extended."

Were she not so practiced; the Mage's face would have been burning a bright crimson. There wasn't a single part of her that had wanted to say those words, but she was bound by the law of the Hollow Kingdom and physically couldn't *not* say it.

Exactly as she had expected, nearly everyone in the throne room began chuckling at the fluffed up implied threat, knowing there was nothing the tiny kingdom could do to the dynasty that had control of more than half of the known world. Taylor let out a groan as the emperor's attention turned to her.

"Even if I cared about some petty local tyrant and his ridiculous laws, the fact of the matter is that *he* broke contract with us first." The emperor strode forward, matching Luke pace for pace. "Simply by sending out mid-level Ascenders to attack the legions of recruits we had sent to the border, back before you destroyed a few of my mountains. So we have every legal right to retaliate as we see fit. Besides… your kingdom is a testing ground, a training regimen only for the weakest of our people. That is the only reason your kingdom even *exists*. Until recently, we've been supplying you with food, materials, and schematics for creating weapons and armor that were exactly what *we* needed you to have."

"Our entire kingdom is a glorified boot camp?" Zed was furiously writing down the information, fully planning on disseminating it if he got out of here alive. "Does it sound like treason? Yes. Would they bring me up on charges, even if it's true? Also yes. If they caught me, would I be hung? *Already there.*"

At this, he nudged Andre with his elbow a few times, winking and nodding dramatically. Not a single person cracked a smile or bothered to give him the attention he was craving. All eyes were on the Murderhobo as he approached his physical match.

As they came within a few dozen feet of each other, the emperor's eyes widened fractionally, and his voice increased in excitement as he spoke. "I'm sensing not one but *two* Domains? What a dramatic increase in power that you've had over the last month, when I last received a report on your estimated capabilities."

The air between the two powerhouses was practically sparking from the sheer tension of the moment, and the atmosphere became so oppressive that Taylor found herself breathing heavily from the strain. Even though he wasn't wearing any armor or carrying any weapons, not a single person in the room assumed that the man assessing the Murderhobo was harmless. "How about it, Luke? Would you listen to my offer?"

"Can't close my ears," the Murderhobo responded casually, still not bothering to look directly at the emperor. "I'm still waiting to hear what my sister wants to do."

"I will personally guarantee her safe passage if she wants to leave." Now the emperor allowed himself to show that he was growing slightly annoyed. Even if he was a calm and rational person, someone didn't survive for thousands of years and *enjoy* being ignored. Taylor walked forward, moving much more quickly than either of the two bodybuilders who were practically twitching their muscles at each other.

The Mage's passage didn't go unnoticed. Dozens of dogs stepped through portals, each of them staring directly at her as she passed by the assembled Ascenders. She kept her eyes forward, making no hostile motions or giving anyone a reason to attack unprovoked.

"Perhaps I can move this along, so all of us are a little more comfortable? Luke, please stop getting closer to the emperor. Even though he is the number one powerhouse of the entire dynasty, you're making his retainers nervous. Cindy, you have a personal guarantee from the emperor, ruler of most of the known world, in front of the people that he needs to trust his word. Please announce what you would like to do, so the rest of us can begin *very carefully* leaving."

For the first time, Cindy looked down, her face troubled. "I... I am not happy to be passed around like a participation trophy. In the Hollow Kingdom, I was told that I would be denied access to my first world to begin Ascension. Here, I am told that I will be a princess, but I have no idea if my powers would be compatible with what is available here. Before anything else... I want to be an Ascender. Is that... something I can do here?"

"Sure." The emperor was once again dismissive toward her. "I straight up *don't care* what you do. The reason the patricidal whelp—who can't keep to the deals his forefathers made—won't allow you to gain personal power is that he fears assassination in his bedchambers. Like I said before, I've got a couple *hundred* sons. As long as you have a good reason, it won't impact me if you very suddenly end up a widow."

"*Abyss*, father. That's dark." Taylor's head jerked to the side, where Prince William stood behind a wall of what appeared to be Druids, going off the plant and leathers that made up their outfits. "Glad to know where I stand."

"What I *do* care about is what your team can offer." The emperor very suddenly flexed, his neck muscles and arms bulging out as he attempted to loom over Luke from his seated position. "What *you* should care about is what I can offer you in return. Actual training, power, greatly reduced restrictions on your travel to your worlds, luxury... the life you should have been living on this world in the first place. Luke, agree to work for me, and I will make you my personal disciple, teaching you the fighting style of the Wild Hunt. Lethal, non-lethal, inducing pain, poisons, assassinations, slaughters. Whatever training you desire, whatever you need. I will *provide* it for you."

He wasn't done, and for the first time since the start of his conversation, the emperor turned his eyes on the other members of The Four.

"Andre, joining us gives you an immediate benefit. You'll fall under our protection, as well as no longer being the Archdruid of a kingdom that doesn't matter. I've seen the miracles that you've been able to produce and heard rumors of so much more. Access to our libraries, our collected data, and *thousands* of years of accumulated knowledge is yours for the taking. Research facilities, assistants, and funding for whatever you need to transform our cities from blights upon the world into natural wonders. Your discoveries would allow us, as a dynasty, to live in tandem with the world around us."

Taylor looked back at the Druid, who was standing stock-still, a look on his face like a deer that had been startled by a hunter. She was expecting him to deny the emperor immediately, but instead he reached up and tugged on the red beard he had been growing, not saying a word. Her head turned back toward the throne and found that the emperor was meeting her eyes directly.

"For you, Mage, I am sorry to say that your world is on the outer reaches of the dynasty. But I will happily make you a deal." The emperor looked around, as though he were searching for something, perhaps a map or a piece of paper to draw on. Finding nothing, he shrugged and turned his attention back to her. "My armies will simply roll over the Hollow Kingdom. Instead of sending in recruits, we will actually step forward and turn it into a vassal state in preparation for full assimilation. You'll be the governor of that province, able to have final say on nearly anything that goes on in that tiny slice of land. You'll only answer to me directly, and will be able to pursue whatever your goals are."

Now Taylor fully understood the conflict that was filling her friends. She had always been nobility, born to rule over people and guide them. There was so much about the Hollow Kingdom that she wanted to change, and having the resources and backing of the dynasty would allow her to implement everything she desired. If he was speaking truthfully, there was no way she would say no... if her oaths would allow her to accept.

"Do you treat Bards better than the Hollow Kingdom?" Zed called out hopefully, a winning smile on his face as he swept into a full, courtly bow. "I have so many amazing and wonderful stories, and I believe that I am the first Bard in history to-"

"You would be assigned to an outer village, where you will stay until you die of old age." Though the words were harsh, the tone was one of bleak regret. "I can feel the power rolling off of you. It resonates with this entire plane of existence, even more so than your Druid friend. He resonates with this *world*, but you... you are a *Bard*."

"Thank you for noticing... your Royal Highness." Zed stood back up, pure exhaustion in his voice.

"Is your country truly such a backwater? Do you not know *why* you cannot be allowed to ascend?" Taylor was surprised that Prince William would put himself in the center of attention once more, drawing eyes away from his father. "Father, at *least* promise him a proper education."

"Do not take this offer the wrong way, Bard." The emperor nodded at his son's point before turning his eyes toward Zed once more. "You would live in absolute luxury, surrounded by interesting people, beautiful women, waterfalls, and hot springs. All you would need to do to have *everything* is continue to *not* increase your level."

Light returned to Zed's eyes, and he let a broad smile appear on his face. "That is *way* easier than nearly dying every single day trying to increase my level! Unfortunately, I am *forced* to decline... if you understand my meaning."

"Ah, yes. The Sigils." The emperor snapped his fingers, and scintillating cages of light surrounded each of The Four. "We need to do something about that, don't we? Otherwise, I will have to start taking offense at your reaction to my very generous offers. Enchanters! Bind them."

"Heard *that* before." Zed chuckled quietly.

Taylor groaned lightly as her Sigil began forcing her to act.

A well-placed injection of mana caused the prison of light to sputter out and fail. "Great. Now we need to fight against the elder monsters of the world."

The lights around Luke shattered with a sound like breaking glass. In the same instant, Cookie came down, only to be blocked by an upturned arm. The Murderhobo had his battle-crazed smile on his face, "I'm so sick of your *words*. Been a while since you had to take what you wanted with your own hands, huh?"

"You know…" The emperor sent his left fist forward in a straight punch, blasting Luke through the air so fast the air screamed around his hurtling body. "…it *has* been. Come, boy. Let this old dog teach you some new tricks."

CHAPTER FIFTY-TWO

- LUKE -

The Emperor's strike to his chest crushed several of Luke's ribs and inflicted a sort of pain that the Murderhobo thought he had been able to accept and move past. In that moment, he was back at the start of the waterfall in Murder World, whimpering in horror at the shards of broken bone that goats had driven into the flesh around a fractured femur.

A split second had passed since he had been struck, and Luke recognized that some kind of Skill had been used against him. His chest armor was gone; his chest was a mess. With a strange feeling of suction, his internal organs reoriented themselves, and the bones moved back into place before fusing into a perfectly reformed system. Even before taking the time to arrest his momentum, Luke let the information from his combat log flow into the forefront of his mind.

Mana Giant has absorbed free-floating liquid mana from your body to initiate repairs!

"*Abyss,* yeah." Luke was extremely pleased with that combination of Skills. Together, with both of them active, it was an incredibly potent recipe for success. Tiering up one of the two in the future was going to be a tricky process, as having half of his blood be liquid mana meant that he would likely explode as soon as Mana Giant was no longer active. "That's a problem for future Luke."

Feather's Flight kicked in, and the air resistance he was feeling sharply increased. His strangely linear momentum from being hit by the emperor was converted into upward momentum, as though the straight punch had instead been an uppercut. There were murmurs of confusion from the assembled Ascenders, but almost none of them were focused on Luke. As far as they knew, the emperor had his full attention on the Murderhobo, which completely alleviated any of their concerns.

Luke realized he was getting to have a true one-on-one battle with a man who was a master of physical combat, someone apparently known throughout the world as 'the strongest'. That part excited him, but there was a small portion of his brain that was attempting to calculate his chances of success and failing drastically. The Murderhobo had two Domain Skills, which, for this plane of existence, was as powerful as they could possibly be. Still, the emperor had been able to easily discern them, count them, and practically discarded the idea that they were a concern.

The ruler had not been the only one who could feel Domain powers. As far as Luke could tell, the emperor had at least *ten* of them.

Even more worrisome was the fact that, if there had been any usage of powers outside of the emperor 's physical body, they had been so subtle that the Murderhobo had not been able to detect them. This wasn't an Ascender who sat around on his throne ordering other people to do hard tasks, like King Vir. This was a man who had woken up one day and decided to build a dynasty with his own hands. Then he had done it for what appeared to be thousands of years of conquering.

He was powerful, he was practiced, and he had a mastery

of his capabilities Luke could only hope to one day achieve for himself. As he dropped down to the floor, his smile only got wider. "What day is better than today for getting stronger?"

Not hesitating for a second, Luke launched himself at the emperor, who appeared to be out for a casual stroll. He led with Cookie, releasing her into the air as an open fist came out and sent her flying off into the distance. He could only hope the emperor wasn't expecting him to let go of his only weapon, so Luke threw everything he had at the immensely powerful individual. His fists flew faster, driving a rapid staccato beat that an entire hail storm would fail to compete with. Marks began to appear on the emperor 's body, but that only put a smile on the man's face.

Cookie came back through the air, having been summoned by Luke's Soul Brand. He finished off his flurry of attacks by hopping in the air, catching Cookie mid-flight, and bringing her down in almost the exact same angle that he had started the fight with. The only difference was that this time, as the ruler lifted his hand to send her flying away once more, Luke dumped power into Zero-point Shockwave, and Cookie rebounded off the air in front of his target instead of being swatted away. As the offending hand passed the point where the Shockwave was being stored in the air, Luke commanded its power to be released.

Damage dealt: 137 sonic damage.

For the first time in their combat, Luke was able to draw blood from his opponent. The blast of stored potential energy hit the man right in the face, as he was out of position to do anything about it. The emperor stumbled back a few steps, looking down at the ground as drips of blood dropped off of him. A collective gasp filled the room as everyone who had been watching what they thought was going to be a mockery of a fight inhaled at nearly the same time. All other motion seemed to slow as the people who were otherwise occupied with Luke's team tried to suss out what had happened.

"How… *fun.*" The words were whispered so softly Luke

wasn't sure it wasn't his mind playing tricks on him again. In that moment, the Emperor jerked upright, a smile on his face that matched Luke's, and a tiny trickle of blood coming from his nose. That wasn't the most concerning thing. No, that dubious honor went to the emperor 's eyes. The sclera of the eyes was turning black, the iris a reflective metallic gold—as though someone had injected the precious metal directly into the sensitive organ—and his pupils turned an even darker black, *drinking* in the light instead of merely allowing light to pass through it. "You'll be a worthy disciple. If you live."

The Murderhobo could feel the change in the air as the emperor activated at least one of his Domains. Intricate stonework that covered the floor was replaced by rugged earth, portions of it even growing small shrubs. The air itself changed in flavor, a deep musk rolling out of it. At the very edges of the arena that had been created with the emperor at its center strolled enormous dogs. They were walking through the edge of the space as though reality had just been distended, and the world that the emperor hunted within came to visit this one. "Neat. That's new."

"You are one of the fortunate few who gets to step into the world of the Wild Hunt without being a Trainer." The emperor 's voice was now a growl, and his throat made a strange clicking sound as he advanced on Luke. "I cannot even tell you how long it has been since someone non-Ascended has been able to make me bleed my own blood."

That made the Murderhobo furrow his brow. "Have you bled someone else's blood before? If you can teach me how to do that, I *am* interested."

"Jokes?" The man's head cocked to the side like a puppy that had just been told the word 'treat'. "Somehow, I didn't expect that from you."

"I don't understand. What jokes?" Instead of an answer to his query, Luke received a slap to his left ankle. His legs went out from under him as he flipped through the air, his hair providing a small cushion as his head was ruthlessly driven into the bare earth beneath him.

The Murderhobo was utterly enraged. He had been able to *see* the attack coming; he simply hadn't been able to react fast enough to defend against it. He had placed almost all of his available points from level increases into Fitness and Resistance, and right now, he was regretting not bringing his Physical Reaction up to fifty points.

Still, his choices in the past had allowed him to survive the hit that he had just taken without sacrificing the limb. That was a pleasant bonus. For only a moment, the bones in his feet were broken. But they were back in place and healed before his face had touched the ground. Unfortunately, now he was down two pieces of armor, as he was still waiting on his cuirass to manifest once more.

Over the next three seconds, the emperor struck him in multiple joints with precise blows, digging through his armor and shattering the flesh and cartilage below. The man leaped back, putting space between them with a satisfied smile on his face. "I managed not to kill you. I *am* getting better at this. Now that you can no longer move, it's time for me to call in my... why, *hello*."

Luke was already back on his feet, no sign of injury on his body whatsoever. "Bum Blast!"

He had activated his Skill with his fist already in position and used the momentum more than any finesse to slam the clenched hand into the 'weak point' that his Domain of the Murderhobo promised existed. Then he dumped mana into the Movement Skill, locking his position to this exact spot. Luke figured that, since he had been able to land a hit here, it was as good of a place to launch his offensive from as any other.

Before he could get another attack in, the Murderhobo was slapped away, four of his left ribs breaking under the attack as he was swatted out of the air at an angle.

Damage taken: 349 blunt.

The emperor was clearly expecting him to need to right himself in the air again, as he had at the start of their battle. Luke reveled in the surprise in his opponent's eyes as his fist reappeared inches from his face. The Murderhobo drove the overhand right punch into the emperor's ocular bone, sending him to the ground where he bounced a single time and disappeared.

An instant later, Luke felt his left arm break in multiple places as he took a hit, then he was once again in front of the emperor, the fist of his right arm driving down. "If I can't keep up with you directly, I don't mind getting reset to land some hits! I'll trade attacks all *day*."

The motion repeated, with the Murderhobo feeling immense pain as his bones were ground to dust, and he showed up once more in front of the powerful man—only for his fist to be caught as if he were a child throwing a punch at an adult. "That's enough of that."

Maintaining his grip, the emperor slammed Luke into the ground, shattering bones up and down his body. Then the Murderhobo was hauled up into the air in an arc over the emperor, to be smashed into the earth once more. Each time Luke was in the air over his rival, his bones would snap back into position and heal. Then, in nearly identical places, they would be destroyed once again as he landed.

The Murderhobo wasn't merely allowing the emperor to do whatever he wanted. Calculating his movement, he summoned Cookie back to him as he reached the apex of his arc overhead, and the emperor stumbled as the enormous Greatmace *thudded* into the back of his head while he was focused on maintaining his form. It wasn't easy to shrug off the momentum of a weapon that weighed over four hundred and fifty kilograms, even if the attack itself didn't contain the power that Luke could put into it with his own hands.

As the iron grip on his body loosened, Luke activated Bum Blast's final stored charge, converting the punch into a backhand that actually managed to send the emperor tumbling to the ground again. The man rested there for a moment, and

Luke didn't hesitate to try to capitalize on the apparent weakness. As he brought his fists down, the closed eyelids of the emperor popped open, meeting Luke's gaze with a steadfast, calm stare.

The Murderhobo's breath caught in his throat as the emperor moved too fast for him to even see, and the pain that struck him the next moment seemed almost distant. He looked down, finding that the emperor 's arm was *through* his chest, almost up to the shoulder.

Luke's momentum had been completely arrested, and he was finding it hard to breathe. The emperor pulled his arm back, lightly shoving the Murderhobo away at the same time. Even as confused as his brain was at that moment, Luke recognized the fact that the emperor was holding his heart in his hands.

"Feces." The powerful ruler actually sounded frustrated as he tossed the sack of meat up and down gently in the air, "Sorry about that. Force of habit. I'm sure you understand."

CHAPTER FIFTY-THREE

"The~e~e *end*." Zed called out boisterously to the tavern full of patrons as he slapped his legs and stood up. One of them in particular snapped out of his trance-like state, his eyes going wide and furious.

Bartholomew sputtered in impotent rage as he tried to draw his sword and attack the Bard. "What do you mean '*the end*'? We all know that there is more to this story. The Murderhobo was seen in the skies above the capital city of the Dynasty of Dogs! You cannot just *end* here; you haven't told us the whereabouts of the queen! How the oaths were broken or why the dynasty collapsed!"

Zed tapped at his chin, a wry smile playing about his lips as he peered out the window of the tavern. "Bartholomew, while I am excited that you are so invested in this story… daylight is nearly upon us. We have a very important event happening, and I would hate for all of us to miss it."

"Daybreak is not for at least another four hours!" Bartholomew pointed an accusing finger at the Bard after realizing that he was unable to draw his sword in the man's presence. "You are intentionally withholding information from the crown! I will be adding this to the list of charges against you!"

"Dear me, I'm practically shaking in my custom jungle-cat-leather boots. Let's see where this would go on the list." Zed pulled a scroll out of his pocket, letting it unroll. It magically extended, eventually reaching the other side of the room and continuing up the wall. "Oh, no! It appears that I just don't have the room to put such a frivolous charge on a list of my crimes. I guess we'll just have to move on with our day."

"Zed the *Bard*!" Bartholomew howled into the open air as he tried to shove his way past the other people in the tavern.

Laughter rang out as Zed bent over in a fit of chuckling. "Inquisitors... always so serious! I'm only teasing you because this is almost always the point in my story where I have been interrupted by agents of the king in the past. As the emperor used to say, 'whoops! Force of habit'. Let's continue what little remains of our story."

With that, Zed allowed a hint of mana to escape his eyes, and the people listening were once more watching the dramatic events surrounding The Four unfold.

———

- ANDRE -

As the emperor held Luke's still-beating heart out in front of him, Andre felt the pit of his stomach drop. He'd thought that he'd been inoculated to the devastation that death and destruction would wreak upon his psyche, but something about seeing one of his oldest and dearest friends dying in front of his eyes made it just that much harder. The fight went out of him, and he sank to his knees as despair overtook his common sense, even overpowering the Sigil that was still frantically attempting to force him to fight.

Now in a compromised position, dozens of layers of barriers and commands struck him, holding him fast in the position that he was currently in. Andre didn't care about any of that at this moment. He could only stare in blank apathy as the emperor began *mocking* his fallen friend.

"You seem to have a miraculous ability to heal through wounds that would cripple other people for life. I wonder if this will be able to slow you down for long." The emperor got his answer an instant later, as Luke toppled over backward, landing on the floor without any attempt at catching his fall. "Ah. So your healing has something to do with your blood, it seems. Well... let's try the next test, then. It's good to see how much he can take, though I do worry that I pushed my future disciple a bit too hard just now."

His words were directed at the assembled Ascenders and earned a laugh from many of them. Andre was currently being held in the air, suspended well above the ground so that he couldn't achieve a direct connection to it. At that moment, he raged against his moment of weakness, wanting nothing more than to destroy these people who would choose to be so casually cruel. Something moved in the periphery of his vision, and he watched as the emperor darted around, lifting Luke back to his feet and shoving his heart back into his chest.

"Now comes the real test." The emperor was speaking quietly, but the throne room had been designed with him in mind. His voice would carry to the entire room no matter where he spoke in it. "Let's see if you can bring yourself back from the brink."

Silence filled the room after Taylor was captured. Zed had been unable to break out of the barrier in the first place, which Andre recognized as an intentional act. The Bard knew he would be unable to survive for any length of time, so his Sigil hadn't forced him to throw everything he had against it, as it had done to them. The emperor waved his hand over Luke's body, and something that he did enhanced the sounds of the internal processes to an audible level for everyone present.

There was some *squelching* as the Murderhobo's meal from earlier in the day was digesting, *bubbling* as gasses were produced, and finally... a powerful heartbeat sounded. One beat, a long pause, another, increasing in speed and depth over the next several seconds. At least one hundred various Ascender Powers were used in the next moment, each of them aimed at containing and controlling the Murderhobo. From the perspective of those in the room, they hadn't acted a moment too soon.

Luke's eyes were suddenly open, and a primal howl of rage ripped its way out of his throat as he threw his body against the powers binding him. To Andre's immense shock, the Spells that were piled on his body started to *snap*, *crackle*, and *pop*.

It took the Druid a fraction of a second to remember that his friend had a Skill that would drain mana out of the air around him, but he didn't realize that it could be used in such a way. He would be a terror on the battlefield against defensive barriers and enchantment-protected walls. Even without further training, the Murderhobo was an effective siege weapon.

"Enchanters, if you will, do your job." The strange bubble in the air that had been created by the Emperor's Domain vanished, and the land around him reverted to its normal stone tile. A half dozen people wearing extremely intricate robes with mystical symbology stitched in them rushed forward and began actively altering the Sigil that had been placed on Luke's forehead.

As they worked, they soon began to sweat. Luke's automatic mana-suction was making their job much, *much* harder. Andre remembered when he'd first gotten his Sigil branded on his forehead and how it had taken less than a handful of seconds for it to be completed. Now, as they moved past the five-minute mark, the first of the enchanters fainted, and the others were hard pressed to pick up his slack. The emperor added a bit of motivation for them, "You'll continue until he is bound, or you are dead. Pick one."

The panicked expressions on their faces turned hard as they leaned forward and began pushing with their scalpel-tools. Now they weren't worried about causing undue damage or keeping the Murderhobo from pain. Blood flowed freely as they cut into his flesh to ensure that the magic was deeply rooted into him. His Sigil was altered, reinforced, then reinforced again.

Finally, almost slumping to the ground, they stood back and gestured for the emperor to do his part. "We were not able to completely remove the previous Sigil, but we were able to over-write it. We kept intact the portions keeping him from Ascending to level twenty and a few other small inconsistencies that must have been created by a botched attempt from the servant territory."

"If it binds him, good enough. Luke, you have been treated unfairly by the king of your country. Now, what you have on your forehead is a much more powerful Sigil, which will bind me to you, and you to me. You are no longer under the geas that were keeping you from accepting my offer. Will you will-ingly swear yourself to me? To refuse is to choose death, and as you have seen, I have the ability to end you easily and perma-nently. To accept is to gain a life of luxury, doing small tasks and favors for me as needed."

"What... do you want from me?" Luke forced the words out, even though his initial inclination was to foam at the mouth and attack the man speaking.

"I want what every leader of their people wants." The emperor raised his hands and gestured around him. "I want power. I want good lives for the people under my command. For the Ascenders to know their place in the hierarchy and to have endless mana for experimentation into enchantments and all sorts of technologies."

Andre's eyes went wide as he realized that this entire quest-line had been manipulated just for the emperor to capture Luke. The emperor had led with wanting all four of them, but it was clear to anyone watching that he was merely trying to consolidate his power.

"We have *half* of the world." The powerful man continued speaking, his voice growing louder and more excited. "With the mana that you can provide to us, we will be able to use the tele-portation arrays as *basic* transportation. No longer will the common folk have to suffer far away from their families, while we are able to travel the world."

Taylor's voice pealed out from her containment. "Luke, all he wants to do is use you to power his transportation system! Then his armies won't be constrained by *walking*, and he'll be able to rule the world from this spot. If you let yourself be bound-"

Any of her next words were cut off as the air around her imploded, leaving a slight shimmery look that didn't allow any sound to pass to her. The emperor pointed at the exhausted enchanters then over at Taylor. "Somebody, please go and work on her Sigil. I think it's a little stronger than the average version that comes out of the Hollow Kingdom."

"Is that true? Do you just want mana to wage war and rule this world?" Luke had calmed down significantly and patiently waited for an answer before he would speak again.

"There is much truth in it. That will be the majority of what we use it for, but only at the start. The rest of it's also true; we will be able to advance our technologies faster. Imagine what I could have done over the previous millennia, if I had access to what you can provide. *Now* imagine what we can do with our current, *stable* base of power and knowledge." The emperor walked closer to Luke, "I *ask* again, and for the last time... will you willingly bind yourself to me?"

"*I*." Luke ground out the words. "*Will*."

"Release our new subject, Luke the Murderhobo-" The emperor cried out with great joy in his voice. The people around him sprang into action immediately, canceling their powers that were binding Luke to the floor.

The Murderhobo finished his statement, "*Not*."

CHAPTER FIFTY-FOUR

- TAYLOR -

She watched with panicked eyes as the enchanters of the Dynasty of Dogs closed in on her, lifting their bloody scalpels with grim determination on their faces. Then, for some reason they came to a stop, confusion on their faces. Taylor had no idea why they had ceased moving, as she'd been cut off from whatever was being said. All she knew at this moment was that Luke was on his feet again, unencumbered by the Spells that had been binding him.

Taylor knew what that meant. He had sworn an oath to the dynasty, and her chances of success in this mission had just been obliterated. Her Sigil was now the only thing she could hear besides her own breathing and the heartbeat racing in her ears, so she was left wondering as to why people were shuffling around in a strange panic. The emperor was making a show of turning around to glare at the Murderhobo, and as he did, the strange auditory barrier vanished.

"-was the last chance I was going to give you to do this willingly." The most powerful man in the world finished whatever he was saying.

"Got that." Luke nodded his head, even as his left hand shot out directly to his side. With barely a ripple in the air, a bright blue portal appeared in the air next to him. "Thanks for removing the binding. I owe ya one."

Taylor's jaw dropped as Luke slipped out of the world and into Murder World, the portal closing behind him smoothly and without leaving even the slightest distortion. Just like that, he was gone. She also knew that there was absolutely *no chance* he was coming back. He had been forced into servitude or trapped in that world for the better part of a century at this point. The Mage also knew that he hadn't really been seeking fights or stronger monsters. No…

The Murderhobo had been hunting for *freedom*.

Ever since they had been forced to return to this world by the commands of the Archmage, the entire time they had traveled together, it had come up in some way in every conversation they had. Unless *everything* about him changed drastically, there was no way he was giving up on the chance he had just stolen. Even if it cost the lives of her, the rest of the team and even his sister.

For a few minutes, nobody said a word. Ever so slowly, the emperor turned back to the remainder of the team and let out a deep, weary breath. "He's going to come back for you, isn't he?"

No one was answering the question, and she could see the air around the emperor begin to distort. Once again, she took the burden of leadership onto herself. "It is… highly unlikely. The Murderhobo has his own, oftentimes inscrutable, ambitions."

"Fair enough." The emperor took a step forward, appearing next to her side before his foot hit the ground. "Yet, 'unlikely' does not mean 'no'. You're saying there *is* a chance. In that case, I hope you are prepared to remain here, in my throne room, until he returns."

"I'm not sensing any movement, Your Highness!" a man with a small puppy on his shoulder called out. Upon closer inspection, the dog's eyes were covered in a milky white film, and it seemed to be either blind or staring at something unseeable by anyone else. "He is merely on the other side of the veil between worlds! It does not seem that he is planning to abandon them."

A satisfied smile appeared on the face of the emperor, and Taylor hoped that none of her team would be so foolish as to explain the reasoning behind-

"*Actually,*" Zed called out, causing Taylor to deflate like a rotting corpse, "As we have experienced, until he comes out of there, it appears he is not moving. But he *is*, I guarantee it. Luke has an extreme time dilation in that world, so by now, he has likely already killed at least a dozen powerful creatures and is working to become stronger."

The emperor looked at the Bard, seemingly weighing his options. "I know you are only telling me this to gather your own Potentia, as having the attention of such powerful people is no doubt bringing great benefit to you right now."

"Yes. Indeed it is, Your Majesty." Zed's bright smile curled slightly, showing a slight cockiness.

"Then feel free to speak, but understand that, if you begin increasing your level, I will be forced to take *permanent* punitive actions against you. Bards cannot be allowed to Ascend."

Zed swept into a bow, and as he came up, he was grabbed by a half dozen hands and had his Sigil carved into. In mere moments, the emperor had bound him with a new, much more powerful Sigil, removing any allegiance he'd been forced to have for the Hollow Kingdom.

Then he told them *everything*.

Soon Andre, followed by Taylor herself, had their Sigils overwritten with the more powerful version that the Dynasty of Dogs had access to. At first, it was greatly frustrating to her. Not only were her accomplishments negated, all of her land, titles, and investments that she had put into the Hollow Kingdom would be stripped away.

It wasn't all bad, as the emperor swore to them that, as soon as Luke was captured and bound, he would still follow through on the promises that he made to them. This came with a caveat that they would need to use all of their expertise, all of their knowledge, to bring the Murderhobo down if he came back and was able to stand toe-to-toe with the emperor .

Hours turned into days, turned into weeks. There was never a single sign that Luke was considering returning.

Months later, Taylor was in the process of studying her new martial art under the instruction of a dozen of the dynasty's finest fighters. She'd settled into her new life, enjoying the amenities, learning the magical formations, and increasing her finesse of using her Characteristics to their utmost potential. The Mage had been expecting the training to be humiliating, but after a rough few initial sessions where her trainers were attempting to test the bounds of her knowledge, they had been extraordinarily professional in their teachings.

Perhaps the fact that she was already at the point where she could simply Ascend if the emperor would give permission, and they didn't want to cause issues with someone who might be able to find them in higher worlds, had something to do with the elegant professionalism. Still, something inside her wanted to believe that they saw a prodigy within her, and they were taking all appropriate measures to ensure that she would be the very best among their best.

A year later, Taylor was considered among the highest-skilled close range Assassin Mages in the dynasty. At the very peak of level nineteen, with perfect Mana Channels, she'd been able to assimilate the information that had been passed on to her. She had been trained in the Arts of subterfuge, murder, poison, and been taught ways to stretch her Spells in ways that would have been absolutely incoherent to her when she walked into the throne room a year prior.

She wasn't the only one. With a cadre of tutors, Andre had been expanding his capabilities right alongside her. In fact, he was often the one in charge of growing the forest she would be training within when she had a mock mission to complete. They had grown closer and had become an official couple months previously. They had yet to go much further than hand-holding or a light kiss, as they were under constant surveillance by the other Ascenders who filtered through the throne room.

Over their entire course of their extended stay, they had never once been allowed to leave the throne room. This wasn't much of an issue, as this still gave them multiple kilometers of space to live, train, sleep, and eat in. For the first few months, she'd been sure they would be slain, if for nothing else other than the emperor 's ire at being kept waiting. Taylor had forgotten at first that he was multiple thousands of years old. Beyond anything else, the ancient monster had cultivated patience to the utmost degree.

In her mind, Zed was the one among them who had the most impressive increases in his personal ability. At the end of each day, his Sigil was checked to ensure that he hadn't devoted any Potentia to increasing his levels. As it turned out, the Bard had no particular interest in losing his luxurious position. He devoted every single point he gained to boosting his Masteries higher and higher. He also learned everything that she did, even if he simply couldn't physically match her in speed, endurance, or combat capability.

Against a regular human, the Bard had become as dangerous as a descending boot was to an ant. More than that, he learned politics, history, and all sorts of courtly manners. Taylor shuddered to think of what would happen if he ever was released back into the world, now able to perfectly blend in at any level of society, from its highest points to its lowest. Luckily, it wasn't something that she had to put too much thought into. She was busy, and when the person in charge of you had the equivalent life experience of an entire *city's* worth of people, there was always more to learn.

A year and a half after she had first stepped into this room, she was once more called to stand before the emperor. This time, she knew all of the proper protocol, which was a strange blend of confidence and subservience. A perfect combination of what her position in a pack would have been, were they the dogs that the vast majority of this country's Ascenders could summon.

Taylor ran her eyes over the powerful man seated on the throne in front of her. Comparing the image before her to her memory of the man from her arrival, literally nothing had changed. Even his hair was exactly the same length, in exactly the same style. Her eyes focused in, and she realized that there *was* one small change: the robes he was wearing had been repaired, stitched where Luke had been able to deal damage through their protective qualities, once upon a time.

"I am beginning to believe that he is not coming back." The emperor sounded completely resigned to this fact. "If what you have told me is true, and I have my own guarantees that it is, then he has been out of this world for a quarter of a century in his subjective time. I have no idea what level of power he would have been able to achieve in that time, but it's likely he found some way to break through the binding of his Sigil and forced himself to level twenty. I am... *frustrated* by this turn of events, but you have devoted yourself to the dynasty with impressive tenacity. I think that it's time for you to take your rewards, and I thank you for your patience in this matter."

Taylor found herself suddenly unwilling to leave. This had been the calmest portion of her life, where she had very few concerns. With the best training, food, and every imaginable luxury beyond privacy, her mind wanted her to refuse this admission of defeat on the part of the emperor. Yet, she could find no fault in his logic. She merely felt sad and found that her friends were mimicking her expressions. This place had become home, and its people had treated them better than they ever thought would be possible.

"As of this moment, I am sending you on the following missions-" The emperor paused, his lips pressing together, then curling upward until his teeth appeared, a wide smile beaming on his face. His eyes narrowed, and his voice turned dark and gravelly. "I had *hoped* this would earn a reaction."

Taylor turned around, utterly shocked to see that *Luke* was standing in the throne room, only a few feet behind them. Even more mind-boggling to her was the fact that he was dressed in well-made clothes, his hair done up in what could pass for a fashionable style, and a dense roiling aura that screamed danger and death filled the air around him.

"It's time for The Four to go. Also Cindy. Time for the five of us to go."

CHAPTER FIFTY-FIVE

"You had twenty-four *years* to plan what you were going to say when you came back." Zed shook his head sadly at the Murderhobo. "Then the first thing you do when you get back is flub it? Not inspiring a lot of confidence."

"Send for the sister." The Emperor's words caught Luke's attention, and he nodded at the man. "Ensure she is not harmed and is prepared to give a full accounting of her time in our care. We have a guest I am *certain* would appreciate seeing her."

"Even before that…" Taylor stepped forward, her arms to the side. "Luke, don't do anything drastic. Let me explain that life here has been *awesome* over the last year and a half."

The Murderhobo listened patiently as she explained the benefits they had been enjoying, the life of luxury that they had been given, and the stream of constant information to which they had access. As she talked, Taylor kept a part of her mind on the location of the emperor, who had not moved an inch since Luke stepped into this world. Even so, she could tell that his forces were mobilizing, and portals were appearing in the throne room one after another as Ascenders swarmed toward them.

"That is wonderful. I am extremely pleased that you have all been treated well." Luke's face was more expressive than she had seen since before he first went to Murder World. "If you weren't forced to take the commands of the emperor, I would even say that it was a good life. But, Taylor… no matter how I look at it, you're just a pampered pet. You've been listening well, so you get treats. You've been trained. Even by your own admission, your leash has been short, no matter how beautiful that leash might be."

At this, the emperor finally stirred once more. "Is that so *bad*, Luke? Is it so terrible to allow someone to take care of you, instead of treating you like a feral beast, like the ruler of the Hollow Kingdom did? My offer to you stands. Join willingly, and life will be wonderful."

"I like things the way they are, thanks. I have no interest in giving up my freedom for what *you* think is an acceptable trade." Luke shook his head, and mana poured off of him in a deluge. The portals that were starting to tear themselves open in the throne room snapped shut. Some even closed while someone was moving out of them and bisected the individual attempting to exit. "I am going to live my life the way I choose, even if that means it's not as 'calm and peaceful' as it otherwise could be."

Taylor watched the stylish Barbarian in front of her, her heart sinking in her chest. He was so drastically different from what she remembered—calm, poised, with an elegant manner of speaking—but all that did was make him three times as terrifying as he had been before. The only other person who had this kind of effect on her was… she turned her eyes to the emperor, confusion filling her mind. There was no smile to be seen, none of the gentle patience he had exhibited the entire time they had been associated.

The ruler of the majority of the known world looked cold, ready to break this obstacle in his path.

"You have made your choice. I hope you *live* to regret it." At the emperor 's words, Andre and Taylor sprang into action, attempting to take down their friend in the most non-lethal way possible. She had been taught by the greatest masters of the dynasty. Andre had learned new, impressive abilities that gave him control over vast swaths of terrain while using only a fraction of his might. Plants sprang up around Luke, moving to entangle him, even as Taylor blinked across the distance and led with her daggers. She knew the man in front of her wasn't going to die easily, so each of her strikes was planned to land in a place that would be completely fatal to someone else.

Luke caught both of her daggers between *the same* two fingers. It took Taylor a moment to register what had just happened, as she'd been aiming at two separate locations: his neck and his pelvis. She hadn't even seen him move, and as her mind caught up with the forced interruption of her forward momentum, the sinking feeling in her stomach turned into dread. "What have you been doing for the last few decades?"

"Becoming *balanced*." Luke's words were almost gentle, and at the end of them, Taylor felt a feather-light touch on the upper part of her chest. Before she could see what had landed on her, she was slamming into the wall of the throne room nearly a kilometer away.

Damage taken: 14 terrain!

She coughed violently as her body attempted and failed to suck in air, finally managing to get a breath in. Taylor hyperventilated for a few seconds, watching as Andre summoned Arthur, his bear, in the distance. The bear had grown alongside the Druid, mutating into a new, disturbing form. Gone was the simple, oversized animal. In its place was a metal-clad war beast —Andre had managed to enter the Fourth circle in the time that they had been training here. Combining his Mastery of the Fourth circle, the metals of the world, with the Second circle, Mastery of animals, he had been able to forcefully evolve his tamed beast in a safe environment.

As soon as she could move again, Taylor was sprinting back toward the fight. Every single one of her movements was perfectly executed, efficient, and flawless in form. This allowed her to utilize her Characteristics to their utmost and flash across the distance nearly as fast as she had been smacked away. Still, there was a question that her brain was screaming at her, and she released it into the world under her breath. "How did he hit me that hard and deal *no* damage?"

Wham.

Arthur the War-clad Dire Bear zipped past her, mere inches from impacting the Mage's face. He hit the wall of the throne room and dealt *quite* a bit more damage than her merely fleshy body had. Metal striking stone and obliterating it, combined with the fury-filled roar of the bear, made it sound as though a wild animal had been let loose in a smithy. Andre followed a moment later, allowing Taylor to inspect the technique the Murderhobo was using.

Somehow, the man was lifting them lightly into the air then pushing them with a force that was applied over the entirety of their bodies instead of at the point that he was touching. Andre flying through the air looked almost comical, as he was in the exact same position in the air that he had been while standing, except for being a few inches off of the floor. Unlike the multi-ton animal that had been flying, Taylor felt confident in intercepting the Druid and swept him out of the air as he passed. They twirled around five times before they had bled off all of the momentum, then both darted back to the fight with a simple nod at each other.

"Enough, it is clear that he is merely toying with you," the emperor stated with a deep sigh of regret. "Sometimes, I forget how *young* all of you are. Some remedial training is in order, to help you understand when you should be stepping away from the battle instead of bashing your face against it."

The Mage felt her legs lock up, and she skidded to a halt. She opened her mouth to tell the emperor that they could continue, but Luke interrupted her, meeting her eyes directly. "Taylor. *Watch closely.*"

Her enhanced brain processed the words, and she understood immediately what he was truly trying to tell her. Not only did the Murderhobo want Taylor to watch the fight and learn what she could, paying attention to what was being said and done... he also knew about her Meta-magic Spell.

Luke was telling her to gather as many Spells as possible. She wanted him to surrender, to join her and the rest of the team in a calmer life for a while, but the emperor had already spoken; ordering her to stay out of the fight.

The mage grimly decided that it would be in her best interests to listen to Luke, even if only to capture his Skills and put them to use on behalf of the Dynasty of Dogs.

The real fight was beginning, and Taylor knew it. She understood that what was coming was going to be combat at a level she simply couldn't hope to participate in or survive against for even a few moments. Not if her opponent was serious about ending her.

To the Mage who had struggled for perfection and power her entire life, the fact that she was the same level as the Ascenders she was unable to touch was deeply troubling. "What is the difference between them and me? Combat experience notwithstanding, is it *Domains*? Are they truly that much more powerful than the lower Tiers? Is this a Characteristic thing?"

"Taylor, you can't do this to yourself." Andre quietly asserted from his position next to her. "Trust me when I say that comparing yourself to other people is a recipe for madness and disaster. Look at Luke, who has been in combat nearly every moment since he awakened as an Ascender. Look at the emperor, who has lived for *thousands* of years to hone his power to this degree."

"Andre..." The Mage let out a light sigh. "It just feels like I am running at full speed and not going anywhere."

"I get it." The Druid turned his eyes to her, and she could see the deep wisdom that he had accumulated over the decades. "But you're looking at the *end result*. We're seeing the power, the skill, the sheer finesse that they can bring to bear. I want that for myself, just as I know you do. Still... we can want what they have, but the question remains. Are we willing to do what they have done in order to get what they have?"

Both of them fell silent as the two muscle-bound warriors clashed, testing each other. When Taylor didn't respond, Andre quietly answered his own question. "I know that I... I'm *not* willing to do that. I don't want to be alone for nearly a century, honing my combat abilities in life-or-death situations the entire time. I don't want to spend thousands of years in one spot, slowly accumulating power, just to hold off on the final step and refuse to Ascend."

The Druid swallowed hard. "The emperor has *ten* Domains and has been an *inhale's* distance from Ascending for centuries. What kind of life do you think he must have lived in order to gather that much Potentia, and what does he fear about the higher realm that he should have *been* in for ten times longer than we have walked this world?"

"Andre!" Taylor gasped at his words; they were right on the edge of treason. In fact, the Druid's Sigil had flared slightly, and the man himself was holding his head in obvious pain. "You can't speak like that! Why *now*, of all times, would you do this to yourself?"

The Druid smiled through the pain, rubbing at the center of his forehead. "Haven't had a moment alone to mention it before now. At least, not when the emperor is focused on other things. I like to speak the truth, and I'm not a huge fan of him making me break my own legs as an apology."

Their conversation ended abruptly as Luke and the emperor separated from each other. The Murderhobo appeared as calm and stoic as ever, but a large frown was present on his opponent's face.

"How are you able to keep up with me? You're level nineteen, as am I. I know the limits of this world, and your Characteristics *cannot* be higher than mine. There is a hard cap to how much we can be changed with Potentia alone!"

"Once upon a time, I was a Mana Giant," Luke offered by way of explanation. "I am sure, with all of the access to information that you have, that you know Characteristics can be trained, as long as you are in a high-mana-density environment?"

"There is still a hard limit to be in this world," the emperor firmly stated. "Not to mention there is a soft cap for what you can train, versus what is required to surge forward in power."

Luke nodded at him, calmly accepting and agreeing with the words being decreed. "Do you know what happens when all of the Characteristic growth which *should* be devoted to higher-value Characteristics... is instead shunted into the lowest of them? It took me a *decade* of pushing my limits to bring my Charisma up to the same value as my Talent. By the second decade, with all of my higher Characteristics capped at where they had been when I started, I could perfectly utilize every bit of them, down to the smallest fractional increase. I'm still not perfectly balanced, but I *am* a lot closer... and I've gained a perfect understanding of what I can do."

"This pleases me." The emperor 's eyes shifted in coloration and reflectivity. "If you're this much better than you were... I get to find your limits once again. Try to survive long enough for me to bind you to my dynasty."

"I'm not going to try to *survive*." Luke's words were sharp, a clear taunt. "I'm a Murderhobo. You're in my way. I'm just going to get rid of you."

CHAPTER FIFTY-SIX

- LUKE -

The last two and a half decades had been extremely informative, giving him insight into what the Characteristics did and what they actually meant for him. Luke had also explored his Domains to a much greater extent, putting time and thought into both of them, not simply treating them as the face value of the Skill would suggest. For instance, with his ability to utilize his World Anchor Domain, Luke didn't need to punch at the membrane between universes anymore.

Over the decades, especially at times when he had been too injured to otherwise pursue different activities, he had toyed around with the Skill. He was still only able to create points of entrance and egress where the world allowed, but he was able to *look* into all other connected worlds whenever he wanted.

At the start, that had been horrendously difficult. Not the act itself... but simply finding the world he wanted to view. As far as he could tell, Murder World was connected to... *everything*. Or, at least every world that used the same style of power that his people utilized.

In fact, there were times where different worlds had *discon-nected* as they went down a different path to power. He didn't know why these became non-connected universes, but something about them had undergone a fundamental shift. Luke had all the time in existence to figure it out, if he wanted to make a study of that in the future. For now, there was an aggressive animal to put down.

The emperor had been testing Luke, trying to see the areas that he excelled in and those in which he was lacking. The last time the two of them had duked it out, Luke's strength was on par with his enemy, if not a little greater. Yet, during battles at this level, *speed* was king. Though they could hit almost as hard as each other, Luke had taken strikes he could see coming but do nothing about. His Physical Reaction had simply been too underutilized to move his body, his Mental Energy too subpar to take advantage of any openings.

The statistics themselves had increased, thanks in part to extreme conditions he'd subjected himself to, such as trying to drink every single drop of liquid mana he could find, chewing on the solid version, and seeking combat in Zones that were lower, resulting in ever-denser mana in the air. But it was truly the fact that his Body and Senses had *not* increased for so long that allowed him to perfect the lacking portions of his being. All of this had been done in order to bring him to a point that he was comfortable fighting his current opponent.

But he'd been caught while testing his ability to peer through the worlds. Somehow, the emperor could tell every time he peeked in and sneaked a look at his friends to see if they were still safe. Luke was unsure what had tipped the emperor off, or if the Murderhobo had just started looking on a regular schedule, but the emperor had been able to figure out when he would be watching and forced him to act. Luke had hoped for a couple extra decades of growth, but he was still pleased with what he'd been able to achieve.

More than that, he had a *plan*. A strategy he believed would give him a chance at success, even though the emperor was still leaps and bounds above him in terms of combat capability.

The Murderhobo's eyes narrowed as he reacted, slapping away a closed fist coming at him from an oblique angle. Cookie swung around in retaliation, his anger and her indignation over the attempted sneak attack working together to generate a blow with phenomenal fury behind it. The emperor blocked with a grunt, getting tossed a half dozen steps back before he came at them again.

"First Domain: Command of the Wild Hunt!" As the emperor spoke, Luke smiled. The fact that he was saying his commands aloud meant that he was in a rush and couldn't take the time to properly form the commands silently. The world was pushed back around them, and once more Luke found himself standing on packed dirt, with strange shrubbery growing around them. "I didn't even get to show you why this Domain is so impressive last time. While I'm here, summoning my trained dogs costs me nothing, and all my other commands enjoy a steep mana discount."

Dogs came running in from what appeared to be nowhere, simply walking through the molecule-thin barrier as if they had just been on the other side of a door. A trio of pooches stood next to each other—one taller than the other two—and opened their mouths to send out a beam attack that coiled and braided together; the three lances of energy combining to form a single unit.

Even with all of his practice and ability to tank attacks, Luke knew better than to let unknown energy touch his body. He danced out of the way, luckily farther than he thought he needed to, as the beam curved toward him slightly as it moved through the air. It passed the Murderhobo, reaching the edge of the Domain and vanishing. Or, perhaps continuing on in the world of the Wild Hunt, but not the Dynasty of Dogs—where it would deal immense damage to the emperor 's palace.

"That was *fun*, wasn't it?" The voice of his opponent was no longer the elegant, kindly sound that normally was exiting his mouth. Instead, it was harsh and brutal, as though the man had slipped back into an accent from an era long past. "Do that again with seventy of 'em coming atcha."

Hundreds of dogs poked their heads into the area, not even bothering to let their entire body manifest in the Domain. As the emperor had threatened, all of them sent various attacks his way. Beams that exuded death like the first, fire, ice, some kind of void-based vacuum that created tearing thunder as atmospheric pressure forced the wound to close after it passed.

All the while, the emperor remained in close range, sending fists, feet, elbows, and knees at the Murderhobo. Each of his attacks were intended to cause extreme pain, weakening the Murderhobo's will to fight. All of his feints and evasions were to allow the beams to pass by without harming himself, or to try and guide Luke into taking a direct hit.

The Murderhobo's combat log was spinning, dozens of messages appearing every second. Luke didn't have to look at them to know exactly what they were telling him.

Damage taken: 0!

It was going to take far more than glancing blows, light scratches, or even teeth grazing against his calves to penetrate his armor. Unlike the last time they had fought, Luke was able to deny a direct strike nearly perfectly. Each time the emperor got close enough that his own flesh touched against the manifestation that protected the Murderhobo, the sovereign moved back with light cuts on his hand from the spikes that his mana formed over him.

Finally, he disengaged and snapped his right hand in the air. Immediately, all energy-based attacks on the Murderhobo ended. "Second Domain, Master of Sound!"

Immediately, the air was filled with a sound Luke knew he shouldn't be able to hear. It sounded so faint that it should have been easy to ignore, but just like his Skill that allowed him to taunt, which was extra effective on goats, he could tell that this was calling something into the battle.

"I don't often get a chance to use this Domain. It's not

supremely useful in my dynasty. But, in combination with my first Domain and my third… it allows me to bring powerful entities to fight on my behalf." The emperor pointed at Luke, and the epicenter of the sound shifted, settling over his body and echoing outward into the world. "Third Domain: Unending Resonance of Metal."

Thunderous howls filled the air, starting with the dogs that had originally been encircling them. They pulled their heads back, vanishing into the world beyond the veil.

Luke knew what was coming, his World Anchor Skill granting him the ability to see through into the heavily connected world that was the Wild Hunt coming into play. That was the only reason he was able to dive to the side as a meteor slammed into the earth where he had been standing, not even creating an explosion as the metal that had struck was simply too *dense*. It penetrated deeply into the dirt, hitting so hard and so fast that Luke would have had the lower half of his body ripped off of the rest if the attack had landed.

"Just making sure… you just threw a ball at me. Now the other dogs are going to want to come and 'play'?" The Murder-hobo shook his head and settled into a deep, stable stance as another of the enormous metal orbs fell out of the sky. "You've been doing this too long. You don't need to roleplay being a dog trainer—it's literally the power set you have been given."

"We all have our quirks." The emperor shrugged with a happy grin on his face. "It is impossible to be number one without being a little… odd."

As the second orb blazed toward Luke's face, he turned and swung Cookie, batting the attack away and sending it directly at the emperor. It missed, as the man easily dodged it. Dozens more started falling out of the sky, and the howling grew louder. The earth began to rumble as a pack of enormous dogs followed the balls that were flying through the sky. Luke took a deep breath, activating Air Warden and completely ignoring the incoming attacks in favor of bringing the fight back to the emperor.

The metal balls blazed with heat, and the friction of moving through the atmosphere turned the surface of them molten. Luke and the emperor devolved into fisticuffs, their strikes being blocked, back and forth in turn. Damage was slowly accumulating on the clothing worn by the ruler, yet there had been no change whatsoever on Luke. The emperor pushed back a few feet as the first of the next round of metal meteors reached striking distance of the Murderhobo. A wide smile was on his face as he prepared himself to collect whatever remained of the man before he could heal through the damage.

"Time to be bound, *Murderhobo*!" The emperor 's glee turned to disbelief in an instant as the meteor that came within a millimeter of hitting the Murderhobo vanished, only to reappear several feet from Luke, moving with the same momentum, but in a straight line at the emperor 's face.

"My turn. Catch."

CHAPTER FIFTY-SEVEN

The emperor took the hit directly, and another two were on the way when he canceled his First Domain to avoid them. Luke landed on the stone tiles of the floor, slightly annoyed that the meteors had been pulled back within the Domain as it closed. A large portion of the area where the emperor had landed was filled with smoke and dust from his impact. The Murderhobo took a deep breath, disliking what he had to do next but understanding the necessity of it.

Damage dealt: 400 heat and blunt damage!

"This isn't even a challenge." He called out the taunt so that everyone present could hear his words. "Here, *watch closely* as I undo my lock on the surrounding space. Maybe, if you have a crowd of Ascenders to show off for, you'll be able to take this fight seriously."

Unlocking the space around himself wasn't as easy for him as dismissing the strange bubble of altered reality was for the emperor. Locking required mana; unlocking *also* required mana. It also took a few seconds for the changes to come into effect, but as soon as they did, portals began opening the length and breadth of the throne room. Dozens of Ascenders, then hundreds, poured in as reinforcements had been called to break through the barrier that had been put in place.

None of that mattered to the Murderhobo. He only had eyes for what was happening on the other side of the room. There was an enormous **clang** as the metal orb, now significantly cooled, was shoved to the side. The man it revealed didn't look anything like the level-headed, calm, benevolent dictator that ruled the Dynasty of Dogs. No… this was the man who had started with nothing in a tribe of nomads who walked the planet thousands of years previous and had killed until he was at the very top of the social hierarchy.

The immaculate white robe fell off of the emperor, revealing furred cuffs on his arms, ankles, and a clearly hand-made loincloth that would never be seen in polite society. "You want me to take this fight *seriously*, do you? You want to attempt to humiliate me in front of my people? Fine, Murder-hobo. I'll be able to complete my grand plans even without you. They may take longer, but what do I have beyond endless time?"

Placing a hand on his chest, the emperor let out a deep, low growl which resembled throat singing, though it was clearly words in a language that didn't belong to this world. Slowly, he lifted his hand forward off his chest by an inch, then brought his hand up, slowly covering his chin, moving to his nose, eyes, fore-head, and top of his head. Wherever his hand passed, fur sprouted from his skin, his features shifted, and an alien presence was revealed.

"To be a king in the Dynasty of Dogs, there is one simple rule." The voice coming from the emperor 's mouth had shifted once again, becoming even more guttural than when he had been nearly frothing mad. "You must defeat and tame a legendary dog. My requirements, as an emperor who commands the kings under me, are more stringent. Tenth Domain, Funerary Rites of Anubis."

The air itself seemed to scream as wisps of light appeared throughout the entirety of the throne room. One of the wisps zipped past Luke's head, the periphery of his vision catching a face frozen in a rictus of horror within the light.

Damage taken: 25 Unknown damage!

"Unknown damage? That is *clearly* some kind of soul attack," Luke muttered at his Sigil with great annoyance. In his moment of distraction, the location of Emperor Anubis had shifted, and he was in front of Luke without any apparent usage of his muscles.

"Just remember," the symbiotic amalgamation of man and summoned dog barked. "You *asked* for this."

Clearly grandstanding for the gathered Ascenders, both of the emperor's hands moved up into the air, elbows tucked at the side and palms facing down, with the tips pointed up at Luke's neck. Then, he simply exhaled through his mouth, which had extended into the snout of a canine.

Luke felt like he had been punched in the chest by the troll he and his team had defeated together in Murder World. For an instant, there was a strong dissociation from his body, and he could see the back of his head in front of his eyes. Then, his perspective slammed forward once more, and blood poured from his eyes, ears, nose, and mouth. The Murderhobo stumbled and clutched at his chest, his body gasping for air as proof that he was alive.

Damage taken: 250 Unknown damage!

Health remaining: 1,215/1,440

"*Already,* you prove yourself far above the average man." The emperor snarled through the side of his mouth, the words slightly distorted due to his mouth and tongue shape being different than usual. "That usually does the trick. Nothing like shoving a soul out of a body to make the brain believe that it is dead."

"Dark," Luke stated with a cough, already moving to crash Cookie through the emperor's head. "Bum Blast! Lock Point!"

Luke spent the next few moments battering the emperor's furry form, then being roughly shoved away, only to reappear an instant later. On the fifth strike, Emperor Anubis landed a direct hit on Luke's leg, and for a split second, the Murderhobo could see a ghostly after-image of that limb trailing behind the flesh and bone of his body. It snapped back into position, but his leg went completely numb, his brain having apparently decided that limb had been sliced off. Then, it was filled with pins and needles as his mind began registering data from his nerves once more.

Damage taken: 100 Unknown Damage!

Damage taken: 110 blunt damage!

"Why didn't you do this from the start?" Luke bellowed as he continued swinging his weapon without slowing down to let his mind process the pain. "Almost no one would last even this long; why do you need entire armies to dominate the world?"

"Every benefit has an equal detriment," the emperor replied cryptically, his muzzle opening wide and revealing a black pit of roiling energy. Golden runes appeared in the air around his mouth, forming a Spell circle for a brief moment before what appeared to be a ball of black tar shot out of the mouth and caught Luke just below the knee of his undamaged leg.

The Murderhobo tossed himself out of the way, assessing the damage he had just taken. To his surprise, the attack had gone *through* his armor and his leg without slowing down, making a sound, or causing any pain. The leg was simply a bleeding stump below the knee at this point. "Nope... don't like *that.*"

Grabbing a loose water skin that was strapped tightly to his chest to make sure it stayed under his mana manifestation of armor, Luke didn't bother to open and drink it. Instead, he squeezed it and allowed the entire container to burst. The entirety of the liquid mana was sucked directly into his body, thanks to his Skill 'You Were Warned'. His health rocketed upward, and flesh and bone were created. By the time the emperor could arrive in front of Luke to launch his next attack, the Murderhobo couldn't be caught on the off-foot.

Cookie came down on his outstretched palms, slapping his hands down just as a shockwave of structured power left, only to slam into the tile below them—the dark stone becoming bleached wherever the power inundated it. A second burst followed the first, missing and causing the emperor to curse. "I admit, in combat, you are well-versed. For how long have you been baptized in the blood of your enemies? I am truly impressed."

"Since I was—*Zero-point Shockwave!*" Luke pretended to answer, only to instead blast the hands coming for his face out of the way. He was shocked as his attack went through empty air, and the illusions of hands faded away like smoke dispersing in the wind. A huge hand, more like a paw at this point, closed around his head, lifted him slightly... then slammed him face-first into the ground, even as a torrent of power raced through the emperor and into the back of Luke's skull. The Murder-hobo screamed in pain as his soul was scoured with power, the only part of his being that had never been forced to take direct damage.

Damage taken: 555 Unknown!
Health remaining: 885 / 1,440.

Now that he had Luke in his hands, the emperor wasn't about to let go. With a shout of effort, he doused the Murder-hobo in the power of his Domain once more.

Damage taken: 555 Unknown!
Health remaining: 330 / 1,440.

Luke was slumped in his grasp, but Emperor Anubis knew he wasn't yet dead. He lifted his head and howled, issuing a command to the wisps who were floating around the room. They rushed toward him, screaming in passing wherever they came close to a living being, flooding into the Emperor and boosting his reserves of power. "It's over, Murderhobo! *Die!*"

"I hereby swear my oath of service to the Emperor of the Dynasty of Dogs." Luke's weak words were barely registered by the crazed Sovereign, but the flash-burning of the Sigil against the palm of his hand caught his attention.

For a long moment, the emperor seemed to consider killing

the Murderhobo anyway. "You fought me right to the edge of death... I should *finish you!*"

Heaving for breath, the monarch forced his hand to unclench, finger by finger, until he had released his opponent. A small, victorious smile traced across his face as he looked at the imprint of his hand burned into the back of Luke's skull, and he took a few more deep breaths before finally releasing his enhanced form.

The emperor trudged back to his throne, completely spent. He turned and sat down, taking a few long minutes to consider the partially desiccated body that was rapidly healing in front of his eyes. "I accept your oath, Murderhobo. I hope you realize the conditions of your time with me won't be as lush as I had once promised. There are *consequences* for your behavior."

"Yeah." Luke used both hands to slowly shove himself off of the ground, a layer of his skin peeling off as he did so. It had fused with the tile as energy raced through him. "I figured that might happen."

"No time like the present." Now the emperor had a wide smile on his face. "It's time to put you to work and complete the grand ambitions of the dynasty."

CHAPTER FIFTY-EIGHT

The emperor motioned for Taylor to walk forward and help her friend off the ground. She did so willingly, gladly, and hoping that she would be able to support her friend during this trying time. A decree came to them as she and Andre lifted Luke to his feet, and she winced at what her monarch had to say.

"I am not offended, Luke. If there is one thing that training dogs has taught me over my long, long life... it is that the best of them, the strongest of them, the ones you most *want* to add to your collection... need to be taught who the alpha is. Now that you have accepted your place, submitting to my rule, for the next year, you will be pampered and given the very best of care. Then there will be ten years of hard labor on the front lines of my expanding dynasty as punishment for your insolence."

"Just going to point this out, not wanting you to change the punishment or anything." Zed stepped forward and bowed to the monarch. "Putting Luke on the front lines of combat isn't exactly a *punishment* to him."

That made the sovereign chuckle, a strong puff of air shooting out of his nostrils. "I didn't say the front lines of combat. I said the front lines of the expanding dynasty. He can use his club or his fists, but he's going to be pounding the ground flat to make roads for us. The absolute boredom should temper his attitude appropriately."

"Where's Cindy?" Luke managed to spit out, trying to ignore the threat of the imminent annoyance. "You called for her, but she isn't here. Is she actually safe?"

Following a simple hand motion from the man on the throne, Cindy was escorted in by a handful of Ascenders, each of them specializing in some form of barrier magic. She looked slightly relieved to see Luke, though there was a core of annoyance in the glare that he couldn't pretend he didn't see. "Great, you're back. Does this mean I can get on with my life?"

"No." The words of the emperor caused five sets of eyes to go wide: Cindy's and Luke's team. "I told you there were consequences for not accepting the deal willingly. Cindy, the marriage will proceed as it had been scheduled, even though it is a tad later than we expected it to be."

"*What!*" Her shout of outrage quickly fizzled away as she remembered where she was and who she was talking to. "Your Royal Highness, I have been nothing but a perfect citizen of this dynasty ever since I was brought here. *Please*, do not punish me for the transgressions of my brother."

"I have spoken," the emperor asserted coldly, callously. "Also, as of this moment, I am issuing a bounty for the safe gathering of your parents. Perhaps, if *all* of you are under my roof, the Murderhobo will be less apt to test the length of his leash."

Luke could feel the cold resentment being sent his way, and he dragged his weary body toward his sister. Each step was difficult, as though he was carrying a great boulder on his shoulders. Although his health had been regenerated, his body was still numb, his mind slightly discombobulated. He hadn't expected the emperor to be able to deal damage without having to deal with his armor, and it had thrown things off for him.

Lost in his thoughts, he barely stopped himself from

running into Cindy. Only a barrier that sprang up between them at the last moment allowed him to stop without taking both of them to the ground.

"Hello, Cindy." Luke looked down into the hot, angry glare of his sister. He swallowed, a very human reaction that startled her. "The last time we spoke, I was... greatly unbalanced. Characteristics do more to your mind and body than your Sigil tells you. Listen... I need a favor."

"I'll do you a favor, if you do me one. Go crawl back into whatever abyss you came out of and stop ruining my life!" Cindy's words lanced into him, and the hot tears that were forming tracks on her cheeks made him close his eyes.

"Not a favor." Gathering his thoughts, Luke reached into a satchel on his hip. "A trade, then. In this box is a powder that is extremely precious. Follow the instructions I have written on a note in there, and you will be able to reach higher heights than you ever imagined."

Taking a few heaving breaths before responding, Cindy's next words came out as a hiss. "Another *gift*? What do you want in return, if this is a trade?"

"I need your necklace." Luke's eyes, tone, and posture were all geared to be pleading. For an instant, he felt incredibly strange. He had never thought that the sub-Characteristic of Charisma, 'Dominate Chance', would appear as something like this. A shift in how he spoke, stood, and even the pheromones that his body would produce. After all, who would look at someone politely begging for something and assume that they were attempting to 'dominate' that person mentally?

"This ratty old thing?" Cindy let out a snort of derision, reached up to her neck, and ripped off her necklace with a single tug. The leather that Luke had once spent years decorating snapped instantly, and she tossed the tiny accessory at her brother. "Take it. It's practically *cursed*! I've had nothing but trouble from the day you gave it to me."

The strange light that seemed to shine out of his sister faded away, and all eyes in the local area were on the shining pearl pendant of the necklace. Luke snatched it out of the air and shoved it in a light blue sack, and the strange feeling vanished. "Thank you. I hope your life will be easier now that people are not constantly trying to figure out how to eat you."

"I'm sorry… *what?*" Cindy didn't receive an answer to her perplexed shout as Luke turned and trudged back to finish his conversation with the emperor, who had been gracious enough to allow him a moment with his sister.

"It's time for you to begin repaying me for my inconvenience." The emperor spoke gently to the Murderhobo, as though he were simply being punished for being irritable, like a child. "You are to report to the enchanters' hall and begin supplying them with liquid mana immediately. You'll stay there until their protected containment units are filled, then you will return to me immediately for your next assignment. If, at any point, you have punched someone, broken something, or tried to flee to another world, you have done something wrong."

Luke took a long, calming breath as he listened. His Sigil flared up, but he resisted it for the moment as he asked the emperor a simple question. "Will you release my sister?"

"I have already told you, Murderhobo. Her fate was sealed as soon as you forced me to act." The sovereign shook his head sadly.

"Please?"

There was a long pause as the emperor 's eyes narrowed, and his hands began to clench. He looked around the room, at the hundreds of peak-level Ascenders who represented the true power of his dynasty. "I have *spoken*, Luke. I've given you my answer. Until your debt is repaid, you will not be getting any benefits."

Luke's chin sank to his chest, and he heaved a great sigh. "Well… I *did* say please."

His head snapped up, his eyes meeting the emperor 's in a steady gaze. His feet, which had been shuffling in an attempt to force him to follow the decree of the emperor, steadied. The Sigil on his forehead flared, released a single, deafening *shriek* of a chime, and broke with a flash of light. Only silence filled the air for the next few moments, as no one felt safe being the one to make a move or speak out of turn.

"You never stripped away the original Sigil; you only over-wrote it. The underlying Quest my Sigil has been forcing me to follow all of these years was to get Cindy back to the Hollow Kingdom, at any cost." Luke took a deep breath and shrugged helplessly. "Well... the fact that I don't have the strength to physically get her out of here, the withdrawing of rewards you had promised, and the conflicting orders that you gave? It seems to me that a pair beats a king, but it takes three of a kind to deny the emperor ."

"I don't understand that reference." The emperor let out a long-suffering sigh as he got to his feet and prepared to deal with the Murderhobo once more. "But I hope *you* understand that I'm not going to let you live this time? Either lay down immediately and allow your Sigil to be renewed, or I *will* ensure that there's not enough of you left to regenerate."

"There's only one problem, *Your Majesty*." Luke closed his eyes, ignoring the Emperor as he closed in. "The Sigils of this world don't function on Ascenders who have attained level twenty."

"What?" The monarch stumbled backward, a strange fear in his eyes. "*No*! You abyssal—you *can't*! Not here!"

"Already did," Luke whispered as golden light suffused him, shining under his skin then out of his eyes. The emperor turned to escape into his higher dimension, only to bounce off the membrane of the world. A nova of light exploded from the center of the Murderhobo's chest, seeming to spread like honey throughout the entire throne room and slightly beyond, coating every Ascender in a thin film of golden energy that squirmed into them almost as soon as it had fully coated their bodies.

"No! There are international *treaties*! Laws! You cannot ascend within city walls, near population centers!" the emperor wailed as he flew at Luke, intending to stop his Ascension by force.

"Bum Blast." Luke was suddenly ten meters in the air above the emperor and locked himself in that position relative to the man. No matter how the sovereign lunged at him, as soon as he got within a few feet of Luke's body, the Murderhobo would automatically vanish and reappear ten meters above him.

Zed looked at his friends, who were watching the show with dawning horror on their faces. "What's happening; why is this an issue?"

Andre had a single tear rolling down his left cheek as he turned his head and looked at Taylor. Slowly, tenderly, he pulled her to him and placed a deep, longing kiss on her lips. "Goodbye, Taylor. May we meet again."

"Wherever that may be," she whispered back, blinking away her own hot tears.

Zed used both hands to grab one of each of their shoulders. "*Explain* to me what is happening right now! For historical reference, if nothing else!"

"What do you think that golden light was, Zed?" Taylor inquired with resignation in her voice.

"It was some kind of energy… and Luke said he was Ascending, so I'm guessing it has something to do with that? Is there such a thing as Ascension energy?" The Bard looked between the two of them, confusion and anger coloring his interactions. "Just *tell* me; don't play guessing games right now!"

Andre took a deep breath and began speaking quickly. "He is Ascending. Legally, in every known country of this world, Ascension must be done in the wilderness. Or, at the minimum, far away from population centers."

"Because of him choosing to Ascend, this plane of existence is forcing him out of it." Taylor took over as Andre trailed off, unable to continue. "Ascending in his next world will have different requirements, and all unused Potentia that he has stored is being squeezed out of him by the world to fuel the movement between dimensions. When this is done around other Ascenders, they automatically absorb some of it, and if there is enough, the world forcefully allocates it to their levels.

Almost as though it's trying to rebalance itself by making that energy be used, instead of causing extra-planar creatures to seek it out and come hunting."

The Bard blinked at his friends as their skin began to glow with a golden light, exactly as Luke had only moments before. Then their eyes began to shine, and soon they were heaving for air as a nova of golden energy coalesced just below their hearts, then exploded out and away from them. "You're telling me that... by choosing to Ascend here, he is forcing everyone *in range* of him to level up?"

"Hundreds of Ascenders at once," Andre grimly agreed, some vigor coming back into his voice. "How many of them do you think allocated their Potentia exactly as we did? Only two points away from reaching level twenty? My bet..."

The three of them turned their attention back to Luke and the now-golden, glowing emperor who was howling like the dogs he had tamed for millennia.

Zed finished Andre's sentence for him, his voice no more than a whisper.

"Surely not... *all* of them?"

CHAPTER FIFTY-NINE

- TAYLOR -

To the Mage's great surprise, the emperor stopped going after Luke, instead falling to his knees and clutching at his head as all of the stored Potentia he had accumulated and not used was squeezed out of him, creating a burst of golden light that likely could have mimicked Luke's. "Centuries. Wasted. Just like that."

Then he began laughing, interspersed with crying and fits of punching the ground. After a few long seconds of this, his head snapped up to glare at Luke once more. Taylor flinched away at the sheer venom contained within that stare. "You have no idea what you have done. What a *cute*, *tricky*, and *clever* plan. Pah. You don't even know it, but you've killed thousands. Millions."

Luke shrugged. "Whoops."

"Your parents are going to be brought here, either way." The emperor 's words came out as a hiss, and Taylor would've been concerned that he would lunge for Luke's throat, if his hands weren't buried up to the elbow in stone from punching the ground so hard. "With a single act, you have doomed my dynasty to collapse. All of the highest-level Ascenders, commanders, leaders, nobility… *all* of them are here, and you're the cause of getting them booted out of this world. There will be no one to pick up the slack, no chain of command. Civil war will begin by the end of the day, and this planet will be torn apart by people looking to fill that power vacuum."

"Yeah, that sucks," Luke agreed easily. "Things happen."

The emperor deflated, apparently resigned to his fate. His skin was growing translucent, and every one of his movements caused enough friction in the air that tiny bolts of lightning were scattering across his skin. "Not to mention the sheer *morass* of Potentia that has just been released into the air. Even now, I can sense thousands of Scars forming in the capital. This world is about to suffer a wave of monsters the likes of which have never been seen in living memory. *No one's* living memory… except for mine. But I guess that doesn't matter now."

Regaining his regal bearing, the man stood up and offered a mocking bow to Luke. "Somehow, I should have seen this coming. You're a Murderhobo. Yet, you never threatened to kill me when I was in your way, instead mentioning that you would 'just get rid of me'. It seems that you had this planned all along. Was it *worth* it, Luke? All of the death, the imminent destruction of this world?"

"Well, you probably should've just let my sister leave when I asked you politely." Luke's words reached the ears of the emperor, and the man started chuckling in absolute disbelief.

"Yeah. *Yeah*… I guess I should have." The air around the emperor shattered as though he'd been thrown through a pane of glass. Over the next half-second, the membrane of this dimension wrapped over the man who had been the emperor of the Dynasty of Dogs and rebounded.

Just like that, he had been banished from this plane of existence.

Something struck Taylor as odd as she watched this interaction. As the emperor vanished, she realized what it was. "Luke… how are *you* still here? You initiated your Ascension far before he did. For that matter, why are *we* still here? We were the next closest to you."

All around the throne room, shouting and screaming filled the air, sometimes in fury, mostly in exultation. Luke nodded at her, as always seeming to be impressed with her perception and comprehension of the insane situations he contrived. "I have a bit more control of my Ascension, thanks to my Domain. I'm holding you guys here as well, but it isn't very hard, thanks to the two of you being bound to the world. It's going to have a lot of trouble kicking you out, and unless we do something to keep this place safe… yeah, I think you'll both tear a giant Scar in this plane."

"I'm surprised at you, Luke." Taylor blinked in shock that it was Andre stepping up to admonish the Murderhobo. "If what the emperor … or whatever he is now… said is true, are you really fine with a wave of monsters wiping out millions of people? Our first, most important role as an Ascender has always been to fight the monsters that will otherwise wipe out humanity. It was the very first lesson Master Don gave us."

"Technically, that was *Taylor* who taught us that lesson," Zed pointed out, much to the Mage's inner delight. She tried not to show the pleasure at his words on her face, but she knew that there was nothing wrong with being happy when people remembered what you had to say. "Wait, no, you're right. He asked a question, then she answered with only one word, 'monsters'. So, yeah, it *was* Master Don giving us the lesson."

"I told the emperor that I had a plan," Luke interrupted them as Taylor started to drive her knife toward Zed's left hand. "You're all part of it, and I truly hope you will be able to help me see it through."

Without saying another word, the Murderhobo blinked out of existence. Taylor looked around, hoping that he had simply charged away, but no… "Luke, you *walnut*! The world won't let you back in if you leave it! Are you *kidding* me! Did he seriously just try to save us all and get trapped out of the world?"

"Nope, didn't go all the way through, just a little bit. Still almost got trapped out; that was close." A grunt of extreme effort reached her ears as Luke reappeared. Andre, Taylor, and Zed stumbled backward as Luke revealed what he had tempted fate to retrieve from Murder World.

It was an enormous pillar made entirely of crystallized mana.

The air around the diamond-like substance began to boil, becoming toxic to most creatures in an instant. "Here's what I was thinking. Taylor, use this to boost the mana you can dump into the Skill you managed to steal off me. I can't overcharge it with power, but I remember you once telling us that your Metamagic would let you add additional mana into a Spell to increase its strength and range, right?"

"Not *that* much." Taylor managed to let the words out of her throat, no matter how hoarse and scratchy they emerged as. "I have no idea how I would even-"

She flinched as a bright red Scar opened in the room, not twenty feet from them. With a scream of glee, a two-headed ogre began shoving through the enormous Scar that had formed, only to receive a blast of pinpoint-accurate ice from Taylor's Astral Triplet. Her training over the last year had allowed her to bend the Spell parameters to condense the attack down to a beam of Stellar Ice, a purple so deep it was practically black, if somewhat hazier than would otherwise be expected.

The ogre fell to the ground, both heads cleanly impaled. Taylor let out a groan of dissatisfaction then turned and nodded sharply at Luke. "I can't make people deal with that sort of thing. We're going to be forced out of here; everyone is going to be defenseless. I will... I will *try*."

"Excellent. Here's my plan." Luke slapped the rapidly deteriorating chunk of mana. "This bad boy can power all sorts of awesome things. Downside: when your Spell takes effect, we don't know how much of the area will turn into locked space. Either way, we're going to be forced out then *locked* out."

He turned and leaned forward. Then Luke gently put his

hands on Zed's shoulders. "Did you manage to get an echo of the Skill from me? After we're thrown out of here, will *you* be able to unlock the world? If you can't, there'll be no more Ascenders. Even the ones who were not thrown out of here will be trapped and will begin losing their power over time. Without regular excursions into higher worlds, they'll begin to age again, like a normal human. If you can't undo that from this side, we shouldn't do it at all. We can just try to gain enough control over our power that we can come back here and join the fight against the monsters."

Zed puffed up his chest and slammed one fist into it. "I've got this, Luke. Don't worry."

"Theoretically, all you'll need to do is activate the unlocking Mastery once," Andre interjected after placing his hands on the ground and communing with the world. "As long as the lock is picked in one area, it will ripple out until it has broken the seal anywhere in the entire world that has been impacted. Just one *single flaw* in the lock is all you need."

"I've got the Mastery," Zed promised them with clear, bright eyes. "I already know what I need to do, and I've got a plan."

"If I could take you with me, I would. I know you can survive where I am going." Luke nodded at the Bard as Andre slammed his hands onto the ground. Taylor nearly lost her balance as a pillar of stone began shooting upward into the sky underneath them. "Good luck, Bard. You'll be missed."

"We *will* meet again, Murderhobo." Zed promised the Ascending group with absolute sincerity.

"Goodbye, Zed. Goodbye Cindy." Luke's voice was as deadpan as usual, but there was at least a hint of sadness in it. "Hey. Zed. Use this if you ever get into a sticky situation, yeah? Don't eat it."

The Murderhobo tossed a small satchel to the Bard, who caught it out of the air and swept his hand up into a salute. The Mage recognized it as the pouch that he had put Cindy's necklace into, but she didn't comment on his giving of a dangerous artifact to a flighty Bard. She had bigger issues, and with her

Sigil having shattered upon reaching level twenty, she no longer had an enforced allegiance to any particular kingdom.

The ceiling was rapidly closing in, and Taylor had a momentary flashback to when they were attempting to smash through the blockade of teeth in order to defeat the Corrupted Nature Dragon. She shivered at that memory and concentrated on the moment. Already, she could feel static building up on her skin as she moved, as the world tried to grind down her resistance. It *would* succeed; the only question was how long it would take.

Every moment that passed increased that resistance, and she began noticing signs of severe strain in Luke's posture. A gasp sounded out, and the pillar came to a shocking halt a hundred feet above the top of the palace ceiling. Taylor looked over to ask Andre why they weren't moving, and hot tears stung her eyes as she realized that he had been taken by his higher world. He was gone. She steadied herself with the memory of the farewell kiss she had gotten from him and the memory of their promise to find each other somewhere in the myriad of higher worlds.

"Ow. Closing that Scar as it formed from Andre getting torn out *really* hurt. Tay. Never... or *right now*." Luke gasped out as he sank to his knees. "Let's get this over with. I've got places to go... things to kill. The usual."

A hint of a smile graced Taylor's face, even though her tears were ceaselessly flowing. "I'll miss you, Luke. I learned a lot from you."

"Hope you... figured out... that you don't always need to have such a stick up your butt." He laughed as her punch to his face failed to send him flying off the pillar. "There's my team-mate—no, my *friend*. I *will* miss you. Don't forget that, sometimes, it's *necessary* to go... Full Murderhobo."

"Absorb." Taylor whispered, the shrieking klaxon call of her Spell erupting from her along with a storm of butterflies, which expanded into a black orb with the Mage in the center. The enormous chunk of crystallized mana was subsumed instantly, and a bar of white-hot *pain* filled her mind as a secondary mana pool was attached to her own.

As of this moment, she only had one and a half minutes before all of the absorbed mana would be released in a single burst, which would add to the growing cataclysm and speed it up substantially.

"Meta-magic." Her words were a whisper in the wind, reaching no one's ears except her own... as well as a Bard who was still listening in at a distance. "Domain. World Anchor."

The Spell *drank* mana, able to accept any amount she could channel into it. Hundreds, *thousands* of points of mana began getting poured into the Spell, which formed as an enormous Spell circle above her head. Three seconds, thirteen, thirty, one minute... the strain of channeling the sheer quantity of power was causing her skin to flake off and turn to ash, and the blood that would have dripped out of her orifices turned to steam and burned cells. At maximum, thanks to the Spell Absorb being at level nine, the peak of Tier five, she was able to contain the additional mana that had been absorbed for up to ninety seconds.

This meant she had already reached two-thirds of her maximum allotted time and had spent hundreds of *thousands* of mana. As far as Taylor could tell... she had barely scratched the surface of the seemingly endless well of mana she had absorbed.

The Spell circle in the air was complete and by its very nature could absorb as much power as she was able to devote to it. She was certain that enough power had been invested to avert the crisis Luke had caused. All local portals would be forcefully closed, then the area would be locked down until Zed stepped forward and turned the key.

But, there was always the danger that the enormous release of mana that would certainly occur when Absorb failed would create issues of its own. The entire capital city, home to hundreds of thousands of innocent bystanders, would undergo a mana Baptism.

Taylor didn't know how many would die from the outburst, and she didn't want to risk them. She also couldn't simply step out of the world and release the excess in the higher plane she would be moving into. There was a good chance she'd be placed in a populated area, and while the people might be able to weather the storm easier than those on this world... at the very minimum, she would have a target placed on her back.

Saving herself, or potentially saving so many others... her eyes widened fractionally as her exhausted mind touched upon a potential *third* option. Devoting a sliver of her attention to her Spell, Earthshaker, she reshaped the stone she was standing on and launched into the sky.

Up she went, higher, and higher, the huge stone that she had used as a base breaking apart and launching a smaller version of itself to continue her one-way trip into the sky. As she drew level with the Spell circle, the world clamped down on her, and she realized that she had lost the protections Luke was affording her. She could see him, far below, as he raised a hand in fond farewell then vanished, off to seek new adventures in another dimension.

Lightning built around her as the world began to reject her, the bonds it had made with her fraying and tearing. As the threads holding her to this world snapped, destruction followed in her wake, her passage unzipping an enormous Scar in the sky, hundreds of feet tall.

With a final moment of concentration, she launched herself upward one last time, only the soles of her shoes now coated in stone. Taylor was out of time, as well as propulsion material. The Mage looked around, nodding when she realized she had reached the height that was necessary for her plan to be a success. As the final second ticked away and Absorb failed, she activated 'You Were Warned' and was fully restored as the mana began to expand outward. A moment later and she would have been destroyed in a flash. A moment too soon, and her blood would have converted to liquid mana.

"What perfect... timing." Taylor smiled, relaxing as she

sank back into the membrane separating the worlds, pulled through without further fanfare.

A dense thunderhead of mana appeared in the sky above the capital, at the center of the Dynasty of Dogs. It persisted for nearly half an hour, swirling like a hurricane as it was sucked into the Spell that was still actively drawing from the pool of mana.

When nary a drop remained, the sky was lit by a Spell Circle of immense proportions, stretching hundreds of miles in all directions. The structured mana activated, the instructions it had written into the world turned into laws that the dimension would impose. Across the entirety of the planet, the influx of mana from other worlds failed in an instant. Every open portal, each puncture in the membrane of the plane, the not-so-rare Scars, even the tiniest of distortions—were outright *erased*.

It didn't take long for the remaining Ascenders to realize they were trapped, deciding that maintaining power meant slaughtering their own kind until a solution was found.

One person watched with a smile as Everything they had built fell apart.

EPILOGUE

Zed beamed a bright smile around the room, as every person within the tavern started blinking and stretching, coming out of the trance-like state his words had dropped them into. "I don't know about all of you... but I just *love* happy endings."

Many people began clapping and cheering, as tales of The Four were always popular. A large section of them quickly went quiet, as they realized that this wasn't the propagandistic, curtailed version they had been expecting. Zed knew what they had been told, the lies that had been spread on behalf of the Hollow Kingdom. All of them, at one point or another, had learned the highlights of The Four's ascent.

The battle that had begun the fame of Andre the Terraformer. How he enriched the kingdom by wiping out an army of invaders and rolling an entire mountain range's worth of resources and donating it to the nobility, doing so proudly, with nary a thought for his own personal wealth.

Zed's own story, which he himself had created, speaking of the trials and tribulations of The Four within the Scarrocco Desert. He had spread their deeds and kept the commoners in the loop of what was happening within their own kingdom. He had brought people together, given them something to strive for. Eventually, that had been spun into a recruitment drive by the kingdom, in an attempt to generate as many Ascenders as possible—to bring them under the yoke of the Hollow Kingdom.

Finally, the tale they had heard tonight, of Taylor the Archmage. According to governmental sources, she had led her team as a strike force against the Dynasty of Dogs, spending more than a year constantly fighting against their armies, only to smash her way into the Grand Palace of Emperor Anubis. From there, she had proven her absolute mastery of Magic by defeating the most powerful assortment of Ascenders the world had ever seen, with some minimal help from the rest of her team.

Until this moment, the people in this tavern had never heard the full, uncensored version of events that had occurred. Firstly, the Murderhobo had always been included in the tales as a source of comedic relief, even as the others in the group strived valiantly to provide opportunity and resources to their people. His antics were supposed to be a counterpoint, a foil that showed the folly of someone with too much brawn and no brains to speak of.

Second, the Archdruid was a known quantity, and his work had been deemed faultless. By the efforts of his own hand and research, he had discovered a race of plant-based entities. He had healed the Hollow Kingdom and had given them the resources to hire mercenaries and train their troops for the last fifty years. As the Hollow Kingdom expanded outward to nearly a third the size that the Dynasty of Dogs had been able to hold for over a thousand years.

To hear him slandered as a bloodcaster... as a manipulated man on the verge of mental collapse, who had practically started his career with human experimentation? This story Zed was selling was a punch to the gut of the common folk... the people who had grown up on the shining tales of the Archdruid. His wisdom, his intelligence, and the desire of the nobility to find someone, *anyone* who could fill the hole that the Terraformer had left in their lives.

Furthermore, the Bard and the Murderhobo? They were just the people who traveled along with the other two, providing support or taking the hits that were needed for the Mage and the Druid to do the work that needed to be done. A surration went through the crowd as they began comparing the tale they had just heard to the stories their parents had told them as children. Very little was matching up.

"Where. Is. The. *Queen?*" Bartholomew managed to speak without throwing himself at the man he had been hunting for decades. "I spent years in the army, being promoted to Special Forces as I proved my loyalty, finally joining the Inquisitors and being trusted with this task by King Vir himself. My entire career culminates in this quest to hunt you down and extract information... and do you even know where she is?"

"Of course." Zed nodded as he chuckled aloud, allowing Bartholomew to relax minutely. The Bard finished his statement. "I don't. Sorry, let me say that again as a whole sentence. Of *course* I don't."

The king's Inquisitor launched himself forward, his fist striking out and... coming to a complete stop against the side of Zed's face. The Bard grinned and waggled a finger at him. "None of that now, my lovely flower is in effect still."

"I've heard your story. I listened carefully." Bartholomew growled at him. "You only generate echoes. Now that you've used this Mastery, it'll be far weaker the next time you do so. If you even *can* use it again. Your time is nearly up."

"Nearly up indeed," Zed stated agreeably. He then waved at the entrance to the tavern. "Shall we step outside and greet your king?"

"*Our* king." Bartholomew stabbed his finger at Zed's forehead, where the Sigil was still clearly branded into his forehead. "Overwritten, but not removed. If Luke wasn't able to escape the brand without conflicting orders, by your own admission... you should still be held by the oaths you made so long ago."

The Bard said nothing, merely smiling and starting his slow journey toward the door. He opened it and stepped outside, with Bartholomew standing behind him, sword drawn and pressed into the small of Zed's back. Familiar faces were in view, and Zed pointed and laughed at them. "Master Don! You've grown so *old*. Vir... tut, tut. In your seventies now, and you never took a queen? Cindy truly did leave an impression on you, didn't she?"

The king declined to speak, merely sitting in the open-top carriage that had brought him here as soon as he had learned about Zed, the real Zed, being at this location. Master Don, hundreds of years old, but only looking elderly instead of ancient, decided that he could speak for the both of them. "Is it true, Zed? Have you held the keys to our escape this entire time? As you say... I *have* grown old. Now, I can say that I am also bitter, but even more than that... I'm tired. I would love to destroy you, but I will instead make you an oath. Break the lock holding me here, and I will escape this world and regain my youth, never seeking to harm you or seek you out."

At this, King Vir stirred, glaring at the man who was likely the most powerful Spellcaster in the entire world. "You are still under the oath to *me*, Archmage."

"Gentleman, no need to fight!" Zed gently chided them. With a sigh, he released his Mastery of Illusions, revealing wrinkled flesh and eyes full of wisdom dancing with mirth. "I fully intend to break the lock. After all, I, *too*, am looking forward to my flesh refilling, my joints healing, and being able to stand as tall as I did back in my glory days."

Master Don looked stricken, and for a moment, mana raged around him. "You *can't* Ascend... no. Forgive me, I forgot myself for a moment there. I don't care anymore. Break the lock, *please*. I don't particularly care what happens here; I just want to go. I want to be free, after working so hard to earn that right."

"*He* wants to be free." Zed whispered softly, sarcastically.

"What great irony fills the air as our time together draws to an end."

"Where is my *Queen*, Bard?" Vir spoke up, finally unable to contain himself. "I heard your tale, projected from the communication stone that Bartholomew was carrying. You were the last to see her, as everyone else in that building Ascended. What happened to her after your team left you behind and rose into the sky on a pillar of stone?"

"I will answer your question because *I* choose to do so." Zed smirked at the frown that instantly covered nearly every face in view. "As her brother left, and the room emptied completely, Cindy opened the satchel her brother had given her, finding enough powdered unicorn horn within to bring her Mana Channels up to the Pristine ranking. We had very little time, so I explained to her what it would do and told her to trust her brother. At that moment, tears flowed from her eyes as she realized that Luke had done so much for her, had risked everything, and she had still treated him so poorly on the advice of outsiders."

He closed his eyes and swallowed his sadness down. "I don't like to see people cry, so I showed her how to open a portal. As it turned out, with the veil between worlds ripping so extremely, she was able to step out of this world and into another before the lock was sealed. She had been intended as your bride and the bride of a prince of the dynasty. No one had ever placed a Sigil on her. As far as I know, she has been living safely, freely, on a higher plane of existence... for who knows how long now."

"Then she is truly gone, and there is no way to get her back." Vir slammed his fist on the side of his wooden carriage and howled. "Half a century wasted. *Wasted!*"

Bartholomew reached forward and ripped a light blue satchel off of Zed's belt. "Your Royal Highness! Not all is lost. In his story, this great betrayer mentioned that the desire your exiled bride exuded came from the trinket this bag should hold! Please, let me bring it to you."

"Proceed!" All traces of rage vanished in an instant; his eyes now filled with a deep hunger. Bartholomew stepped forward, pulling open the satchel and releasing an enticing glow from within. Everyone in the area paused, staring at the light. The Inquisitor pulled out a single pearl, all traces of the necklace it had once been on nowhere to be seen. "That's it! This *feeling...* this is what she bewitched me with! Bring it to me immediately."

"No!" Master Don interposed himself between the Inquisitor and the king. "This might be a trick, a trap of the Mindbender! All of this could be a ploy to assassinate you; that is what makes Bards so feared! As the Archmage of the Hollow Kingdom, I am invoking my right to inspect this magical artifact. I believe it's having a detrimental effect on your mind."

The Sigil on the Archmage's forehead went flat, almost like a solid metal. No matter how the king shouted at him, Don was able to ignore the commands while he snatched the pearl out of Bartholomew's hand and shoved it into his mouth. A wide smile shot across his face, then it faded as he realized what he had just done.

"He never intended to assassinate the *king*. That weakling can't put up a fight." There was one person who still had a huge smile on his face, and it wasn't Zed. Bartholomew dropped his hand, which he had purposely held open and out, close to Master Don. Over the next few moments, his skin shifted slightly, his bones realigning themselves. There stood Zed, as he had looked thirty years previously. "Mission complete."

With that, the doppelganger collapsed into dust.

In the next instant, Master Don's body dropped to the ground, his head having detonated. Almost everyone stared at the situation, completely aghast. King Vir was the first to react as the reality of the situation Don-ed on him. "Archmage Don has perished... that means you dropped the field of safety you were creating!"

"Yes, because I needed my mana for something else." Contrary to his expectations, not a single person tried to attack the Bard as he lifted his hands into the air and activated one of his oldest stolen echoes. "World Anchor... *unlock*."

There was a ripple in the sky above them. The paltry amount of power the Bard could bring to bear was nowhere near enough to shatter the lock in a single push. But it was enough to make a flaw. That crack was visible above them, and every Ascender in the king's army sucked in a breath of fresh air as new mana from another plane of existence flowed into the world for the first time in half a century.

Crackle.

Everyone's eyes were on the sky as that crack spread, echoing out farther and farther, until the entire sky was lit up with lines of light. The joy and exultation etched on their faces turned into concern, and all eyes turned back to Zed as a golden nova of light radiated out from him, only reaching a few feet in each direction. It was then pulled straight down, as though it were rainwater being sucked down by the dry earth around him.

"You... did you just reach level twenty?" King Vir threw open the door of his carriage and stormed out, striding up to the Bard as though he were going to be the first one to launch a fist into his face. "All of this time, you could have left...? You could have Ascended? Why *now*? Why did you wait? Why did you do this to us, to the world?"

By the end of his miniature rant, the King was shouting in Zed's face, but the Bard maintained his composure and merely let a bright smile show on his face. "No, you have it all wrong. Tonight was the night I finally *earned* enough Potentia to Ascend. Didn't you see that golden Nova? I had practically no excess to donate to the world. Without getting a chance to tell my story to the king and his entire army, courtesy of my Doppelganger and the communication stone that you put in his hand... well, who knows how long that would have taken?"

"I trusted him. Bartholomew proved his loyalty time and time again!" Vir's voice was despairing as he whipped around and began slowly walking to his carriage. "After all of this? I walk away with nothing?"

"Well, we'll see." Zed's words didn't sound promising to the king. Instead, they struck the old man as cold and malicious. "Do you not know the stories, kinslayer?"

Ever so slowly, King Vir turned around. "What do you mean, Zed?"

"The real reason Bards are so feared?" Zed waved his hands to the side as though the answer was obvious. The earth itself started to glow around them, the color brightening until it appeared that the ground all the way to the horizon was coated in golden sunlight. "The tales that are told to children are that everyone should bind Bards because of their ability to influence minds. Even so, in the hundreds of *thousands* of years that our world has been here, why am I the very first Bard to begin to Ascend?"

The cracks in the sky grew wider, and light flooded into the world. It was met with a wall of golden light that lifted off the surface of the ground and continued until it met the cracks in the sky. There was a sudden motion, and everyone felt a jolt in their stomach as though they had suddenly fallen a few feet.

Every eye was drawn to the fact that there was a new star in the sky, and various planets could be seen orbiting it. The cracks in the membrane of the dimension rapidly healed, leaving the new view for all to see.

Zed's smile grew darker. "I made a friend, long ago, who explained many truths to me. A Bard is reliant on the Potentia they can gather from the people in the world where they're born. There *is* no higher world for them to go to. When they Ascend, when *I* Ascended, I took all of you with me. The world is mine."

A deep *thrum* shook the air and the earth as the cracks in the sky fully vanished. Dense mana rolled down out of the sky, visible due to the sheer air pressure it created as it came toward them, creating an instant deluge as the water in the air was displaced.

Vir sank to his knees. "The entire world is about to go through a mana Baptism. All of the lives that your friends saved, all that you did… just to throw it away? The survival rate is going to be *minuscule!*"

"It's all worth it," Zed mockingly consoled the king. "I have it on good authority that, by surviving, I have no choice but to be an Annihilator Ascender. Once upon a time, you used us as pawns to consolidate your reign. Now I get to use *all of you* as a stepping stone to begin my journey to level thirty."

"It's all about power? That is… that's out of character for you! Isn't it? Someday, won't your friends come for you? Won't they hunt you down for what you've done to them? To their families? To their *world?*" Vir shook his head. "No, there's more to this. There must be. What were you given, what were you promised?"

A portal tore open next to Zed, and soft, scratchy jazz music poured out of it. Zed smiled as he heard the sounds that he associated with his mentor, music he hadn't heard since their stay in the desert. "Why, Vir… of course I want them to come find me. We're going to *need* Luke, if we're going to save the multiverse and reach the source. As to what I was promised for my services…?"

"You may not believe it, but my new friends didn't just promise me the *world.*" The Bard looked up into the sky, the dozens of planets revolving around the star reflecting in his eyes. There was a gentle smile on his face as mana wrapped around him, and his skin began to rapidly tighten. His body was fully renewed, and in only a few minutes, Zed looked exactly as he had when he had fought his way through worlds with the Murderhobo half a century ago.

"They promised me *Everything.*"

ABOUT DAKOTA KROUT

Author of the best-selling Divine Dungeon and Completionist Chronicles series, Dakota has been a top 5 bestseller on Amazon, a top 6 bestseller on Audible, and his first book, Dungeon Born, was chosen as one of Audible's top 5 fantasy picks in 2017.

He draws on his experience in the military to create vast terrains and intricate systems, and his history in programming and information technology helps him bring a logical aspect to both his writing and his company while giving him a unique perspective for future challenges.

"Publishing my stories has been an incredible blessing thus far, and I hope to keep you entertained for years to come!" -Dakota

Connect with Dakota:
MountaindalePress.com
Patreon.com/DakotaKrout
Facebook.com/TheDivineDungeon
Twitter.com/DakotaKrout
Discord.gg/mdp

ABOUT MOUNTAINDALE PRESS

Dakota and Danielle Krout, a husband and wife team, strive to create as well as publish excellent fantasy and science fiction novels. Self-publishing *The Divine Dungeon: Dungeon Born* in 2016 transformed their careers from Dakota's military and programming background and Danielle's Ph.D. in pharmacology to President and CEO, respectively, of a small press. Their goal is to share their success with other authors and provide captivating fiction to readers with the purpose of solidifying Mountaindale Press as the place 'Where Fantasy Transforms Reality.'

Connect with Mountaindale Press:
MountaindalePress.com
Facebook.com/MountaindalePress
Twitter.com/_Mountaindale
Instagram.com/MountaindalePress

MOUNTAINDALE PRESS TITLES

GameLit and LitRPG

The Completionist Chronicles,
The Divine Dungeon,
Full Murderhobo, and
Year of the Sword by Dakota Krout

Metier Apocalypse by Frank G. Albelo

Arcana Unlocked by Gregory Blackburn

A Touch of Power by Jay Boyce

Red Mage and
Farming Livia by Xander Boyce

Ether Collapse and
Ether Flows by Ryan DeBruyn

Dr. Druid by Maxwell Farmer

Bloodgames by Christian J. Gilliland

Unbound by Nicoli Gonnella

Threads of Fate by Michael Head

Lion's Lineage by Rohan Hublikar and Dakota Krout

Wolfman Warlock by James Hunter and Dakota Krout

Axe Druid,
Mephisto's Magic Online, and
High Table Hijinks by Christopher Johns

Skeleton in Space by Andries Louws

Dragon Core Chronicles by Lars Machmüller

Chronicles of Ethan by John L. Monk

Pixel Dust and
Necrotic Apocalypse by David Petrie

Viceroy's Pride by Cale Plamann

Henchman by Carl Stubblefield

Artorian's Archives by Dennis Vanderkerken and Dakota Krout

Vaudevillain by Alex Wolf

Made in the USA
Coppell, TX
12 July 2024

34550649R00254